An
inverted
Sort of
prayer

An inverted Sort of prayer

A NOVEL

CHRIS F NEEDHAM

N_1 O_2 N_1

CANADA

*Publisher's note: This book is a work of fiction. Names, characters, places and
incidents are either the product of the author's imagination or are used
fictitiously, and any resemblance to actual persons living or dead,
events, or locales is entirely coincidental.*

Library and Archives Canada Cataloguing in Publication

Needham, Chris F.
An inverted sort of prayer / Chris F. Needham.

ISBN 0-9739558-0-5

I. Title.

PS8627.E43I5 2006   C813'.6   C2005-907204-0

Printed and Bound in Canada

Now Or Never Publishing Company
11268 Dawson Place
Delta, British Columbia
Canada V4C 3S7
www.nonpublishing.com

With thanks to Gene Derreth, Corbett Enders, Angie Long,
Mark Nishiguchi and, especially, my family.

In memory of Pauline Baher.

For having the wisdom to see that a boy will dream,
And the will to see that boy awake a man,
This book is for Lori.

*'Everything dramatic is in the nature of an appeal,
a frantic appeal for communion.
Violence, whether in deed or speech,
is an inverted sort of prayer.'*
                    —Henry Miller, *Henry Miller on Writing*

*'Do you know, sir, what it is to have nowhere to go to?
One must of necessity go somewhere.'*
                    —Fyodor Dostoevsky, *Crime and Punishment*

BOOK ONE

CHAPTER ONE

THIS IS WRONG. These are not my words. Or rather, these are my words, but you have to remember that as you are reading them you could also be writing them down.

This, too, is wrong. It was not Montreal but in fact Mannheim where I first met Chris De Boer, and I was playing, more or less, for Adler of the German Elite League as I recall. I met him at a bar that, back when I'd initially arrived in that country, I'd developed the habit of getting kicked out of quite regularly, and consequently I'd not returned to in some time. In the parlance of the profession I was what was, and still is, called an enforcer. Don't think that I'm all that much impressed by that as a title, although it would have meant all that much more to my father.

Now I don't remember what all he was wearing that night, but I do remember that Chris was standing behind the bar when I first took notice of him, chatting quietly with some seemingly good-natured skinheads on the other side. It was Saturday night and we had just lost that night and afterwards, tired of speaking broken German and wanting to be alone a while, I had come in for some Greyhounds and some televised Hong Kong horseracing to calm my nerves a little. Heaven, I believe the place was called, but try not to read too much into that either. After the Greyhounds I hooked back several shots in succession with this teenaged, unabashedly implant-ed, seemingly permanently sunburned waitress, and then told her I must be going. She had been toying with the idea of the two of us going off somewhere sunny for the weekend, but I told her I must decline. I'm not very good company these days, I assured her, but she didn't seem to care one way or the other. So then I suggested she join me in the washroom for a quick puppet show, but then she didn't seem all that impressed with such acts of exhibitionism either.

"Well then I know a girl around here who might like to join us," I said, at which point she took a drink from her tray and tossed it against my face. Ignoring the attack, I brushed the beaded moisture from my chin. Then I went on in English: "Henrietta used to be a man, but knows everything you need to know about being a woman. He really is a lovely girl."

The waitress tossed another drink at me and walked stiffly away. Fortunately they'd come from a recently abandoned table and contained little more than ice by the time they made it onto me.

Something pressed against me from behind—it was De Boer, or as I knew him then, de bartender, and he was standing on my side of the bar smiling politely, breathing lightly, one hand clasped firmly over my shoulder.

"Hey weren't you barred from here a few months back?" he asked in English, stifling a yawn with his forearm. "Someone told me you were barred from here a few months back."

"Who told you I was barred? Günter? The chef? Really? Well fuck Günter the righteous chef," I said.

He frowned. "He's only a fry cook."

"Seriously? Then he's a liar. A fryer and a liar. A frying, lying, good for nothing cook," I said, not really knowing where I was going with this, and not really caring either.

I returned to my drink and my steadily increasing hate of all things fried until a certain gesture shattered my resentments: the bartender was offering to buy me a drink. "Think of it as a congratulatory drink," he said, grinning good-naturedly. "You know, for your reincarnation so to speak."

He returned behind the counter, poured a Greyhound, and set it down before me on the bar. Then he introduced himself as Chris De Boer, a name that, I must admit, meant absolutely nothing to me at the time. We shook hands. I thanked him very much for the free alcohol, and then asked if he'd seen the game that night. He said he had, indicating with a nod the television in the far corner of the bar.

"It wasn't a very good game though."

"It wasn't, no."

I took the straw from my drink and placed it alongside the others on the bar—twelve straws. It would be time to be leaving soon.

"So what do you think about the trade?" he asked, wiping mechanically at a section of the bar. Not knowing which trade he was referring to, and not wanting to appear too out of touch, I didn't answer, choosing instead to taste my drink and draw my head down between my shoulders until what I thought was a reasonable amount of time had elapsed. Now there is this popular misconception amongst those without money that those of us with money have little or no interest in receiving a free drink. But in reality it is just the opposite. Poor people enjoy spending their own money. Wealthy people enjoy spending other peoples' money. Both cases being a simple function of principle and pride. And besides, this was a Greyhound, my signature drink since back in the Sault, this time, though, made with pink grapefruit juice. I really developed a thing for the pink grapefruit juice back in Mannheim.

"You don't sound too German, Chris," I said, routinely flexing my fingers and cracking my knuckles, and he was about to respond to whatever it was I meant by this when someone called for him to start a Guinness. Guinness is poured very slowly, at least when poured properly it is, and while the Guinness was pouring I watched Chris slowly work his way down and around to the far side of the horseshoe-shaped bar. To be honest, he was hardly remarkable in his appearance, except in those most conventional of ways—hardly the horse to hitch your sum total of hopes and dreams to anyway—and yet it was surely the breeding that engendered the appeal and eventually the obsession, and I suppose that for most of us that was more than enough. He was youthful and athletic looking. He kept his dark brown hair quite short. The smile he used was nice enough—that is, whenever he managed to smile with more than just the mouth of it, it was. He was handsome, not beautiful but handsome, and then just enough to be in danger of manifesting his fantasies in some obscure way. In the end, then, Chris De Boer was certainly a study in something, although I have no idea what, and yet with everything that is being written and said in conjunction with his father's recent death I feel it imperative I come clean myself.

He returned and finished the Guinness and handed it over the bar. Someone else said something else and he smiled, blowing off the joke with a nod. By and by he was back to leaning against the bar directly across from me. Heaven was not all that busy that night and there was plenty of time for procrastination that I could see.

Finally, as I had nothing really interesting to ask, and as he had nothing really interesting to say, he turned his attention to the glass washer, taking out glasses and arranging them against the back bar in neatly ordered stacks. Eventually he returned, this time with a copy of *USA Today*.

"I can't believe it," he said, indicating the front page photograph of two girls crying.

"Can't believe what?" I asked, not caring, determined to preserve my overwhelming ignorance of that gender intact.

"Another kid opened fire on his classmates," he said. "I can't believe it."

He looked like he was about to say something more, but then decided against it, and looking to reinforce my position of ignorance I pushed the paper away. I was proceeding on the admittedly dim theory that if a customer did not ask a question, well then a bartender would have nothing to say. But then he took a drink from a coffee cup and I asked what was in the cup.

"Same as you," he said, and I was led by way of association to the question of which brand of vodka he used, to the conclusion that it was probably one of the premium varieties. One great thing about drinking is that after a while nothing exists of the world but thoughts about drinking. It is also interesting that thoughts about drinking often lead to more actual drinking which, for the drinker, is the entire reason for being. And that is when you know you have drunk too much: when you can no longer tell the difference between them. And so, just to be sure, I stopped thinking. Although I did continue drinking just in case.

Chris looked like he wanted to say something again, and so, yielding to the pressure, I asked what he was thinking about, and satisfied with my degree of curiosity he pointed to the photograph in the paper. "That kid going on a killing spree at school."

"So?" I shrugged, still refusing to think, still confused with this trying to ascend so suddenly from the depths of a good vodka-drunk to the knowledge of something in reality you do not wish to understand. Someone called for a drink and failed to get one. I watched that someone stomp angrily away. And suddenly, struggling heroically in the face of overwhelming odds, I found myself scrambling to find something in the way of wisdom to impart here.

Beating me to it, Chris tapped the photograph and observed, "It's like when you're driving down the street and there's a car coming towards you in the other lane. Well now what's to stop that car from suddenly veering into your lane and hitting you head on? Nothing. That is, nothing but a set of values instilled in that driver, instilled in that car, instilled in that system of mechanical humanity bearing down on you at over one hundred clicks an hour."

He paused, suddenly aware of just how intently I was looking at him. He wanted to know if I was listening and I was. After all, here was the first real hint of genuine conversation directed my way in months, and on top of that it was in English as well.

"Honestly now," he continued, "what's to stop that driver from pulling hard left on the wheel and plowing right into you? What's to stop him from flying right over that little white line and hammering you head-on? Nothing but a phantom set of values based solely on what someone else somewhere else believed to be somehow right and wrong." It was like every morning when I went off to work in my hunter green Ford Taurus, he maintained, I was engaging in what was little more than an act of blind faith. Faith in the fact that driver coming towards me was not going to suddenly decide to run me off the road. Faith in the fact that driver had been raised appropriately and with the proper amount of instruction, and that his belief in the sanctity of life had not been violated at some point by his society's failure to deal with those issues he held most sacred somehow. Faith in the fact that he was not insane. In the fact that he was not a manic-depressive. And that he was not out on a mission of vengeance against his former employer who, it just so happened, drove something resembling a hunter green Ford Taurus himself. Faith in his problem solving skills. In his ability to know right from wrong. In the values of those people who taught him right from wrong, and those who taught them, and so on and so on and so forth ad nauseam. Faith in the values of the carmakers. In the values of those subcontracted to design and build the steering system for those carmakers. In the braking system. In the fuel system. In the values of the guys on the floor who build those systems et cetera. Faith in the roadwork. Faith in the weather. Faith in the fellow who made his latté that morning and that, for minimum wage plus tips, he would not take out his own frustrations and vengeful intentions on our hapless driver here. Hell, faith in the fact my own Taurus wouldn't suddenly jump the line and run headlong into his. "In other words," Chris said, "blind faith in the values of an entire society not to break up and suddenly let you down."

"Is that all?" I said sarcastically—I said a lot of things sarcastically that season, that being my sarcastic season—to which he replied "Pardon?" but I was in no mood to compound the obvious mistake of speaking out of turn with the further embarrassment of explaining myself herein. Instead I hovered thoughtfully over my drink, wondering whether I'd just been told an interesting anecdote about religion and all its various incongruities, or whether I'd just been told the bartender had recently survived a minor car accident of some sort. Since it was no big deal either way, I decided to forget it, and as you can see, I did not. I did, however, start to think about my next drink, and whether or not I should offer to buy Chris one.

He studied me a moment, then stepped forward again. "That kid's classmates, they had faith you know. Sure they did. That kind of faith that led them to school that morning and into the sightlines of a seemingly normal, obviously disturbed, automatic rifle-carrying kid. That kind of faith in a society's values that very much let them down." It seemed to Chris that our entire culture had been raised on a mother's milk of blind faith, and although he wasn't quite sure, he thought perhaps the best-before date on that sort of thing had pretty much expired of late.

He said something else—I forget what—and then, almost as if feeling my glassy-eyed disconnection somehow transferring itself to him, and wanting no part of it, he acted as though he hadn't said anything, and I acted as though I hadn't heard anything, and as soon as he moved away to the glass washer, which was immediately, I glanced up at the television and started thinking about horses again.

Finally, seeing as we were in need of some sort of relief here, comic or otherwise, and seeing as I was relying on a bartender to explain to me what I didn't understand about myself, I tried obstinately to yawn. It was an unequivocal success.

"So what you're saying is, you're gay," I said, yawning blatantly once again, and believing it. As a final defence against understanding I have always taken refuge in scornful superiority based on size, sex and sexual preference, and this occasion in Mannheim proved no exception. He looked at me, blinkingly, as the big-breasted, drink-tossing waitress called out for another round behind him. Someone else called out for something else and failed to get whatever he was after as well. In terms of service, Chris was a rather poor bartender in my opinion.

"And besides," I said, "it's the yellow line."

"Pardon?"

"Yellow line. You said white line, but it's the yellow line that separates heterogeneous lanes of traffic. White lines separate homogeneous lanes of traffic."

He smiled, arching a sceptical eyebrow for emphasis. "Homogeneous lanes of traffic, huh."

"Homogeneous lanes of traffic, my friend."

He backed away to the washer, stopping just long enough to pour the waitress some wine. I pressed on.

"So what you're saying is, you're having a little trouble coming to grips with all these shootings."

"No, what I'm saying is, I'm having a little trouble coming to grips with *faith*."

Well almost any display of genuine spiritual contemplation draws a stunned tribute from me, and when I had no response to what he was saying he shook his head despondently and drifted quietly away. Eventually, however, he returned, and finished what he had to say by telling me what it was he really wanted to say.

"I mean do we trust something because it's true? Or is it simply true because we trust it."

"Trust? Who said anything about trust? I could have sworn we were talking blind faith here."

"Homogeneous heterogeneity."

"Pardon?"

"Same difference," he said.

I finished my drink. Chris offered to buy me another but I declined—faces were starting to smudge and the walls were closing in. I stood up and thrust myself clear of the counter, all the while watching the television in the far rear corner of the bar. I was thinking about the horses back on my mother's family's farm.

He returned with a bottle of *Cuervo 1800* and poured out two shots. He picked up a glass and said, "Gentlemen, to blind faith."

"To getting blind," I said, and we hooked back our tequila together.

Still wincing from that shot, he poured out two more. "To the piss," he said.

"To the piss," I repeated, and we hooked back our tequila together.

He poured out two more.

"Gentlemen, to the Caps."

"The Caps?"

"Yeah, the Capitals."

"The *Wash*ington Capitals?" I said. "What the hell for?"

"Well, for picking up the rights."

"Rights? What rights?"

"Christ, don't tell me you didn't know."

He placed his shot glass on the bar and opened the *USA Today* to the Sports section.

"There," he said, pointing. "They just picked you up."

"You're kidding."

"Nope. Look, it's right here in black and white. 'Washington signs Bill Purdy of Mannheim Adler.' Congratulations, Bull, your prayers have been answered. You've been granted one last reprieve from the china shop of the world."

CHAPTER TWO

SO AS YOU are about to see, Montreal was in fact the second time I hooked up with Chris De Boer. Admittedly that too took place in a bar, and while he was not working that night he was definitely drinking as though he were. It was the beginning of November as I remember, some ten months after being traded out of Germany, and I was in town with the Capitals to meet the Canadiens for the second time that year. Arriving a full forty-eight hours prior to the contest, pre-game ritual dictated that a couple of the guys and I head out that first night for some drinks. We ended up at this martini bar called Purgatoire, a smoky little jazz joint on Ste Catherine Street I had been tossed from for good a great many times before. As far as bars went, Purgatoire was a good one, and whenever I passed through Montreal I always tried to include a stop there. I was rarely, if ever, disappointed. The staff at Purgatoire never remembered who I was and yet, oddly enough, always remembered how much I liked my Greyhounds.

My trade from Mannheim to Washington had not really been a trade at all. Not in the familiar sense of the word. The Capitals had simply chosen to sign me when no one else would. I was pleasantly surprised. The last thing I thought I would be doing that year was returning to the National Hockey League, let alone to a playoff contender. And although it was only the league's minimum salary they would be paying me, and although they would ultimately trade me, getting a chance to play at the highest level again was not something I would ever take too lightly. I was forty now, and while, by and large, still benefiting under the tutelage of my old buddy Stan, really beginning to feel the effects of my age. I had discovered traces of blood in my urine some three weeks before, and not really knowing or trusting the Capitals' team physician yet, had flown up to Hartford to see Stan, who discovered, along with the blood, a newly developed arrhythmia, or irregular rhythm of the heart. Stan asked how much I was juicing and I told him, and he made me cut it back. Way back. So far back in fact that I began to feel it was having no real effect whatsoever, and so I cut it out completely. But it didn't matter. Not really. Because by now I was spending the vast majority of my time in the press box with two young rookies named Carl. Because both their names were Carl I called the one Hot Carl. It doesn't matter which. The point is, I was playing what was beginning to look more and more like my last season—again—and I was playing it up in the press box of all places. The Capitals had a good young enforcer named Craig Simon that year, as well as a trio of decent young middleweights—of which Carl, not Hot Carl, was one—and with the new rules being introduced into the game of late there was rarely any need for more than two of us to dress for any given show. So there I was, perched up high in the press box, managing to get on the ice and fight maybe one game in four.

They kept me around because I was good in the room. It is always said of role-players like myself that we are good in the room—good in the corners, good along the boards, good in the bar, and good in the room. To be honest, I have never met an enforcer of whom it was not said that he was good in the room. But I liked it. I really did. I liked being good in the room. It was always best if you could somehow get it goin' on, but if you couldn't get it goin' on, then ranking a close second was gettin' good in the room. Being good in the room endeared you to people, it really did, and they even let me wear the 'A' when I played, and there is just so much that can be said about that. There is just so much that can be said about that, understand, as pretty much anyone can be given one of those on any given night. Still, if you can't get it goin' on, then I suggest you get good in the room, and as promptly as possible too. So there you had it: a good in the room kind of guy with traces of blood in his urine splitting time between the press box and the penalty box. Sometimes I think my entire life has been spent in some box.

When I'm with people who aren't hockey people, I don't like to be treated like a hockey player. That requires clarification. What happens at the rink should stay at the rink. Better. Often times people like to talk to me about my being a professional athlete, and having to talk about being a professional athlete all the time can really get on my nerves. Don't get me wrong, I fully understand the role of the professional athlete in modern society (as fully as something so absurd as professional athletics can be understood anyway), and I do appreciate the sheer height and magnitude of the pedestal on which he has been placed, and further, the size and weight of the gilded cage into which he has been flung. That is not my concern. What is my concern is that my free time away from the rink remain just that. And that was one of the things that first drew me to De Boer: he was more, what, sympathetic than the others. As sympathetic as the others insisted themselves to be.

He seemed to be preoccupied with ideas. Or else he had a strange ability to read your thoughts. Whatever the reason, he rarely spoke to me about my professional life unless I was the one to bring it up. I was not a nice man back then. I was not a decent sort of human being. I beat men up for a living and then went home and beat my women. And yet the absurdity of making a living from such a life, it was not lost on me. I knew that I was not a role model. I knew that mine was not a proper way of being. Nevertheless, I had learned early on in my career that if I dropped my gloves and fought, people would like me. I learned to drop my gloves a lot. And yet when I was with Chris De Boer I always felt as though there was something more to Bill Purdy than simply an enforcer. And something less. And I like to think that was why I took to him so readily: next to De Boer the stigma of being the Bull meant next to nothing anymore.

I remember I was dabbling secretly and somewhat sporadically in the art of writing at the time, and in doing so, even though it is presently somewhat unfashionable to do so, reading frequently the

American writer Ernest Hemingway. I remember I was reading him a great deal really, and, as I recall, had taken to speaking in tough understatements from the corners of my mouth from time to time as well. Naturally, that sort of thing was always happening with me. Now I have heard, from a variety of different sources in fact, that this is not all that uncommon a phenomenon, neither all that unusual nor strange, and therefore cause for no undue concern. So be it. But despite all assurances to the contrary, I still can't help but feel that there really is something special to this transformation, something I really haven't been able to put my finger on till just now: when you spend so much of your time in the box, you learn to spend a great deal of that time in your head. And I have always spent a great deal of time in mine.

Hemingway, I have been told, is arguably not all that good a role model for the novice writer easily influenced by works of literature, hardly any good when he is a hard drinker, never any good when he has tendencies of violence towards others, but, naturally, a very good line of furniture. And having discovered his line as late in life as I did, I liked to think that I was safe from any adverse effects it might have had on me if, say, I was younger. Now I am not so sure. That Hemingway could deliver is a well-established fact, and one is always wise to guard against any antiques gathering dust in one's attic, no matter how expensive, inspired, or reasonably well-crafted. And so guard I did. And if speaking in tough understatements from the corners of my mouth was going to be the worst of my crimes, then so be it, I would be a better man for it. Or so I thought at least.

Just to be on the safe side, though, and because my father hated him so, I tried to supplement my literary laundry list with some openly American, but in reality closeted French Canadian Jack Kerouac. Christ Almighty, what a papist load. And yet here was the only other writer I was reading with any regularity when I finally hooked up with Chris De Boer that second time around. So there they were: the two brand names, the two trademarks, the two apparently outdated but nonetheless co-opted literary luminaries that if I were diligent, not necessarily intelligent but diligent, I would not only outgrow, but with any luck cheerfully transcend—at least insofar as my fictional wardrobe was concerned. There were worse places to be in life than a sort of expatriate paradise—of that I was certain—and furthermore, that to be lost as such was indeed to be beatified and therefore suffering from not all that incongruous a condition. That was tough to fathom when you first really thought about it, not necessarily difficult but tough, but despite that toughness I thought about it anyway. Besides, in those days, I really didn't have all that much else to do. There were Carl and Hot Carl of course, but then those two weren't quite enough company for themselves, let alone for anyone of even marginal intellectual aptitude. So there I was, in a gap of sorts, feeling hemmed in on either side, floating free but at the mercy of almost any force exhibiting sufficient strength to move me, returning once more to that bar in Montreal from which so many times before I had been barred for life.

Purgatoire was housed in the basement of what appeared to be a very old rundown warehouse, one that had, in all probability, been designed to look like that. The room ran long and narrow, and the bar ran the length of the left-hand wall. There were tall metal stools at the bar, comfortable looking chairs and sofas arranged along the opposite wall, and a grand piano situated atop a raised platform at the far rear end of it all. Naturally a tall young hipster hunched studiously over the piano, while beside him a horn player blew soft ironic phrases from afar. Next to the horn player sat a drummer and maybe another horn player or else someone thumbing the bass—I cannot quite recall. Neither can I recall what kind of horn the man played nor the style in which he played it, but, like I said, I do recall it playing very softly and ironically somehow. Situated along the brick walls were these enormous black and white prints of boxers, freckled brown now with smoke and age. Old-time boxers. Famous boxers. Boxers I recognized and had seen plenty of times before—whose names escaped me now as they had so many times before. Taking no notice of these ghosts of pugilism's past were those equally two-dimensional members of that new young hipster set, trying hard to look as patronizing and poor as possible, yet completely oblivious to the rest of us. They had that certain aesthetic quality the young have now of all looking exactly alike. The air was sweet with their various cheap perfumes and corner store colognes, not unlike the entire street of Ste Catherine we had just descended from.

As he saw me approaching, the doorman's eyes flashed over me. Then he gave me the nod. They were always doing that, those door-men, they were always giving me the nod like that. But I liked that nod. I really did. I would even like to think that I could give that nod one day—that is, if I were ever to make it out of this little predicament I'm in.

That night I was out with Hot Carl and my roommate on the road, Jim Fischer, an altogether decent defenseman with a face like a fist and a colon to match, and before we made it to Purgatoire he made us make a quick pit-stop at Chapters bookstore so that he might try and take a crap. Chapters, Jim maintained, was an excellent place to move one's bowels on account of all that good Starbucks cof-fee and reading material they had in-store. Better than a club, at any rate. Jim hated taking a crap at a club, he often said. And so, waiting for Jim's bowels to move, I flipped through a self-help book by Mary Lou Retton, ex-Olympic gymnast. I forget the title of the book, but I do recall it being particularly informative, albeit on which subject I have absolutely no idea at this point.

As I said, though, we did eventually end up in Purgatoire, man-aging, quite by luck, to secure a soft, plush, low-slung sofa and chair arrangement directly opposite the servers' station halfway down the long narrow bar. A waitress arrived immediately to take our order. She was very tall and extremely thin and appeared, from her itali-cized body language at least, to be suffering through a very long evening. I smiled wide-eyed and Grover-like as she squeezed her way through the throng, and that seemed to disarm her momentarily.

"Bon soir," I said.

"Bon soir," she sighed, picking something unseen from the crotch of her short black dress. I smiled again, this time at her Frenchness, at her waitressness—at her crotch, to be honest, current-ly undergoing a good grooming at approximately eye level—and finally at her perfectly frank indifference to my existence. I remain to this day firmly convinced that waitresses are the only really worth-while women left in the world.

Hot Carl said, "Hey," then stretched, yawned and wheeled alto-gether too casually on Jim and me with a "What say, boys, coupla jugs?" further shattering any illusions of our feigned indigenousness. Jim nodded, and I asked for a Greyhound, adding "With the pink juice!" just as the waitress squeezed away to the next low-slung sofa-chair combo along the line. I wasn't sure whether she'd heard me, and suddenly became quite irritable. That was when I first heard this voice from the next sofa, this voice I recognized, accompanied by much loud liquor-fuelled laughter. Trying hard to start something, Hot Carl naturally told whoever it was to keep it down—an altogeth-er absurd request considering the current volume of the environment, understand.

"You got some sorta problem?" Hot Carl then inquired in his traditional idiom, and the voice sighed:

"Well you, now, I'm guessing."

Hot Carl went to stand up, and I told him to shut up and sit down. Hot Carl was young, just a month past twenty-one, and had recently taken up trying to impress me in public. It was a bad habit to be sure, one for which I was at least partially to blame, as I had allowed it to go unchecked for some time now, and so it was that I had to treat him harshly now and then.

I turned to apologize to our neighbours for Hot Carl's misbehav-iour, and that was when I noticed it was Chris De Boer that he'd been baiting. Chris smiled drunkenly and hoisted a martini—a red marti-ni with what looked like cranberries in it—and then we shook hands. He said that he'd been following my career, and furthermore, that of late he'd been following me around from city to city. Naturally, I found this last admission a little strange and more than a little discon-certing—but admittedly in a rather exciting and flattering fashion—and I thanked him for his interest, however dubiously or haphazard-ly inspired. At this point he invited me over to his sofa where, unless I was mistaken, he was translating the horoscopes from a local

French paper to a pretty young woman in a blonde wig. I could tell it was a wig she was wearing by the way the hairline ended so abruptly at the temples and neck. I remember wondering if she had cancer. I remember wondering that as, aside from carefully pencilled-in approximations, she had no eyebrows or eyelashes to speak of, and how because of those somewhat glaring omissions I couldn't help but stare. Staring like that, I remember quite clearly how I thought she did have cancer, and how the thought of that made me quite sad. Not that she had cancer, mind you, but that she'd try so hard to hide the fact. And I remember that sadness because other people were staring too, and their staring made me want to hit them, and wanting to hit someone—actually *wanting* to hit someone—well that always made me feel bad. The young woman caught me staring and I smiled softly. She smiled sweetly and I was glad.

Such profound observations made me forget where I was. Suddenly, though, I came to, and found myself watching De Boer gulp down the remains of his red martini and call out immediately for its successor. His forehead was sweating, and his features glistened sharply in the conical overhead light, while at his elbow stood a stack of three or four paperbacks tied together with a single red elastic band. I asked what all he was reading and he showed me *Lovestiff Annie.*

"Ever heard of it?" he winked.

"You know, I have," I said. "And it's a good one."

"Is it? I can never tell. To me it seems rather, well, malicious."

Malicious? That irked me. "Why do you say that?" I asked.

"Well I'm not altogether sure, Billy. Perhaps I was just curious to test your reaction. I'm a man of unquenchable curiosity, people tell me."

"I tell you what," I said, "that's something I try to avoid completely."

He handed me my father's book minus the elastic band, and I dutifully flipped through the pages a moment prior to politely handing it back.

"Keep it."

"I couldn't."

"Come on, consider it a gift. Besides, it's of no use to me now anyway."

"I already have a copy though. An original hardcover actually."

"So have this shitty second-hand copy too," he said. He was smiling now and I smiled too. He looked over to see if the young woman beside him was smiling, but she was not. He stopped smiling and I stopped too.

I flipped through the familiar pages again. "So then this is my father's book."

"Yes, I think we established that."

"No, I'm just thinking out loud is all."

"Well then maybe you should think about something interesting," he laughed.

I tucked the book away as another friend of his returned from the bar to take a seat in the chair alongside. "Billy, this here's Shannon," Chris said. "Apparently he's in love with my wife. Go ahead, Shannon. Tell Billy here how in love you are with my wife."

"Shut up with that," Shannon scowled as the woman blushed beneath her wig. He tilted his head a little to one side and back. "I mean it," he said, "shut up with that."

Shannon was short, perhaps the shortest black man I'd ever met, with a broad white gash of a grin running the width of his face and a thin pink slash of a scar slicing the bridge of his nose. His hands were stubby. His neck was thick. And his severely misshapen ears jutted out from the sides of his asymmetrical head almost as if trying desperately to escape it. Shannon and I shook hands waiting for Chris to introduce the woman in the wig, but he chose not to.

De Boer's table was being serviced by the same waitress as ours, and she soon returned with a tray laden with drinks. Hot Carl bought mine as well as all the others, I think. Next he ordered us four shots of Yukon Jack, followed by another four, and then another four after that, the jerk. The young woman in the wig smiled sadly at his overtures and I smiled too, and then in jest I asked if all the shots were for her. She answered quite sincerely that she thought they were probably for Shannon and her husband, and maybe even for me too.

"So no more Mannheim?" I asked Chris, flexing from my knuckles the stiffness that bore witness to the general inactivity of recent weeks.

"God no, no more fucking Mannheim," he said, arranging on his face a look of drunken disgust. "Not that it's your fault of course. Not entirely anyway."

I nodded as though I understood the joke and we scanned the crowd together. I asked if they were expecting someone and Shannon told me, quite frankly, the former prime minister. I looked at Chris. Chris looked at me. And that was when the full magnitude of his family name first really hit home for me.

"Say," said Shannon, steering me back to unfortunately more familiar matters, "are you by chance related to the Purdys who make the chocolates?"

"No," I answered with deliberate slowness, "I'm not related to the Purdys who make the chocolates."

"Too bad," he said. "Good chocolates." And then: "Hey, you know Nigel Warren? Nigger plays down in Florida?"

"As I recall, there are plenty of those in Florida," Chris put in, drawing an impatient glance from Shannon for his efforts.

"I meant for the Panthers. Nigger plays hockey," explained the latter to me.

I told Shannon that I knew Nigel Warren. Or that I knew who he was anyway.

"Say, didn't you two square off just last week?" asked Chris while petitioning another drink from a passing waitress.

"More like two weeks ago, I'd think."

"Nigger's my cousin, see," claimed Shannon proudly.

"Oh but can't you tell, Billy? Shannon here loves him. Go ahead, Shannon. Tell Billy here how in love a brother you are."

"I said I love her like a *brother loves a sister*," retorted Shannon decisively before pivoting to me. "Well he's not really my cousin, see. Pop's his godfather, that's all."

"An offer he couldn't refuse," I replied, and together we nodded slowly and jutted our chins a while.

"You know you broke the nigger's nose," continued Shannon at length.

"Yes, well, he had an extremely hittable nose," I said.

"Still, he throws pretty good."

"Yeah, he throws pretty well."

"And we love him for it too," Chris added, watching with critical interest as I tipped the candle onto the table to form a graphically phallic shape with the wax. "I mean it's vitally important that we all declare our brotherly love for each other's wives."

"Nigger, will you *please* shut up with that?" Shannon said, shaking his asymmetrical head from side to side. I was really very far behind them, especially with all this love and nigger business, but, for the moment anyway, decided to let it pass.

I pushed the depleted and flickering candle aside. "He does throw pretty well though. Nigel, I mean."

"Yeah, but you put a beating on him."

"I beat him, yes."

"Soundly."

"Very soundly, yes."

"Man, that's some fucked-up shit," muttered Shannon in drunken disbelief, at which point a holster-clad shooter girl came squeezing through the crowd. At De Boer's request she poured us each an ounce of Ouzo. We all took one except for the woman in the wig. The shooter girl took one though. Evidently word soon spread through the ranks, as before long another bottle-slinging shooter bandit came squeezing through the crowd.

"Say, you ever notice how all the niggers in the league are freaking goons?" Shannon observed, having waved this latest offer away.

"Not goons," I said. "I don't like that word 'goon.'"

"Fine. En*forc*ers then."

"Not all," Chris said. "There's that one in Boston remember."

"And Edmonton too," I said.

"Actually Edmonton has two. So does Buffalo for that matter."

"And Phoenix."

"Got sent down," Chris said, shaking his head.

"Really? That Williams guy?"

"Oh yeah, sent way down."

"But most," Shannon suggested.

"Oh sure, most. Same with the natives though, eh Billy?" Chris said with an ill-behaved smile, provoking the woman in the wig to push him hard on the arm in protest. "Aw come on," he told her, "I'm sure that's what they're calling themselves now."

I was shaking the cubes around the bottom of my glass when Hot Carl piped up from behind—I told him to keep quiet as I was speaking with friends. Never interrupt me when I'm speaking with friends, I added. And immediately he turned away, believing, as he always did, anything I told him, especially when it involved my supposed acquaintances.

Shannon sighed, "Yeah, but all the Indians cling together'n shit, like they all got some sort of pact or something. Check it out: you never see the Indians fighting one another. Never. Yet the niggers, they're always pounding the living daylights out of one another like it's the only thing they can do." He paused, reflecting on the unnatural, clearly racist injustice of it all. "I tell you what, though, that's one crazy fucked-up game. I mean smack a nigger in the face with a stick and get five minutes. But *call* him a nigger and get suspended outright."

"Oh and I suppose you've got a better game in mind?" Chris said, wiping sweat from his forehead with the back of an arm. "Oh don't you dare say basketball. Please, for the brotherly love of God, spare me my own prejudice and don't you dare say basketball. Christ, that's novel."

"Novel nothing. Don't you go profiling me."

"Hey, you quit acting like a minority and I'll quit treating you like one. You're not exactly living in the Projects, Shannon. Although naturally I'd love you like a brother if you were," Chris smiled, and together we drank in silence as tribute to all this brotherly love going around. In the meantime Shannon looked at me, then at the woman, then at De Boer, and finally threw up his hands in hopeless appeal. Mission accomplished, Chris turned his considerable intoxication on me. "So, Billy, do you want to come to Costa Rica with me or what."

"Costa Rica. Why Costa Rica?"

"Why the fuck not? I'm telling you, it's beautiful down there. They love you like brothers down there." He cut his eyes Shannon's way so that the woman in the wig pushed him hard on the arm again, but he only laughed and said something that sounded like Hauko.

"Sorry?"

"J-A-C-O. Jaco. They've got this town there called Jaco Beach where they make, bar none, the best sandwich I've ever had."

"Sandwiches, huh. Boy, now if that's not reason enough to go," I said.

"And there's this hotel called the Copacabana too," he went on, his pupils fixed not on me but on a boxer on the wall beside me. "Swear to God though, Billy, the Copa-fucking-cabana—with this great little swim-up bar. Remember that, Shannon? Sure you do. Remember how we swam right up to those stools, those cool little stools right there in the goddamned pool? No? Ah well, what the hell," he said, "maybe it wasn't you.

"Backwards though," he continued. "Costa Rica, I mean. Like least a century removed. I mean they're Catholic and everything, but still promiscuous as all hell too." Someone kicked him beneath the low glass table and he jumped, wincing suddenly at the woman in the wig. "Hell, why go to Jaco when there's plenty of good tanning beds right here?" he said, moving her to a sad sort of smile. "But then again, it's probably all different now. I mean everything's different now. Nothing feels quite like it should."

"*All* right," Shannon said, rolling up his big white eyes. "All right, now we get it, people. You see, Billy, your fellow white man here is presently struggling under the weight of his semi-annual spiritual crisis. Don't worry, though, he'll get through it. He always gets through it—for the ladies. Sorry," he said to the girl.

"Hey, he's Indian," Chris said, tipping his chin at me.

"Half maybe."

"Still half more than you and I put together, I'd say."

"Whatever," Shannon said, dismissing my pedigree completely. "Still not some maximum minority busting his ass for minimum respect."

"Oh come now. You know I love you like a brother, Shannon."

"Oh *please*. You don't love anything you can't pull your exalted little missionary act on."

"On the contrary, I'd love you like a nigger any day."

They blinked at each other a while, and in time Shannon rotated my way. "So hey, I was wondering, do you switch sides? Or do you always pin the same cheek."

Briefly I felt the anger swell up inside, more at the presumed intimacy than at the implied accusation of it all. "Switch. You have to switch," I eventually replied.

"Why, one side'll get bigger or something?"

"Something like that, yeah. And too much scar tissue builds up besides."

"Side effects?" he asked, provoking the woman in the wig to push Chris hard on the arm yet again, in a roundabout effort, it would seem, to bring an abrupt end to Shannon's tactless line of questioning. "Side effects?" he repeated anyway, stroking his chin.

"A touch of the rage maybe. You know, when people get to asking me a lot of personal questions."

I winked at the woman in the wig, and she smiled shyly as I hooked back a shot. As anticipated, the Yukon Jack locked my jaw, and for a moment I had to fight just to remain outside all that alcohol.

"No disrespect of course," said Shannon. "I was just wondering is all. I mean don't they feed that shit to racehorses?"

"Used to anyway. And hey, if you're interested, I did start pissing blood just the other day."

"Seriously? Are you fucking serious? That—that's terrible, man."

"Well I'm sorry to disappoint you," I said, adding for the benefit of no one in particular, probably the girl, that my health was my business and no one else's, some sawed-off nigger's especially.

Later, when I returned from the bathroom, De Boer and the young woman were nowhere to be found. Shannon, however, he was still there, having since moved up to a stool at the bar. I asked where Chris was and Shannon told me he was gone. His father had sent a car for them and they were gone.

"But what about Costa Rica?"

"Sorry?" said Shannon, forced to shout over the noise of the crowd.

"Chris and I, we were supposed to go to Costa Rica for sandwiches together."

He looked at me blankly, shaking his curiously shaped head from side to side, and so I returned to my sofa and to my seat next to Hot Carl and ordered myself another Greyhound—a triple this time. And sitting there waiting for my drink to arrive, I studied the boxers on the walls, wondering why I could not recall any of their names. I thought the one was perhaps Sugar Ray Robinson or else a young Cassius Clay, but I was still very much unsure—his face was distorted by his opponent's fist and he looked to have been knocked unconscious already. Alongside this photograph, inexplicably, hung a copy of the Mona Lisa, smiling in her knowing way. I wondered what she could possibly be smiling about, smiling that way. And then, very suddenly, it hit me.

CHAPTER THREE

I HAVE NEVER cared all that much for fighting, and in fact thoroughly dislike it now, but I learned it painfully and practiced it diligently—at first to get my career on track and later on to keep it rolling. I must admit there was a certain comfort to be had in knowing I could take care of myself in most any given situation, and furthermore, knock most anybody down, but true to the craft I tried my best to keep it on the ice, and in that I was successful, or for the most part at least I was. After being selected by Chicago in the National Hockey League's entry draft way back in 1978, it was hoped that with soft hands and decent speed I would step into my scorer's role immediately to help solidify a dwindling attack, and, with my size, add some much needed grit to the Blackhawks' suspect right side. It didn't quite work out like that. In training camp I was promptly overmatched—I squared off with seasoned heavyweights Stu Timmins and Ray Rhodes twice, and they each beat me soundly both times. This experience served only to increase my distaste for fighting, and I was promptly cut, forced to spend that season and the following two bouncing around the minors hardening my hands and honing my craft. Then, in 1981, at the deadline, my playing rights were traded to Hartford for future considerations, and knowing that at the ripe old age of twenty-three I might not have too many shots left, I took advantage of the opportunity the only way my no longer soft hands would allow. On my very first shift of my very first game I fought Buffalo's Todd Brown, an altogether decent middleweight and notorious tough guy, and dispensed with him easily. Next shift out I ran their goalie, running him out of the game. And by the end of regulation I managed to fight and beat each and every man they threw out at me, including both top enforcers, making my way to the box a total of five times. From that day forward I toiled fifteen straight seasons as the Whalers' premier heavyweight, dropping the gloves whenever it was required, slipping on those of the field surgeon, taking apart each of my opponents with the cool clinical detachment of the seasoned hatchet man. All told I missed only thirty-two games over that span, the majority of which were suspensions, and so it came as somewhat of a surprise when in the summer of 1996 the Whalers decided not to renew my contract.

Needless to say, there was little interest in a thirty-eight year old enforcer with bad hands and tired legs. In fact, as far as the National Hockey League was concerned, there was absolutely no interest whatsoever. My career appeared to be over at that point, and with it, my stumbling second marriage as well. Brought up on misdemeanour spousal assault and battery, I was sentenced to four hundred hours of community service at the Boys & Girls Club in Hartford, only one hundred of which were ever served—a long-time season ticket holder and assistant district attorney managing to see the remainder waived. And six months later, restraining order firmly in place, divorce all but complete, cut off from my two children and paying their mother a hefty chunk of alimony and child support, I moved home to Lethbridge, Alberta to play right wing on my brothers' team in the local beer league. And that was when my old Junior coach called, from Germany of all places, promising a full-time job if I would only agree to have both hands surgically reconstructed, and furthermore, remain dry for the entire campaign. After much contemplation I consented—to his first request, that is—and went under the knife for the first time in my life. And so, seven months later, there I was skating on Mannheim Adler's third line in the German Elite League, fighting rarely, drinking excessively, pooling my many off-ice hours in some of that city's more notorious bars and strip clubs whose only real romance was their names.

Because of the liquor I mistrust my memory to a great extent, especially when the images hold together, and I surrender now with

great reluctance that until I met Chris De Boer I'd always had this
sneaking suspicion that I'd never really lived at all. Until he bought
me that first drink in Mannheim, I thought that perhaps I'd made it
all up. That perhaps I'd simply asked for a pair of skates as a young
boy, and that for being so insolent as to ask for a pair of skates as a
young boy I'd been snatched from my boyhood home near
Lethbridge and placed in one of a succession of small boxes for the
rest of my life. Naturally, I was correct in this belief, or for the most
part at least I was, but as was always the case with belief there is always
more to it than typically meets the eye.

Through my dead mother I am a non-practicing member of the
Kainaiwa, or Blood, Blackfoot Nation, and through my dead father,
by way of his, of the Black Irish Canadian Catholic one. There aren't
all that many of the former remaining, and with any luck even fewer
of the latter, so I think that perhaps I am of a dying breed. In the
town of Lethbridge where I first attended a non-residential school,
and where I first played organized hockey, no one ever made me feel
race-conscious. In fact, no one ever made me feel like a half-breed,
a mistake, and hence any less a citizen than anybody else until my
coach, the local Catholic priest, was sent east to Sault Ste Marie and
the Ontario Hockey League and my father sent me there to play on
his team. Still, I took it pretty well, I think. I never did let it get into
my head. I was a big boy, a confident boy, and something like that
was never going to box me in.

As a young man I was never all that interested in girls to be honest, never like my teammates were at any rate, and so it was that, after
signing my very first professional contract, lacking any sort of frame
of reference, I married the first pretty girl who was ever really nice to
me. I don't mean sexually nice—I had met many nice puck-bunnies
in the Sault—but genuinely nice. Decently nice. *Respectfully* nice.
Rena seemed legitimately interested in the things I had to say, in the
things I liked to think and read and dream about, and I really did
appreciate her for that. Unfortunately Rena and I were separated just
three months later. Sometimes with Rena I got to beating her up pretty badly. That struck me. Up until Rena I thought I had been an

altogether decent fellow, even an altogether noble fellow, but as it turns out I was very much a rotten son of a bitch. After Rena I tried to forget about girls for a while, and I did, managing to remain unmarried for close to six years before finally giving in to an aging predator named Louise who, with the clear and notable exception of my mother, sported the blackest hair I had ever seen.

Louise was very strong and direct with me, and for that reason we were very much in love. I was twenty-seven at this point and in my prime as a hockey player: I had money, really a great deal of money, a good wife, two children on the way, a blossoming domestic happiness I had never really counted on and, perhaps most importantly, a recently acquired awareness that I could drink less and less and yet still have a hell of a time anyway. For five straight years my life was perfect. For five straight years I was a good man. And it was under these circumstances that I first came in contact with steroids, became an addict, and eventually went through the hell of withdrawal, thereby gaining the necessary motivation, if not the very real need, for something I had never really felt before.

I had discovered Stanozolol. Or more accurately, had it recommended to me by the Whalers' team physician, Doctor Perry Kittles. Everyone called him Stan, though I have no idea why. Actually maybe I do know why. Anyway, it was the summer of 1990, with my life in hockey seemingly winding down, when Stan informed me that if I were willing to quit smoking, begin a program of regular physical fitness and with it, an injection of two hundred milligrams of Stanozolol a week for twelve straight weeks—repeating the cycle after a brief one month hiatus—I could probably count on adding another season or two to an already distinguished professional career. I had never used the juice before, and to be honest, it had never really occurred to me as something to try, but another season, well that sounded awfully good to me—life after hockey proving such an intimidating prospect for prospects like myself—so many of us having never known anything else, or else having forgotten everything else entirely. And so it was that a new training regimen, combined with that wonderful magic cocktail Stanozolol, sounded to me like a hell of a plan. The effect was uncanny. By training camp three months later I managed to add some twenty-five pounds of solid muscle, and perhaps more importantly, managed to bring my skating back to where it had been a decade before. My coaches were impressed. The owner was ecstatic. That year I fought everything that moved.

It was my best season ever: twenty-three goals and four hundred forty-eight minutes in the penalty box, a mere twenty-four off Dave Schultz's all-time record. They even did an article on me in *Sports Illustrated.* Now I shall forego the embarrassment of telling you the article's title, but I will say that the accompanying photographs, one in particular, were widely published in the weeks immediately following the season as heartbreaking evidence of a latter-day aboriginal success story. And the Whalers, all they did was reward me with a five-year, three-point-five million dollar contract. And then of course the Stanozolol stopped working.

Well it did not exactly *stop*—the weekly doses were simply no longer having the same desired effect. So I doubled the dosage. Then I tripled it. Soon I was taking two hundred milligrams of Stanozolol, stacking it with one hundred and fifty of something called Deca Durabolin, throwing in another fifty of Dianabol or Winstrol or whatever else was available for good measure—a total dosage of four hundred milligrams—and taking it, in conjunction with some female fertility drug called Clomid, *every day.* Needless to say, those were some very strange days indeed. But alas, not even the holy grail of cocktails can halt time forever, no matter what the proof, and so it was that in the summer of 1996, with my contract up, my second marriage over, and my knuckles shattered from hammering up against so many helmets for so many years, that I again found myself contemplating life after hockey—something I was very much afraid of and completely unwilling to accept of course. And so began my latest resurrection, first in Lethbridge, Alberta and later Mannheim, Germany, whereupon I finally met the late prime minister's youngest son in Heaven and my life began anew.

CHAPTER FOUR

THE THIRD TIME I hooked up with Chris De Boer was in Vancouver, British Columbia. It was the early spring, a few months after our not so impromptu reunion in Montreal, and the Capitals had flown into town to face the Canucks for the first and final time that year. For the previous two weeks I'd been living with the rumour that I might be traded away at any time. That was what the trading deadline was like for fringe players like me: forever on the block when it came time to fine-tune the playoff-bound machine. Now early on in my career, say, back in my prime, I would never have been let go by a playoff-bound team. For even though fighting was already somewhat of a rarity in playoff hockey by that time, the enforcer was still very much a necessary ingredient of any winning recipe. A policeman, if you will. A bodyguard. A lurking threat of retribution for all those insistent on taking liberties with your so-called players of skill. But here in the twilight of my career I had no such expectations. Here in the twilight I had become somewhat redundant and therefore expendable—good in the room but mediocre on the ice—a penalty box-prone instigator considered too far gone to be anything but a gamble. And so, just hours before the deadline, things were getting rather tense around the room. Trade deadlines were always good for some tension around the room, and if you happened to be good in the room then the deadline was the time to step up and get in goin' on, as it were.

However, when I returned to my hotel room that evening, there was a message waiting for me. Chris De Boer, having evidently followed me to Vancouver, said he wanted to meet up with me as soon as it was convenient, that night if possible. I was to meet him at the Devil's Advocaat right near the hotel. Well that's a smart name for a bar, I thought. In fact, as far as bar names went, I thought that was the smartest one by far. When I arrived there was quite a queue however.

"He's not there," announced a voice near at hand, and I wheeled to find approaching from across the street a man smiling kindly, laughing lightly and tipping back a can of Coors Light, all while stretching out towards me an eager friendly hand that I should clasp.

"Who's not there?" I asked, unable to place the fellow, and therefore fighting the immediate urge to realign my scepticism here. He was young, younger than I was at any rate, somewhere in his late twenties maybe, tall and handsome and clean-cut, radiating a sort of collegiate affability.

"Who's not there?" I repeated, enduring his seemingly endless shaking of my hand. In fact, he shook my hand so hard and long that I began to wonder whether or not I'd recognize it when I finally got it back.

"Chris," he said, draining the last contents of the can before tossing the empty into a nearby bush. "He's already at the Roxy. Come on, though, we'll hook up with him there."

Curious as I was, I asked who he was and he said Fisk. I could see Fisk was expecting some sort of recognition here, and feeling obligated I was expecting to provide it, if only to bring about an end to this somewhat painful impasse at which we'd so suddenly arrived.

"Fine, have it your way then—Fisk," I said, and with that he finally let go of my hand, only to take me by the elbow instead, manoeuvring me down Nelson, across Granville, and through the gauntlet of young scruffy beggars waiting to accost us there. For whatever reason one young woman caught my eye, catching it in such a way that rustling up a few dollars, whatever was in my pockets anyway, seemed like a small price to pay for the chance at our striking up a pleasant conversation. Unfortunately it turned out that she was Québécois, and therefore uninterested in any such exchange, and so in the end it remained very much a one-way transaction—as if the French are capable of doing business any other way.

Managing to emerge relatively unscathed from the rash of beggars and panhandlers with which we were subsequently plagued, we eventually approached a bar with a bright red neon sign overhead. *The Roxy*, it said, and there was quite a queue at the front door. Conveniently, though, the doorman gave us both the nod, allowing us to pass without our wasting any more time outdoors.

The Roxy was a good bar. In retrospect, I might even say it was my favourite bar by far. It was long and narrow like Purgatoire in Montreal, although quite a stretch longer and not nearly so narrow. In fact, now that I think about it, the Roxy was nothing like Purgatoire in Montreal except for how it catered to the young and pretty, and how it used the pink grapefruit juice in its Greyhounds. Three steps in we hit the wall of noise, then the wall of people, then the first bar where a bald Arab bartender seemed almost too pleased to have us around. Fisk (whose given name, I soon found out, was David) shook the bartender's hand and gestured my way, and the bartender shook my hand and gave me a long deep nod indicative of nothing insofar as I could tell straight away.

"Name's Shar," he said in a suddenly stringent and businesslike tone. "Tomorrow night you play, right?"

"Tomorrow night, yes," I replied in much the same way.

Shar nodded deeply again and clasped his muscular brown hands together solidly over mine. I asked where De Boer was, and shrugging he told me "the fucker" was around. Fisk ordered two double Greyhounds and two bottles of beer along with two shots to make up the round. Shar popped the caps off the bottles, poured two stiff double vodkas and topped them up with grapefruit, then splashed out three punishing shots of Jim Beam and tallied it all up at a ridiculously cheap seven dollars. Fisk handed Shar a twenty and told him to fuck himself and keep the change. Shar laughed and kept it. We chatted some more about this and that and then the three of us hooked back our shots together. Fisk and Shar touched fists. Shar and I touched fists. Then Fisk and I touched fists—for symmetry, I suppose.

The bar was busy, extremely busy, and the band had yet to take the stage. I followed Fisk along to the rear of the establishment where, if the crowd was any indication, a small sunken bar was apparently all the rage. He offered to take my coat and I allowed him the pleasure, watching as he placed said coat, together with his own, in the hands of the stunning blonde bartender currently hovering about at crotch level. She in turn placed the coats somewhere beneath the counter. Then she and Fisk shared a joke about something as she poured out three great big shots together.

"What are these then?" I asked, allowing myself an indulgent albeit appropriately aloof smile at this point of my night's adventure.

"Kamikazes," said Fisk, and we hooked back our shots together. Licking the remains of Kamikaze from my shot glass, working hard to get my tongue all the way down to the end of that stubby little brat, I glanced around. Everything was as it should be—that is, other than having a member of a former prime minister's immediate family around. Meanwhile, the tartness of the lime and Triple Sec, together with the vodka, made the bone of my jaw ache all around.

"Busy night," I noted, flexing my fingers and cracking my knuckles.

"Industry night," said Fisk.

"Is that why the prices are so low?"

"No, that's just the Arab. Sharif likes to rig it so that he makes a lot of dough."

I asked once more where I might find De Boer. Fisk said he didn't know. I thought about asking whether this was some kind of con—I'd had that experience before—but just as quickly as the idea occurred to me just as promptly was it lost, for just then another guy came up, this guy quite a bit shorter than either Fisk or myself, introducing himself as Gavin something-or-other—I forget what. I watched his eyeballs pinball over me: head to chest to shoulders to arms. Gavin was an actor apparently, and according to Gavin himself, quite an accomplished one at that.

Fisk and I spoke of Gavin in a quiet condescending manner while the latter was off at the bar fetching us drinks. He was wearing a red leather jacket with the word *Roots* embroidered in bold white letters across the chest. For those who still didn't get it, the word *Canada* had been no less discreetly emblazoned across the back. Apparently, whenever it was foggy anyway, it was Gavin's idea of a good time to have his photograph taken, in black and white no less, either walking coolly down the street with a cane, or else sliding forth from shrubbery with a samurai sword clutched up threateningly alongside his head. Whichever fiancée he was sporting at the time received the reward of taking the photograph, I guess. Evidently Gavin really liked to get engaged. Six times he'd taken the plunge already, only to get cold feet within a few days. He was twenty-seven years old and, apart from what I've presently portrayed, confined himself to being belligerent in a variety of ways.

Gavin returned shortly with three double Greyhounds and three more shots—red ones this time—and we three hooked back our shots together. Then Gavin dropped his empty glass to the floor. The music was too loud to hear it land, but believe me it did, and as it shattered about my shoes Gavin proceeded to growl something derogatory in the direction of the stunning blonde bartender still hovering about below.

"That's a real gift with the vernacular you got there, Gavin," I said, and suddenly he looked at me as if seeing me for the very first time, all the while trying hard to resemble that celebrity he hoped to hell he could be just one time.

"So why not just go someplace else then?" I inquired of Fisk, feeling Gavin's antagonism reach out to meet and steadily reciprocate my own.

"We would, except that we're rather limited by the geography of Gavin here's sexual history. Or is it the history of his geography, I don't know." Either way, Fisk explained, Gavin here had demonstrated, on a variety of occasions and with several different bartenders, a rather remarkable and disturbing fondness for having his anus played with. Which was, actually, no big deal, Fisk told me, as having a girl slip a finger up your ass while she performed oral sex was apparently about as explicit as shaking hands these days.

With that in mind, then, my host and I moved out to the main front room where, having managed to reduce his head sufficiently in size in order to squeeze it through the crowd, Gavin eventually condescended to making it a trio once again. It was my round, and at Fisk's suggestion I returned to the front bar to see the Arab, Shar. By now I was beginning to collect the usual amount of attention from the various occupants of the bar, that kind of attention a bona fide hockey player always receives in such a bona fide hockey town. It's not like that in the States. At least with hockey players it's not. Now certainly they never miss out on an opportunity to celebrate their celebrities, but having spent the vast majority of my career on American soil, I've come to realize that the professional hockey player, culturally speaking, ranks just behind your typical roller-derby magnate and monster truck virtuoso. So be it. That kind of attention has never meant all that much to me as it is. And yet it remains part and parcel to the scene here in Vancouver, and therefore deserving of particular mention: young women pressing themselves against me, and young men measuring themselves against me too.

I was a large man back then, there is no getting around that. I was a large man and, coupled with that, a recognized professional athlete, and being as such necessitated a certain responsibility, even an obligation, to fulfill the more elemental expectations of that assignment. When you're a large man, people come to count on you, even need and expect things from you, and either you learn to deliver on those needs and expectations or else learn to face the wrath of a considerably less than enthusiastic review. That much I discovered at my first professional camp way back in '78. I was to fight and fight often, and I was to win—or else be banished back to the farm for an unspecified length of time. I mean my God, entire swings of momentum were hanging in the balance here—indispensable fruits of an enforcer's endeavours. Yet it is a different game now. Vastly different. For now it's not so imperative that the enforcer deliver just so long as he remembers to snarl.

There is no mystery to being big. The business of bigness is an easy read. I remember clearly how different life became for me when

I first entered puberty, and again later when I first started taking Stanozolol in 1990. Even then, the transformation, it was not lost on me. I mean it was obvious—I knew exactly what was happening right away. For instance, I was immediately aware of the fact that if I were to enter a room chest-first in a nice tight shirt, I would receive immediate gratification for the effort. Whether it be envy, lust, intimidation or repulsion, immediate gratification was there to be had. You make a statement like that, entering a room chest-first in a nice tight shirt, and things immediately become clear, unquestionably so in fact. Yet this certainty, this absolute confidence and clarity, is not always available when you enter that same room an average man. No, when you enter an average man, you have to rely on the intangibles to promote you from the margins of life—intelligence, charm, wit—a difficult proposition to say the least, at least for someone like me it is. Entering this way the lines of certainty become blurred. Entering this way lacks immediate gratification. And immediate gratification was what the juice was all about.

Now there are plenty of myths that surround and saturate the steroid business, and the steroid user perpetuates these myths each and every time he steps out in public. For instance, a lot of nonsense has been written about the various side effects steroids come saddled with. If you believe these reports, one shot in the ass and a glance in the mirror reveals your testicles all but shrivelling up and falling to the floor like rotting fruit from a tree. Come on. Barring massive doses taken over extended periods, there are absolutely no negative effects to steroid use whatsoever. Another myth concerns the air bubble in the syringe. Please. If shooting an air bubble into your vein could kill you, there wouldn't be a juicer left alive (including, of course, your narrator). Truth is, the fewer the comforts the juicer has at his disposal, the fewer the interruptions to his discipline he is forced to endure, then the deeper he is immersed into the rigors of his addiction, the more he feels himself at home in that world. His morale is higher; his sense of self is greater. And yet at the same time he learns to gamble somewhat with his health, to risk something permanent and potentially even lethal, and as a result of that kind of existence becomes altogether indifferent to the outside world.

And that is the reason I love liquor. Or one of the reasons anyway. It's more like an idea. An idea of a place. A place in time where the roads are frozen and the air is clear and cold and dry—a place of mountain chalets and smoke-filled cafés, of long Indian trails and longer Indian summer days, of cottages along the lake where the rooms come cheap to offset the loss, the opportunity cost, of days spent staring out the window and waiting for the ice to break. Literature is steeped in alcohol. Inebriation is one of the all-time great subjects, and certainly one of the most difficult to write well. Those who do not like it, or who have been scarred or frightened by it, are always very wary of it and try to make it seem foolish, or disgusting, or something in the way of a disease, when in actual fact it's something very irreplaceable in all of us. We all know it's bad to drink. But sometimes it's necessary to get drunk. And anyone who says it's not is a liar, or at best mistaken, I think.

Seen in that light, then, booze is very different than juice. Juice takes discipline, while booze is the escape from any discipline and, in the short term anyway, manifests itself almost exclusively in the spirit—thus that particular nickname, I take it. Juice, on the other hand, proceeds as a muscular dialogue, teaching the user facts of general validity, and the abuser the facts of life. I have learned nothing from the use of alcohol. But I have learned a great deal from the abuse of steroids. I have seen strength and power doled out in weekly syringes and monthly cycles. And I have experienced the shrinking of the body and the agonizing self-loathing of withdrawal—followed by the growth and associated pleasure when juice-thirsty muscles drink from the vial. The continued use of steroids, the discipline and the addiction to that discipline, exists as a self-stoking fire, a nuclear reaction at the muscular level contained only by the user's reluctance to strap yet more horsepower onto an already overburdened chassis. For the juicer, when he stops growing he starts to die. So he never stops growing. Perhaps all pleasure is growth, I really don't know, but to shrink, or even to remain in stasis, is, for the steroid addict anyway, to wither away in relative exile. Now he may from time to time complete a cycle, thus staying the growth for a while, but he will always get back on the juice. It's almost impossible for the juicer not to get back on the juice. It's the discipline he can't leave behind.

As usual, I considered all these old ideas and some newer ones besides, in forms now framed by low-cut shirts and high-cut skirts and, on the outermost margins, some semblance of the Canadian flag. The alcohol was beginning to turn me now. Shar rang me up three double Greyhounds, and poured out two shots of Jack Daniel's on the side. We conversed a while about the plight of the hometown team, agreeing, wholeheartedly, that while their chances of making the playoffs this year were virtually nil, they might just make a run and slip in the backdoor somewhere.

"That being Gavin's forte," said Shar snidely, holding up his shot for a toast. "Gentlemen, to the anus."

"To the anus," I said, and we shot back our Jack together.

"You boys leaving us out?" protested Fisk from behind, having draped one of his long limp hands over my shoulder by this time. For all his good intentions, I was seriously beginning to dislike Mr Fisk and the seemingly sterile yet somehow faggy way he copped a feel. And as much as I found myself disliking him, I was really beginning to detest his anal little actor friend here—my natural axis of liquor-induced bliss forever at the mercy of my juicer's more combative gravitational pull.

"Just give it a name," Shar shrugged.

"Four more," I told him, feeling my face piling up in the periphery of my vision from all these strained speeches and forced smiles. "Red ones though. I like the red ones," I said, taking two twenties from my wallet and slapping them down on the bar. Shar asked if I wanted change and I told him, as was the custom apparently, to go ahead and fuck himself.

Shar smiled fiercely and poured out four shots—in highball glasses this time—saying in a mock East Indian accent, "Put yourselves outside of that, you assholes," and we four assholes choked down our shots together. Scanning over the heads of the crowd, Fisk winced continuously as he sucked the last remnants of liquor from his gums.

"Must be gone."

"De Boer? Yeah, gone," Shar told Fisk over the band's annoyingly discordant preparations. "He fucked off like an hour ago."

I looked at Shar. "I thought you said he was here though."

"I did. He was. But then he fucked right off when he heard you were on your way over."

Gavin wheeled me about by the shoulder. For reasons unexplained he was laughing terrifically hard now, but in a very abstract way—wide-mouthed and silent—and watching his head roll back off its jaw like that I wondered just how much effort would be required to cram my fist all the way down that deep dark hole.

Grabbing a bottle from the back bar, Shar discharged three shots of cheap blended scotch, declining one himself. "Don't be ridiculous," he said in the same exaggerated accent as before. "I have to work, you ridiculous cocksuckers."

We three cocksuckers hoisted our scotch. "So let me get this straight," I said to Fisk in an oddly imploring tone, "Chris is gone?"

"Appears that way, yep."

"Did he ever get to Costa Rica?"

"Sorry?" he said, lips hovering poised and ready over his glass.

"Costa Rica," I repeated, riding out a sudden surge of self-disgust. "Did he ever get to Costa Rica."

"Billy, he's gone there several times."

"I meant the last time—after Montreal," I continued, unable to stop myself.

"Oh sure. He, me and Shannon went. I mean I assume we went. As I recall I was a little drunk at the time."

We hooked back our scotch just as the band began to play in earnest. There were two women singing in the band backed by four male musicians, and they were called the Shaved Pussycats, I think. And as I stood there watching the Shaved Pussycats work the crowd, I began to imagine De Boer, imagining in him I saw my own fractured adolescence come rushing back: voices of my brothers slung down along the Blood Reserve's riverbanks on lazy hunting afternoons, daytrips from the Sault on down to Paris and even Woodbine to watch the horses run, and summers back on the Alberta family farm assisting in the branding of a new one. With De Boer I imagined all these things—I had to—because in him I saw not one of these things, and had nothing else to do.

CHAPTER FIVE

FISK AND GAVIN had left. Suddenly and without notice they were gone. In their place a pretty young woman named Melanie—not my Melanie but theirs—a pretty, young, church-going Melanie with burgundy hair, large even teeth, and a rather unfortunate sexually transmitted disease I never really discovered the source of. Presently a writer by choice, and a bartender and legal secretary by necessity of course, Melanie had actually taken a stab at being a lawyer at one time—that is, until getting caught up in the mutual admiration society of David Fisk and Chris De Boer somewhere along the line. Actually, having purportedly attended law school for no other reason than to learn how to write crime, Melanie of late boasted an impressive resume of mostly food and beverage-specific employment, as well as an escalating contempt for the world in general. Whenever she got around to the business of complaining about Chris, which she inevitably did, Melanie was always very practical about it—but then every axe to grind has to have its handle, I guess.

Somehow I feel I have not yet adequately revealed the character of Chris De Boer. Perhaps this is due to the fact that he has yet to reappear in the narrative, I really don't know, but at the risk of redundancy I feel it imperative to further illustrate that character here. Until Chris fell in with his wife, he was positive, along with his friends and family, that he would never amount to anything in this life. On the contrary, until he fell in with his wife most everyone, including Chris, stood convinced that he was well on his way to a life's accomplishment of zero. Now this is not to say that he was a born loser—obviously not in light of his family's longstanding wealth and rank—but simply that the effort, or else the passion to produce that effort, prior to his wife's arrival, had simply never been there. And yet exhibiting as he did the age-old habit of the drifter, if not the actual virtue, any or even all of what I am about to tell you might have been at work well below the horizon of his character long before the advent of Jennifer.

If he was in a crowd he would offer nothing of note to stand out, and yet he was always an accomplished actor, forever an exceptional liar, and really very funny in ways I've not yet found the means to bring out. He wore shorts a great deal, even in winter, but he wasn't really or even remotely stupid. On the contrary, he was intelligent, often to a fault, and that it seemed for so long that he would never amount to anything in this life made that seem all the more tragic somehow. But then he fell in with Jennifer, his wife, and everything about him changed, or else the perception of everything did, until, in the end, people felt as though he'd simply been playing ignorant all along. And as if to confirm this theory, even after hitting the pinnacle of his notoriety, he was always very nice about it.

As I have mentioned, he was nice to look at. He cared about his body and liked to keep it in shape. In this way, then, he managed to retain about him a timeless undergraduate charm while everyone else around him seemed to depreciate at a fairly standard rate. He moved always on the periphery, his gait a smooth and slightly bowlegged skate, and yet he was always at the center of things, where everyone, including me, seemed to assign him with uniform aim and considerable haste. When he looked at you, it was as though he was looking right through you, and yet he always made a point of listening to whatever it was you had to say. Not that De Boer was any great politician himself. On the contrary, he only spoke when he had something to say, something meaningful anyway, which often left considerable gaps in the conversation that you felt obliged to step into in some way. And while in his peers he experienced no immediate reflection of himself, he carried around all these shadows as if it was his responsibility, and his alone, to show them the light of day. He was a contradiction then, and however loath he would be to admit it, an artist in every way. Except for the fact that he understood without acknowledging his understanding that while a life of spiritual fulfillment could indeed be achieved by the artist, there was a life far more lucrative to be had by he who simply acted like one.

Perhaps that's why I felt such an immediate and absorbing attraction to his mistress. I liked Melanie. In fact, spending on her the amount of money I did that night, I like her a great deal to this day. And because I liked her so much that night it was of course inevitable that I would eventually make an ass of myself in some way. I did not disappoint. Believe me, I was grand. Soon enough I was forcing myself in behind the bar, pushing Shar and the other staff aside to pour not only my own drinks, but any and all others I thought might help boost my appeal somehow.

As might be expected, such a transgression didn't go over so well with the staff and management of the Roxy that night. As might be expected, it rarely did. My being a bona fide hockey player in a bona fide hockey town carried me along for a while, but not nearly long enough, and eventually the staff's cool amusement fermented to a fairly caustic disapproval and disgust.

At first Shar and the other bartenders played along quite amiably, even good-naturedly, but soon enough the bouncers were moving in, eager to negotiate a quick and more or less violent settlement to this large and drunken issue currently weaving about behind the taps. They circled in on me rapidly, stepping in smoothly and en masse, collapsing down upon me an aggressive muscular trap. One placed a hand on my shoulder, and I immediately brushed him off. Another made a grab for my arm, and I pushed him off too, slapping him in the face with an open palm. Someone suggested they call the police, but in the end they must have decided against it, no doubt determined to solve this crisis themselves in order to maintain not only any displaced Roxy pride, but the high level of entertainment all those of regular attendance had no doubt come to expect from such a fine establishment.

A large skirmish ensued. Not so large a skirmish as you might expect, especially considering the sheer mass of the combatants involved, but still altogether quite impressive, and before long I was being ushered out the front door equal parts pushed, punched, dragged and kicked. Once outside, the bouncers of course informed me that I was barred, if not for life then perhaps a good deal longer—funny, that—and in turn I cursed and swore that I would never return to their lousy bar anyway, as if the choice were still mine at this point. This was also highly typical, if not for the content of the message then certainly for its context, at which point I went about raising the kind of ruckus one quite rightly reserves for such paltry scenes as this. Eventually, however, growing tired from all this posturing, I swore a few more times and staggered off, eager to cap one more successful night with perhaps one more nightcap someplace else.

I turned right off Granville and headed east down Smithe. It had rained since my initial expedition into the Roxy, and my feet stumbled along through deep dark puddles hell-bent on tripping up and embarrassing me at some rapidly approaching, as yet unspecified point. The streets were busy. The sidewalks were crowded. And cars and people were pitching through my narrowed field of vision at odd aggressive angles, in seemingly arbitrary divisions, running up and through any provisional ceilings I might have placed on their activities in order to retain some semblance of balance for the moment. I tried diligently to focus, first on one blurred face then on another, in the faint and desperate hope of somehow regaining some of the equilibrium I'd left behind me at the bar. It proved tough sledding. But in the end I was rewarded for my efforts, managing to navigate the sidewalk slowly and deliberately, if a little awkwardly and unsteadily, it being all I could do to keep from falling flat on my face—not that such an application would have proved wholly inappropriate in my case. Finally I vomited and felt a good deal better. I didn't know where I was going and, to be honest, doubted she even cared.

By this time I had discovered Melanie shuffling along beside me, her arm slung neatly through the nook in mine. I slammed to a tremulous halt on the sidewalk, and wiping blood from my nose, heard myself say something to the effect of, "You didn't have to come, you know."

"Oh I know," she said, and we continued along arm in arm as before.

"He always just takes off like that," she said after a time.

"Yup, he sure does," I told her.

"I mean he always just runs off without checking with me first."

"Yup, it's almost as if he's got a mind of his own, the bastard."

Here she chose to say nothing, and the silence, it began to drag. Fortunately someone said hello, and I turned to find Chris De Boer after that.

"Well *hello!*" Melanie said, groping about for my hand. "Why, Chris, are you *stalk*ing me? *Are* you? It would really mean a great deal to me if you were stalking me."

De Boer and I exchanged drunken pleasantries as Melanie and I continued along hand in hand. Intoxicated as I was, I still managed to focus in on him here and there, sauntering along fists thrust deep in pockets, one forward, one back. He looked a little cold in his shorts and T-shirt, the latter reading *Potter's Vodka* in small red letters across his heart and STAFF in large white letters across the back. Almost all his shirts said that.

Melanie asked where his coat was, and glancing about as if hoping such a minimum of effort might make it suddenly materialize, he mumbled, "No idea. Must've left it in the limo."

"Limo? What *limo.*"

"Yeah, Gavin, David and some of David's friends rented us a limo," he said, turning to me. "Should've been there, Billy. It was hilarious."

"Thanks for the invite though," Melanie snorted.

"It was sort of spontaneous," he laughed.

I wondered whether Chris was going to ask me where my jacket was—I was suddenly aware he would—but then for some reason he didn't, even though I thought he probably should. I thought I heard someone calling his name from back up the street somewhere, and managing to struggle around, found no one to warrant the notion, let alone the effort. And so I continued along, breathing in, breathing out, trying hard to keep my stomach lining from somersaulting out.

Melanie sighed, "Actually I'm glad you're here, Chris. Really. I've been meaning to talk to you." Suddenly she turned to me. "What the fuck? Billy Pretty? Do my eyes deceive me? Well listen, Mr Pretty, perhaps you could help me. It seems I'm having a little trouble figuring things out. You see, nobody gives a sniff anymore. Who gives a sniff? Nobody. And this one here"—she indicated Chris— "well he doesn't bother coming over anymore. Nor did he call when he got the fabulous news about the book. Well that takes the cake, I say. Yessir, that's the full-on cake-taker, I'd—"

"Book? What book?"

"*What* book? Why, *the* book, Mr Pretty."

"Actually it's Purdy."

"Pardon?"

"Purdy."

"*What?*"

"So he's a writer too," I continued on instead.

"Well of course he's a writer. I mean we're all writers really. And who can blame us, really. I mean literary fiction's the only really useful language." After all, she said, where else could you claim economy to account for a description completely devoid of substance. Obscurity was subtlety, punctuation was arbitrary, illiteracy was but a form of poetic license, and if you were completely wrong in your take on things, you could always cry irony to save a little face.

"Mel, we really shouldn't—"

"Quiet, Chris," Melanie interrupted. "I'm talking literature with Mr Pretty here."

She told me how, on the strength of family connections and a first draft punched out in a little over six weeks, Chris had signed some enormous book deal, and how he hadn't even bothered to call her. Well did I know what that said to her? Did I know how that made her feel? It said he didn't remember where it was he'd come from. It said he didn't care how it was she felt either.

"Ap*par*ently," she said, taking me firmly by the arm and thrusting me forward, "he doesn't think we're together anymore."

"Come on, Mel, I—"

"Dammit, I'm not finished!" she snapped, lacerating him with a series of scowls. "So anyway, Mr Pretty, what do I have to do? Do I have to call up his sweet little blessed wife to find out what's happening? Do I?" Well that was exactly what she did by God. She called up his nauseatingly sweet little blessed wife—"a real saint this one, a real *soldier* of the Lord"—and had I any idea how *that* made her feel? Had I? I said I hadn't, and that I had no idea what the hell she was talking about either. Well she would tell me. "It made me feel like a real whore."

"Whore, huh."

"Yup. An honest to God whore."

We walked along some more.

"Look," she said at length in her overly loud, entirely unnatural, and now slightly exultant voice, "could I talk to you? It would really mean such a great deal to me if I could just talk to you. You're such a good listener though. Really, though, you are. You see, I've got herpes. Yeah I do, I've got herpes, and Mr Chris here, well he's part of my research for the cure. Which is unfortunate of course as we haven't had a conversation like this in years. He doesn't *listen*, see. He *hears*, but he just doesn't *listen*. We have absolutely no emotional intimacy."

She dragged me along by the arm three steps ahead of De Boer. "Listen, do you like him? I mean do you really even *like* the former prime minister?"

I struggled around to find the former prime minister's son. He was still there at that point too. "Why, don't you?"

"Don't I? Why I think he's just *char*ming! Absolutely *char*ming! In fact I always have—haven't you?"

"Well I—"

"Let me ask you this though," she continued. "Do you keep your campaign promises? Do you? No, don't answer. Honestly, though, you don't have to." Because, according to Melanie, I really had no need to keep my campaign promises. Just so long as I promised I never would, she explained, I would never actually need to.

"You understand how it works then? Do you? Well then perhaps you could help explain things to Mr Chris here. You see, our Mr Chris here doesn't seem to know how to keep a promise to anyone anymore. Oh he'll marry you, sure, but does he bother trying to remain faithful to you? Hell, no.

"Listen, though, do you know how we met, Mr Chris and I? He was being charged. For assault. Well of course he was. He was being charged for breaking the jaw of this poor Rick the Roofer character." Oh I'd like this one, she said. I'd appreciate this little anecdote for sure. Poor Rick the Roofer, why he had to have his jaw wired shut. But I was not to worry, as eventually Chris got off, slutty ol' Mel here (her words) making certain of that much herself.

"Oh I'm not being rude, Mr Pretty. You make that face, but honestly that's the very last thing I'd want to do. I'm desperate to make an impression, that's all. Really, I am. First impressions are all the rage these days, I assure you. But I digress. It's always better to digress a little of course, but then again, maybe I digress a little too much too.

"It's just that no one cares enough anymore," she continued. "Everyone's so superficial, aren't they? Aren't they, though, Chris? No one bothers to search for the truth. It all lacks *value*. No one has *faith*. Oh you should hear this hypocritical prick, Mr Pretty, talking about faith as if it were a brand new word." And I should have seen him too, apparently, especially the day he came strolling into her office in his Puerto Rican tuxedo—"I'm not kidding, he looked like a jean sandwich"—and on his way to a wedding too. Well did I know what that sort of thing did to a woman in Melanie's condition? Had I any idea what all that denim did for a girl with genital sores? 'But he's so *cuuuute*!' one of the little pincushions around the office actually had the audacity to say to her one day. "Yes, a real stitch of eloquence, this one. A real sucker for the syllable, this girl. Quite the little Hoover too: every Friday night meant downing another quart of the boss's throat yoghurt in the photocopier room."

She paused, and we continued along into the night-time blur, drifting south on dark, dreary Richards Street. Wheeling around, I was disappointed to find that De Boer was no longer with us. Melanie pitched a tremendous sigh, shaking her head sadly back and forth. She had been sailing along quite splendidly, but opted now for a slightly different tack.

"And now he wants to leave me of course. Oh but that's jumping the gun, isn't it. Bad little gun-jumper. You know he once told me we'd be married though?" Well naturally he had. I was to be assured that he was very old-fashioned that way. And Melanie, why, she was utterly conventional of course. In fact she was chockfull of conventionalism—I was free to confirm it with anyone—because she was Catholic of course. "My day's just one big twenty-four hour guil-tathon," she observed. "But then I suppose that's beside the point."

Again she sighed, this time quite transcendently, and me, I sighed as well. Then she continued on sheepishly, but with this pretence of being coy.

"But then, to be sure, I am an utter canyon to cross these days. Chasm really. And I *am* the great big Jesus-lover too naturally. Oh yeah, love JC. Can't get enough of ol' JC. And I don't believe in sex outside of marriage anymore." Well of course she didn't. Who did, really. What with loose lips sinking so many proverbial ships. "I mean what am I going to tell the lad? 'Step right up and take your shot, big boy? Roll the proverbial dice? And hey, be sure to steer clear of the saddle sore?'"

She told me how Chris had always said he'd introduce her to his father, and how he'd never actually done so. Not once. So now how old a story was *that*, I was very rhetorically asked. How old a story was *that* when the wretchedly diseased Catholic girl fell hard for the former prime minister's son before falling even harder for the floor. Those classics, though, they never went out of style. Not when their themes were just so darned easily recyclable somehow. But then that was the life Melanie had chosen for herself, as I could see for myself by tuning into any Oprah episode. Yes, according to Oprah anyway, Melanie here had literally begged for it lifetimes ago.

"So what do you think of *that*, Mr Pretty? Do you think *Jennifer* begged for it lifetimes ago? Do you think *Jennifer* begged to get cancer, and get it twice, so that *Jennifer* could learn from it and further evolve? Oh I doubt it. After all, no one bothers evolving anymore. It's so passé. But then that's karma for you: everything that's been done before. It's a simple little digression, Mr Pretty. Oh but if I could only digress a little more."

"I remember I met his wife," I managed to slip in at this point. "In Montreal."

Well that was good, she said. That was good that I remembered. For the history of this particular disease was the history of the wife in question. He'd brought it back from Europe, she told me. Yes, he'd brought it back from Europe in a moment of weakness and spiritual liberty. That moment of weakness and rebellious pride all those who led such lives had to deal with eventually, an accident that was to be expected from all such extracurricular activity, and an end to the party life for all those former prime minister's sons whose wanderlust had led them too far from chastity. "'Hail Mary, Mother of God, the Lord is with thee. Blessed art thou among women and cursed is the fruit of thy womb,'" Melanie pseudo-quoted me. So now I could see why my once omnipotent saint here had become again, at least for a time, a great practitioner of discipline and purity, limiting his crusades to an impotent circle of one. "'Behold Saint Christopher,' I say, 'and go your way in safety'—but then who can blame him, really. Certainly not us mistresses, Mr Pretty. No, not us mistresses whatsoever. After all, we have our own faithlessness to deal with, our own lack of discipline, let alone this fabulous new STD."

We stopped outside some bar, but it was closed, and so we continued along down the street, Melanie push-pulling me along by the arm for now.

"Oh I'm so mad, Mr Pretty. Who's mad? I'm mad. How mad? So mad. Still, I wouldn't marry him now for the world." Naturally she would, though, despite the fact that she was playing into a massive stereotype—bad little hip-hop, flip-flop, but otherwise conventionally Catholic girl. It was just that, while writing his book, Chris had begun to think that he really didn't need her anymore. Then again, he needed new material, she supposed. Apparently a girl with open sores wasn't all that consistent with cutting edge fiction anymore. She was in need of some better character traits, that was all. Some deeper flaws. And even a little more digression as well. Perhaps if she slit her wrists she could somehow manage to make the cut. And there we had it! Literature! Not only a sly pun, but perhaps even a little foreshadowing as well. "Oh hallelujah," she said. "Heavens to Betsy, we've turned the corner. Oh but I'm not letting you get a word in edgewise am I, Mr Pretty. After all, we're supposed to be having a little talk here, aren't we? A bit of a chat. A wee bit of a digression, nothing more."

I just looked at her.

"You say nothing. Good. It's intelligent to say nothing. It shows breeding. And specialization. And one should always specialize in this day and age of reckless breeding." It was all about knowing more and more about less and less until pretty soon you knew everything there was to know about nothing. And that was logic for you. And a certain degree of sophism too, to tell you the truth. "Christ, say something, Mr Pretty. No, say nothing. People speak too much as it is, and I already speak enough for both of you."

I said nothing.

"And now this whole book thing comes up," she sighed once again, somewhat subdued. But then she'd always known it would. You hung around those De Boer boys long enough and you tended to get a feeling for the plausibility of such implausible scenarios. And oh, they were going to celebrate so, but instead she just got drunk. It was so very foolish to get drunk in public, though, didn't I think so? Didn't I though? Well it depends, I told her. Alas, but it was true. And it was literary too. And by God, literature was filled with drunken fools. That is, according to Melanie here.

"Isn't that true? Isn't it though? Oh I'm absolutely clever. Nothing like a little passive-aggressive digression into the Arts to make oneself feel awfully clever though."

Melanie looked at me, blinkingly, and I sighed into the breach, not really knowing whether to make a run for it or just lay still.

"I never did like children much though," she eventually went on while clutching my arm, releasing me of the burden of making any sort of decision here. "So I suppose that made it easier. To break up with me, I mean. Creative differences, you see." Now naturally if she *were* to have children, she'd have to go on this special pill so that the little bugger didn't pick anything up on the way through. They break out in times of stress of course, and what could be more stressful than squeezing another human being through your pelvic girdle.

"Possibly this," I said, indicating where her fingernails were about to pierce the skin of my inner arm.

"What? Oh sorry," she said, tightening her grip even more. "Oh I'd've made a great wife though, Mr Pretty. I'd never have gone frigid between the thighs. I'm very reasonable that way. In fact I'm chock-full of reason. Reason and conventionalism. As a matter of fact I've had it grafted onto my DNA." And that was another myth apparently, religious women and frigidity—"Let all men pull asunder what God hath joined"—that's what she said anyway. That's what she'd always said. In fact, she was surprised she'd ever bothered to say anything else. Because she'd never really been interested in anything else. Perhaps, though, she should have been. In hindsight, it might have saved her a lot of strife. It certainly would have saved her on the medical bills anyway—like poor Rick the Roofer. "Oh, but that's just spilt milk-crying. And spite."

"You're almost through," I told her, wincing against the pain of her grip.

"Yes, almost finished," she said. "But do you know *how* to keep a woman interested, Mr Pretty? Do you? Tease her. That's it. Just tease her to the point of never quite giving her what she's never quite been willing to live without." And that way she kept searching, I was told. She kept searching and searching and craving that which she knew must exist out there somewhere, because she'd read it in a magazine once or else on a bathroom wall somewhere.

"It's a shame."

"Yes it is, a real shame—like Atwood's nose," she said. Oh there she goes again, sounding awfully resentful—she was sorry about that—simply a digressive slip, nothing more. They just sort of snuck up on her. They really did. But then a big ol' Jesus-lover like herself ought to have been able to accept such things in a more calm and dignified manner, didn't I think? Didn't I though? Well Jesus would have, I told her. But then again, Melanie said, she was a bit of a throwback. Yes, a bit of a throwback player of sorts. "Hey, isn't that what they call you, Mr Pretty? A throwback player of sorts?"

I stopped walking. She stopped too.

"You know, you're destroying the image I have of you."

"What image is that?" she asked, fixing me with a sober, significant look.

"The one of you being not entirely too old and bitter."

"Well I'm not old."

"But entirely too bitter."

"Not entirely, but yes, still bitter," she admitted.

"So then maybe he was tired of that too."

"Oh you think so, Mr Pretty? You really think so? Well perhaps he was. Perhaps he was just a little bit tired of ol' Melanoma somehow." Then again, he was probably just *bored*. Yes, that was it—that was surely it—he was probably just *bored*. "I mean if he was, well then I'd certainly understand. I mean I'd know exactly how that feels. Boredom is the stigma of our entire generation of course, and De Boer, well he considers himself our generation's stigmatic spokesperson."

CHAPTER SIX

WE STARTED OUT again. Someone called out, this time from right close by, and we lurched our way over to a slutty looking woman on the corner rapidly applying eyeliner. I asked what she wanted and, putting her makeup away, she stated with somewhat theatrical elusiveness, "Now that would depend on what you want, chief."

In retrospect, I should probably have realized that she was entirely too ambitious to be a prostitute, especially in that prototypical prostitute sense, as in truth she seemed far too together to have ever had to consider such a lowly occupation as this. She was intelligent, she was presentable, and she appeared to have a serious passion for her work. She actually seemed to have a fairly good attitude about the whole thing, even going so far as to offer me Kleenex to wipe the drop of dried blood from my chin, and so I decided that we should speak closely. Very closely in fact. Her name, she said, was Cat—"that's with a C not a K, chief"—while proceeding to take a good step back.

Thanking Cat for the Kleenex, I introduced myself as best I could—not so poorly considering what all had been poured into me to this point—and then introduced my girlfriend too. Melanie was very intrigued with Cat, keen on understanding the price point one utilizes in such a profession, whereas Cat, for her part, acknowledged that it was by no means a perfect science, but that the system she'd stumbled upon in Vegas certainly possessed its merits, a system that, due to local attitudes and current market conditions, she was unable to employ to full potential at present.

"One, two, three, four," she said. "Handjob, blowjob, sex, half and half."

"What the hell's a *half and half*?" I asked, leaning in closer—apparently too close as she proceeded to take another good step back.

"Something you're never going to see, chief, unless you settle down, all right?"

"So let me get this straight," Melanie said. "You get a hundred dollars just to jerk a guy *off*?"

"I did in Vegas, honey, and that's not the half of it. You've got to judge the client, see—his clothes, his mannerisms, his hotel room, his car—so that if the situation warrants, you play the scale. Say, two, four, six, eight. Or three, six, nine, twelve."

"And what scale would I rank?" I asked, having struck what I believed to be a most sophisticated pose. "You know, just for interest's sake."

She gave me the once over, and then reported at length: "One, two, three, four."

"You must be joking. I mean check this out." I removed my false front teeth and grinned like an idiot.

Cat looked at me vacantly. "One, two, three, four," she repeated, and together we enjoyed a good long phoney chuckle over that.

"Seriously though," she said, stepping up close, "you're a tall drink of water, chief. You a ball player or something?"

"Thumthing like that, yeth."

"He's a throwback," Melanie threw in, watching with interest as I put my teeth back in. "A digression. Go on, Pretty, tell the nice prostitute lady here what it is you do for a living."

"I'm a fighter," I said. "I fight people."

The word 'fight' had a curious effect on Cat. "What people?"

"Other people like me."

"Well in that case then, make it two, four, six, eight," she said, turning to Melanie with a complex and impatient sigh, as if she'd been providing sexual release for men of violent means all her life without pause. "Professional athletes, they're all such high maintenance. Them and actors and the rest of that overpaid lot."

"Why's that?" Melanie asked.

"Well because they've been spoiled, honey. They've been jaded. Gold-diggers like you—no offence—have been throwing yourselves at these boys so long that their sense of what's sexy has been knocked irredeemably out of whack. Believe me, I've had more than one cast member of *Da Vinci's Inquest* beg me to stiletto his balls," Cat assured us both before turning her full attention on me. "So how 'bout it, chief?" she asked, steadying my arm with a tight grip of fingernails, painfully reminiscent of Melanie's grip earlier, although not quite so acrimoniously inspired. "You want me to stomp on your sack? Or has the little lady here got you covered tonight."

"Fat chance," Melanie snorted. "He can stomp on his own god-damned sack."

"I'm fine, thanks. Really," I said, trying to convince them both that I was hardly disturbed by that.

Cat saddled up before me, arms crossed, all too confident that I would not fall back. She was tall, really very tall, with a fantastic reach, and with her narrow head up this close to mine I could tell she was wearing a wig. Having fondled my genitals for several seconds now, she reached up inside her coat, searching diligently for something in the vicinity of her armpit. "Come on, chief," she purred.

"Yeah, come on—do it, Pretty," Melanie slurred. "Do it for old Mel, okay?"

"Do what? What exactly is it you want me to do here?" I asked, having fixed a wavering finger at Melanie to better enunciate some already forgotten point.

"One, two, three, four," she said. "Take your pick."

Cat cuddled up closely under my arms. "Look, just because you seem so nice, I'll make it one for a blow, one-and-a-half for the whole show—plus tip of course."

"Thanks, but I'm really not interested."

I felt I was quite done with the idea, but then evidently Cat was not quite done with me. She cuddled up closer.

"Come *on*, Pretty, you have to," Melanie pleaded. "It's imperative." She actually used the word 'imperative.'

"Really?"

"Abso*lute*ly," she said. And then, out of respect for any and all professionals in our midst: "I get to watch though."

"Whatever tickles your fancy, honey."

"But where?" I had to ask.

"Well there's a comfy little spot right down this alley here," Cat suggested.

"Lovely, I'm sure."

"Oh like you've had better," Melanie said, blowing her bangs from her forehead.

"You know, I'm not even sure I have that kind of cash on me," I must have mentioned at this point, which Melanie in turn must have taken as an invitation to thoroughly probe my pockets for loot. In no mood for resistance, and even to further facilitate operations, I lifted my arms, and eventually she emerged triumphant.

"You have sixty-five here," she reported upon tallying up the take. "Is that enough?"

"Almost, honey, but not quite."

Cat seemed hopeful, pulling hard for us.

"How about a handjob then? Christ, he must have enough for a handjob. Hell, he could give him*self* a handjob," Melanie huffed, handy herself with the word, if nothing else.

"Gentlemen, give yourselves a *hand*job!" I parodied, but it didn't come off quite like it ought to have.

Cat shook her head despondently. "I would prefer a little more, to be honest."

Frustrated, Melanie pouted about for a spell. Then an idea struck—you could almost hear it strike—and rummaging through her own pockets she suddenly emerged with two crumpled, rather sorry looking twenty-dollar bills.

"Congratulations, we're in business!" Cat cheered, and shook each of our hands in turn. And it was at this point I realized that I did not have my coat, a matter, suddenly, of paramount importance in this or any other world.

"Ladies, I don't have my coat," I announced. Stunned, they both regarded me in silence. Then they laughed, shrugged and together sallied alleyward, leaving me to lumber along in their wake, a little bit cold and quietly disturbed.

"I'm serious, ladies. I don't have my coat."

"Well where *is* it then?" Melanie asked.

"Back at the bar. Fisk left it with the bartender."

"We'll get it later then," she told me, and we continued along up the alley as before.

"You know, you can't just push me around like this, Mel."

"On the contrary, Mr Pretty, I'll push you around if I want to push you around. You're my push-around," she told me.

Finally we came to a halt alongside an overflowing dumpster.

"Oh it's everything I thought it'd be," I said, "and more."

Cat smiled in an arguably almost catlike way. "So what was it we settled on then, chief? Handjob, was it?"

"Yessir," I said, and Melanie looked around for something large to hit me with.

"No way!" she protested, raising a smooth muscular leg to poke me hard in the stomach with a toe once, twice, instead.

Cat seemed incredulous, even insulted by any notion it could have been otherwise.

"Actually, it was a 'hundred for a blow' as you so eloquently put it before," I said, to which she sagely if obliquely replied, in a southern accent entirely absent otherwise:

"Hey, ugly's ugly, chief. She still ain't goin' to the dance no matter what dress you happen to put her in at home. But then I suppose I must've," she conceded with a sigh. "All right then, a two-for-one it is. And that's what you get for doin' deals with professional athletes," she added in a theatrical aside to Melanie. "Forever bringin' their A game when it's time for contract negotiations."

Melanie pooled our funds together and passed them over. Cat took the cash and placed it in her purse. As for me, I continued to worry about my coat long after the rest of the police showed up and ruined everything.

There I was, surrounded at once by a whole host of officers both uniformed and otherwise, along with the token pair of cruisers complete with all the flashing lights and wailing sirens anyone with a penchant for prostitutes has always half-expected to eventually be overwhelmed by. Standing there like that was all very embarrassing to say the least. I didn't know what else to do. Melanie, though, for her part, started in immediately, first on Cat and then on the other officers, as they carted me off in handcuffs to one of the awaiting cruisers. She was citing how inadmissible it all was: how they knew as well as she did that any charge relating to a transaction brokered in such a fashion would never hold up in a court of law. Now whether that is true or not true I will not pretend to know, but after hearing it, those officers most recently arrived were suddenly some very friendly sorts—very polite and extremely efficient—and the one recognized me suddenly and wanted to chat some about the prospects of the game the following night. They were both big fans, he said. He also wanted to ask me about some changes the league might be making to the crease rule the following season. We probably would have gone on to discuss the instigator rule and free agency and how both, in reality, were a calamity for the league in particular and the sport in general. I was annoyed enough.

Just then De Boer and Fisk showed up, and together proceeded to grin down through the rear window of the cruiser in which I was currently housed. Chris was eating a donair. They both were, in fact. I asked if I might have a bite of one of these donairs, and Chris tried his best to sneak his in through the open door of the cruiser to my awaiting mouth (my hands were handcuffed, remember) only to be thwarted by the overly diligent watch of one of the polite efficient officers up front. Chris frowned at the officer. It was difficult to tell whether he'd been drinking, whereas with Fisk it was something of a foregone conclusion by this point.

"Christ, those are some uncomfortable looking uniforms," Fisk told one of the officers. "Really, though, I've never seen that much climb on a pair of pants before. I mean seriously, that is a hell of a lot of crotch, no?"

"Well this sucks," I told Chris as Fisk rambled on in that vein. He agreed that it did suck, and speaking of sucking, changed the subject to my attorney.

"Yes, Melanie," I sighed, watching her further criticize Cat across the way. "She's a handful, isn't she."

"She certainly is."

"Certainly has a way of carrying the conversation anyway."

"Yeah, well, she's an opportunity too, if you're interested."

"Opportunity for what?" I asked, but before he could answer the officer filing the report in the passenger seat told us both to shut up. He turned up the radio.

Afterwards, having conversed briefly with his partner, the one officer came around to my door, removed my handcuffs, and told me I was free to go. I asked if they might consider driving me up to the bar to retrieve my coat, but he told me not to push my luck. I suppose there were worse ways of finding out. And so it was that the Bull ended his short tenure as a Washington Capital and began his much shorter one as a Vancouver Canuck.

CHAPTER SEVEN

Canuck: *n.* 1. a Canadian. [Slang.]
      2. a French Canadian. [Slang.]
      3. a kind of Canadian pony or sinewy small horse. [Colloq.]

THIS FROM WEBSTER'S Dictionary, Second Addition, an ancient green tome of my father's I was in the habit of carting around from city to city, season after season. The west coast of Canada is hardly French, and since we weren't paying tribute to anything even remotely equine—our jersey featured a rather angry looking whale for a logo—I suppose we were celebrating Canadians, albeit in a fairly derogatory way, something I could very much relate to being exactly half Kainaiwa. So be it. The Bull was not one to rock the boat. Not that way. Besides, when you enjoyed the kind of home-ice advantage I did, you learned to look forward to the road trips.

Having borrowed the handle from one of the local standing stallions, it was my father who first encouraged others to call me Bull back when I was still a youngster. He thought it would stick in their heads. It would also make me seem slightly mythical, he maintained, as there were not all that many native kids playing organized hockey in those days. In his mind, it would also compel people to think of me in a more friendly way. About that time I started growing, and so naturally the nickname grew with me.

It was my mother, however, who first informed my brothers and me of our lineage—secretly, objectively, and with an economy of emotion that left little room for rebuttal in any way. I remember her being sick at the time. I remember her being sick because she made it seem as though she herself were free of this particular ailment—we children having simply contracted a kind of unmentionable childhood disease, the very notion of which she would never so much as consider disappointing our father with.

Now there is a tendency to do one of two things when confronted with one's genetic roadmap in such a way: hold to it unwaveringly, or else run hastily away. These two extremes aptly describe my two brothers, if not still, then certainly for a time anyway. John ran. John ran hard, and long, and in my opinion runs even still, to this day. I can't say I blame him though. Not really. Not anymore. For in those days being branded a half-breed was not the spiritual expedient it seems to be now. In fact, having inherited much of our mother's more sublime physical makeup, John could have passed himself off as five-eighths, three-quarters, or possibly an even more liberal fraction if he had wanted to. If he had known how to. If they had tried. But John wanted no part of it. No, John wanted nothing more than to be pure white. And so, upon discovering his pedigree, he immediately and without hesitation forgot it entirely. Or so it seemed anyway. He never did acknowledge it to Teddy or me, and indeed, never spoke of it again. Now I like to believe, alone and at night, that this was the real reason he got locked up. I don't believe it of course, but still I like to believe it, the difference here being practically negligible in most practical respects, I find.

And while my older brother ran, my younger brother sprinted— back. It was all rather embarrassing to say the least. For from that one quiet instant on Teddy *was* Indian, even managing to smuggle around on his person a homemade tomahawk for most of his aborted high school campaign, for the express purpose of showing it to the easily impressed whenever it suited him. Unfortunately, from a purely physical standpoint, Teddy could not have been less suited for the part. Perhaps it was the pale white skin, or else the bright blue eyes, or even the Purdy family curse of a constantly cursing mouth, for whatever the reason, whatever the cruel twist of chromosomal fate, Teddy was no more Blackfoot than, say, his father was. Both packed the temper, both lacked the patience, both understood nothing when it came to sustaining their spirituality over time. Now this is not to say that I am embarrassed of my heritage—I most certainly am not—but simply that, in my family at least, Black Irish and Blood Indian seemed to mix with all the tenderness and success of, well, Irish and Indians every other place, I guess. Who was Teddy kidding anyway. It was almost as if—no, it was *exactly* as if—he was trying to brave our father head on. And for that Teddy got locked up himself, though much later on.

But I was determined to be different. In fact, I was so determined to be different that I managed to end up right where it started. Right where she left me. Right where I began—in the middle. In no man's land. Tied to the earth and surrounded by ice. Alone. Asocial. A man.

CHAPTER EIGHT

AFTER INDUSTRY NIGHT at the Roxy, after the trade, alleyway arrest, reunion and subsequent release, I dragged my ass from my hotel room down to the arena the following morning to say good-bye to my old teammates and to introduce myself to some new ones again. I gathered my gear from the visitors' dressing room (the Capitals' equipment manager had been kind enough to pack it up for me) and wandered along through the underground tunnels until I found the dressing room belonging to the home team. On the wall outside the door, in large black letters, was written something inspiring about commitment. Funny, too, considering, and too bad I cannot regurgitate it here.

I met my new bosses, or boss, I should say—the head coach pulling double-duty as acting general manager in those days—and I remember wondering if he'd changed at all since coaching me in Hartford more than a decade before. Difficult to tell that morning. He did seem pleasant enough though.

He told me to take a seat and I did. He spoke slowly and deliberately as always, meditating over each and every word he considered somehow more appealing and impressive than the rest. He did this, naturally, to intimidate people. He had long held a reputation for it. I had long held it in high regard myself, but now no longer gave it much thought either way. He told me I was the kind of player any man would be lucky to go to war with, and if that wasn't cringe-inducing enough, that I was limited, but that I was his kind of player. To be, um—competitive now, he explained, it was imperative a team be able to roll four good lines, and roll them fairly consistently as well. And due to all the new rule changes being introduced into the league there really wasn't any justifiable, um—rationale for carrying a designated hitter anymore. The rules have changed, Billy. The business has changed—evolved—it's that much more disciplined now. The balance of a game simply doesn't hang on the outcome of one particular brawl anymore.

He looked at me and smiled, widespread fingers rebounding buoyantly off the pads of their manicured counterparts. "Billy, are you ready to play tonight?"

"Tonight? Yes. Absolutely yes, of course—Mark," I lied, and in turn seemed to discover the fountain of youth that night, even though it was probably just the fistful of amphetamines working their way around my already speeding intestines. I was not angry at having been traded. If anything, I was pleasantly surprised. I relish the opportunity for reinvention, I always have, and a good crisp trade has always presented the most effective forum for that. This is not to say that I was about to make any drastic changes to my game plan—I wasn't about to quit fighting or anything like that—all I mean to say is that the relocation to a new team, a new city, or even a new country has always provided the necessary excuse, if not the mechanism, to reinvent myself in an entirely new and increasingly engaging light.

That night, my second shift out, I ended up standing alongside my successor Craig Simon near center ice. He was leaning over, hands on stick, stick on knees, long straight hair hanging down around his chin in sweat-soaked spikes. The television time-out gave us an opportunity to talk things out.

"Sure strange seeing you in that jersey, Billy."

"Strange to be seen in any jersey these days," I said, pivoting on my left skate blade a fraction of an inch, etching progressively smaller circles into the ice.

"What's he like?"

"Mark? Seems all right."

"Still the same?"

"Still the same. No reason to go changing with a winning percentage like that."

I skated some more circles as Craig fell silent a while.

"Listen Craig," I finally said. "We have to go tonight."

He glanced up from under the rim of his helmet with a kind of bovine amazement. "What, you and me?"

"You and me, baby."

"I don't wanna do that, man."

"Come on," I said, "it'll be fun. Consider it a favour. Consider it a means of direct action on behalf of your primary benefactor."

He shook his cow-like head slowly from side to side. "I really don't wanna do that, man."

"What, you think you might em*barr*ass me, Craig? Is that it? You think you might actually *beat* me?" I tried to say this with just the proper amount of tension, eliciting the expected response of pride.

"Yeah I do, but that's not why," he said, standing up straight. Christ, Craig must have been up over seven feet tall on skates.

"Why then?"

"Because it just ain't right."

"What, Indians don't fight at night, is that it? Look, I need this."

"So what?" he shrugged. "It still ain't right."

"Oh fuck that," I said. "You're no more Indian than I am."

"Yeah, well, you're the one who keeps bringing it up, so what the fuck is that."

He leaned forward from the waist again, shaking his big head from side to side. "Look Billy, I just don't wanna do that. Fight Carl. Fuck, fight Hot Carl. Fight—"

"You fought me at camp."

"That was different."

"Yeah, you needed a job."

"That's right," he said, and again stood up straight. I could tell I was getting to him now. I could tell because he was beginning to shift his weight nervously from skate to skate. Craig was always rather easy to read that way. He was always so very concerned about his balance, and for very good reason, I would say.

"And so I did you a favour," I reminded him.

"Yeah, you did. You did me a favour. And believe me, I appreciate that."

I rotated the blade of my skate a fraction of an inch further, gliding over to his side. Eventually he leaned down to join me, hands on sticks, sticks on knees, heads hanging down side by side.

"So now I need a favour from you tonight."

And that is how these things come together. True, it is not always so orchestrated. And true, the outburst is more often than not triggered by anger and pride. But more often than you might think, we who are involved, we know what is coming, we understand the situation at hand. All it takes is that little look, that subtle glance, that expression of recognition and we are game.

Now upon meeting a player outside the arena it is nearly impossible to say, with any degree of accuracy anyway, whether or not he is of quality fighter material on the ice. Typically the more quiet and calm he is, the less nervous he seems and the more disciplined he behaves, the greater the likelihood he will turn out all right. The better a fighter is, the more confident he is, and consequently the less he needs to bluff and hide. All exterior signs of aggression are signs of bluffing, and bluffing is a technique of avoiding combat whenever possible. So go ahead and talk your game. And when you are through talking your game, go ahead and learn your craft. Combat requires discipline. And discipline requires poise. And upon dropping the gloves, the truly capable fighter gives little or no warning before launching his attack, and having commenced operations, never even opens his mouth during the entire course of the fight—other than to draw a breath or to bare clenched teeth—and in the end, having finally been separated from his opponent by the linesmen, skates off to the box as modestly as possible, leaving the opponent with the best possible image of himself, mouth clamped shut against the flow of blood now pressing at his lips.

The world the fighter inhabits is a crystalline world unto itself, but one in which all other worlds, both real and imagined, are to some degree reflected. And like any world, that of the fighter reveals its nature to be at least partially repugnant. At that particular moment, then, my world was composed exclusively of my opponent, his fists, my own fists and me, and all that existed of me were questions about my opponent, his fists, and a way in which I might inflict my own on him. It is one of life's little blessings that we occasionally get to stand apart from ourselves and witness our creating something meaningful, even if it is only a fist to face relationship of sorts.

When the whistle blew, Craig and I wasted little time before throwing down and squaring off. We circled, Craig removing his elbow pads first the one and then the other, sending them spinning off to remote corners of the ice. I did not hear the whistle blow again to stop the play, nor did I hear the crowd rising collectively to its feet. I did not hear our teammates sliding in to form the quiet cage around us, nor did I hear anything but the breathing and the scraping of my opponent and his skates. This, then, was that last moment of crystalline perfection before our brittle little world shattered to bits, along with all of Craig's silly little reservations regarding our similar reservation heritage.

Me, I stand quiet and motionless before a fight, my hands held low, an old habit of making my opponent come off like a showboat by comparison, not to mention disguising a strong left hand. As for Craig, he fought more like a boxer on the ice. At least he tried to start out like that. Still, he'd learned early on in his career that, in a fight, the difference between the right decision and the wrong decision was about six inches—or the space between your ears—and you were always wise to work on your habits before your habits started to work against you. We circled some more and closed in, each of us trying to gain the upper hand.

There is a real art to fighting on skates, the basic components being threefold—strength, balance, and grip—all three of which require equal mastery if one is going to be at all effective in such a difficult forum as this. The first component, strength, is of course self-explanatory. It takes a strong man both mentally and physically, not only to maintain that level of energy, but to dole it out effectively as well. Short and straight is definitely the rule of thumb here. Short and straight is always the most efficient way to maintain a maximum purity of line, and in doing so, minimize the gap between fist and face.

The second component, balance, may be the most significant, structurally speaking at least. Balance is lost, and found, in the hips—as goes the means so go the extremes. For starters, a wide stance is good—difficult to get knocked off your feet like that—toes slightly out, knees bent, hips held in under the body, allowing the momentum of the action to send you spinning around a central point. Tight and effective, good balance can be the one crucial difference leaving you standing at the end of the tilt.

Thirdly, grip. Just as important as balance but far more complicated, it is with grip that so many rookies make their rookie mistake. Overly concerned with landing the money shot, typically the overhand right, too many young fighters forget that this is in all probability their opponent's number one weapon as well—they'd be better off improving their use of the cloth instead. Instead of establishing an effective grip on the opponent's jersey, thereby limiting that opponent's mobility and effectiveness, a less accomplished fighter typically holds on for balance, for life, or merely to generate power. Typically, say, with two right-handed fighters, each gets a good grip with his left hand out near the right shoulder of his opponent's jersey (out too far on the arm he risks being pulled off balance, while in too close to the chest he risks the very bone structure of his face), thus nullifying any undue generation of power, speed and punishment on his opponent's behalf, all the while trying with any amount of twisting, pulling, pushing and the like to get his own right free and clear. Typically. Because it's when a left-hander is involved, or else a right-hander of greater experience and ability—say, one like me—when the complexity, speed and beauty of the dance tend to grow together almost exponentially.

Now while it's true that the enforcer requires a variety of attributes and skills in order to excel in this line of work, above all he needs a good left hand. Any enforcer worth his jersey will tell you a fight is won more with the hand controlling the cloth and guiding the opponent than with the one feeding in the ham. The game of grip is a game of small advantages. This could be a slightly better development in grip, or perhaps even a slightly safer head position (typically tucked into the grip arm's armpit), but whatever the case, whatever the improvement and however slight, when several of these seemingly insignificant advantages are added together, suddenly control has been established. And when a fighter has control, his opponent, to break that control, must be willing to sacrifice something else.

Now there are plenty of misconceptions that influence how people perceive, and execute, the hockey fight. For instance, most people believe that the most competent fighter—that is, the enforcer—simply out-punches his opponents, and while this is certainly often the case, it is certainly not the rule. Neither is it necessarily true that he outthinks them. The situation is uncertain, the information ambiguous, and the hockey fight is about controlling the situation at hand. The fighter wants to determine his own future, and for that he needs clarity, not clairvoyance. So the real issue becomes not how far ahead he can think, but indeed, how he thinks insofar as his head is concerned. It's not fighting unless you are looking for instant answers to immediate questions, even if the questions are posed on the forward face of an advancing fist.

Craig and I came together in the middle of the face-off circle, spinning slowly, grimacing expertly, clinging to each other's jerseys for a time. As mentioned, Craig was tall, really very tall, with a fantastic reach, and because of that it was in my best interests to stay in close and underneath. Craig knew I threw both hands rather well, and he did well to guard against it. Much clutching, struggling and grabbing ensued.

Now there is something truly odd, detached, and even humorous that happens to a fighter the moment he engages an opponent in a fight: he gets excited. And I was excited, but managed to keep my hands cool and under control despite it. I was excited because, no matter what the experience of the fighter, there must be some slight transition, translation or sudden visitation upon the spirit once the body engages a fellow mortal soul in combat. In a fight, one moment the world is clear and accurate and the next it has disappeared entirely. And yet, knowing all too well the damage a hard plastic helmet could do to my knuckles, and not expecting Craig to remove it himself, I managed to work my hand up the back of his head and dislodge it with a free finger. We spun around some more, breathing and wrestling, foreheads held together in a slipping sliding press of uneasy satisfaction. And then, when I was good and ready, I pulled back and unleashed hell.

Now if you have never seen an enforcer in a fight, you have never seen the job reduced to its essentials. I hit Craig hard with a series of quick rhythmic jabs with the right, short and straight and piston-like (imagine the fist as a piston, the arm the rod that connects it, and the entire shaft of the torso cranking into the stroke), alternating to my left as soon as he upped his guard. It should be noted here that small shoulder pads are a must for the enforcer, allowing a greater range of motion in this critical area, as are oversized sleeves and the willingness to condition one's knuckles between games to the point of permanent disfigurement and perhaps even surgery at some later date. We traded punches for a time, each of us feeling out the other—one rhythm superimposed on the other—and at some point during the sequence Craig accomplished the removal of my own helmet, proceeding to land a series of heavy overhand rights to the back of my skull—hardly at all damaging from this close range, mind you. Then, from my position in close, I flashed his own jersey in his face, blinding him momentarily, before jerking back and away violently, hitting him repeatedly with the right, again short and straight. I crossed him up. By reaching across with my right to secure his jersey up near the opposite shoulder, I was able to free up my left to let fly short and straight. Off balance now, Craig pitched backwards, then forward again violently, leaning over at the waist and scrambling to remain upright on his skates. And it was here I knew I had him. Looking down over the top of his head currently wavering about near my waist, I let fly with a series of hard punishing rights, finishing him off with an arcing, rather stalwart, uppercut left to the face. And as quickly as it began it was over and so, foregoing the satisfaction of one last free shot to the head, about to leave my opponent behind on his hands and knees to glide gracefully off to my perch within the Plexiglas walls of my penalty box prison to serve, quite contentedly, the five-minute sentence befitting my crime, not to mention a rest I most definitely deserved by this time, all to the fairly brazen applause and chants of "Bull!" from my eighteen thousand-plus newfound friends and admirers, I was very suddenly, rudely, and without any regard for the enforcer's code, popped squarely in the back of the head.

Someone jumped me from behind and managed to get my jersey up over my head. And if this weren't an unfavourable enough turn of events in itself, it soon grew exponentially worse. Allowing my arms to hang up—or down, as it were—past my head, the jersey came off quickly as my unseen combatant was wrestled away by one of the linesmen, and before I knew it I was paired off with some kid—as it happened, the very same visor-wearing, fresh-out-of-American-college Canadian kid I'd been traded for the night before. Lord knows how, but at some point during the ensuing struggle the slick little bastard managed to get in a pretty good shot, opening up an old scar over my right eye. Seeing the blood, I went berserk. No exaggeration, I went mad. Off came the pads, off came the undershirt—stripped to the waist and leaking blood, the league's worst nightmare sprung suddenly to life. It is difficult to remember what happened next. Although I do admit to borrowing someone's stick somewhere along the line.

Poets and artists are forever talking about the moment. But it is really the fighter who experiences eternity turning on a dime. No one can say, with any degree of accuracy anyway, what the moment is until the whole world is seen compressed onto the face of a fist and that fist is coming at you at high velocity and then it is gone. I shall remember that little son of a bitch forever. I shall remember trying valiantly, if desperately, to get at him, as the beating I was going to lay on him, in the advent I could catch him, was going to be nothing short of absurd. I shall remember skating around recklessly, swinging my stick fiendishly, first at one Carl then at another in hot pursuit of that little son of a bitch, the fact I hardly recognized my new teammates as just that, teammates, only adding to the confusion of it all.

And I shall remember that little son of a bitch whirling and swirling about me, an irksome little gnat managing to remain forever just out of reach, yet most annoyingly, and effectively, quite directly in my face. I shall remember the chasing. And the running. The players fighting. And the crowd cheering. Just as I shall remember the whole world disappearing behind a bright wet veil of red.

CHAPTER NINE

LOOKING BACK NOW, I suppose the strangest thing about that group was not so much their robust dedication to the bar, but indeed their rare dedication to De Boer. In fact, they were so ridiculously possessive of the man that I was forced to shrug it off as simply the overzealous protection of quasi Canadian royalty. And so I was not put out nor even surprised when the rest of them decided to show up that following afternoon for coffee. I had chosen this coffee bar in particular because it was located just down the street from the Sutton Place Hotel I was currently negotiating to make my permanent home. I had chosen coffee in general because of this vague and sentimental idea I had that every once in a while it might be nice to share with someone. I was reading the two local newspapers when they all showed up, first the *Sun* and then the *Province*. Born of a single agency, both papers reported the same hockey news, albeit in slightly different styles—the *Province* in an at best grade-seven reading level—so I went with the *Sun* first. Both papers really put it to the Bull, both as a player and as a man. I felt a genuine dislike from the one writer, but then that was hardly out of line. Often times when these writers really put it to you like that it was simply for the sake of the paper. But other times, those times when the hate was not an optional hate, it took some time and even some effort to swing them over. The trick here was to coax them down gently from hate to contempt, and once at contempt, pity and even compassion were never all that far out of reach. And when the hate was an optional hate you never had to worry. You could always rely on the intrinsic adoration of the readership to rise up, write in, and waive that option entirely.

After I read the *Sun* I started in on the *Province*, which I was about halfway through when De Boer and his entourage came rolling in. I recall I was camped near the fireplace by the window, mulling over my latest suspension resulting from that little stick-swinging incident the night before, when their collective arrival forced me into devising some casual new pretext for spending some quality time alone with De Boer. Prior to that, if I moved my head to just the proper place, I could restore a certain semblance of symmetry to the previous night—not that I had any great desire to relive the events. That the game was changing—or *evolving* as they so annoyingly enjoyed informing me season after season, suspension after suspension—there really was no doubt, although it seemed to me they were simply evolving it way too goddamned quickly these days. After all, that little stick-swinging fiasco the night before would never have even made the news a decade ago, let alone the highlight reel, and now they were literally calling for my scalp. Were they really so hypocritical? That was what they paid me to do. That was what they had always paid me to do. And for my life I could not understand why they would choose not to acknowledge that here. Of course I could though. Mine was a dying trade. The heavyweight, it seemed, an endangered species. Gone were the glory days of the gallant enforcer. Gone were the days of respect and pride upon the blades. These days it was all corporate boxes, television revenues, bottom lines, and faggot hockey. These days anyone could play the heavy and make it pay in spades.

"No thanks," Chris said when I offered to buy him a coffee, and that was that. Meanwhile, with Gavin and Melanie up at the bar, Fisk flopped down onto a nearby couch copied, I heard it said, straight from the coffeehouse set of *Friends*.

"Suspended indefinitely," Fisk said, scratching his head. "Well now that's rather harsh."

"Yes, and get this: coach tells me to stay home from the road trip to collect my thoughts. Collect my *thoughts*," I said. "Whatever the hell that means."

Fisk uncoiled himself tableward in an effort to extract a magazine from the stack, only to come up about three inches short. Defeated, he flopped back into the couch, the collar of his T-shirt pulled up over his mouth; his attention, like De Boer's, gravitating steadily to the enormous buttocks of the barista bending over behind the bar.

I flexed my fingers and cracked my knuckles as they continued to watch the fat girl spill Frappuccinos. "So, Chris, how's the wife?" I eventually asked in a spirit of reclamation, concerned our coffee date was not going anywhere close to according to plan.

"Oh she's cleared up somewhat. How's the blood in your urine?"

"Oh she's cleared up somewhat too."

"So you're not juicing anymore?"

"Not anymore, no."

"I could tell," he said, and it hurt.

I returned my coffee cup to the table, only this time to a slightly different location. I felt the previous location with my hand—the table was still warm with retained heat—and so I allowed it to cool entirely before returning my cup there again.

"Jennifer and I are separated," Chris told me as my clandestine little thermal experiment continued.

"Why? What happened?"

Before he could answer, however, the others came loping back from the bar, Melanie with an oversized latté in hand, and a green tea-ed Gavin with a tight red Washington Redskins toque pulled down snugly over his oversized skull.

"So what made you decide to write a novel?" I asked in a spirit of eager curiosity and chatty candour, at which point Chris took a deep breath and answered:

"Same reason anyone writes a novel. Prestige."

"Really? That's it? That was your entire motivation?"

"Well that and to debunk the prevailing De Boer myth," he admitted.

"*Ah.* So you wrote a book about your father, did you. Well won't Daddy be pleased."

"Well it's actually quite malicious. Misogynous, I guess would be the word. Apparently that's why nobody would publish it."

"How do you mean."

"Canlit," Melanie put in.

"Sorry?"

"*Can lit*," she repeated, enunciating each syllable for my doubtful benefit. "You know, 'Canadian Literature.' Of course it's all clit-lit these days," she insisted, blinking away a loose eyelash, placing it ever so gently on the arm of the sofa.

"I'm not kidding," she continued. "It's like you've got to be some sort of Lebanese lesbian alcoholic from Nova fucking Scotia if you even *hope* to get published these days." It was true though, she said. There was great demand in certain literary circles for the memoirs of sexually abused minorities from the Maritimes these days. It filled quotas. It reflected culture. It got you various government grants for all the customary politically correct reasons apparently. Of course it was always best if you could be self-deprecating in your writing. Such humility reflected a catharsis of one's own soul. Objectivity, of course, was crucial. You had to be doing it for the good of literature somehow. Frank talk about forays into child prostitution—that too seemed to be in great demand in Canadian literary circles—and if you could somehow find your way to exposing the sexual dysfunction of certain prominent and elder members of white literary society while you were at it, so be it, that was always good for exposure too. As were the marriages you broke up. The systematic sexual harassment you exposed. And the lesbian love triangles you put together. Naturally, you were sure to drop names. That way you were assured of being sued for libel and hence, gaining a broader notoriety as well. You used profanity. Recited dialogue verbatim.

And for heaven's sake, remained wise beyond your years. An old soul. "I'm telling you, it's fucking discrimination," Melanie said. "Or else it's reverse discrimination, I don't know."

"Or maybe," I felt compelled to point out, "women are the only people who bother to buy books anymore."

"Yeah, that's it," Gavin remarked with straightforward insincerity, his eyes all but hidden beneath his ridiculously low-riding toque.

"Shove it up your ass," I told him. "I hear you're into that. And what's up with the disguise by the way? Afraid the great actor might get recognized in public?"

"Fuck you."

"That's beside the point," Melanie interrupted.

"Excuse me?"

"That's beside the point."

"Yes, but closer than you might think," I maintained, feigning acquaintance with all things literature-related, thinking she might somehow be impressed.

"Oh *please*. We've already anointed Sarah McLachlan as some sort of, what, poet laureate, so what's next? The mandatory study of the philosophical hypotheses of one Alanis Morisette? Give me a break. Just give me a goddamned break. I mean if I have to digest one more catalogue of family recipes or bolting bride memoir, I think I'll puke."

"Wow, noble *and* ironic. How Catholic of you," I said. I turned to Chris. "So you, what, wrote some sort of nasty novel about women, is that it? Well no wonder no one wanted to publish it. Plenty of books never get published. The vast ma*jo*rity of books never get published."

"So?"

"So for starters, what the hell does it prove, *failing* to get a book published?"

"But he is getting published," Melanie corrected.

"That's exactly my point: it *proves* nothing. He *is* getting published."

"But not by a *Canadian* publisher," she intoned, as though I was an infant or an idiot or perhaps, I held out hope, an idiot savant of some sort.

"Right," I said, trying to digest this mess. "So let's just forget for the moment that he wrote the thing in six weeks."

"All right," Gavin said.

"No offence, Chris, but six weeks isn't really a great deal of time to output a finished manuscript, former prime minister's son or not."

"You're right there," Fisk admitted.

"So here it is then, this nasty misogynous novel, and Canadian publishers won't publish it."

"That's correct," Melanie said.

"Because he doesn't have a clitoris."

"You either have one or you don't."

"Really?"

She shrugged. "Anyway, that's what we suspect."

My initial response to all this was simply to bury my face in my hands, where I would remain for the longest time, unable to find the necessary phrases or even the words to properly express myself herein. Finally I said, "Well that's the biggest load of shit I've ever heard."

"And that," Melanie said, "is Canlit."

She was failing to get my point.

"Look," I said, shuffling forward in my chair, "everything else aside, have you ever considered the fact that a book written by a bartender tends to beget its failure to be published? Has it ever occurred to you that perhaps those concepts are not entirely mutually exclusive?"

"It's occurred to me, yes," Melanie said.

"But you still don't feel that has any merit in this case."

"Of course not. Look, the publishers up here rejected it for all the wrong reasons, just as you knew they would."

"What, and the Americans accepted it for all the right reasons?"

"Actually no, they accepted it for all the wrong ones," Chris said.

I must admit I was altogether thrown by that. And in truth it suddenly occurred to me that I was asking all these questions under the mistaken notion that these people had something to gain from their contribution.

Eventually Fisk and Melanie left for work, leaving my good buddy Gavin behind, flexing the one side of his face for some unseen camera nearby. However, neglecting for a moment his duties as nemesis, he soon wandered off in search of someone else to annoy.

"Is it really that hateful?" I asked Chris point-blank once Gavin had wandered a fair distance off.

"Yes, it is. Or it was. Truth is, it's actually rather tame by today's standards. Though it's well-written," he added, "so I guess that makes it worse somehow."

I shook my head. "I must be missing something here," I said, "because this really makes no sense whatsoever."

"Well there's something else you should probably know, Billy. Something the others—don't."

"Good Christ, there must be."

"I took it word for word from your father's book."

"*Lovestiff Annie*? Are you serious?"

"Yup."

He looked at me a long time. He was waiting for me to say no, I suppose.

BOOK TWO

CHAPTER TEN

EDWARD PURDY WAS not always the rotten son of a bitch I grew up knowing. In fact, up to and including the summer he first met and married my mother, the summer of nineteen fifty-something, I suppose he might well have been regarded as a somewhat respectable sort of one.

Born in the town of Paris, Ontario in 1922, he migrated to New York at the tender age of eighteen to attend Columbia University and avoid the war, and upon graduation, after short stints in Denver and various points southwest, returned northeast to Hamilton and the role of staff reporter for the now defunct *Tribune*, where he wrestled his way up to the assistant editor's desk before finally usurping the senior editorship by the rather junior age of thirty-one. Pushed into action by his colleagues (for their benefit, I'm sure, as well as his own) after having developed a certain notoriety over the years as a somewhat shrewd and tactful writer, he soon left his position at the paper to take the journalist's seemingly inevitable sojourn into the would-be-novelist's sabbatical. And it was during this latter tour of duty that he first met and fell in love with my mother.

Now that is not entirely true. Yes, he did meet my mother on the Blood Reserve near Lethbridge that summer, but he certainly never fell in love with her, not in any ideal sense of the term. And there is almost no chance whatsoever, having impregnated her after a long night of drunken revelry, that he was forced to wed—my father was many things but he certainly wasn't one to fall for that chicanery. No, looking back now I stand convinced it was a business decision. A career decision. A pragmatic, if rather dubious, would-be *novelist's* decision. You see, my father knew all too well that to write about something, and to write about it well, he needed to know it, he needed to experience it firsthand. And it was that desire—that singular desire for script, I'm afraid—that led him into my mother's arms that night, and kept him there, neglecting her, for years to come.

I remember I was twenty when it happened. I remember I was twenty because I was still living with my coach in the Sault when, having just been drafted by Chicago, I called my father's barn-loft apartment to tell him the good news and no one answered, and no one answered the following day either, nor the day after that when they found him dead of a heart attack—one of those garden variety jobs typically reserved for those far more deserving of such a neat and speedy departure. I didn't bother to attend the funeral. I didn't need to. At the time I recall his passing meant little to me as we were no longer as close as father and son should be. But to this day I still wish he would have known that I'd been drafted. It would have meant a lot to him to know that I'd been drafted. And yet as much as I disliked him then, and even now, that was not always the way—we are not born with an innate wisdom but with an innate trust—and trust him I did for that was the way. Actually, I do have some fair memories of my childhood, even some fond memories, only a portion of which could have possibly been contrived. No, we did have some good times together, my father and I, even some great times together, and from time to time these long empty days it's one or two of these I like to look back upon as well.

First and foremost my father was a writer, really a very good writer, as even today his words ring true, as hauntingly honest and sincere as ever—or as honest and sincere as words can ever be. An unflagging loyalty to his profession and its ethics had instilled in my father a deliberate and exacting attitude regarding his reportage of the facts, and conversely, an increasingly opportunistic and conniving one regarding his dealings with their softer human subjects. And so it was a 'bold new artist' his peers referred to when *Lovestiff Annie* first appeared on the bookshelves back in 1956. And an 'anguished and profane poet' by those of a more, what, romantic temperament maybe. But unfortunately for Edward Purdy, and in turn his wife and children, with the arrival of the bolder, newer Beat Generation and with it Jack Kerouac's more anguished and profane *On the Road*, in which the much celebrated author lampooned my father by means of the Hemingway-imitating character Roland Major, all those passionate supporters who in the beginning had read or misread my father's sparse taut style as the discipline of a modern-day master, suddenly they became his most zealous critics, writing off his 'minimalist saltpan' as throwback, hack, and even fraud, and just the sort of ham-fisted maliciousness to be expected from such a would-be literary Grey Owl. And so it should come as no surprise that he only ever published the one book. Almost a quarter century of writing and he only ever published the one book. And in the meantime he built us kids a backyard rink the pride of the entire reserve.

He simply converted one of the old holding pens, itself a perfect square, which doubled as box for box lacrosse in warmer summertime weather. In truth, all that was required insofar as any reconstruction was concerned was a levelling of the horse-trodden earth, and then the water was pumped in from the adjacent lake and that was it—instant rink—and believe me, that ice was smooth. Not as smooth as Northlands in Edmonton perhaps, but certainly as smooth as the Gardens and even Joe Louis. And whatever the sport, hockey or lacrosse, my father drilled us for hours out there. I remember him standing grey-haired in the entrance of the barn bellowing incessantly at my brothers and me. And I remember it was some time in the late Sixties when my mother first got sick. I remember that because it was around about the same time that my father moved out to the barn for good.

Now it's true that my brothers and I would have preferred to start learning how to play the game of hockey by taking hold of one of those magic totem poles and slapping a few pucks around, omitting entirely anything in the way of preparation, technical or otherwise, but it was not by way of fun, or indeed play, that we were introduced to our father's game. No, if our father had his say, no one who did not know how to skate would be allowed to desecrate a rink by playing on it. And so we skated. And skated. And skated. Now I could probably go on to tell you how my brothers and I first learned the advantages of the wrist shot over the slap shot, and the art of blocking the shot, but then this story isn't really about hockey. Nor is it really about brothers. It is, however, about a father. Or at least to some degree it was.

Now adhering as he did to certain fundamental rules, my father was very certain about various universal matters, one of which, surprisingly or not, was baseball. My father loved baseball. And believe me, I understood—I was *made* to understand—how it was that baseball had become the thinking man's game. How with its capacity for infinitude, with its boundlessness of design sprawling out and past a few critically placed bags and baselines, the five-four-three double play had become, and remains today, among the most artistically perfect phenomena ever triggered by the hand of man. My father taught me at a very early age how it was that baseball, with its complexity of games within games and sheer magnitude of traditions and cultural spin-offs, had evolved into something far more than just a sport. But as much as he loved baseball, as much as he revered and trusted it, that was nothing in comparison to how he felt about hockey. And my father was a passionate old man.

Those other so-called men of letters, they could keep their nostalgic reminder of all that once was good and still could be again. My father wanted his frozen reflection of a world gone mad—a Cold War—of what had come to pass and seemingly always would be then. Perhaps it was the environment he grew up in—Paris's frozen lakes and winters without end—but somehow he was just not cut out for the game of baseball. For my father, the puck always carried more currency. For Edward Purdy, the skate always cut to the chase. And yet despite all that, and despite all that I would endure for the discipline of hockey, there was always the discipline itself.

CHAPTER ELEVEN

WHEN NOT PLAGIARIZING my father's one and only novel, the youngest of the late prime minister's three sons worked nights at a bar on the corner of Burrard and whatever no more than a stone's throw south of my hotel. Operating as a kind of ultra-modern shrine to classic literature and rock, the Devil's Advocaat was a popular little room far from the modest little room it had first appeared to be upon my recent arrival in town. Catering once again to that indistinguishable but eye-catching twenty-something crowd, the Devil's Advocaat offered a truly exhaustive list of expensive and cleverly named martinis, ensuring all therein that while there would never be any chance of stumbling upon something even remotely unattractive, there would always exist ample opportunity to pay handsomely for the convenience.

Still, enjoying as much popularity as it did, the Devil's Advocaat really was a tiny little bar. In fact, so tiny and so popular that I immediately hypothesized that a bar's success was related quite inversely to its measure. Take Heaven in Mannheim for instance: very large and hardly popular. Purgatoire in Montreal: long and narrow and proportionately popular. The Devil's Advocaat: extremely small and undeniably popular. The Roxy being the lone exception to this rule of course, but so long as there were rules I imagined there would always be one of those.

There was the usual queue when I arrived that night, but luckily the Indo-Canadian doorman recognized me and was more than happy to nod my way inside. I felt sorry for those unlucky few left to list out there in the night. Not because they had yet to be picked, mind you, but simply that they would even bother to try. How demoralizing to be passed over in such a manner. How agonizingly stupid to leave oneself open to such a defamation of character. In those days how anybody stood in a line-up—in any line-up—was forever beyond my ability to understand.

I squeezed my way through to the bar where De Boer met me with a cold pink martini.

"What's this?"

"Here at the Ad it's referred to as a *Seminole Squeeze*," he told me. "But anywhere else it's just a double Greyhound, shaken and strained."

I found a seat at the bar. The drink was strong, really very strong, and it stung a trail of pink fire all the way down to my groin. Glancing around, I noticed the usual number of people beginning to take notice of me. Still, it was good to smell the smoke again; to feel my core fill up with Sault again. I settled in as Chris wiped down the marble bar with a cloth. The music was loud, and I was forced to ask him to repeat himself on several occasions early on. I was not angry at his having stolen my father's work. On the contrary, I was pleasantly surprised. Now at one time or another since, I have probably considered the subject of plagiarism from most if not all of its various angles, including the one that all words and phrases remain exclusive property of the author (except, of course, those the plagiarist finds altogether irreplaceable and therefore entirely irresistible), but at the time, beyond all the other reasons I had stockpiled, I was actually very keen to see exactly how far this con could go, would go, and in turn, anticipate all those opportunities made suddenly, intriguingly possible.

De Boer had actually written some stuff of his own, three complete novels in fact, and excluding perhaps the third one—I've not yet read the third one—they were simply not that well done. Unfortunately it takes just as much effort to write a poor novel as it does a good one, and De Boer's problem, I think, stemmed from the fact that he had read too much J.D. Salinger too early on. An innocent enough occupation for the rest of us, too much Salinger could often prove disastrous for the writer, especially the one still early in his development. For the young writer to take Salinger as his mentor was to invite sheer disaster, especially that of the later works. The early stuff was okay; it was the later stuff that caused all the trouble, especially when taken first. The style of the language was simply too rich, the character of Seymour Glass just too well described, the Buddhist mysticism too intense. That was what did it then. The mysticism. The mysticism of J.D. Salinger was simply too potent to leave alone with the young writer unattended. The result, more often than not, was even more mysticism, only this time of an altogether poor design, emanating out of an ornate writing style further complicated by whatever pseudo-scientific jargon had managed to capture the interest of our as yet undiscovered messiah at the time. Little good has ever come out of thinking like a messiah, and even less from trying to fly like one. Now having since read his first two books myself, I must say that Chris was absolutely correct in his analysis of them, and in his decision not to publish them, but back then I wish he would have afforded me this information himself. As it was it came indirectly through Mitch.

Mitch was a friend of Fisk's, one of many such friends Fisk kept around for any such situation as this. An overweight corporate insurance salesman and neophyte pimp of about my age, Mitch displayed a robust and dedicated passion for American cigarettes and overproof Jamaican spirits. Mitch was in the habit of drinking and pimping at Fisk's bar, but on this particular evening had set up shop here. What for exactly, I had no idea, though I got the idea early on that Mitch really enjoyed the fact that he could spend such a large amount of time amid such a pretty group of people and, except in a roundabout way, never have to pay for the pleasure. Which was odd, as Mitch was one of those moderately annoying drunks for whom it was always very important to be seen picking up the bill. Drinks, dinner, cab fare—just so long as it was repeatedly acknowledged, he was more than happy to be taking care—a habit that would no doubt hamper his pursuits in his two chosen professions, I was sure.

As mentioned, Mitch was overweight, not so overweight as to mention it twice perhaps, but in my mind still overweight, with small, soft, almost feminine hands forever fluttering up around his chubby face, receding jaw and cauliflowered ears, one hand telling the story, the other hand underlining all the important words. Penance, no doubt, for the sin of being a pimp, Mitch always seemed to be sporting some rather large oval sweat stains under the arms of his dress shirts, and his soft feminine hands (devoid, like the rest of him, of any and all suspicion of bone), when not fluttering up around his ears, were either aggressively engaged with his chubby, sweating glasses of overproof rum and Coke or else squeezing the last vestiges of life from a perpetually dying smoke.

"Never seen a bar with books in it before," I mentioned to Mitch at one point, having skimmed over the contents of the nearest bookshelf. "Never known good drinking to be all that conducive to good reading, I suppose."

"They're all cut down though, see?" Mitch wedged his cigarette into the corner of his mouth so as to extract a book from the nearest shelf without compromising his grip on his drink. And he was right: each book had been hacked down to within a raw ripped inch of its binding in order to fit the shallow mock shelving. I extracted one 'book' from the shelf, *The Ultimate Horse Guide*, and began flipping through, plucking various words from the only remaining margin. 'Preferred colours,' 'proportion,' 'predominant characteristics,' 'breeds,' 'powerful quarters,' and even 'profuse feather' being those that recurred most often; those and 'strength' and 'stamina' naturally. Eventually a sharply dressed Asian filly pressed in beside me, tilting in to announce her arrival with a certain sniffing satisfaction and, arguably, the blackest mane I'd ever seen on a girl.

She asked if I played for the Canucks.

"Actually, I'm the heir to the Purdy's chocolate chain," I told her, returning the horse book to the shelf.

She smiled good-naturedly, perplexedly, and finally not at all.

"I was suspended indefinitely," I explained in a conspiratorial whisper.

"But you do play for them."

"Oh yes, you definitely have me there."

She frowned and told me that, in her opinion, I wasn't very good this year.

"Your candour, how refreshing," I said, at which point I ignored her so that she might soon go away. She did. Meanwhile Mitch took a drink, and I winced as the burning tip of his cigarette undershot his eye by no more than a fraction of an inch.

"She's looking for a date, if you're interested."

"Really, Mitch? You think?"

"Yep, she'll make someone a hell of a good *wife*," he said, left hand firmly underlining 'wife' so that I fully understood the implication. "Thing is, she's not completely—onboard with the idea yet." He hesitated. "Like I said though, I can get you a date if you're interested."

"No thanks," I said, searching her out amongst the crowd. "She's a little too, what, emaciated," I suggested, having located her at last, to which Mitch nodded his staunch, sweaty-pitted agreement while extracting from his cigarette a long punishing drag.

"Used to be an actress back in Korea. Commercials, that sort of thing. It was chocolate bars mostly, but—"

"Really? What kind?"

"You know, commercials. Like on TV."

"I meant what kind of chocolate bars, Mitch."

"Oh, right," he said. "Oh Henry maybe. Or maybe it was Mr Big, I don't know." Tapping his cigarette over the ashtray and thoroughly stirring the results, Mitch studied the ashes for meaning as if they were a Korean character to be decoded. "Either way, it was definitely one of those bigger bars," he concluded.

"All in preparation for her new career, I suppose."

At this point I let Mitch know that his tie was dipping into his Appleton and Coke.

"So out within the year, hey," he said, shaking his tie dry.

"What's that."

"De Boer's book. What else is there?"

"Those two there, I'd say."

Mitch followed my nod to the two men hanging around the end of the bar, the one sporting what could best be described as a fireman's moustache, and the other a tight-fitting turquoise sweater. I watched their hands gesturing frantically under the light. Reminiscent somehow of Mitch's, albeit even more animated in fact.

"Check out those two," I said.

"Yeah, they own the place," Mitch said. "Actually, that one with the moustache, he came out to his family just the other day. I hear they're taking it pretty hard."

"Not as hard as he is, I bet."

Mitch laughed, coughed and finished his drink in one greedy gulp, then nodded stoically for another to immediately take its place. Mitch, I would learn, was always doing a great deal of stoic nodding at the bar. It was part of what he felt to be the pimp's system of authority somehow.

The moustachioed one asked De Boer something I could not make out from here. Whatever his response, both owners started laughing, no doubt overjoyed to be offered such a rare insight into the heterosexual world. De Boer winked my way as he leaned away to the glass washer, and I smiled down into my pink martini and routinely ordered another.

"Let me get that."

"Thanks, Mitch. I've got a tab."

Just then the owner in the tight-fitting turquoise sweater shouted out to De Boer something about the three best feelings in life. I will not go into detail here, but suffice to say it was one of those witticisms some of those people tend to feel the need to put out there from time to time. Excusing myself from the bar, I went off and found the ex-Korean actress and budding Canadian prostitute sitting alone at a nearby table, and explained how these two potential 'dates' were awaiting her arrival down the end of the bar. This, I thought, would be incredibly funny.

"Excuse me?" she said, and I felt my ears turn a telling red. Finally she laughed and touched my arm. "I'm joking," she said.

Craning her neck, she managed to spot the owners through the mass of bodies in between. "And here I thought they wouldn't be into someone like me," she frowned, leaning forward, prompting me to peer down the vacant front of her dress, fittingly paltry compensation, it turns out, for having ventured this far from the bar in the first place.

"Oh I think perhaps they are," I said.

Pushing off the rest of my embarrassment, I asked Gracie—that was her name, Gracie—if she would perhaps like to join me up at the bar. She said she would and that she was a really big fan. I disregarded the latter, but when she repeated it I politely informed her that she should really go to hell.

"Ex*cuse* me?" she said, her eyebrows plucked so severely that her agitation seemed to arrive at me almost obliquely and from the remotest corners of her face.

"I'd prefer you didn't play me up like that."

"But I honestly am a really big fan."

"I understand that, Gracie. I do. But I'd still prefer you treat me like any other john."

I sat down at the bar, and Gracie shoehorned her way in between my thigh and Mitch's arm. She ordered a virgin Pina Colada, and Mitch ordered his Appleton and Coke. Me, I just ordered the usual, and then turned my attention to the deeper contemplation of the two owners still hanging around the end of the bar.

"I got that one."

"All right, I got the other one."

"The round, I mean. I got the *round*," Mitch said, pushing my drink toward me.

"Oh," I said. "No thanks."

"It's mine."

"I said no thanks."

But again he nodded and again he got it, managing to out-Mitch me once again.

We listened to Neil Young and stirred our drinks, watching the two owners hold court at the end of the bar. The one with the moustache was watching De Boer. Naturally he had that look of expectation about him. The other one was watching me, I suppose. I shifted my focus to Gracie, and to her tight black dress constructed mostly of some sort of synthetic sheer material. She was pretty, not so pretty that she came off as anything more than an emaciated, expatriated ESL student looking to earn some extra cash, but still fairly pretty in a high-cheeked, weather-beaten, forlorn and elfin way. Bored, she shuffled about on her stool, offering me a view of her overly Asian anatomy in parts. I laughed and she asked me what I was laughing at, so I told her again to go to hell.

"Well screw you," she pouted, pivoting Mitch's way. "I've read about you."

"Watch it, you'll be reporting on me next."

"So how come you got suspended?" she asked over her shoulder, eyes wrinkling up at the corners, quite vexed.

"Oh I, uh, experienced a bit of a mishap the other night on the ice," I told her, at which point something burst from Mitch's face.

"What kind of mishap?" Gracie asked.

"Oh you know," I said, watching Mitch closely for any further signs of imminent detonation, "myself and another encountered a slight misunderstanding as to the details and implications of what was, by rights, a lifelong binding contract."

Mitch burst again, free hand up aflutter around his ear lending strength to the impression of having finally expended something quite impossible to withhold. I realized, then, that this was his laugh I was witnessing. As an ensemble, a remarkably unattractive performance.

"I *love* hockey fights," Gracie beamed.

"Really," I said. "Good for you."

"I do though. There's nothing else that even comes close."

"Extolling the virtues of my occupation, Gracie? How nice. I wish I could do the same for you."

She smiled wryly. Then she asked, "Tell me, who's the toughest you ever fought?"

"Jim Beam, no question."

"Who?"

"I joke. Billy make joke."

"Seriously though."

"Oh, Semenko maybe. Twist probably. But then Brown, he was good too. . . . Now Probert, he was difficult for a time—and Domi. Yeah, Domi can put on quite a show when he wants to."

"Now Probert," she reflected, "does that mean he's anti-Ernie?"

"Pardon?"

"I joke. Gracie make joke."

"Right. I get it now," I told her.

She frowned almost maternally, disappointed in my uptake. "It's too bad about that instigator rule though. I mean the fighting, it's the only thing that keeps the players honest anymore."

"Yes, well, you certainly seem to know your hockey, Gracie. You and Don Cherry, real aficionados you are."

"Real what?"

"Aficionados. It means you have great passion."

"Oh I do," she smiled, all too Muppet-like to be seductive. "I have great passion for all the contact sports."

From his position on the other side, Mitch burst again, and I watched his cigarette just barely graze his eyebrow as it completed another reckless orbit of his head. He refused to blink, so I blinked for him. It was to become something of a routine of ours in the months ahead.

"Oh yeah?" I said. "What else you got passion for, Gracie?"

"You," she smiled. "I've got passion for *you.*"

"But you don't know anything about me."

"I know you've played for three whole teams now."

"Four."

"*Four?* Really?" she said, managing to knit her overly plucked brows together momentarily.

"Well sort of, sure. Well maybe not, maybe three," I conceded. "Depends on how you look at Chicago."

"Four. Wow. That's a lot."

"Gretzky's on his forth," I told her.

"Yeah, well, I believe Gretzky's won four cups too. How many have you won?"

"None."

"Ha. You see? I knew that too."

She finished her virgin Pina Colada with one long muted slurp, palm-over-glass providing all the necessary soundproofing required to clandestinely accomplish the task.

"Still you're lucky you're not bald," she said at last.

"Why do you say that?"

"Well because you wear a helmet. Hockey players are always going bald because of their helmets—it's scientific fact."

"Huh. I never thought of that."

"True," she said, having spent one last, long, largely contemplative moment thoroughly stealth-slurping the bottom of her glass. "And hey, I used to eat at his restaurant in Toronto too. Gretzky's, I mean."

"Oh yeah? So then you live in Toront—"

"Studied the menu too," she continued. "All his records and stuff. Like ninety-two goals in one year. I honestly do know my hockey, Billy."

"Wonderful. So then you live—"

"He's so good, even now."

I sighed. "He does see the ice well, true."

"What's that mean?"

"It means he sees more of what's happening than the rest of us do. You know, like the bigger picture shining through."

Gracie seemed to like that, and dropped the subject for now.

"So then you live in Toronto?" I asked again, finally given the opportunity to string the words together.

"No, here. In the West End. Why?"

"How long ago'd you come over then?"

"From Korea?" She shrugged. "Five years or so, I don't know. I remember I was pretty young at the time."

"You speak pretty good English for only having been here five years, Gracie."

She considered that a moment, and then: "You think I'm *lying*?"

"Hey, easy now. I just can't believe you speak it better than I do, that's all."

Mitch ordered another round. In the meantime, another girl came up to rub up against Gracie, a rather lame attempt to profit by proximity no doubt.

"Mitch brought me over," Gracie explained once the girl had reluctantly moved on. "But then when I got to Toronto I figured I'd make more money out here in Vancouver."

"Prostituting yourself."

"Yeah, you could call it that, I guess. Figured I'd take advantage of this whole Hollywood North thing, just like everyone else is. Unfortunately, though, there's just not much of a demand for Asian girls, so Mitch got me into this massage therapy course."

"Massage therapy, huh?" Chris put in from across the bar.

"Yeah, here I thought you were working the whole hooker-with-the-heart-of-glass thing," I told her, at which point she smiled glibly.

Chris asked if he could crash at my place that night.

"Absolutely," I said. And then, trying not to sound quite so damned enthusiastic: "Why, what's wrong with your place?"

"Wife needs it," he explained.

I nodded deeply, thereby conveying my unfortunate understanding of the often overwhelming needs of the recently estranged spouse. "Stay as long as you like."

"And it's heart of gold by the way."

"Sorry, Gracie?"

"It's hooker with the heart of *gold*," she said. "Not *glass*."

"My mistake," I said. "I apologize."

Chris moved off down the bar to fix some drinks. Meanwhile I turned to Gracie, studied her a while, and tried to picture her with Mitch. I tried to picture what all they had done together. I tried to picture what all she knew. And right about then I must have figured that, as a visual aide, she would more than likely do.

Standing from my stool, I leaned in close to her shiny black hair and told her to meet me in the washroom. A minute or so later she joined me in the second stall.

"How much?" I asked over the rasping piped-in *Rush*, hoarse now with excitement as Gracie slowly closed the door behind her. She did not answer, not immediately anyway, choosing instead to survey more closely the lay of the land and the situation at hand. Finally, adequately pleased with the working conditions, if not with the actual work itself, she informed me that in fact it was bought and paid for, much to my surprise.

"What do you mean?"

"It's completely paid for," she repeated, twirling as though to show me her dress.

"Chris bought this?"

"*No*, Dad did."

"Who?"

"Mitch," she said.

"You call him Dad? *Nice*," I said, chuckling down into the palms of my hands.

"Hey, what's so funny?"

"This, Gracie. *This* is funny."

"How come?" she asked, long thin hands balanced on slender hips, one hip kicked out just a fraction too far.

"Never mind," I said, forced to shout over the speakers, suspended just overhead, currently pounding *Tom Sawyer* deep into my head. "Tell me, who exactly should I be addressing here."

"Dress?"

"Yes?"

"I *told* you," she said. "It's paid for."

"Right. Sorry. So what is it that *Dad* . . ." My voice trailed off as her lips curled back to expose two crowded rows of stubby white teeth.

"Now that would depend on what you want, chief."

I eyed her sceptically, wondering whether or not I should make a run for it.

"What? What's wrong?" she asked.

"I was just wondering whether this was some kind of set-up or sting or whatever, that's all."

"Huh?"

"ARE YOU A COP."

She did something then to convince me beyond all reasonable doubt that she was definitely looking to become a bona fide prostitute.

I told her to take off her dress.

"What? No way."

"Take it off," I told her.

She crossed her arms emphatically. "Not gonna happen, big fella. No way."

"I thought you said it was paid for though."

"It is."

"So then take off the damned dress."

"Hey man, this is an Armani. *This* is a nice dress. And listen: I don't strip. That's just not what I do. You want some sort of show, go hire your*self* a prostitute."

She unzipped me, bent down and began, but nothing happened.

"You want something else?" she asked after what she evidently considered to be the obligatory amount of time.

"What else?"

"Anything else."

"I don't know," I told her, and she smiled knowingly.

"Well I think maybe Dad's hoping you will," she said.

I explained to Gracie what it was I wished she would do, or rather, what I wished she would watch me do, and despite another expression of what seemed like truly genuine sorrow she dutifully consented, flopping down onto the edge of the toilet seat to recline in bored observation against the attendant paper dispenser.

I tried to get it going, but nothing happened.

"Is it going to get big?" she asked at length.

"That's the general idea," I told her, trying to think over not only Getty Lee but the heightened thud of blood in my ears to what Mitch would do to her, and then to what some of my teammates over the years would have done to her, but still nothing happened. I began to grow frustrated.

"Relax, would you?" she said in what was surely not, but surely seemed, a very condescending tone.

"Sometimes it takes a little more with guys like me."

"Some ego you got there, Bull."

I swore a little more, and tried once more, as she settled in against the toilet paper dispenser, conserving her strength for the long hard struggle ahead.

"Maybe you had too much to drink," she offered up eventually, failing to ease the least bit of my frustration. Breathing deeply and evenly, but without the least shred of dignity, I ignored her and tried again, this time with eyes closed. Still nothing happened.

"Here, let me help."

I pushed her hands away and zipped up, and then told her to get the fuck out.

"Fuck you," she said and I slapped her face, skipping her forehead off the left stall wall. She looked up at me defiantly, looking up through tussled black hair. I thought about smacking that defiance clean off, but then thought better of it in the end, I swear.

"Look, I'm sorry, Gracie. I really am. And I think maybe you're right: I think maybe I've had a little too much to drink tonight."

"It happens," she said. And I knew it often could.

CHAPTER TWELVE

"THIS ONE'S ON me."

"So I heard."

"You and Gracie, I mean. It's on me."

"I understand," I said. "You're quite the pimp, believe me."

He didn't blink, so I blinked for him. Then I asked for the bill that had already been paid apparently.

"Blondie."

"Pardon?"

"Blondie," Gracie said, blowing partially digested burp-breath down the vacant front of her dress. "You called me a hooker with a heart of glass. Well that's a Blondie song."

"That so? How the hell would you know?"

"That one there told me," she said, indicating with a nod the owner in the tight-fitting turquoise sweater. I laughed long and hard as Gracie put forth her best rendition here, listening as my laughter, and her singing, carried together throughout the room. The bar was busy, the dance floor was crowded, and all the stools had been pushed aside. There were so many people packed in so tightly around me that no one seemed to notice me spitting down onto the concrete floor. I had already vomited once, having managed to contain it all the way to the washroom only to find a queue at the door, as a result of which I was relegated to spilling out into the shallow shelf space provided by the swift removal of some radically abridged but arguably improved Robertson Davies novels. Still, with a little more time I was sure I would eventually come around. I mean I would eventually have to come around. I wasn't thinking about my earlier shortcomings either. In fact, I had placed them completely out of mind. Not even Gracie's enduring presence gave me pause, let alone cause, to feel unwell. I was sure it was just a one-time thing and besides, I'd learned from two marriages and a handful of affairs that a woman's self-esteem with regard to such matters was brittle at the best of times as well.

Both Fisk and Melanie had arrived some time ago. Both tended bar at the same restaurant these days, and having gotten off early but nevertheless to a late start personally, both were looking to get drunk as rapidly as possible.

There was some commotion at the bar, and it was with a great heave of sadness that I looked up and discovered, standing high atop the marble with a bottle of liquor in each hand, who else but my own personal barman De Boer. A line was forming behind me, snaking its way out towards the dance floor. Evidently, and despite all my drunken objections to the contrary, I had been designated first go. Spinning me around, Chris placed the back of my head down against the wet marble bar. Briefly his face appeared above me in silhouette, swimming in the halo of lights beyond. I opened my mouth and liquor poured in. I took in all I could—I took in a lot—but when I could not possibly take in another ounce my head shot up off the bar and coughed. I coughed down onto the floor. And wiping my face with the back of my sleeve, I accepted all the congratulatory back-slaps and cheers those gathered in so closely around me evidently deemed the compulsory score.

Sweating profusely, I stumbled clear of the bar and all the activity there. At some point it became clear that someone was yelling into my ear, and turning I found who else but the owner in the tight-fitting turquoise sweater.

"Who's your agent?" he was asking, his plucked muscular forearm draped snugly about my shoulder. He leaned in to nuzzle his unshaven cheek against my sweaty forehead, and wrenching myself free I told him I didn't have an agent, not anymore. Then I sighed heavily, feeling my stomach pitch over. I sighed again, certain, for the moment at least, that the liquor was going to remain down there somewhere.

"Why not?"

"Why not what?"

"Why not have an agent?" he said.

"I negotiate my own deals, thank you."

"And hey, you negotiated for the league minimum, so then maybe you should, you know?"

He laughed and nuzzled in again, and again I tried to wrench myself free.

"Nice sweater," I said.

"Thanks. I'm told it really brings out the red in my eyes," he winked, waiting for me to laugh, and when I didn't laugh, said more seriously, "Listen, I used to play. For the Blazers. Up in Kamloops."

"Wonderful. Could you do me a favour?"

"Yeah, the Loop," he mused, his breath pouring over me like warm sweet booze. "Played defence even though I was a little too small. . . . Of course I could skate though. Man, could I skate though. Sometimes I wish I could just strap on the pads again just for the contact. I sure do miss the contact, you know?"

"I bet you do. Now listen—"

"And the hazing," he continued. "Holy *shit*, the things we used to do. God, you have terrific forearms, you know that? You really do."

He displayed for me his left wrist then, and the tattoo of scars running around the base of the hand. "Broke it in two places, see. There and—there. Went to hit some guy in the face and hit the glass instead—*wham!*" He flexed the wrist several times. "They rebuilt the bone with a piece of my hip, hey, so imagine—"

"Listen—"

"—if I hit someone now, it'd be like a rock!" he exclaimed triumphantly, and began to run in circles small at first but progressively larger as he went along, eventually running off into the crowd in search of Gracie, singing *Heart of Glass* at the top of his lungs. I remember feeling a great deal of disgust just then. Not so much for what he was, mind you, but more for what he had bothered to say.

Sometimes I hated the way everyone always seemed to have an opinion on my given employment situation. And just as it had passed, the feeling was rapidly re-established, and I suddenly began to vomit a great deal once again.

It was not my finest hour. Hands clasped more or less over my mouth, I stumbled off to the toilet spewing forth through fingers, shouldering past various strangers in search of the first available stall. Unfortunately there were no stalls available, and so I was forced to gut out into the sink in front of them all. Someone suggested I try something—God knows what—but I wasn't about to go out on a limb just now, and finally Fisk came in and found me drifting off to sleep in a pool of my own bile between the second stall toilet and the third stall wall. He helped me to my feet, and together we stumbled out into the bright lights and slashed-down books of an unusually quiet and empty bar. I asked what was wrong and he said nothing, nothing at all—the bar's closed, that's all. Apparently, according to Fisk anyway, the upside-down margaritas had ended some four hours before.

He set me up with some water at the bar. The Indo-Canadian doorman eyed me sceptically, but at De Boer's suggestion decided it wouldn't be in his best interests to force any sort of confrontation here. Gracie and the two owners continued to sing *Heart of Glass* over and over, although with neither the volume nor the exuberance of before. Mitch drank coffee. Fisk helped clean the bar. And with me was Melanie of course.

She said she desperately wanted to go down to the Penthouse. Desperately? I said. How desperately? Desperately enough, I found out. I said as desperate as I was I didn't know where or what the Penthouse was, and Fisk informed me that the Penthouse was in fact a strip club down on Seymour. I told them I had no desire to see more, but that one of the owners there might be willing to play the part of voyeur. Mitch said women. I said what? Mitch said women strip there.

In the end, however, we all headed off to my hotel. Naturally the doorman asked if he could come along too, but I told him I didn't think that was such a good idea just now. At some point during the ensuing mêlée in and around the front door we managed to hail ourselves a pair of cabs, and driving the two or three hundred feet down the street to the hotel managed to upset that pair of Indo-Canadians as well.

How we all got past the doorman at the hotel is anybody's guess. Perhaps I threatened him. Or perhaps Mitch paid him. But in all probability it was a collaborative effort that saved us. Dragging Melanie down to the pool, I offered Chris the key to my room, and together with the two owners he, Mitch, Gracie and Fisk all ran up to the room to raid what little was left of my mini-bar.

Melanie and I stripped naked and scampered into the pool. Melanie was constructed with a great deal of curves, and to my surprise was rather amply, if somewhat unevenly, breasted too. But in the end it still wasn't any good. I explained to her alcohol and its renowned performance-impairing effects.

"It happens," she said. And I knew it often would.

So then I took the approach of servicing her explicitly, this despite the fact I knew her to be saddled with herpes and all the rest of that baggage, to which she responded curtly, "This ain't the Pepsi Challenge there, Bull."

That said, I promptly disengaged from her larger left breast, allowing her to drift more or less unmolested to the stairs.

"My grandfather died today," she told me after a time, afloat on her back, uneven breasts pancaking into her armpits.

"I'm sorry," I said, qualifying this rapidly with, "About your grandfather, I mean."

We floated about some more.

"So how'd he go then?" I finally asked.

"Oh," she sighed, "peacefully in his bed of natural causes."

"Good Christ, who does *that* anymore."

After a prolonged silence she told me how her grandfather had actually been a pretty good guy.

"I'm sure he was."

"How come?" she asked, bolting suddenly upright.

"How come what?"

"How come you're so sure he was a good guy?"

"I was just being polite," I replied, and that seemed to appease her somewhat.

Eventually she sighed, "He really was, you know."

"I bet."

"Fuck you," she said, and I assured her I was joking, and some time later she asked me why we always assume things like that. "You know, that they're always such good guys when they die."

"Oh you mean the mechanics of it. Well probably because that's the way we feel they ought to've been while alive."

"Yeah, probably. Still, they're not always, you know. Sometimes they're just—awful."

"That's true."

"Are you, Billy?"

"Awful?"

"A good guy?"

"Oh sure," I told her. "I'm very good-guy material."

The next morning I was asked to vacate my room at the Sutton Place Hotel. Apparently Charlton Heston, having registered as a guest that night, had borne witness to some of the more suspect activities in and around my room (the popped champagne corks he likened, not surprisingly, to shotgun blasts), and in turn had lodged a rather severe and hostile complaint with hotel management. I didn't attempt a defence. I didn't need to. Gathering my few belongings, settling the bill, and wiping the dried puke shrapnel from my shoes, I checked into another hotel, this time the Pan Pacific down on the water, where they placed me in an eight hundred-dollar-a-night room called *Jade*. That was what the room was called, *Jade*, and in their italics too. No number on the door, just *Jade*, opening up on a veritable cavern of a room. For a hotel room it really was enormous, with a great high ceiling, a great huge bed, and a balcony running the entire width of the hotel from which I enjoyed a tremendous view of a body of water known, according to the in-room literature, as Indian Arm. The only complaint I had with *Jade* was the television alongside the hot-tub forever fogging over. Nevertheless, I loved *Jade*. I really did. In fact, with the balcony being so long and the ceiling being so high, I immediately called down to explain my rather unique situation here, inquiring of the manager-on-duty if I could perhaps remain indefinitely, as it were. She accepted without reservation. They even offered me a special weekly rate. I explained how that was unnecessary in light of my employment situation, but then they insisted I take it anyway.

Both De Boer and Fisk had the night off work, and so we ended up at the Roxy for a drink. As for me, I was no longer barred, my sentence having been suspended on account of my newfangled status as Local Hockey Hero. In due course two young women joined us. The one I soon recognized as Toni Childs, part-time actress and ex-child porn star. The other, it seemed, was her protégé somehow. Toni bought us a round of shots, and after that so did her pal. They were both a little too crass for my liking, both a little too weather-beaten and worn-out, but still rather amusing to have around, I found out. Toni had been on and off with De Boer years ago, and at times still seemed to fancy herself his one and only girl.

We were drinking in the back room of the Roxy at a glass-topped table next to the sunken bar. Fisk was explaining something of no particular interest to anyone that for the volume of the Shaved Pussycats and this one other thing I was admittedly finding it a little difficult to pay much attention to just now. I was preoccupied with the protégé's handiwork beneath the glass-topped table. She noticed me watching, and I noticed her notice me watching, at which point we shared a quiet chuckle.

Across the table, Toni Childs was moving in aggressively on De Boer. To be honest, he seemed completely uninterested. I began to wonder about him some more. Still he decided—that is, if it were all right with me—that we should probably get back to the hotel as soon as possible. We called a cab, and Fisk and the protégé hopped in front while Toni, De Boer and I rode in back. Chris, though, continued to display little or no interest, and eventually Toni turned her considerable attention on me. Her hair was coloured a very improbable blonde, evidently self-induced, as when I asked where she'd had it done she said everywhere imaginable, and that back in the room she'd probably do me too. I shrugged at Chris to see if it were all right. He laughed and wished me good luck. I kissed Toni Childs on the face and neck, but then there was little more that I could accomplish here in the confines of the cab. When we arrived at the hotel, Fisk managed to Mitch me on the cab, and so, once we were safely installed in *Jade*, I called up room service and, with an air of fiscal impunity, ordered up four bottles of champagne, two dozen bottles of beer, a bottle each of whatever liquor was on the menu, and last but not least, just to one-up that affable bastard Fisk, a double order of raisin toast for one of the girls. When the liquor finally arrived, I tipped the waiter outrageously and we all immediately set to—Fisk and De Boer shaking up shooters with some water glasses found in one of the washrooms, and the girls tonguing each other and, inexplicably, the remote control for my stereo system. I turned up the stereo by hand—and after the first real complaint turned it down. I did not want to lose hold of *Jade* just yet as I was growing rather fond of her particulars now.

Eventually Toni hopped up onto the bar and hastened to remove her blouse. In back of the bar was a mirror in which I could plainly see my hopeful face looking on. Patches of purple dots peppered my eyelids and the soft tissue surrounding my eyes. I thought perhaps I was experiencing some sort of allergic reaction, but when I deferred to De Boer he told me that it was probably just bruising from the effort and strain of so much vomiting the night before. Meanwhile, out on the balcony, in clear view of everyone, the protégé was trying hard to remove Fisk's pants. Toni purred for Chris to come join her up at the bar, but he said no, he didn't think so, not yet. So then she tried to put on a show. Something from her childhood perhaps. It did not come off too well, and she began to grow angry and called him a faggot. You little fucking faggot, she said. Chris did not respond, and so she maintained her superior position both literally and figuratively, verbally molesting him from the bar. Still he did not respond. Finally she called out to me instead, but I insisted I watch, if only for a while, as in reality I wasn't quite ready to reveal my latest injury just yet. I suppose it was funny. It had to be funny. I mean of all the rotten ways to be injured this had to be the funniest one. Especially in a situation such as this one. And sitting there watching a naked Toni Childs curse De Boer from the bar while her protégé wrestled Fisk's pants into submission, I tried my best to recall a funnier one. It was difficult, but then I think I did come up with one. It certainly had a funny name in Indian anyway. As I recall, that was about the first funny thing I learned from them.

Eventually Toni slid down from her perch on the bar and staggered out to the deck, untouched raisin toast in hand. Soon she joined in alongside the protégé. Together they made quite a tandem. I tried to watch. It was fun to watch. But then I began to grow angry just the same. It wasn't easy. It would never be easy. But I thought it would be workable eventually. Maybe it will come back, I told myself. Maybe it will partially come back. Or maybe it's over for me completely. But I didn't have the feeling that it was really over. I only had the feeling of a young girl, or what I thought a young girl must feel like, who thinks this blemish she has will last forever.

Fisk was naked now except for his socks and shoes, and I watched as the long lean muscles of his back pushed and pulled, bunched and released, straining his pelvis up into her. I remember wondering how much more the protégé could take as he was really starting to give it to her. Behind me, on the sofa, Chris refused to watch. I wondered what was wrong with him. Perhaps he's still hung up on that other one, I thought, that one without hair that he'd married. Meanwhile, out on the deck, they continued steadily on course, all three moving in one upon the others until there was but one rhythm remaining—she was the picture of industry, this girl. I knew enough to appreciate the effort, but still to swallow it like that seemed an awfully big pill.

And finally, but not all at once, they were done. Naturally, they all sat around chatting for a spell, but then nothing really gripping materialized there. And so we all decided, at Fisk's suggestion, that since it was only eleven o'clock, and since there was nothing else to do, we might just as well get back to the Roxy for one last quick cock-tail or two. There was quite a queue when we arrived by taxi, but nat-urally we paid it no heed. We immediately made our way to the sunken bar in back where we ordered several shooters and plenty of Greyhounds, backing those up with round after round of single malt scotches just to be sure. Still it wasn't any good. Fisk and the girls went off to dance, leaving me alone at the table with De Boer. But still it wasn't any good. I finished my Greyhound and hooked back a scotch, then announced that I should really be going soon.

"Where to?"

"No idea," I said. "But far, far away from here, you can be sure."

"Was it that thing back at the hotel? Look, Billy, I'm sorry about that. I am."

"Don't be. Really. It's no big deal," I assured him, and he nod-ded to the girl behind the bar that we were in desperate need of another round over here.

"Really, it was no big deal," I repeated just as the Greyhounds and shots arrived, and together we sat and drank in relative silence, watching a group of young Asian men play pool. I wondered if any of them knew Gracie. And then I wondered that I should care.

"So what is it then? The suspension?"

"Not really, no. No, I've been suspended before."

"It's this town then, I can tell. This town can get to you some-times."

"I do find it kind of boring, true."

"It's not a bad place," he said. "Not one of the worst places to come home to. And home is where the heart is," he added inconceivably.

I looked at him. "Well now that's profound, Chris. You ought to put that in the next book you plagiarize."

He cast me a peculiar glance. "I thought you said you were cool about it."

"I am, I am," I assured him, and together we drank some more.

When someone won the pool game, and the subsequent shout-ing died away, Chris smiled, "Now if I ever write another book . . ."

"You're not going to then?"

"I don't think so, no. No, I've already said everything I wanted to and besides, I think your old man said it best." He laughed heartily at that, eyed me shrewdly, and then laughed heartily once again, at which point I asked if he was going to publish any of his own books after this one and he said no, no, they'd've already crucified him for this one by then.

"But you said your last one was good."

"It is. In fact it's very good. Although hardly provocative enough to warrant the title, 'Former Prime Minister's Son's First Published Work.'" He dunked his straw into his glass several times and told me that when you first start to write, the stuff you write is invariably shit. But the secret, he said, the secret so many fledgling authors fail to realize, is to keep writing that shit. Keep writing that shit until you *are* the shit. "Because by this time, see, you have your very own style, your very own voice, your very own personal *brand* of shit, and man that shit is yours and . . ." About to say something more, he shook his head when he found he was wrong, then started over: "The point, I suppose, is to remain consistent with the effort. Yes, the consistency of your shit is of paramount importance, Billy. And then they call it literature of course."

"So you write like shit," I said. "Wonderful."

"No, what I'm saying is, I *used* to—in the beginning." But then naturally he believed his shit was beautiful. In the beginning all writers believe their shit is beautiful—the writer's anal stage of development, he called it, I think. "And later on, with my second book, I continued to write like shit, and in turn discovered it was exactly that. And finally, with the third book, I actually began to write quite well, but still stood convinced that it was shit." He considered this a moment, then concluded his lengthy but largely impressive attempt at what I suppose could be, if you'll pardon the pun, analogy: "It's the maintaining of this third state of mind that ensures a writer continued success, I think."

"And now?"

"Pardon?"

"And now?"

He sighed. "Well let's just say it took three books for ability to finally catch up with ambition."

"Meaning?"

"Meaning I now have plenty of ability but very little ambition."

I stood to leave.

"Where are you going?"

"No idea," I said. "Home to watch the highlights maybe."

"They lost."

"Really? What was the score?"

"Don't know. Lost though. Heard it in the cab on the way over." He stood along with me. "Toni's not bad, you know. I mean I know she comes across as a bit of a bitch, but she's actually not that bad."

I offered to pay the bill.

"Look, I really am sorry, Billy."

"Forget it. And besides, she treated you a hell of a lot worse than she did me."

I tossed several twenties back onto the table as we picked our way through the pushy backroom throng towards the crush of equally inconsiderate humanity out front. Once outside, in lieu of a cab, we walked along in the general direction of the hotel. We didn't feel like waiting for a taxi. One grew tired of waiting for taxis in that town. Chris asked why I didn't get myself a car now that I'd be staying in town a while, and I told him I didn't have a driver's license anymore.

"What? What's so funny?"

"Nothing," he smiled. "Really, it's nothing."

"What? I know how to drive."

"No, it's not that, it's just—just such a *cliché*. You're such a cliché, Billy, you really are," he said, and when I objected, held up his hands for clemency. "But then no more than the rest of us are.

"I mean look at us," he said. "We get drunk. We take trips. We quit good jobs and tend bar to furnish some wanton delusion of actually writing for a living." They were all intelligent, he said. They were all experts. They 'jammed' and spoke subversively of a culture they had no real chance of changing. They were all overeducated in regard to topics of no critical importance to anyone, let alone to any of them. They were pathetic and pitiful, the lot of them. They were pathetic and pitifully obvious in every ironic attempt they made to become something alternative, radical, and new.

"Not Melanie."

"No, es*pec*ially Melanie," he said. "You know what we are, Billy? Expatriates. All of us are. Disenchanted cultural expatriates. Christ, even syphilis is making a comeback, so why not just go live in Paris and be done with it."

"So why don't you then?"

"Believe me, I tried," he said. "Too expensive though. And you know why it's too expensive, Billy? Because it's all been done before. All this counterculture and coffee-shop rebellion, it's all been done before." And now there was nothing left but the build-up for the tourists. Because they were all the same. They were nothing new. They were all built-up, every last one of them. "And you know what else? We're all Indian givers too."

I just looked at him.

"Well you know what I mean."

"Actually no, I don't," I told him.

We were in the banking district now, moving steadily amidst towers of concrete and glass. We strolled silently down the sidewalk to the roar of distant engines, listening in anticipation of the attendant squeal of spinning tires. There were few people out on these particular streets at this time of night and, for the time being anyway, we walked along in silence side by side.

"So, Indian givers," I said eventually, but he didn't seem to hear me. Instead, gathering steam, he started to pace around in circles, shooting from time to time a reproachful look at me.

"You know what bores me, Billy? The word 'no.' Yeah, the word no and people who say no bore the hell out of me. And not just those who say no, mind you, but all these other mindless drones that try to stand in my way." And you can bet the mindless bored him. As did the overly mindful naturally. Not to mention the seemingly inexplicable fact that Led Zeppelin's mind-numbing *Stairway to Heaven* was still seeing regular airplay in this day and age. Music television, that bored him a little bit, as did watching television in general and listening to FM radio in particular and reading anything other than the sports section of the newspaper. That said, he was bored of the slam dunk, the home run, tie games after overtime, teams with less than five-hundred records still making the playoffs, White House visits by the Stanley Cup champions, adulterous presidents, semen-stained garments and thus, to paraphrase, what little was left of the American Wet Dream. He was bored of waiting for the green light, reaching for the brass ring, and believing in the oneness of everything; old souls, children wise beyond their years, and capturing the zeitgeist of anything. He was bored of the Ten Commandments, the Eight-fold Path, the Seven Deadly Sins, the six degrees of separation, the one Golden Rule and any and all dialogue one was forced to share with a washed-up hockey player concerning the struggle and the pain and the ultimate futility of really trying to create something original. He was bored of waiting—for anything. And everything. For anything and everything worth waiting for had already been built over and built up and was thus entirely fucked up and *that*, I was to understand, remained his entire motivation.

CHAPTER THIRTEEN

HE RETREATED A few steps and, with the toe of his right boot, traced a figure onto the concrete sidewalk. Then he retreated a few steps more, traced yet another figure, and another, all the while bent low and silent, as if studying his work in progress somehow. Finally he stood upright, bringing an abrupt end to the invisible lesson.

"To be honest, though, I really don't know why I'm doing this. Not anymore. And it's not like I admire the writer's life or anything. Other than sleeping in of course." The truth of it was, the life of a writer was none too glamorous. Actually it was rather pitiful, if you asked him. You spent your whole life struggling to achieve, and then maintain, some sort of precious isolation and singularity of voice, and you struggled and struggled and then what? Woke up one morning to find yourself being photographed in a grey turtleneck Christian Dior sweater.

He leapt high to snag hold of the lowest tree branch. "No, it's not the reality that's important, Billy, it's the image. The idea. The *illusion*. Yes, it's the illusion of the writer we cling to everyday, and not the writer himself."

Eventually his grip gave way and he fell back down to earth. He said, "But then I guess you already know that. You of all people know that."

"And if I objected?"

"I can't imagine you would."

"But if I had?"

"You haven't."

We turned a corner. Eventually we crossed the wide grey lanes of Georgia Street and stopped outside a bookstore. It was dark, but not overly dark, and standing there side by side our reflections fit together nicely in the frame of the window. Someone walked by and offered us ecstasy, but naturally we declined. I watched the man drift away around the corner, removing his ecstasy forever from our lives.

Peering into the bookstore window, we examined the titles beyond the glass. "You do read don't you, Chris? Or are you bored of all that as well."

"No, I read," he said. "I get some of my best material that way."

When I failed to take the bait, he frowned and pressed his face against the glass. I must say, it bothered me that he understood my father so well, and more, that he understood him better than I did apparently.

"You don't seem too excited about it, Chris."

"Well it's not my book, Billy."

"So why do it then? It's crazy. I mean you know they'll find out eventually."

"Yes, I know."

"So then what do you hope to accomplish?"

"Enough."

"Enough to what?"

"Enough to know I was once crazy enough to try, I guess."

A police car roared by and up the street, sirens wailing, and I watched the red and blue flashing lights rise and fall in rhythm with the rising falling road.

"To avoid detection you might want to adopt a pseudonym then," I suggested. "Milli Vanilli perhaps. You could blame it on the rain for instance."

"Yeah," he mused, "that'd be all right."

"You know, Chris, people don't take kindly to having their illusions shattered. It's like a cardinal sin. And you could get in a lot of trouble before it's all said and done."

"I could, yes." He stooped to scan another row of titles beyond the glass. "I honestly don't see how anyone can actually pay these kinds of prices for books," he said at last.

"So how'd you get my father's then? Steal it?"

He stood up. "It's not *stealing*, Billy."

"Well it's plagiarism. And plagiarism is theft."

"Yeah, well, I'm sorry you feel that way."

We started along again and later, after some more discussion on the finer points of literary ownership, he said he wanted me to accompany him to New York at some point. "You could be my agent," he said. "You know, my handler. My 'representation' so to speak."

I shook my head.

"Why not?"

"Well for one, Mr Vanilli, you already have an agent," I said.

"Well yeah, a *lit*erary agent, but believe me when I tell you she's entirely too old and boring for the likes of you and me. I need some-one—else," he said.

"Well I know absolutely nothing about publishing. Or agents. It's an entirely absurd proposition," I said.

"And that's why it'll be perfect. I mean it's perfectly absurd. Honestly, though, what's more absurd than writing a book? No offence, Billy, but *Lovestiff Annie*? It's not even that good. I mean it's good, but it's not *that* good." The scenes came off as contrived at best, the dialogue was outdated, and come on, no one mistreated the Indians like the Spanish—hell, everybody knew that, he'd bet. "But you know what, Billy? I bet it'll sell a million copies. In fact I know it will—or would," he said.

We passed a bar. There was a band playing in the far rear cor-ner, and a great many taps lined up behind the counter. I noticed my team playing on the television, a repeat of the Toronto game from earlier that night. I thought I might like to stay and watch a while, but then Chris thought he saw someone he knew so we kept walking along for now.

We strolled across Hastings Street where, cocooned in a sleeping bag on the corner, a young woman sat biting with that panhandler's infinite patience what little was left of her fingernails. She had a cat along for company and, not surprisingly, asked us to spare her some change. De Boer had no money, at least he said he had no money and that neither had I, but then I felt like being charitable, if only to impress him in some small way. I offered the girl a dollar, which she accepted with disproportionate, somehow disparaging appreciation. I felt condemned in some way. And as we moved away, Chris informed me that, unless he was mistaken, she was an intern doing research for the local Liberal MLA.

We walked along again.

"What about your wife?" I eventually asked, eager to find some new weakness to fit myself against.

"What about her?"

"Well what does she think of what you're doing?"

"Jennifer has no idea the book's not mine. No one does—but you," he said.

I felt a tinge of satisfaction at that—followed by the inevitable guilt and then regret on behalf of my old man.

"Look," he said, "Jennifer doesn't want this. Jennifer doesn't *need* this. Believe me when I tell you I've already given her way too much as it is."

"You speak in tongues," I said.

He crouched to retie his boot. Several eyes on bottom led to three pairs of buttonhooks up top. He untied the knot, adjusted the tongue, adjusted it again when he discovered some discomfort with it, and then started from the bottom cinching the laces tight. When he arrived at the buttonhooks he again cinched the laces tight, wrapped them once around his ankle for good measure, and then tied the knot at last.

"She simply doesn't want what I have to offer anymore," he said, having tested his work with a few quick leaps and hops. "Maybe after the first time she did, but not now. Believe me, Billy, you get tapped on the shoulder like that—and tapped twice—it changes things.

Skews things. Demystifies and deflates things. But I tell you what, she was one wild woman back then. After the first time, I mean. She was like this, this—well she was larger than life is what I mean."

We crossed the street in the direction of the hotel lobby, passing romantically lit pools, intricately shaped hedges and, waiting patiently alongside the road out front, annoyingly long taxi queues.

"It started in her cervix," he said, coming to an abrupt halt, seemingly fascinated by a spot of gum there on the sidewalk. He positioned the toe of his boot delicately in the centre of the gum and pressed down steadily, as if it were a button to be pushed. "And you tend to believe, once someone goes through something like that, that they're suddenly going to have this handle on things the rest of us don't. Like they're suddenly going to have this all-encompassing knowledge the rest of us aren't yet privy to. But then soon enough they're right back to sweating the small stuff just like the rest of us do. But then you can't really fault them there either," he said, shrugging. "Billy, do you have any idea what chemotherapy can do to a girl?"

"Some, yes," I said, and although I was unsure exactly what we were talking about, sensed vaguely the vicinity to which we were headed.

"It robs them of their cycle, for one," he said, speaking slowly and so lowly that it was an effort just to hear. "It robs them of their cycle so that they don't get their period anymore." And her hormones were suddenly so messed up that her flesh became all raw and irritable, so much so that she actually found it revolting whenever he tried to touch her. "And pretty soon, well, pretty soon you can't touch her even if you wanted to."

We moved through the lobby of the hotel.

"Back then," he said, "back before it happened the second time, I mean, I guess I always had it in the back of my mind that she might get sick again someday." He shook his head once, and then continued on in the same cadenced way. "But then I never did dwell on it, I don't think. I mean I never did let it get into my head." Still, it was strange the things you tended to think about when someone that close to you went through something like that; the things you tended to think about when you weren't even really trying to. And Chris, he made a point of not thinking about it much, but then he thought that was probably part of the problem too. "It was such a terrible lie, Billy, it really was. But then what else can you really tell a girl?"

Nothing, apparently, and since nothing much was going on at the hotel café, we decided to head out for a drink, ending up back on Hornby Street at a place called the Bacchus Lounge, I think. The Bacchus Lounge was very dark and red inside: there were dark red wooden tables with candles on them with plush red velvet couches and chairs alongside, and there were pretty young waitresses in short red uniforms taking orders from wealthy silver-haired citizens of pride. Naturally the citizens were smoking cigars and laughing and calling one another 'sir' a great deal, standing for a lady whenever it seemed appropriate—which really was too often, I feel. We took a seat over near the window. No one came over to take our order though, and so we moved on up to the bar instead. For himself Chris ordered a Cosmopolitan, and for me a martini that tasted vaguely of raspberries. When we finally received that round we immediately ordered another, followed it up with a Greyhound for me and a Bailey's coffee for De Boer, and then quietly asked for the bill. And all the while we were drinking, the little immigrant manager kept coming over to speak to me in an accent with which I was completely unfamiliar. He came to check on me, and to talk and smile knowingly at me, and every time he did so I pretended to take no notice of his company. He was focusing on me because, generally speaking, he focused on all the citizens this way. And he was focusing on me in particular because, unlike the late prime minister's son, he thought he recognized me in some way. Unfortunately he wasn't sure from where it was he recognized me, and for that kind of attention I really wasn't in the mood just then. One had to be in the mood for that kind of attention, and as I wasn't, I turned my own to the bowl of orange-coloured snacks on the bar before me. I picked out the straight pretzels and the square Shreddies and something else that was tubular but tasty. This scene, the one with the little immigrant manager talking and smiling knowingly over my shoulder as I picked through the bowl of orange snacks before me, carried on for some time as he kept on coming and I kept from listening until finally he sent the waitress over to see what, if anything, could be done for me. She asked if everything was all right. I told her everything was fine. She said her manager had expressed some concern, and I told her quietly to ask her manager to go to hell. Hell? she said. That's correct, I said: straight on down to hell. The waitress laughed and said she'd like to, but that she'd of course be fired if she did. I gave her twenty dollars for the trouble and told her to forget it, at which point she placed her hand on my shoulder and smiled in that same managerial, knowing, almost Mona Lisa-like way he had.

I liked the Bacchus Lounge. I appreciated its lounge-like qualities. There were a great many paintings mounted on the walls, each depicting a scene of drunken merriment, as well as a black, stoic, rather rotund pianist mounted beneath one of the larger, more colourful ones. Because of the candlelight it was difficult to distinguish his facial features from the shadows, but I once saw him respond enthusiastically to a laughing call of "Sir!" from one of the wealthy silver-haired citizens and so I was certain, for the moment at least, that he was very much alive. I wondered quietly and to myself if they ever called him that when they had not been drinking their brandy and smoking their cigars. Probably not, I said out loud. After all, these citizens had all those other names from all those other times for people of his particular pedigree and pride.

"Excuse me," said a voice, and I turned to find a handsome clean-cut fellow of about De Boer's age whom I took to with that instant suspicion and then carefully constructed aloofness I'd learned to employ in all such similar situations. We shook hands. He and Chris shook hands. I too shook hands with Chris. And finally the young man pointed to a pretty young woman smiling and waving from her seat over near the window.

"My wife and I just wanted to say we think you're, you know, you're . . ." Hesitating, the young man wrung his hands. I could tell he was sincere by how genuine and unassuming he was behaving, let alone this thing with the hands. "We're big fans and we just wanted to say that we think you're—you're *innocent* in all this," he said, just now stumbling upon the word. I nodded thanks, wondering how long our conversation would last, and then nodded to his wife for good measure. The young man nodded too, but then didn't go away as I was hoping he would.

"Listen, would you two like to join my wife and me for a drink?" he ventured, having finally worked himself under the burden of posing such a question, thereby separating himself from the herd.

"Well I don't know," Chris said, grinning slightly but mischievously. "How about it, Billy? What do you think?"

I shrugged, "Actually, we've already asked for the bill."

"Oh," the young man frowned. "Maybe next time then."

"Maybe next time, yes," I assured him, expressing a rough approximation of genuine sorrow for being unable to take him up on his generous offer just then.

We shook hands again and I nodded to his wife. She smiled awkwardly as her husband eyed me sceptically, just now turning to walk away. Abruptly he returned. "You know, you don't have to be such an asshole about it."

"Sorry?"

"You don't have to humour me," he snorted simultaneously. "It was just an offer. Just an invitation for a fucking drink."

"Look," I said, but he told me to forget it, raising his hands in mock surrender.

"You're the player. Have it your way—Player," he said.

"Everything is fine over here?" asked the little immigrant manager from his perch atop my shoulder.

"Everything's fine," I said, looking the young man squarely in the eye. "We were just leaving."

"Yes," the young man said, "the Player was just leaving. We natives were getting a little too restless, I think."

"Oh fuck you," I said, and the young man straightened, his arms going rigid, his fists opening and closing in the light. I stood from my chair and he retreated a step. We stood a second or two more just like that. Suddenly De Boer moved in and shoved him to the floor.

To his credit, the young man scrambled immediately to his feet, only to have De Boer shove him hard to the floor once more. By and by the swarms of silver-haired citizens arrived, and quickly and effectively and with much shouting, bravado and ballyhoo, separated the two combatants to remote corners of the establishment. No punches were thrown. All faces were saved. Nevertheless the little immigrant manager asked the young man to leave. I told the manager to forget it as we were already leaving ourselves. And checking the billfold to ensure I had left enough money for the waitress, I moved towards the door with De Boer. The little immigrant manager followed along apologizing, and I told him to let it go.

"You do not worry for next time," he said. "Next time that man, he is barred."

"All right, you bar him good then," I said, and we made our way over to the Roxy after that. Once inside, having bypassed the queue, a leering Shar caught us cold at the front bar, offering up a round of shots. Whiskey this time, lukewarm and in tumblers, and we three hooked back our punishment together. After two more shots, feeling the music and the alcohol squeeze in around me, Chris and I moved off into the crowd in search of Fisk, eventually finding him alone on the dance floor with the collar of his T-shirt pulled up over his mouth. Toni Childs and her protégé were apparently long gone. Fisk had not seen them leave. He had been worried about the two of us going off and leaving him too, he said, and I assured him that we'd never so much as consider it. And the very next morning, for absolutely no reason whatsoever, he and De Boer left for Costa Rica without me.

CHAPTER FOURTEEN

SOMEONE CALLED MY name from a nearby table, and turning I watched a husky fellow of about my age come lumbering up. We overshook hands, and I was about to inform him that I had no pen when he introduced himself as Jason Carpentier, my friend.

"Sweet Jesus, the Bull," he said, scraping back a chair. "Sorry to hear about the suspension."

"Yeah, well, you know how it is."

"Have they given you a court date yet?"

"No, but it's looking like community hours again anyway," I said.

We sat and nodded a while. Since I had seen him last Jason had put on plenty of weight, and his hair had receded aggressively— Gracie's helmet theory, it seemed, sprung suddenly to life before me. His once strong chin now lay hidden within the considerable flab of his whisker-infested throat, and he was definitely overweight for one his size—I was tempted to call him fat to his face. Jason had been drafted a year before I. He had never gone on to be all that great a player for the Rangers—a sort of poor man's Messier—but always rather industrial in a limited sort of way.

I asked Jason what he was up to now, and he shrugged and said still selling athletic equipment. I was going to ask which company he was selling for, but then the way he made it sound made me think I was probably supposed to know already. We talked some more about this and that and then I decided that I didn't want to talk with Mr Carpentier anymore.

"So," he said, catching me by the arm as I slowly rose from my chair, "any plans for retirement?"

"What the hell, Jason. What the hell."

He pulled his hand away apologetically, stuttering, "I didn't—I didn't mean—"

"Listen, I know exactly what you meant," I told him.

In the weeks that followed my suspension I spent most of my time at David Fisk's bar. He and Melanie worked the downstairs lounge at Stone's Steakhouse and Cocktail Bar, an upscale eatery on Robson just west of Thurlow. Robson Street was where those riots took place after the Canucks went to the Stanley Cup Final back in '94. There would be no such riots this year. Still, there were always plenty of people on Robson as there were plenty of restaurants and bars around. Also, there were plenty of coffee bars and stores where plenty of overpriced merchandise could be found. I liked Robson Street in general because there were always plenty of girls around. And I liked Stone's in particular because you could sit at the downstairs bar and still order food from the upstairs menu—I ate the vast majority of my meals right there.

The lounge at Stone's Steakhouse and Cocktail Bar was very long and narrow. There were black and white photographs on the walls of contemporary celebrities like David Bowie and Madonna as well as the compulsory number of classic Beatles and Elvis Presleys. A vintage red Harley Davidson sat upon a raised dais high above the bar. The counter of the bar itself was in-laid with sheets of stainless steel scratched with steel wool, the scratches forming a sort of wave pattern running the entire length of the bar, the bar itself running a long smooth wave the entire right-hand side of the lounge. Stone's was always very busy, especially at night, except in the afternoons between two and five. During the afternoons I'd often come in for a late lunch and read the copy of my father's book De Boer had given me in Montreal. I usually got the very last seat at the far rear end of the long scratched steel bar. But not always. Sometimes this little Asian guy with a laptop managed to arrive ahead of me and take it for himself. Whenever he did, I didn't raise a stink, but simply took the very last booth directly across from the far rear end of the scratched steel bar. Whatever the situation, bar or booth, it was imperative I be sitting at the far rear end of the establishment as hardly anyone ever bothered me there.

Stone's used the pink grapefruit juice in its Greyhounds. In fact, Stone's used arguably the freshest most delicious pink grapefruit juice around. The fact that double Greyhounds could be had there on the cheap probably had something to do with my liking it so very much as well. Instead of ordering a double Greyhound, or even a single, I simply ordered something called a 'Malibu Martini' on the rocks. Stone's always had their martinis on special, or so it seemed, and their martinis were always doubles. Now paying full price for Greyhounds made little difference to someone like me, but someone else with, say, a more moderate means of income might just benefit from such information, more so with Stone's recent mention in successive issues of *Condé Nast Traveler* ('World's 100 Best Bars You've Somehow Never Heard Of—Till Now' being the title of the first article), and therefore I feel it imperative I mention something here. If folks are going to spend that kind of time and money in there, they might just as well save themselves a few dollars in the process, I feel.

On this particular day, Fisk started at five. Melanie hit the floor at five-thirty. And having spent the previous hour or two walking around Stanley Park avoiding people like Jason Carpentier, I of course was there when they punched in. There had been a zoo at the park at one time, but now, thanks to pressure from various animal-rights activists, only the aquarium remained open to the public. However, not wanting to support such an inhumane enterprise, I spent a few quiet minutes at the zoo at what would have been the monkey and the bear exhibits, but which were now the BC Hydro Salmon Stream Project—a manmade stream replicating the salmon's natural spawning bed—but then began to feel silly just standing there staring at an empty stream, and so took to chasing some squirrels over near the totem poles instead. Along Georgia Street on the return trip into town, I came upon a poster of the great Gordie Howe endorsing take-out food for a local chain of restaurants, smiling in a knowing way. I knew that smile. It was the same sort of smile the little immigrant manager had on reserve for the worthy at the Bacchus Lounge, as though there were a very deep secret between the two of you, a rather shocking but very real secret that only he and you could fully comprehend. Both he and Gordie smiled as though there were something outsiders would never really understand about your little secret, as if this granting of citizenship or that endorsement of take-out food were somehow lewd to those not in the know, but to you was simply an age-old passion better shared. You didn't speak much. You didn't need to. It was simply the pleasure of discovering again and again that little secret for which you both held so much passion. Smiling in their knowing way, both Gordie Howe and the little immigrant manager let you know that they alone would always understand your little secret, and would never dare expose it to anyone outside your little band.

Seeing Gordie Howe smiling that way on that poster made me feel embarrassed. But then I always felt embarrassed for Gordie Howe. True, they didn't have much in the way of a pension back when he played, and true, he was none too intelligent, especially when it came to negotiating his contracts, but seeing him smiling that way on that poster made me think of Jason Carpentier, and no one in my position should have to think about that. I began to wonder what I would do after retirement. I began to wonder when I would. My old Junior coach had once told me that I might make one hell of a coach one day, and since plenty of guys I knew were coaching now (Dave Schultz was coaching now. Wayne Gretzky's brother was coaching now. Hell, Wayne Gretzky's brother was coaching Wayne Gretzky's *other* brother now.) I thought I might just add my name to the growing list as well. Either way, coaching or not coaching, I certainly had no desire to end up selling used cars or worse, sporting goods like Jason Carpentier. And I certainly wanted no part of Gordie Howe's latest claim to fame, peddling shakes and burgers to a largely white trash customer base. Not that there was any danger of that happening anytime soon. Even if I were willing to, there would be no recruiting the Bull's cut-up mug for any widespread poster campaigns. And anyway, Gretzky would never pimp his image like that. I wondered what Wayne would do after retirement. I wondered when he would. But then maybe they would not allow it. Maybe he was just too good. And maybe he already meant far too much to the rest of us than any hockey player should. Thinking about my old Junior teammate, I thought about our old Junior coach as well. I thought about Chris and I thought about my father and thinking about the both of them enabled me not to think about Gordie Howe or Jason Carpentier anymore. And I think it was probably right then and there that I decided I'd rather just be a writer after all.

Anyway, I soon made my way back to Stone's Steakhouse and Cocktail Bar. Mitch arrived soon after I did, nodding for a drink as soon as his pants hit stool. Mitch was in a good mood, and hence his hands were soon dancing up around his ears. Apparently he'd landed a big account that day (in which business I could not say), and because of that he was very much ready to drink. I appreciated Mitch for that. For Mitch there was never any shortage of reasons to get thoroughly Mitched on any given day.

We chatted and drank and within the hour ordered dinner. Mitch had one of the steak dishes, I think, and I ordered my traditional pre-game meal, pasta with chicken. Fisk brought and removed each of our plates, providing everything that was necessary to navigate from one end of the meal to the other, ensuring each drink was full or else arriving shortly with a refill. Fisk was a good bartender. I might even say he was the best of the bunch. He was certainly the only member of that ambitious little group without any megalomaniac misconceptions as to exactly what his role was in this life.

Throughout dinner and drinks and afterwards, coffee, Melanie came around the bar to chat or laugh or else simply to sip at her soda. She seemed genuinely happy to see me, even interested in the things I chose to talk about, and so we talked and laughed as she came around the bar and placed her hand casually atop my shoulder. She was wearing a crisp black button-down shirt and bright colourful tie with black slacks and black apron. This was the Stone's uniform—they all wore it—even the managers most days.

We were sitting and drinking in our customary way when Mitch gave me a nudge, nodding in the direction of the newest arrival halfway down the long scratched steel bar. I recognized the man as that Latino actor who, back in the late seventies and early eighties, had risen to television prominence playing a sexy, roguish California highway patrolman before dropping out of the limelight just as far. We watched that Latino actor chat with Fisk. He was wearing a black leather jacket of course. Most everyone wore leather jackets in Stone's in those days—the crowd was quite a bit older than at my usual hangouts, and for that there was always a great deal of skin hanging about—mostly in the way of middle-aged lawyers staring down the low-cut fronts of their secretaries' blouses. These lucky beneficiaries, along with the usual bevy of escorts on seemingly contractual display at Stone's, weren't nearly as leathery as their bene-factors, although still fairly smooth and tanned in an oily sort of way. And despite the fact they were all rather made-up for my liking, they'd all been upgraded with all the right accessories in all the right sizes.

We watched that Latino actor a while. Apparently, according to Mitch anyway, Sylvester Stallone had been in the other night as well. Evidently Stallone was quite a short man, a fact I found altogether surprising, if not for the outright fraud of it then certainly for the cin-ematic fabrication. And as he stood at the bar drinking water from bottles he apparently chatted with the bartenders a great deal. None of this is part of the story of course, but then I thought you might like to know what ol' Sly's been up to.

Mitch explained how that Latino actor was in town filming some made-for-television sequel. Evidently he'd been over at Planet Hollywood for an autograph session earlier, but no one had bothered to show up for that either. Now he smiled very seldom and only at women and the cut of his leather was very traditional. He simply sat at the bar drinking what I assumed from the porcelain white cup to be coffee, smiling the Latino version of the knowing smile at those few remaining women who still managed to remember what it was he was trying so hard to forget. I thought I remembered how he, too, used to beat his wife, but then that would be considered hearsay and even libel, I'm betting.

The television over the bar was showing hockey highlights. The fellow documenting the highlights seemed rather small. I asked Mitch if he was really that small or if it was simply an effect of the television—a sort of Stallone-in-reverse perhaps—and Mitch informed me that the fellow was indeed that small, and that it was in fact all part of his charm. Flexing my fingers and cracking my knuckles, I watched the small charming fellow talk about hockey. The program was close-captioned, and so I was able to read along with his rant, reading how, in his opinion, it was becoming increasingly evident that the Canucks' management and ownership were trying to punish the fans of this town. When a team traded away decent young talent for an old warhorse like Bull Purdy better suited for the glue factory, it had some real issues to deal with apparently. This indefinite suspension is a blessing, he said. This guy Purdy's hands are so bad he can hardly hold onto his hatchet, let alone the fistfuls of money he steals every night. And if the Canucks' brass think they can continue raising ticket prices while throwing out this kind of recycled trash night after night well then . . . I stopped reading shortly after that. Mitch pretended not to have noticed. I thanked him silently for that. He looked at my hands. I looked at them too, turning them over slowly under the light. Purple and dark to the knuckles, and then white and marbled after that, in some places the hair would never grow back, while in others I thought it just might. In those years immediately following the surgery such a hope had seemed entirely unrealistic, although now of course you can see that I was right. Mitch underlined the fact that they seemed to have no trouble at all holding onto my drink or, for that matter, my stick the other night. I maintained that, stick or drink, the damned things gripped it like a vice. I would probably not mention any of this here except for the fact the small charming fellow from the television sauntered into Stone's not an hour after that.

When he finally noticed me sitting down there at the very far end of the bar, I told him he'd done a heck of a show that night. He seemed a little surprised. I thought about hitting him right then and there, but then realized that such an outburst of aggression outside the rink would probably prove unwise. This clarity of thought lasted all of two seconds until his wife came sauntering in. She was really very young and altogether very pretty and obviously way too much woman for him. And so I could think of no good reason not to do my best to embarrass him. On my way to the washroom I pushed him from his stool to the floor. A crowd gathered and dispersed as he scrambled back onboard, at which point I pushed him hard to the floor once more. Again the crowd gathered and again it dispersed as again he scrambled his way atop his stool. I was about to push him over once more just for the hell of it but then the hostess announced that his table was ready upstairs. I watched the little fellow negotiate the stairs with that small man's wounded pride. And I watched his wife brooding along in his wake. Neither of them seemed all that impressed with my actions. Nor, for that matter, did that Latino actor, it seemed.

After all that we tried to start the evening in earnest, but it wouldn't come off without a fight. Mitch and I decided to switch venues when Melanie finished her shift around nine. On the walk over to the Devil's Advocaat, Melanie hailed us a cab. In this way, then, we ended up down at the Penthouse instead, and in the front row secured three seats side by side. The first girl up was thin, really very thin, too thin, and being so thin up top she kept her bikini top on for most of the set. Knowing her best feature was undoubtedly her ass, she took to showcasing it from every conceivable angle, stance and position. The last song, as I recall, was something along the lines of a Bon Jovi ballad. And as she sang along with Jon and squirmed about on the stage, I was surprised to see so many young women in attendance. So many young women of approximately the same age as my Mel. They simply sat and stared and drank their watered-down drinks, taking in far too much of the show. That the Penthouse was at least half as popular with women as men in those days made me think there might just be something to this affirmative action phenomenon after all. Still, they were just so determined to be taken as genuine contemporaries that they were all but missing the point of it all.

After an hour or so at the Penthouse, we made our way over to the Ad. When we arrived there was naturally quite a queue, but then naturally we paid it no bother. True to form, however, and for absolutely no reason whatsoever, Mitch slipped the doorman ten dollars on the way by.

We set up around the bar and proceeded to get quite drunk. Melanie was frisky ever since our shift at the Penthouse, and her hands were soon wandering up and down the inner expanse of my thigh. Recently returned from Costa Rica, Chris too was in a very good mood, and the drinks arrived even stronger than usual. Gavin showed up some two hours later, followed finally by Fisk just prior to last call. We ended up meeting up with some of Fisk's work friends, and we all ended up having a fairly good time. At one point, though, I glanced over and found, much to my surprise, my coach saddled up beside me. He asked me what my next move might be. I said without knowing how much I said that I was actually thinking of writing a novel.

"Really," he said, nodding sagely. "You know, you never really struck me as the type."

"Well first impressions can be deceiving, Mark. Take yourself for instance: I even thought you might like me."

"You know," he said a little later, gazing thoughtfully at the ceiling, "that's something I always thought I might like to do one day. After I finish with hockey of course. What we need is a, um— conscientious hockey book. One, say, that Kinsella might write. There's just not enough quality material out there anymore," he frowned, pounding his fist against the bar to further lament this lack. "That Kinsella, you know, he wrote about Natives himself."

Here he looked at me for something like patriotic approval, and in an obliging mood I stared back as stoically as possible.

"What was that one he wrote? That one they made into a movie in a cornfield?"

"Shoeless Joe?" I said, sucking back the last of my drink.

"No, no, that's not it . . . Field of Dreams," he said, snapping his fingers. "That's it. That's the book we need, a Field of Dreams—but for hockey of course."

"Like that television commercial then."

"Ex*act*ly like that television commercial, Billy. Exactly," he said, and proceeded to pound the bar into submission once more.

"Let me ask you something though," he went on. "Do have many contacts in that area of, um—expertise?"

"I do have a few, um—favours I could call on, sure."

"Well that's good, Billy. In fact, that's outstanding. You cash in some of those favours and you write that goddamned book, all right?"

"It's settled then," I said, and pounded the bar triumphantly. He stood slowly from his stool. I stood slowly too. We shook hands, and he smiled compassionately.

"You know, Billy, some players, after they leave the game . . ."

"I'll be fine, Mark. Really. I have the book. I really only need the one book."

"And I hope that works out for you. Believe me, I do," he said. "But just so you're, you know, aware, the organization does have a program in place for its retiring players that you might be interested in looking into. A transition course, if you will. To help make the, um—adjustment now that hockey's over. And hey," he said, suddenly upbeat, "right now I know of a position available with a local group marketing sporting goods and apparel."

"Thanks, but I'm really not interested."

We shook hands and I walked out of the bar, walking along in the direction of the hotel. I walked under cover and out of the rain but still, by the time I arrived under the high vaulted ceiling of the hotel lobby, I was soaked right through to the core. I sat down at the café and ordered a drink. I would have had a Greyhound, I think. Yes, I would definitely have had a Greyhound as it was a Thursday, and it was a Thursday when they told me that Gretzky, too, had retired from the rink.

CHAPTER FIFTEEN

THE FIRST CALL came from a lady named Cathy. Cathy was Chris's literary agent. Cathy said she had some suggested manuscript revisions or whatever from the publisher worth reviewing, or rejecting, whatever the case may be, and she wanted to make sure she had the correct address to which to email them. Chris wasn't in at the time, so I read the address to her over the phone. Cathy said that was the address she had all right, and so I told her to go right ahead and send the suggested revisions over. She asked who I was and I told her. That seemed to alarm her a little. After that Cathy didn't call so much, choosing instead to email her suggestions over.

The next call of note came four days later, from the publishers themselves this time. That was an exciting call as I remember it, the fact that it initiated from New York itself simply adding to the romance of it all. Naturally both De Boer and I had been to New York in person, myself of course on several occasions, but as with any illusion the illusion of New York was far superior to the original. Chris happened to be in that time, and thus took the call himself. I forgot to mention that he was living with me now. His wife, it seemed, required exclusive use of their apartment. I supposed it was just as well. But if he was going to stay, he said, he wanted to help pay the rent. He felt obligated to pay his way. Oh sure, I laughed, obligated to pay your way with an advance earned on my father's book—how noble. But I was half-joking of course and told him that he could stay.

Around this time Fisk mentioned that we should probably make our way up to Whistler at some point. The day after that he rented us a car. Despite my repeated suggestions that we could probably afford something a little more extravagant than a Dodge Neon—certainly something a little less Spartan—Fisk politely inquired what for? After all, he said, the roads were good all the way up this time of year, not to mention the fact the car would be sitting at the cabin most of the time. Besides, he went on, for four guys with no skis on a trip to Whistler, small and Spartan was just the way to go.

Before we left, Chris went out to see Jennifer at their apartment located in this little seaside town close to the border. In truth, the town of White Rock was known more for the colour of its citizenry that for the colour of any stone—but then that's not really part of the story here, so I won't delve into that matter any further at this point. In those days, Chris was getting out to see his wife every second week or so, and when he did it was never for the better—he always returned feeling rather low. As for me, I never really saw her face to face. In truth, except for that one brief encounter in Montreal and this one other time that I will eventually get into, I never really saw her at all. Actually, now that I think about it, my having seen so little of her probably had a great deal to do with my general indifference to her deteriorated health and welfare. Seldom did he speak of her, though seldom was she far from his thoughts, and on those rare occasions when he did speak of her I tended not to listen very carefully, if at all. I suppose I could have been more concerned about it, certainly more bitter or confused about it, but then it simply never struck me to be that way. I mean the fact that I was unable to act on any given sexual impulse was probably for the best anyway. After all, it wasn't as though I had some outstanding track record back then. It wasn't as though I had ever really been meant to be with a girl. And it wasn't as though I had not seen it coming from a great distance off. It wasn't as though I had ever expected it to work out in any other way. Besides, Melanie and I, we had it all worked out. We had our own little con going on. We were keeping up appearances, one might say—and one did—and if nothing else we were being very selective with whom it was would know any differently. If a thing were fundamentally correct, she assured me, then lying about it was never going to make a difference either way. It was all just as well. I'd gotten the idea early on that due to her disease and her religion she never really enjoyed it anyway.

From Vancouver, the highway north to Whistler wasn't all that good a highway, although not so bad as people have made it out to be. It was narrow in places, often hewn straight from the cliffs alongside Howe Sound, but decent enough to drive in the end. The country was barren and rocky much of the way up, and there were evergreens along both sides of the road. And further up, where the highway finally shifted east and inland from the Sound, a steep rocky gorge emerged on our left. There were trees in the gorge, evergreens again, with eagles perched up high in the branches. Here and there, crosses and flowers marked the sides of the road where carloads of travellers had evidently gone over the side to their deaths. Further up there appeared patches of snow. But it was old snow, and dirty, and occurred only in crusty grey patches alongside the winding road. I could see how the highway could be regarded as dangerous in the advent it was snowing, but in this good spring weather the trip came and went without incident or peril.

Halfway through the trip, the road came down over a steep narrow crest before flattening out into the town of Squamish. Chris had driven the first portion, and now Gavin took the wheel the remainder of the way. Naturally I was none too excited having the actor along, but soon we were back in the mountains anyway.

Throughout the journey into the mountains, we drank beer from cans and listened to music on the radio. After the radio cut out we just drank beer—collecting the empty cans for recycling, naturally, good responsible citizens that we were. Prior to Squamish, Chris indicated a place called Porteau Cove where he and his family had once gone scuba diving. There were three sunken ships down there somewhere, he said, one of which was an old minesweeper apparently, the one marked with buoys farthest out in the cove. I asked what that had been like, diving in the dark like that, and he said somewhat uncomfortable and, in his experience anyway, very much like married life.

The road was well-graded here, cut smoothly into the adjacent hills. Beyond Squamish, though, it meandered its way through a narrow forested area before stepping up into wide rugged constructs of barren stone. The road managed itself fairly well through these obstacles before negotiating its own release further along—somewhere deep in the mountains purple and dark to the snowline and then white and marbled in the sun beyond. Beyond these mountains I saw a second range of mountains, these ones slightly lighter in colour with their peaks covered in even more snow, beyond which stood a third range of mountains I couldn't tell if I really saw at all.

After the rugged stone stretch there were once again evergreens along both sides of the road, as well as a stream cascading down through the gorge on our left. The nearest evergreens were still and clearly defined, while those further up the sides of the mountains blended and swayed in a green continuity that ended in a crooked line at the crests. Chris alluded to a place called Black Tusk nearby where he and his family had once gone hiking. He told me of this lake in the vicinity, or else a series of lakes, the most unearthly blue he had seen in his life. The colour of the lake(s) had something to do with the minerals in the water, he thought, although he wasn't entirely certain of that. There were fish in the lake that you'd often see jumping, he said, and an old wooden bridge that crossed the water at its narrowest point. After that he told me of swimming in the lake as a teenager with his father. He told me how cold the water was, and how his testicles had sought to crawl up inside his abdomen for protection and warmth. And lastly, he attempted to explain what it was like to look across that stretch of clear, cold, impossibly blue water in the middle of August and see, from the mountains beyond, a great white glacier sliding down—but I couldn't really picture it, to be honest.

Eventually we came to this place I thought might well have been Whistler, but apparently was just the old Gondola base. Perhaps ten minutes later we hit Whistler proper, and I could see what all the fuss was about. There wasn't much in the way of snow remaining in the village, and hardly any on the lower portions of the slopes. There was some snow on the mountains, however, collected here and there in dirty swollen mounds, and higher up there was even more snow, from which I could see the ski lifts occasionally separating themselves. From a distance I saw the cobblestoned village of alpine hotels and chalets stuffed down between the two great, gradually clarifying peaks. On closer inspection I began to recognize the emerging build-up of the place—that emerging slickness and foreign quality—but for all that there was still a romance to it, still a feeling of nostalgia to it, so that I didn't mind being conned in such a way that day. I enjoyed the feeling of the mountain sun against my face and the feeling of the mountain air scraping out my throat and lungs. I enjoyed the slanted mountain roofs and the painted mountain signs and the colour of the cobblestones in which the streets of the village had been done. I'd read somewhere that there were over twenty-seven thousand licensed seats in Whistler one could order a drink from, and I pictured myself ordering a drink from every single one.

We were staying in Mitch's cabin just south of the village proper. Mitch himself hadn't accompanied us on the trip as it was a Tuesday, and he had to work Tuesdays apparently. To be honest, I was glad he hadn't come along as his considerable bulk would never have fit into our little Dodge Neon. Not that Mitch the Pimp would ever have stood for our renting such a ridiculous lemon.

After a few drinks in front of the fire at the cabin, we decided to make our way into the village proper. Of course I insisted we eat at the Chateau Whistler, as in those days I had a genuine fondness for large extravagant hotels in general and those with counterfeit French names in particular. On this last premise alone they agreed, albeit insisting that we drink at the Fairway Hotel afterwards. They knew the bartender at the Fairway, they said. Ralph was the fellow's name. And as luck would have it, Ralph poured five-ounce Long Island Iced Teas—one ounce each of vodka, gin, rum, triple sec and tequila. Fisk explained how he and De Boer had taught Ralph to tend bar incorrectly when the latter had first returned from the Olympics the year before. Ralph was this skier who, having tested positive for marijuana, managed to play the second-hand smoke card and thus, incredibly, retain his gold medal. Though a fine athlete, a good liar, and an exceptionally good source of pot, Ralph had always been rather thick, Fisk insisted, and because of that they'd been able to take full advantage of his pours early on. And although Ralph had since learned the proper way of preparing his Long Islands, he still poured them the old way for Fisk and De Boer—out of a sense of nostalgia, I suppose. I think it was because he was a gold medalist that I briefly considered telling Ralph that I was a novelist. But then, in the end, because he was stupid and supposedly bankrupt, I think I decided against it. I had to admit they were awfully good Long Islands, though, and so instead of lying about my being a writer I went one further, saying that if I were ever to play for the Islanders, I would make that drink my signature one. And yet, despite numerous attempts, we couldn't come up with a decent Canuck concoction.

After three rounds with Ralph at the Fairway, we migrated north to the Cinnamon Bear Lounge. The Cinnamon Bear was located in another hotel nearby, the name of which I can't quite recall just now. Once there, just to be different, De Boer and I drank red wine. Gavin and Fisk, however, true to their natures, stuck to their guns and their Islanders for now.

I have always appreciated a good wine drunk. A good wine drunk is different than any hard liquor drunk, as vastly different as a hard liquor drunk is from a beer drunk, and of wine drunks, a red is often quite different from a white. A good red wine always brings out a certain romance, even a certain light-heartedness, and because of its disposition slips down all too easily, raising you up gradually to a most dizzying and nauseating height.

The next bar on the tour was the new Buffalo Bill's. The new Buffalo Bill's was not nearly as good as the old Buffalo Bill's, they all made a point of telling me, repeatedly, but for all intents and purposes would suffice. As it was a Tuesday, there was no queue when we arrived, and inside it was still quite dead. We chose four seats side by side at the very far end of the bar, at which point Fisk handed over his Visa card. We started out on a steady diet of double gin and tonics, supplemented here and there with the occasional shot. Soon enough we were all quite drunk and swearing profusely, and for that we had to be warned on more than one occasion to tone it down somewhat.

Other than to use the facilities, I doubt I got up from my stool more than twice the entire night. Buffalo Bill's must have filled up rather quickly, if covertly, as I recall wondering when it had gotten so crowded. The steadily encroaching throng certainly made for a good shift, however, one in which we all worked diligently at our craft. But for all my good effort, not to mention Fisk's good credit, I still managed to drink myself sober by the end of the night.

Throughout most of the evening, Gavin sat directly to my right talking glibly into my ear. Chris and Fisk were out of sight when he decided to inform me of his newly discovered affection for my girl. Evidently he had no working knowledge of our pseudo affair, or if he did, then certainly didn't care about it.

"Melanie came over last night," he told me at one point.

"What for?"

"What do you mean what for? Come on, Buffalo Bill, you know exactly what for."

"So why are you telling me?"

He shrugged, smiling. "Just being chummy and fun, that's all."

"Well I don't believe it," I said, having just removed myself from that category.

"You don't believe what?"

"I don't believe she's that kind of girl."

He split open at that one, his head laughing back off the hinges of its well-oiled jaw. Meanwhile, out on the dance floor, Fisk toppled over on some poor girl, sending them both sprawling to the floor.

"What do you mean?" Gavin said once his mouth had closed sufficiently in order to properly formulate the words.

"I mean I think you're full of shit."

"Come on," he said, splitting the difference between amazement and amusement.

"Hey, that's what I think, Gavin. I honestly have to believe that you're lying here."

The next day, we were all up out of bed by early afternoon, at which point Fisk and Gavin went out in search of coffee and scones. While they were gone, I listened a while to some of Mitch's impressive collection of pornographic videos—the television picture was out—trying to imagine what possible contortions could illicit such impossible responses. Eventually growing bored of that, I wandered back downstairs to find De Boer's bedroom door slightly ajar. Inside, the bathroom light was on. He had a short orange towel wrapped snugly around his waist and he was attempting to shave in the fogged-up mirror.

"No fucking clue," he snapped when I inquired about Melanie and Gavin.

"Hey, no need to be an asshole about it," I said, and he looked around half-shaven a moment before returning once more to the mirror.

"I think maybe he's just busting your balls on that one, Billy."

"Lying sack of shit."

"Oh no, don't you get like that," he said. "Don't you dare get like that this early on in the trip." He smacked his razor sharply against the side of the sink. "How'd you happen to hear about it anyway?"

"Oh, so it is true then," I said.

He looked around again, not bothering to say anything, and then eventually returned to the mirror. "Thank God I don't have to put up with friends like that."

"Why do you say that?"

"Well I must have introduced him to Jennifer a dozen times before he ever bothered to get her name right." He tested his throat with a thumb, studied the results, and then carried on as before. "Besides, Gavin's David's friend, not mine."

"David's a fine one himself," I mumbled experimentally.

"Excuse me?"

"Nothing. Forget it. How the hell'd you ever get hooked up with that faggot anyway?"

"Gavin? Like I said, he's Fisk's friend, not mine. What's this all about anyway?" he asked.

"Oh just something he said to me last night."

"About him and Mel? Well in all honesty, Billy, I'm probably not the best guy to ask about that. Besides," he said, rubbing additional shaving cream onto his cheek, "it couldn't have been all *that* bad."

"Hey, you weren't the one stuck beside him all night."

"Come on now, you could've gotten off your ass and danced with those girls like the rest of us."

"Oh which girl, Chris? The fat one you humiliated?"

"She wasn't *fat*," he frowned, and I laughed.

"Yeah, well, you certainly broke her heart," I said, taking a small measure of pleasure as he winced in the mirror over that.

"Was it bad?"

"Awful. Just awful. We passed her on the way out and she looked, in all honesty, quite suicidal."

He shook his head with seemingly genuine regret, and then moved on to his sideburns after that.

"You shouldn't have humiliated her like that," I added a moment later, unwilling to let it go just yet.

"Well now if that's not the pot calling the kettle black."

"And you really shouldn't have just blown her off like that."

Placing his razor gently on the side of the sink, he rotated slowly away from the mirror. "And since when did Billy Purdy's morality concerning the treatment of women become so fucking superior to mine?" That said, he picked up the razor again and returned to the mirror, this time, though, in reverse, employing the adjustable side mirrors in order to better execute the shaving of his neck—a difficult, oftentimes dodgy manoeuvre. "And besides," he said, "I thought we were having this hate-on for Gavin here."

I shrugged. "I just didn't think it was too cool what you did to her, that's all."

"Well Billy, neither did Mel."

Our eyes met briefly in the mirror. "Hey man, no holding out on me now."

"Look," he said, abandoning the side-mirror manoeuvre, "even if I did know the sordid details of your relationship with Melanie—which I don't—it still wouldn't be my place to comment either way. That stuff's between you and Mel and that's it, okay?"

He splashed cold water against his face, and then checked over his work in the mirror. Finally, convinced he was finished, he took the towel from his waist and patted himself down with pleasure.

"There's really not all that much to say," I said quietly, lowering my eyes, cracking each of my knuckles in turn. "About me and Melanie, I mean."

"So what's the problem then?"

"I don't know . . . I just don't like Gavin too much, that's all."

"Well no one does. Not even Gavin, I suspect. And hey, he's leaving town soon anyway, so you're free and clear for a while yet."

I glanced up. "He is?"

"Yup. Got himself a gig out near Winnipeg somewhere."

"Really? What's it called?"

"Mission to Mars."

"What's it about then?"

"Mission to Mars."

"How long's he gone for then?"

"Not really sure," he said. "Maybe eight weeks, maybe more. After Winnipeg his agent expects him back in LA though."

I smiled. "Wow, that's great."

"For him or for you?"

"Well for him—and for me," I said.

"You know, he's really no threat to you," he said, dropping his towel to the floor.

"Yeah, well, you didn't hear what he had to say about Mel."

"Hey, so what. So the fuck what. So what if she did go over to his place," he said. "You know as well as I do what girls like that are all about. And listen, I don't know if anything's going on between Melanie and Gavin—I really don't—and to be honest, I really don't care. Maybe she did go over. Maybe she didn't. And maybe she simply thought it would do him some good, or whatever." He looked at me and shrugged, "I guess what I'm really trying to say is, would it really be so bad if they were?"

"I suppose not. But then it sure wouldn't hurt to know she felt something for me too."

"Oh grow up, Billy. Christ Almighty, you sound all of fifteen years old."

"Believe me, it wouldn't have hurt all that much back then either."

"Listen," he said, shouldering past me into the room. "She does like you. She does. But you have to remember who you are. Melanie's a smart girl—she reads the papers, she watches television—she's heard all the terrible Bull stories."

I sighed. "Yeah, well, it'd sure be nice to get a clean slate every once in a while."

"Wouldn't it though."

"You still love her then?"

"Melanie?"

"Jennifer, you idiot."

"Oh, sure," he said. "Of course."

"And Melanie?"

"Not really, no. Not anymore. Melanie and I are just—just friends," he said, smiling at the word.

"Is that it then?"

"Shouldn't it be?"

"She just seems to be, you know, holding out for you a little, that's all."

"They always want what they can't have, Billy. It sounds far too simple but it's true." He shook his head wearily and continued, "Look, that woman wants it all. She really does. And she's the most deserving creature to ever walk God's green earth, just ask her. Oh you laugh, but it's true. I'm not just romancing her up here—she was it. She was certain she was the next daughter-in-law of the former prime minister."

He stroked on some deodorant, hoisting one arm then the other. "You know what the best thing about Melanie was though? She was the only person ever willing to tell me the truth. If I was ever out of line she'd tell me." He hesitated. "But then I guess that's what I've got you for now."

"Then why break it off?"

"I told you, I'm just not interested anymore."

"Is it her, you know, her condition?"

He shook his head. "No, not at all."

"There has to be something though. I mean there has to be. There *must* be."

"There isn't."

"But you can still do it."

"What, like impo"—he managed to slur into—"oh yeah, I can still do it, sure."

I looked down at the floor. "She told you then."

"She did mention something about it, sure."

I watched him rummage through his pack.

"But with you it's not like that," I said at length. "With you, you can, but you simply choose not to."

He didn't say anything. Instead, delving deeper into his pack, he found his underwear and stepped into them, then went about pulling them up into place. And finally, once he'd shifted himself into position, he pulled on his standard shorts and T-shirt.

"With you, you can, but you—"

"You act as if I have a choice in the matter, Billy."

"Well don't you?"

"Look, please don't ask me to start having intercourse again just to make you feel better."

We didn't speak of Jennifer again in Whistler. Nor did we speak of Melanie. The last thing said on either subject came as we walked out of his room that day.

"I never told you, you know. What Gavin said happened. I never told you Melanie came over."

Ahead of me, on the stairs, De Boer stopped dead. "Look," he said, speaking directly to the stairs ahead, "Gavin's a son of a bitch. He really is. He's a pompous son of a bitch and I really couldn't care less if you popped him one. I mean that. He's a bastard, he makes me sick, and as far as I'm concerned he can reap what he sows. So if it'll make you feel any better, Billy, go right ahead—don't fight it— go right ahead and pop him one. Just don't come crying to me with your petty love life problems. To be honest, that's something I really don't feel the need to share with you right now. And if you want her, then for Christ's sake, take her. Just don't get caught up playing the victim too long."

He stood there a long moment, his back to me on the stairs. Finally he turned around. "Look, I'm not being facetious here. There's no irony to what I'm proposing. Hit him. Hit him hard. Hit him repeatedly. For Christ's sake, take his head clean off for all I care. Just get it over with and move on. Please. If not for your own sake, then for mine."

He sighed. I sighed. And then we stood together on the stairs for a time.

"You're killing me, Billy. You're absolutely killing me here."

The silence grew increasingly uncomfortable until, finally, when I could no longer stand it, I managed to say with a certain successful exuberance, "All right, let's go tie one on."

"Yes, let's," he said. "Let's go tie one on at lunch, all afternoon, and all night tonight as well. Let's go out and level this silly little village to the ground. Let's do it, Billy. Let's get drunk. Let's get so drunk we can't even remember what we've done."

That second night in Whistler was a strange one, yes, but for us at least didn't come off anywhere close to according to plan. The Longhorn Saloon was offering a concert that night—some American band called Jacket!—and we bought our tickets at lunch and returned for the show later on. Jacket! had just taken the stage when we arrived, and everything seemed to be going fairly well. Unfortunately, though, the drummer died after just two songs, simply collapsing down on top of his snare drum. The paramedics arrived in record time, but it was still too late—apparently he was dead by the time his head hit the ground. We were told to return the following morning to collect our reimbursements for the tickets, but then in the end we decided against it, as any monies forfeited were to be used to send the drummer's body back to the States, they said. He'd been American apparently, and they were shipping his body back to the States. It was awfully difficult to throw a decent wake at the best of times, let alone for a foreign drummer. And so it was, for us at least, that the second night in Whistler was a quiet one.

*   *   *

A week or so later, back in Vancouver, I was finally brought in on criminal assault charges stemming from that little stick-swinging incident over a month before. Apparently, according to the officers that came to arrest me anyway, the little sports reporter I'd pushed off his stool at Stone's that night was pressing his very own charges as well. Well good for him, I said. And when I asked the one officer placing me in handcuffs what exactly I'd done to warrant such abuse, he didn't answer—neither one answered—though the one did tell me to shut up on more than one occasion. The other one, the one with the handcuffs, had evidently decided that the rough approach here would work best. Each time I tried to talk to him, he offered my wrist a painful twist, and so I eventually told him that we should really all try to get along here. Finally the other one told him to ease up a little, and after that we all got along quite well. Naturally I wasn't surprised. I've always had the knack of bringing out the worst in any city's finest, I find.

By and by we arrived at the flat fortress-like police station down on the corner of Hastings and Main. It was a large station, and very well maintained, especially for that part of town, and once inside, the officers led me down a steep set of concrete stairs to a room with a sign overhead that read 'Cell Block Area: No Firearms Allowed.' Here we were buzzed through a steel mesh gate into a plain eggshell white room, where I was left in the care of yet another officer emanating an insurmountable boredom. This officer, too, evidently felt no affinity whatsoever for the professional hockey player, although in truth he did seem genuinely impressed that I could both spell and write my name so well. I cursed that, cursing my luck at having stumbled upon such a difficult batch of policemen, and eventually I was fingerprinted and photographed by the hockey-hating officer in a very routine and systematic fashion. I recalled how, the first time, I'd found it strange that I would sit for the photographs. I'd always thought that I would stand. And when I asked about this, the hockey-hating officer informed me that I watched way too many American cop shows, and then gave me a court date for the fourth of July. I told him I was very much obliged. His actions here, I assured him, spoke very well for him as a citizen in my eyes.

Chapter Sixteen

The Girls Looked at me. I looked at the floor. Naturally I was embarrassed as I didn't know what to do with that anymore. Big reader. Jesus Christ. It was a stupid thing to say about someone in conversation, and not something you could work with very easily somehow. Christ, I was embarrassed. As embarrassed as any writer would be anyhow.

The one girl, the one standing beside Gavin, asked me something I can't quite remember now. I do remember, however, that she was standing beside him with her hand clinging loosely to his shoulder, while Gavin's was wrapped snugly around her abdomen. Naturally they were both drinking homemade red wine, both from great huge glasses she had made. In fact, most of those in attendance that night were young midriff-baring women drinking homemade red wine from great huge glasses she had made. They congregated in the kitchen, assuming positions with backs against cupboards and oven, from which, at intermittent occasions and seemingly at random, one would call on another to join her in the only available bathroom. Once in the bathroom, it was presumed that they would fuss and bother in front of the mirror until such time that it was deemed the next shift was due to take over. The rest of the time they stood with backs against cupboards and oven drinking wine of dubious quality. And this was the scene I was privy to in the kitchen that evening at Gavin's going away party.

Gavin said, "Isn't that right though, Buffalo? Aren't you the big reader now?"

"I don't know, Gavin."

"Sure you do," he said. "Come on, just for interest's sake, what are some of those big books a big reader like yourself tends to read nowadays, huh?"

I winced as I couldn't think of one. Not one. I thought that was really strange back then. I think it's even stranger now.

"You just watch," Gavin said, "pretty soon he'll be writing too. I mean look at him: he's probably working on something as we speak. In fact I know he is; I can see his lips moving."

"Buffalo Bill!" chanted the girls together. They were all still looking to me to brace the conversation, and not knowing what else to do I took a good long drink of wine, smiled goofily, and said:

"Shove it up you ass."

"That's too easy," Gavin said. "Come on, even *you* can come up with something better than that."

"Fuck you."

"Better! Now really articulate it. Use your instrument."

"I'm serious, Gavin. Fuck off."

"Oh that's good," he grinned. "With language like that we'll make a writer of him yet."

My ears began to turn red. I don't know what happened next but Gavin said, "Alas, but words fail our big reader yet again."

"Leave him be," someone said. "He's embarrassed."

"Yes, leave him be," said someone else. The room fell quiet. Suddenly I felt like telling Gavin how fat he looked. I don't know why I wanted to tell him that—he most certainly wasn't fat—but then I thought it might hurt him just to hear it. Alas, I couldn't come up with a genuinely clever way of saying it, not with all these young girls around. 'You look fat' definitely wouldn't do it. No, it would definitely have to be something better than that. Suddenly I had it: 'What's the deal, Gavin? What's the role you're playing in this movie you're shooting out in Winnipeg, a fat *ass*-tronaut?' But then he started talking again, and unfortunately my window of opportunity closed shortly after that.

"He's not embarrassed," Gavin chuckled. "He's beyond embarrassment. Hell, he's a professional *hockey* player for crying out loud. Even worse—an enforcer. A *goon*. Yup, Buffalo here's the last of a dying breed. I mean look at him. Look at his hands—all chewed up and useless from all those forgotten battles. Well what did they prove? I mean honestly now, Buffalo, what did they all prove? They might just as well be ancient history now, don't you think? But then history is written by the victor, they say, and, well, what the hell, you won most of yours didn't you."

I didn't say anything, but went about cracking each of my knuckles instead.

"Well of course you did. Of course you won. But now that I think about it, when was the last time you even *touched* the puck, huh?" Because that was the point of the game was it not? To touch the puck? To score? So when was it then? Could I even remember? And would it have mattered if I had? Now that was a good question: *Did* I even matter? Had I ever? Could I even be considered a functioning member of society now?

"*Now*," he said. "Now there's something Buffalo here's a little, what, ill-equipped to deal with, don't you think? Don't you though? Wouldn't you say he's a tad bit—now how shall I put it—*shy* in the basic life-skills department somehow? How 'bout it, big fella? Wouldn't you say you're a tad bit—now how shall I put this—*obsolete* now that hockey's over?" Actually, what the hell was I going to do with my life now that hockey was over? Write a book? Was that it? Good God, he hoped so. Because really, who had use for an experienced winger. A good *mucker*. A decent *grinder*. Someone good in the corners and good in the room and all the rest of that crap as well. Who was going to want a goon like me to come work for them at the firm downtown. "Say, isn't this stuff great?" he said, and following his lead the girls all took good, long, contemplative sips of wine from the great huge glasses the one had made.

Gavin continued on. He was interested, he said. He was keen. He was actually very concerned about me now. What was I going to do with my life? What was I going to do to affect that very small sphere I inhabited? "Drop down and block the shot, is that it? Or just drop the gloves and be done with it."

It was an interesting question, and I glanced around for some way in which I might not have to answer it. A gaggle of young buxom wine-drinkers blocked any thought of making for the door, and naturally the bathroom was currently off-limits to those of my gender.

"So tell me. Please. I'm begging," Gavin said. "Tell me what it is you're going to do with your life now that hockey's over. Play golf, is that it?"

"I don't play golf."

"You don't play—oh dear. But I thought every hockey player played golf," he said. He thought it was part of the contract. In fact he'd seen as much. We held tournaments. We invited celebrities. We raised money for charities in our own names in order to take advantage of generous provincial and federal tax breaks. "So come on now, Buffalo—I'm concerned. In fact I'm frightfully concerned. What the hell is it you're going to do now that hockey's over?"

"Don't worry about me."

"Oh but I am, you see. I am worried. I mean Christ, look at you. Hanging around here with people half your age. Who invited you anyway? What the hell are you even *doing* here? Surely it's not to see *me* off. So what is it then? One of these?" he said, indicating his harem with a wide sweep of his hand. "*No.* No way it could be one of *these*. And you can quote me on that, Bill. You can quote me on that, you great big reader you."

At that point the front door slammed mercifully open, revealing the party's latest arrivals, while at the same time breaking Gavin's stranglehold on the girls' collective consciousness. His apartment was small, boasting an impressive looking exercise machine but little in the way of actual furniture, and prior to their arrival, with the dozen or so bodies already in place, the apartment had been filled almost to capacity. Over the entrance to the kitchen a banner was strung. 'GOOD LUCK ON MARS,' it said. Yes, good luck, Gavin. Good luck and Godspeed, my fine old friend.

De Boer and the others came rolling in, releasing some of the tension and hostility that had been building over the previous few minutes of baiting. They were already quite drunk from having worked all night, and the sheer volume of their voices offset the somewhat delicate situation currently on display in the kitchen. I was glad they were there as I'd arrived too early. Or else I'd come too late. Either way, I'd been reading at the café under the high vaulted ceiling of the hotel lobby and now my timing was suffering considerably. The café at the hotel served good aperitifs and excellent cappuccinos, and enjoying them as I had I'd allowed the time to get away on me. It had been good reading, and the crowds passing by on the imitation street out front had made for good people-watching, and the café life had all been rather like I'd imagined it would be. Still, the time had gotten away on me, and now my own timing was off considerably. You should start wearing a watch, I told myself. But then really, who wears a watch these days. Certainly not us Indians. No, us Indians have our own internal clocks. Who came up with that? Some fucking Irishman no doubt.

Chris and Fisk set themselves up on the living room sofa while Mitch made his way into the kitchen. Gavin was pretending to talk Yiddish to the girl beside him while Melanie stumbled about in a haphazard way. With her was a husky woman approximately my age, with a large square frame hidden under a loose-fitting sweater and a large square face suspended from a high ridge of dyed blonde hair. Forcing the two of us to shake hands, Melanie said, "Billy, I want you to meet my big sister, Nina. Nina, this here's Billy Purdy, ex-professional athlete extraordinaire."

Nina's big green eyes lit up as she looked me up and down, her face a rapid-fire series of cocaine-fuelled contortions and gestures highlighted by a terribly bright jaw-grinding smile. She grabbed my arm and gave it a squeeze. Then she patted my testicles just so. "Oh but God bless him, Mel, if I weren't married I would."

"Well I would if he could," replied her sister rather coldly.

Melanie whispered something to Nina then, and together they giggled a while. I grew angry, not overly angry but still fairly angry, and in the meantime Nina looked around with that terribly bright smile of hers. "Would you look at all these pretty people though? My God, they're all just *gorgeous*! Oh but I really must be going. Sanjeev's just going to *kill* me for being out so long, you know."

Her focus gravitating towards the girl currently draped about Gavin, Nina approached her after only the slightest hesitation. "What's your name then? Tracy? Well God bless you, Tracy," Nina said, and proceeded to fondle the girl through her sweater. "Now what size are you? Come on, tell me. Thirty-six C, right? Am I right? Oh you must be. I mean everybody's a thirty-six C these days."

Tracy giggled, but didn't answer. I'd gotten the idea earlier on that she received a great deal of attention this way.

"Thirty-eight D!" offered up one of the other girls finally, and Nina's face lit up.

"You're joking. Oh you're absolutely *joking*! I don't believe it. I mean I *can't* believe it. You must be lying though. God bless you, though, thirty-eight *D*? I mean it can't be. It *mus*tn't be. Oh I really must be going though. But first let me see your back." Nina grabbed Tracy by the shoulders and swung her around. "Oh well, maybe, I don't know," she shrugged, swinging Tracy back around. "You look so *small* though. You *do*! And so *petite*! People think I'm big-breasted, but I'm really just big-boned. See?" she said, taking hold of Tracy's right hand and clamping it securely over her left breast. "Mind if I smoke though?" she asked, turning to triple her chin at me. "No? God bless you though. My husband's friends, they don't smoke of course. No, they're all so damned healthy and *anti-tobacco*. Believe you me, bunch of Paki puritans the lot. But that can't be!" she said, pointing in horror at the clock on the stove. "Oh I really must be going though. Sanjeev's just going to *kill* me for being out so long, you know."

Instead of going, though, Nina fumbled through her purse in search of cigarettes and lighter, and having finally located her tools, lit her Marlboro and inhaled heavily before thoroughly groping Tracy's thirty-eight D's some more.

"God bless you, but I really can't believe you're a D. Oh well, you get what you get. Me, I'm not big-breasted though. I hate that. Not that I'm flat or anything, but that everyone just as*sumes* I'm packing around so much more because of my little sister and all." She checked her watch, then checked it again. "Oh I really must be going though. Check this out though: this one time I was in Greece with my husband, Sanjeev. Can't remember which island—Mykonos maybe. Paradise probably. Anyway, there I was, just sitting on my blanket on the beach, and this one chick, well she's got tits like *this,* and a butt like *that,* and she's wearing this tiny little pink bikini that wouldn't make the rest of us decent enough *floss,* and then you know what she does? Takes it off. Oh yeah, she just takes it off and runs like this to the water"—here Nina pranced across the kitchen—"and this little Speedo-wearing wop she's with, or dago, or whatever the hell it is (the Australians have a funny name for them, but I can't for the life of me remember what it is), he's got this little jar of cream that he spreads on himself like this, and this, and this, and then he pulls off his Speedo and spreads it on his thing! He did! I'm not joking! There he is, with his big ol' horse penis hanging right smack-dab in my face, and I don't know how I should take it—I mean I certainly had no idea how *she* could take it—but, well, what the hell, if you're going to cook it in the sun that long, I say slap some mustard on and stick the goddamned thing on a bun."

Everyone laughed, and Nina took advantage of the break to further fondle Tracy through her sweater.

So there she was, Nina explained, on the beach, in Greece, trying to look inconspicuous and avoid the Greek horse penis when suddenly she turned her head right into this beaver. "Beave!" she cried, indicating with the flat of her hand to her face just how dangerously close she'd come to the beast. "Like right there! I turn my head and nothing but *beave*! And red English beave to boot. The worst. I mean talk about your red herring. Talk about your bush league. There it is, all huge and curly and red and right there! Right in my face! As red as the head of the dick of the dog, I swear."

Nina took one good long drag off her Marlboro as everyone waited for her to say something more. "I'm phoning now!" she said, disappointing all, adding in a brief aside to me, "My husband's his biggest fan, you know."

"Gavin's?"

"Gavin? Who the hell's *Gavin*? No, David," she said. "Loves David. Can't get enough of David. Talks his bloody ear off too, I might add. God bless him though," she sighed, staring glassy-eyed at the ceiling, "he considers David to be God's great gift to us all." That said, she grabbed the phone and punched in the number, shouting out, "David, I'm phoning Sanjeev now!"

Fisk wandered in from the living room to receive the cordless phone. And watching him meander off towards the door and the hallway beyond, Nina leaned heavily into her Marlboro once more.

"Listen," she said, graciously expelling the smoke to the side, "Billy, is it? Yes? Well listen, Billy: God bless you. I mean that. Now have you ever in your life seen such a pretty group of girls? Look at me." She grabbed my face and pulled it down to hers. "Now look at that one there." She turned my face to the kitchen. "That Tracy one with the tits. But wait, who's that boy she's with?"

"That's Gavin. He's an actor. We're friends."

"Oh but he's something isn't he. God bless him, he's prettier than she is."

Releasing my face, she studied Gavin vigilantly.

"Anyway, I really don't get out all that much. I'm really not all that much of a drinker, truth be told. Of course I *can* drink. I simply choose *not* to drink. Anything I might have seen though?"

"Pardon?"

"Your actor friend there, what's his name—Kevin—has he been in anything I might have seen?"

"Maybe," I shrugged. "I really don't know."

"He's sure pretty though. Prettier than she is anyway. Look!" she said, and brought my attention to Tracy's midriff now that her shirt had ridden up sufficiently to reveal it. "She's got a *scar*!"

"Probably not something she wants you to bring too much attention to though."

"Oh come on. Check this out." Nina wheeled about to hike up her own sweater, revealing a thick pink scar running the length of her spine. "See that?"

"I see it."

"Touch it."

"I'd rather not."

"Come on, touch it."

"I don't think so."

"Suit yourself," she shrugged, wheeling around again and dropping her sweater. "Scoliosis. Pins and rods, the whole works. God bless you for having all of those though," she winked, and proceeded to pat my testicles over and over until finally, feeling entirely overwhelmed, I made my way out to the living room where Chris and some girl sat chatting on the sofa. The girl was wearing a short orange dress and her straight brown hair hung unevenly across her shoulders, while her face was made up with some sort of make-up in order to induce the impression that she was not, nor had she ever been, afflicted with this particular skin condition she so obviously was at present. She was drinking red wine and she wanted another. Her eyes wanted for very little, however.

"Shauna here's got schizophrenia," Chris informed me as I sat down in the chair opposite.

"That so?" I said, trying to sound placid in case this was simply another joke at my expense.

"Apparently. She was just telling me."

"Wow, that must be hard," I said.

Adjusting her dress, Shauna shuffled forward to the edge of the sofa with a sudden air of cheerful confidence. On the wall behind her, amid a bevy of Gavin's notorious black-and-white fog shots, hung a photograph of the host relaxing on this very sofa with some girl's head in his crotch, his hand raised in fraternal greeting towards the camera. Judging by the colour of the hair, I thought the head might well have belonged to Mitch's girl Gracie, but from this perspective it was difficult to tell.

"I'm learning to live with it though," Shauna smiled, her teeth covered in a network of flashing silver metal. "Now I know what you're thinking and you're right, it is—it is hard—but you have to be open about it. You have to be. Otherwise you'll go around being afraid all the time. I've got schizophrenia, and that's it. I've got schizophrenia, Billy, and I'm learning to live with it." The absolute worst thing you could do to anyone, including yourself, was to be dishonest about it, she said. "And hey, with the medication I'm on it's hardly a problem. More a minor inconvenience than anything."

"Still, that must be hard," I said.

I flexed my fingers, cracked any remaining knuckles and then, snapping a prolonged silence, blurted out something to the effect of, "That girl in the kitchen there has herpes. And her sister there had scoliosis when she was a kid."

Shauna looked at me, visibly taken with this intelligence. "Oh yeah?" she said, blinking repeatedly, glancing about hopefully with a strange disjointed grin. "Does she suffer from any—oh what's that phrase—residual psychological scars?"

"Well Billy here's got scars," Chris put in. "Show her, Billy. Show Shauna here some of your wonderful residual scars."

"I'd rather not," I said.

"*Please*," Shauna cried, having placed a long, thin-fingered hand on my thigh. "You must."

"Must I?"

"Please."

"All right," I sighed, and pulled up my pant leg. "See that? And that? That one there's where they rebuilt my knee."

She drew her finger lightly across my kneecap where, had I had one, the scar surely would have been. "What happened?" she asked.

I nodded profoundly. "Blew it out a few years back."

"Oh I'm sorry," she cringed, covering her overly metalled mouth with her hand.

"Forget it. Besides, it's not your fault. Or is it?" I asked warily, trying to be funny. She traced her finger lightly across my kneecap again.

"It's healed rather well. I mean you can hardly even see where they went in."

"Just goes to show how really bad it was," I said, and Shauna shook her head with tremendous sympathy at what was, for her, the brutal irony of the thing.

"Show her some more, Billy," Chris said. "Show her that medal of yours."

"What medal?" Shauna asked, head on a drunken swivel between us.

"I didn't bring it with me," I shrugged, wondering where he was going with this.

"No matter, those badges of honour there are medal enough," he quipped, turning to Shauna. "Though we're still holding out for the chest to pin them to of course."

I lowered my pant leg. No one spoke. I was actually hoping Shauna might touch me some more.

"I've got some more scars," I said, nudging her gently in that direction.

"Really? Where?" she asked, and I offered her my knuckles. I doubted she would be all that impressed.

"You know, I really don't see much of anything," she reported at length.

"You're joking."

"I'm telling you, they look fine," she shrugged, and retreated deeper into the sofa.

I began to grow angry. "Look closer," I said, and she did, leaning forward to hunt carefully over the various crests and valleys, only to shrug good-naturedly once again.

"I really don't see much of anything."

"You don't see that. And that. And that one there," I said.

"I told you, Billy, your hands look fine. I honestly don't see anything at all."

I hit her then, open-handed and across the cheek, and her head flew back to rebound off the sofa—for a moment it stood transfixed in the air. I waited for it to come. It seemed to be a long time coming. Then it came. Here it comes—I watched her hair fan forward onto the table. I turned to the kitchen but no one seemed to have noticed, immersed as they were in one of Nina's grand tales. And so I turned slowly back to Chris and Shauna, wondering as to the repercussions here. He didn't say a word. Neither did she. And then her cheek flushed pink as her eye began to weep uncontrollably.

"I should probably go," I said, and stood to leave.

"Tell him I'm sorry," I heard Shauna cry out behind me. "Tell him I was just trying to make him feel better."

"Hold your horses," Melanie said, catching me by the arm at the door. "And where do you think you're off to, mister?"

"I have to go."

"I don't think so. We haven't—"

"Look, I have to go, all right?" I told her, and pushed past and out the door. I was outside on the street before Chris caught up.

"You're bleeding."

"What? Where?"

"There. From your hand."

I held the hand up under the light of the street lamp, and watched the blood run down across the palm. "Well would you look at that. I must've caught her braces."

"Good to see you used the left though."

We walked along a while.

"You think she's all right?" I asked a little later.

"Shauna? Oh she'll be fine. Shauna smacks of someone who's been smacked around before."

"Still, I shouldn't have just up and lost it like that."

"No, you shouldn't have, Billy. You definitely shouldn't have. But hey, she's gotten over worse things from better men, I'm sure."

We walked along the sidewalk through a long quiet tunnel of blossoming trees. There were pink blossoms all along the sidewalk, and the street alongside, still wet from the thunderstorm earlier that night, reflected deep and black in the soft amber lamplight flickering down through the trees. A few blossoms clung to the dripping branches, but otherwise the branches remained as naked as their trunks and as darkened by the rains of the season. Although it was only just past ten the streets were relatively quiet, and despite the storm it was rather warm and lovely and felt very much like the spring. We walked along the tunnel of trees gazing up at the lights of the apartment buildings and, far above the lights of the city, the brightly illuminated alpine ski runs.

Eventually we turned left onto Denman, passing a collection of crowded restaurants and cafés, heading south and away from Coal Harbour and Indian Arm in the direction of English Bay. As I said, it was a nice night out, not too cold and pleasant for walking, and we were deep in the heart of the West End.

"That's it, Billy. Put your shoulders into it."

"What do you mean?"

"The way you're walking," he said. "Hunch any further forward and you'll be scraping your nose on the pavement."

"It does the trick."

"Trick? What trick?"

"Lets them know I'm not gay."

"Christ, you don't think they can tell already? My God, you all but exude intolerance."

A breeze came up, and Chris slung his fists deep into his pockets, one forward, one back. "Okay, enough," he said, coming to an abrupt halt on the sidewalk. "Enough posturing on my behalf—it's pathetic. I know you're not that much of a redneck and besides, they can tell."

"You better believe they can tell," I said.

We continued along past several streets blanketed in pink, eventually stopping outside Delaney's coffeehouse. I looked down at my hand to where the blood had dried, and inside Chris wiped it clean with a cloth. I flexed the hand several times to see if the bleeding had truly stopped and it had—there was no more blood on the cloth. The fellow taking our order smiled, and trying to be nice I smiled back. He's definitely not one of them, I told myself. I mean his hair was streaked blonde and he certainly had the look—he was clean-shaven, tanned, and in fine athletic shape—but you could still tell he was working on a con. I could tell anyway. I had that ability back then. And he knew I had it too. He knew I knew it was a con he was working on, and so he didn't bother playing it up any more than he had to.

Chris asked what I wanted and I told him. "Regular black coffee for me," he said to the streaked-blonde conman behind the bar. "And a tall homo milk latté for my tall homophobic friend here."

Unmoved, the conman repeated the order to another one working the espresso machine. I continued to watch the first one. He knew I was onto him. He wouldn't meet my eyes with his own. But the other one, the one making my coffee, well I suppose he only wanted what had always been denied him. I suppose we all wanted that. Turning to the window, I squinted out onto Denman, looking both at the glass and through the glass, seeing both myself and through myself—one image superimposed on the other—the image of the one behind me blending with those out there before me on the street. That was what this thing with De Boer and my father's book was like: confusing like that. No, that was too artistic. Definitely too elegant, ornamental and artistic. But it was like that. At least something like that. After a fashion, at any rate.

Receiving our coffees, we returned outside. Up ahead we could see English Bay. There were plenty around when you took the time to notice, and ahead I could see the pretty patterns of city light reflecting off the surface of the bay. We walked past the gas station and down towards the water. Suddenly a crowd of them came running up behind us, running very closely together. There was nothing coming up behind them, but they were certainly running as though there were. Eventually they all went out of sight around a corner. At the last second, however, on the turn, one fell and scraped his knee. He scrambled up and continued on as before. We went along and past and I pretended not to notice. They were all still running together though.

BOOK THREE

CHAPTER SEVENTEEN

A FEW WEEKS later, again for no real reason whatsoever, we flew off to New York, Chris and Fisk and I. I had fully intended to begin my sentence that day stemming from my two assault charges, but obviously couldn't now that this whole New York thing had so conveniently gotten in the way. A man had called a few days before—I forget his name and title—and in the end, with a plea of no-contest, I was sentenced to forty hours community service at Canuck Place, a hospice for terminally ill children in Vancouver somewhere. Evidently they were still under the illusion that I would be playing again at some point. I harboured no such delusions however.

We flew first class—my treat—and the boys seemed genuinely impressed. De Boer recommended the Woodward Hotel at fifty-fifth and Broadway where he and Jennifer had stayed a few times previously. Truth be told, it wasn't much of a hotel. I'd been ready to book us into the Waldorf, but then Chris said this Woodward was decently located, with a reasonable proximity to Times Square, and he and his wife had really enjoyed themselves, so in the end we landed at LaGuardia and took a taxi in from there.

It was a grey muggy day when we set down in Manhattan, with the peaks of the World Trade Center (this was back in '99 remember) lost in the thick underbelly of a dark menacing cloud. We checked into our hotel and made our way up to our room, a suite on the eleventh floor. As for luggage, we didn't have much. Fisk was the lightest packer, followed closely by De Boer, with the Bull, I'm sad and somewhat embarrassed to report, pulling a distant and somewhat cumbersome third. Regrettably, both Chris and Fisk refused to bring anything other than jeans and T-shirts, a fact that would hinder us from trying more than a handful of bars and clubs I was interested in drinking in this time through.

It was a large suite, with two bedrooms and a fold-out bed in the living room, and the one window afforded us a nice view of Times Square down Broadway past the Ed Sullivan Theater, and the other an equally impressive view of our unfortunately fat and exhibitionistic neighbours. Somewhat surprisingly, the Woodward was a member of the Best Western chain. In truth, it seemed far too old for that. But as far as old hotels went, I was assured this Woodward was quite an historic one, and as such room service was provided by a delicatessen somewhere offsite. As well, we were the beneficiaries of some rather elegant looking passes to a nearby gymnasium. Of course the hotel would normally have supplied such amenities itself, but since the Woodward was such an historic edifice, we were granted the pleasure of finding them someplace else. I had grown used to a great deal more to be sure, and the Woodward wasn't quite up to the test of comparison, but despite all its shortcomings it was still quite a good hotel, and I quite enjoyed my stay there.

Having arrived with no real itinerary, we decided to walk around some and maybe give old Dominic a scare. Dominic Reid sported a variety of titles, but had made his name as a literary publicist for those already public figures bent on seeing their private thoughts transcribed for the world. I had talked to Dominic by telephone on several occasions, and he had invited us, if and when we found ourselves out this way, up to his weekend house in Bar Harbor, Maine. We were drinking dark beer at the Times Square Brew Pub when I called him at his office that day. He wasn't in so I left a message, and his secretary called back right away. She offered a variety of ideas as to where we might try finding Dominic at that hour, but neither Chris nor Fisk seemed all that interested in leaving just yet. They wanted to stay put in Times Square. I thanked the secretary for calling and for being so helpful, and told her we'd probably be here at the brew pub for the foreseeable future. Still, I felt obligated to question our decision. I mean here we were in New York, and of all the places we could be drinking we choose a brew pub smack in the middle of Times Square? Times Square wasn't even Times Square anymore. Most of the better joints were gone. But it wasn't any use, they weren't going to budge, and so I leapt in the best I could considering the circumstances. It rained most of the afternoon and well into the evening as well.

Some time later, good and drunk, we wandered south along Broadway towards Battery Park and the Staten Island Ferry, pit-stopping at Dempsey's Irish pub along the way. For an Irish pub it sure was clean, and empty, but it did have a nice long bar with plenty of taps poking up out of it, and so we decided it would do, for the time being anyway. We sat at the bar opposite the taps and watched the financial reports scroll across the bottom of the TV. Fisk made friendly with the bartender, and tipped her ridiculously, and when no one was watching she pretended not to notice our helping ourselves to her beer.

After our stint at the pub, Fisk purchased us a dozen cans of beer for the road. And later, beer in hand, we sat outside on the benches of the Staten Island Ferry watching the Statue of Liberty slide slowly in and out of view. We watched her appear then disappear, first to starboard then to port, and as we watched her sliding slowly by De Boer tried his best to back out.

"Let's go to Costa Rica," he said. He was staring up at the orange lifejackets stored in the compartments overhead. "Let's go to Costa Rica right now."

"But we can't."

"Sure we can, Billy. Let's go to Costa Rica and forget this whole fucking thing. If we catch a plane tonight, we can be on the beach tomorrow."

"Yeah, Jaco's good," said Fisk. "But Manhattan's better."

"All right, fuck Costa Rica—the Netherlands," Chris said. "Let's catch a flight to the Netherlands. Actually, I've got this cousin there that . . ." He paused as the Statue of Liberty appeared once again to port. "I'm just not sure what I'm doing anymore," he said at last, and

I suppose I could have let him go right there. I mean I knew he was speaking to me—not soberly perhaps, but specifically—and I suppose I could probably have let him go right there. Why I felt the need to push him I don't know. Of course I do though. And the fact he was starting to take it so hard really didn't alter that requirement any. Although I do admit that I did consider it. I can honestly say that right then and there, drinking beer on the Staten Island Ferry and watching that lady slide slowly by, I did consider letting him walk away entirely. After all, it was at heart a joke, at best a bad joke, and a terrible sort of way to go about being with people when you really considered it in its entirety. But there was more to it now. There was more to it than simply one former prime minister's misfit son. So I let him dangle. Sitting there watching the Statue of Liberty slide slowly by, I let him wait. And there were many such statues on the ferry that day. Sisters and daughters, mothers and granddaughters— hundreds of them really, stoic and serene, staring silently ahead—so many in fact that I began to wonder if women ever really died at all. Women whose ability to love and trust now lay crippled beyond repair, whose best hope for survival now lay in numb detachment commensurate to their capacity for pain—as if living such a life would ever get them anywhere. It does that to women. Marriage, I mean. It casts them together to keep them alone, when all would keep is that tenderness, that fleeting moment of tenderness lost somewhere in between. The men it simply kills. And those it cannot kill it numbs. And these sisters and daughters, mothers and granddaughters, they gather themselves at the tender places where it cannot kill them, but where it numbs them, until there is nothing left to cling to but the numbness itself. And as I said there were many such statues on the ferry that day.

After the ferry, we took the subway back to the hotel—we missed our stop, however, and ended up at Central Park instead. From Central Park, we made our way up to a bagel shop on the Upper West Side where we split a half dozen raisin bagels, after which we stumbled upon this little Mexican restaurant where we drank Coronas and tequilas at the downstairs bar. Then we just went back to the hotel. All in all, I found the trip rather disappointing until we left for Maine two days later. I had expected that being on the road with the likes of Fisk and De Boer would have proved more intriguing, or at least more exciting, but instead we just sat around drinking most of the time. I mean the drink was fairly good, as was the food—the company was certainly good—but all in all I found the experience somewhat boring and therefore a little disappointing. I chalked it up to the grand old lady herself, New York, bloated out beyond all possibility of repair. Now maybe I was being unduly cynical here, but that was simply the way I felt back there. I did feel stoic. I did feel small. I did feel very much alone. Right then and there I felt as though I was this last remaining warrior—this last remaining warrior from this last remaining tribe—a refugee cast adrift from another age and presently lost in time. I was this exile, this last remaining exile, and pardon the simple analogy, but I felt just like this statue sliding slowly by.

CHAPTER EIGHTEEN

"FIRST WIFE DIED of that. Poor thing had it in the lungs."

"I'm sorry."

"Don't be. Anybody had it coming it was definitely first wife. Ran off with my brother, the cow."

Pulling steadily at his nose with thumb and forefinger, Dominic proceeded to sneeze for a spell.

"Dairy man by trade," he muttered through his handkerchief once the bulk of the attack had passed. "Operates his own truck just north of you somewhere. Town called Terrace. Familiar?"

"Vaguely."

"Yes, well, brother of mine delivers dairy products up there. Milk, cheese, ice cream—that sort of thing."

"Sounds like a swell gig."

"His run alone sometimes four hundred pails a week."

"Four hundred pails a week, huh. Well that's a heck of a lot of ice cream, isn't it."

"Yes. Yes it is. . . . It's the Injuns though, Billy. Apparently the Injuns just love their ice cream."

"Injuns?"

"Indians. *Aboriginals.*"

I nodded, and together we gazed out over the water a while.

"So, what, only Indians eat ice cream?" I asked a little later.

"Of course not, just more than their share. Yes, real gluttons apparently. Can't get enough apparently. It's the same in any Third World country, they say."

"I had no idea."

"True," he said. "Nothing better than a bucket of Ben and Jerry's for your typical Third World countryman these days. Absolute Heaven for him apparently. Cone, bowl, sundae, banana split, milk shake—the list goes on and on really."

"You sure do know your ice cream, Dominic."

"Yes, well, I've a brother who drives a milk truck, don't I."

"Yes, I suppose you do," I said.

Pulling steadily at his nose again, Dominic prattled on in a sudden fit of English charm. He'd been missing that up until now. He'd been missing almost all of it as he kept it saved up for all those hours he spent on the telephone. And so it was that he got up to dance about the stern of the boat, just managing to lurch about instead.

In person, Dominic Reid was far less flamboyantly British than he was on the phone, although still very much the conventional drunken caricature of everything British I have ever come to know. He was quite old—you could see it in his face—maybe even past seventy, with thin, starkly white hair tossed over the top of his narrow sunburned skull, and liver spots staining his elongated hands and arms. Tall, gaunt, and severely loose-jointed, the latter making him seem even more intoxicated than he typically was, Dominic was charming—not so charming that you thought anything but a con— but really very charming in an impeccably suited and scarfed, expatriated Englishman in New York sort of way. He had a nice second wife as well. Aimee was also transplanted English—Welsh, she said—and she was in decent shape for a woman in her early forties nearly full-term in this her first pregnancy. Along with Aimee, Dominic had managed to acquire himself a Manhattan apartment, a house in Bar Harbor, and an enormous Lincoln SUV, not to mention a slick little fishing boat, the *Pilfering Patricia* (renamed, it seemed, right after his first wife divorced him and well before she passed away), the exact sort of fishing boat I would purchase if I were ever to get around to getting out of here.

The town of Bar Harbor was actually quite small, but it came with wide open streets roofed with great leafy trees, the names of which, till now, I've never really had the time to get to know. An East Coast tourist town in every conceivable sense, Bar Harbor still boasted the ocean and all its associated recreational activities, along with those few remaining residents still extracting a legitimate livelihood from its depths. On seemingly permanent display, on seemingly every tree-lined street, were plenty of cozy hotels, scores of restaurants, and coffee shops and bars galore, along with some pleasant green scenery through which the sun played down at just the proper angle and intensity for one's leisurely mid-afternoon stroll. In the mornings, before sunup, I would often arise and fix myself a Greyhound, then watch from the veranda those few remaining fishing boats motoring out under a slowly illuminating sky. And I would watch the seagulls follow those boats out to a certain point before turning back abruptly and heading for land. Off they would go, those few remaining boats, until I could no longer distinguish one from the other along the thin blue line of the horizon. Or until I grew too bored to bother watching, in which case I would make my way back upstairs to the bedroom I shared with De Boer. Eventually he, too, would rise, all squinty-eyed and stretching, and together we'd make our way down to the kitchen for coffee, or else out for breakfast somewhere. Aimee would sometimes waddle around and worry us up something herself, and other times she was far too hung-over to bother. But those times we did manage to make it out for breakfast were my favourite times by far in Bar Harbor.

Up near the center of town stood an old grandfather clock where the local teenagers would often gather at dusk. They would pull up in their cars and trucks one after another, then pair off on the surrounding lawn to make out en masse, and although the elderly folks shuffling on past would often shake their heads in shock at such brazen displays of youth and lust, I knew they were really only shaking them in bittersweet memory of it all. Sometimes, if I were out walking with Aimee, or else stumbling home from one of the bars, I'd stop off at the old grandfather clock to watch the kids neck or else to think about things I'd never really thought about before. And it was here that I seriously began to consider Fisk the alcoholic he so obviously was by now.

It was one evening after dinner when it finally struck me. We'd just come from the restaurant when, sitting with his back against the old grandfather clock watching two prepubescent teens grope their way towards second base, Fisk said we ought to try just one more place before packing it in for the night. There was this bar called Tony's nearby that we really ought to give a go, he said. Tony's, he said, would be the ideal spot for one last quick nightcap—as if any of us, including Fisk, were in need of any more alcohol at this point, that is. In truth, we were all fairly tired from a long morning at the café, followed by an equally long afternoon and evening at the restaurant, but one after another we all caved to his request—if only to see the day through to its appropriate conclusion, I guess. And anyway, he really only wanted one last quick nightcap—hardly a crime worthy of punishment in this booze-soaked little part of the world.

You must try to understand what a truly sociable and handsome drunk this David Fisk was in those days. He was one of the best I have ever seen. And when one was as sociable and handsome as Fisk was, the intoxication all took place in the face, it seemed. He was sitting beside me at the table when it happened. His face was arranged very near to mine. I remember clearly the hot metallic stench of his breath, and the equally offensive flow of his speech, as together they blew so harshly into mine. Turning so that the flow might impact more my shoulder and back than my unprotected neck and face, I tried my best to endure the barrage, unfortunately without much success. When I eventually succumbed, turning face-first into the gale, I saw that Fisk's eyes had begun to narrow—not vertically but horizontally—each drawing gradually in upon the other in the very center of his face. Beads of perspiration appeared along his upper lip and forehead, and a darkness surfaced under the sinking bridge of his nose. All around his skull the skin drew back tightly, and when I asked if he was all right, Chris explained how that last shot had gotten him—by the balls, he said. Hoping Fisk might pull the collar of his T-shirt up over his face, thereby relieving me of the burden of observing it, not to mention the curbing effect it would have on his breath, I asked again if he was all right and Chris shrugged, "He's fine. That's just what happens when he overdoes it," or else something to that effect, and sure enough all returned to normal within a few seconds, the spell broken, the omen passed, leaving only the steady stream of belligerence as evidence of its ever having occurred in the first place. And that was when I knew for sure that Fisk was an alcoholic, and really a rather nasty one at that.

Eventually Aimee waddled her way home for the night, allowing us boys to make our way out in the *Pilfering Patricia* for some apparently much needed "guy time." We were heading out for some late night fishing, Dominic insisted, although naturally he was in no condition to pilot the boat now. He asked De Boer to drive instead, and once far enough removed from land to suit his own unspoken requirements, Chris killed the ignition so that we drifted about with the current. The moon was out, the breeze was down, and listening to some Frank Sinatra on the CD player, we rolled slowly with the ocean's swell. I fixed two rods, hooking, weighting and baiting each before reeling them off with the downriggers to depths at which the digital fish-finder indicated there were massive concentrations of fish just waiting to be hauled up and onboard. Then I positioned each pole in its slot on the gunwale within easy reach of my seat in the stern. I had no idea what it was we were fishing for, and doubted the fish were all that concerned. Still, this was the first genuine fishing opportunity I'd been presented with since arriving in Bar Harbor, and I wasn't about to let it pass by untested. The ocean was calm. There was little or no breeze. The *Pilfering Patricia* rolled steadily with the ocean swell. And as I sat there in the stern dipping my hand into the current and bored beyond measure, it suddenly occurred to me that Sinatra might well have been a closet homosexual.

"Tell me, Dom," I said at one point, "do they have that phosphorous stuff here?"

"What do you mean?"

"You know, that phosphorous stuff. In the water. Do they have that sort of thing here."

"Oh you mean phospho*rescence*," he said, wobbling back towards his seat in the stern, swaying almost regularly and in rhythm with the ocean below.

"Yeah, that's it. Phosphorescence."

"Well that's it right there."

"Where?"

"On your hand. *That's* phosphorescence."

"Oh," I said. "I guess I was expecting something more."

Dominic sat, lit a cigarette, and took a good long drag before pointing the burning end in the direction of Fisk's limp carcass currently spread-eagled across the bow. "His story then?"

"There's really not all that much to say," I said, watching the phosphorescence wash over my scars. "Mr Fisk doesn't make all that much of an impression, I'm afraid."

"No?"

"No, not really. Though he is a bit of a drunk, no question." Fortified by the liquor, and therefore feeling exceedingly conversational, flattered as always by the elegance and faint theatricality of my host's attentions, fraudulent though they were, I explained how, at one time, Fisk had been one hell of a drinker as well as an excellent bartender, not to mention a valuable and faithful friend. But now, as Dominic could see for himself, he was just another addict on the long rough road to oblivion. Stripped of all pretence, that was the unfortunate reality of his condition.

"Anyone can be a drinker," Dominic said, scowling his old man's scowl, an expression of truly English indignation.

"No, anyone can get *drunk*, Dom. It takes a measure of dedication to be a drinker, I'd say."

We sat and drank and watched the rods flex with the current, Dominic smoking his cigarettes in religious succession, myself dipping a hand into the pinpoint scintillation of phosphorescence in much the same manner. He offered me a smoke, but naturally I declined, citing how much it irritated my throat since giving it up a few years back. And so I took a bourbon instead. And here we were fishing off the coast of Bar Harbor, Maine, speaking high-handedly of alcoholics in the bow whilst in the stern drinking bourbon straight.

"So why is it called Bar Harbor?" I inquired after a time.

"Eh? Oh because of the sand bar, I suppose."

"Really?"

"You sound disappointed."

"Well I thought it might have had something to do with all the, you know, all the bars they have in town."

I listened to Dominic's laughter reverberate out across the water.

"So you're like this, what, this spin-doctor then," I said when he was not quite finished making fun at me. He looked at me soberly.

"Oh don't be so callow, young man."

One of the rods bent a fraction further, but nothing of importance materialized. Meanwhile, up on the bow, alongside a prone De Boer, Fisk rolled over, passing gas to the distant shore. Dominic, too, gassed on like never before, explaining how Chris obviously understood the very essence of effective storytelling as he kept the narrative voice as simple and straightforward as possible (this in reference to the admission I'd made earlier, in private, that I too had been working at becoming a writer for some time now), and although there was something of a backlash brewing against such stoicism, Dominic felt it would expire soon enough under the weight of its own verbosity. He leaned unsteadily but grandly towards me to explain, at close range, that writing stories was but trimming trees into totem poles— "functional, clean, straight: reminiscent of God's originals, but prettier and without all that extraneous foliage to unbalance them"—and that the truly gifted writer understood not only how to establish fundamental creativity and believability in his characters, but how to trim away all the excess in order to forge a stronger tighter core as well. To that end, it was not so crucial what was said, he knew, but that which was *implied.* A character needed scars—"not just any scars, but the right *types* of scars"—and the appropriate opportunities to display the sources of these scars as well. In other words, he needed soul. More than anything, a character needed soul. And to establish soul, Dominic said you must allow your character to write himself. At least to some degree you must.

We sipped our bourbon a while. This speech is coming in on a high plane now, I thought. Too high even. I wondered if Dominic shovelled this sort of shit for all his clients. No doubt he would. Hell, he would have to. After all, that's his job.

"What strikes me most about him though is his innocence."

"Chris? Oh, yes, he all but exudes that sort of thing," I said.

"*Exudes*," Dominic repeated, clearly relishing the word, the tone of which he appeared to have missed. "And what's more, how all the preoccupations and anxieties that typically burden the young artist seem completely lost on him." It was almost as if—no it was *exactly* as if—Chris really didn't care one way or the other.

One rod flexed momentarily, then straightened out once more.

"Publishing is such an archaic business," Dominic sighed, gravely instructive once again, having prefaced this remark with a brief review of the general state of literature in the world today. "Oh very archaic indeed. Literature, by design, has always moved exclusively in the high country, but by design of that high country has always moved rather glacially as well." And there was little demand today for great writers. Good writers, true, but not great. The old grew older and the young grew younger and, well, there was simply no corrupting the corrupt anymore, he was afraid. It was all lowest common denominator stuff now. No one was willing to pay the price anymore. And although decent introspective people started writing books, Dominic said, it was only the truly narcissistic that finished them somehow. Now certainly the technology had changed, but the fundamental idea was still in place. It was still putting one's ideas down on paper for others to read. It was still reading left to right. And the fact you thought you had something important enough to say that others ought to read it was still one hundred percent ego all right.

I watched Chris make his way back towards us. Upon his arrival in the stern, having noted the rods, he reeled them each in, and with that animal-lover's zeal and a large knife acquired from a cupboard, severed each of the lines just above their leaders. Once finished with his modifications, he again ran out the rods, this time, though, minus their hooks, baits and weights, much to my disappointment of course.

"Tell me, what do you think of the book?" I asked our host as Chris made his way forward again.

"Oh it's brilliant," answered Dominic automatically, intent as he was on the tangle of bait and tackle presently swimming about in the bottom of his boat. It was brilliant and it was malicious and it was hauntingly reminiscent of all the greats—savage, noble, intelligent, inappropriate—out there on the fringes full of pride and love and bitterness. "Oh the world needs its writers, Billy. And it needs its monsters, too. It needs its rapists and its murderers and its buggers and its bastards—especially when they resemble even remotely Richard Gere." The world needed to know such entities were out there, he said, unwilling to be bought, or else unwilling not to be, refusing to live according to the rules set out for the rest of us to heed. The world needed to know such entities were out there, so it invented them. It invented the illusion, you see, and in turn the reality to fulfill that illusion, like some sort of self-fulfilling prophecy, or novel of the same. To dream about and hope for. To glorify and worship. To immortalize and love. And to vilify and blame. To reach for something more and to break the rules again. "In the absence of any genuine gods a person will always elevate his own," Dominic said. "And I'll tell you this, Billy: while we may absolutely love our lives, we'll always love someone else's just a little bit more."

From off to the west I could see the faint lights of Bar Harbor reflecting out over the water. Meanwhile, having pried off his shoes, Dominic stumbled about in his socks trying to locate pen and paper, and failing to do so, retook his seat instead, looking suddenly old, tired and defeated, replaying a few key phrases under his breath in hopes of recalling them again at a later date.

"Now tell me about this Jennifer," he said at length.

"His wife?" I said. "They're separated. Oh yeah, and she has cancer too. I think that maybe she's getting over it now, but then again I'm not too sure."

Dominic narrowed his eyes keenly, seeking some sort of unsolved mystery here.

"What I mean is, I really can't say, with any degree of accuracy anyway, whether or not I've really earned the right to know."

Just then, having heard the direction the conversation had taken, Chris came bounding back to settle into the only remaining seat in the stern.

"De Boer," said Dominic. "Now that's Dutch obviously."

"Yes, it means 'farmer.'"

"As in the war."

"No, as in farming."

"Damned romantic war really," Dominic sighed. "Might even say the last romantic war. We English were there incidentally."

"Weren't you though."

"Yes, we English were there in an effort to 'bestow rights upon the slaves.' Whatever for," he chuckled, "I have no idea."

"Perhaps because we Dutch felt every man had the God-given right to beat his own black man," Chris suggested.

I thought I felt a fish tug at one of the rods. Foolish, of course, considering how they had no hooks to speak of anymore.

Making his way up to the wheel, Chris started up the bilge pump and flipped on the lights, at which point somewhere below me an engine groaned suddenly to life. I gathered in the rods as we returned to shore, and three days later, upon our return to Vancouver, Dominic called to tell me in his telephone voice that his wife had successfully delivered a baby boy. Apparently he was a healthy boy, all strong and long and not at all out of sorts like I'd envisioned he would be. I'd seen the face of addiction. I'd felt the forewarning of David Fisk. And with the luck we'd had with foetal-alcohol babies in our family, that's what I was afraid Aimee's might just be.

CHAPTER NINETEEN

A MONTH OR so later seemingly not much had changed. We were still living in the hotel and we were still proofing *Lovestiff Annie*, but then we were still drinking every night and most days and still behaving as though everything were normal. It was easier not to look ahead to the inevitable conclusion, especially with the momentum building like it was, but then feeling it building and knowing that you felt it made the entire process seem all the more surreal somehow. We never discussed the building of the con's momentum any more than we discussed the inevitability of its conclusion, as anything that built in such a way was hardly worth discussing at any rate, never in depth, and not at all with any reason. De Boer was still taking it pretty well at that point. He was well past his first interview by then, the one with the local entertainment weekly, the *Georgia Straight*. It was a small article to be sure, offering little in the way of detail, but it did prove effective for its size, accompanied as it was by that rather clever headline and, as I recall, a rather clever photograph as well. It was that grainy, black and white, rather Gavinesque photograph you still see popping up from time to time. That one of Chris standing seaside in nothing but his T-shirt and jeans, gazing out, one supposes, upon the various fascinating and significant things a Writer perceives in what the rest of us see as a typical incoming tide.

Dominic worked almost exclusively from his offices in New York. Editors, he said, forever hungry for fresh copy, loved to break the story on fresh young talent, and break him they did for that was the way. *Vanity Fair* was to be the key of course, that large and, by and large, effective key to the greater American market campaign, and the *Georgia Straight* was considered small enough and Canadian enough to be of precious little consequence at that point—or so at least the Englishman maintained. But trading on the De Boer name was hardly Dominic's idea to be honest. As much as he has been the one to take the fall for all this, I assure you it was hardly his inspiration at all. From the very beginning they seemed more intent on publishing the former prime minister's son than publishing any book. And so it came as little surprise, least of all to me, that this particular package was the package of virtues selected to endear him to the general public. With such a proven track record it surely seemed a logical course of action at the time, one that would surely strike a deep and lasting chord with the American collective consciousness, even if an absurd device to sink to in order to keep what was once such a proud tradition crawling. Chris knew they would. Hell, he had always known they would. And when they did he played it out like any good Canadian kid should.

And this, of course, was the point of the exercise. Or for De Boer at least it was. I mean look at him. Look at what they did. Not that it would have made one bit of difference. Not in the end. For the publishing of fiction was a dying trade. That the game was changing—or *evolving* as they so annoyingly enjoy saying—there really was no doubt, although it seemed to me they were simply evolving it way too goddamned quickly these days. After all, *Lovestiff Annie* would never have even made it out of the slush pile a decade ago, let alone onto the bestsellers' list, and now they're literally calling for a sequel. And for my life I can't understand why they choose not to acknowledge that here. Of course I can though. The writing of fiction is a dying art. The writer, it seems, an endangered species. Gone are the glory days of the literary novel. Gone are the days of respect and pride upon the page. These days it's all corporate campaigns, book clubs, bottom-lines, and clit-lit. These days anyone can play the poet and make it pay in spades.

As for the Englishman's contribution to all this, I do admit that he facilitated the idea somewhat. I do admit that the carpet-bombing media blitz to which you were eventually subjected was entirely his campaign. But then that was just his job. That was simply what he did. He paid out the disbursements and he purchased the magazine space and everyone felt that much better for it, I believe. And even though he encouraged Chris to be himself in his interviews, I got the idea early on that it was only because Dominic knew exactly what the manifestation of that self could be, would be, and in turn, exactly how it would play out to the lowest common denominator of the lowly common scribe. But then Chris understood all that himself. Not only how to establish fundamental creativity and believability in his character, but how to trim away the excess in order to forge a stronger tighter core as well. To that end, it was not so crucial what was said, he knew, but that which was *implied.* His character needed scars—not just any scars, but the right *types* of scars—and the appropriate opportunities to display the sources of these scars as well. In other words, he needed soul. More than anything, his character needed soul. And to establish soul, he knew he must allow his character to be written for him. At least to some degree he must.

America loves Canadians, Dominic said. America is slightly amused and at the same time deeply mystified by Canadians. This overly glorified suburb of itself; this strange and graceful nationette forever in need of maintaining its autonomy—even at the expense of an ever-increasing ambiguity—well America loves the comedic underdog, Dominic said. And Canada is the comedic underdog, Dominic said. And it was as such that, timely and politically incorrect book in hand, his handsome, clean-cut, politically-affiliated client would come waltzing down over the border to take his rightful place in that heartfelt space from which the rest of us had been barred outright. And that was it. That was Dominic. That was the extent of his supposed crimes. And if there was truly something he was guilty of in all this, it was simply being in the right place at the wrong time. Just for the record, I have no idea how much they were paying the Englishman for his services, but it seems to me that he was worth every red Canadian cent.

So that was how it started. And Dominic was right—desperate for copy indeed—soon we were getting calls almost every other day. Everyone from the *Georgia Straight* to *Maclean's* magazine to a CBC television program entitled *Booked on Saturday Night*. *Booked* wanted to have him on as early as possible in the new year, they told me over the telephone. I asked why they wanted to wait until the new year, and they told me that was just their policy. They didn't want to profile a writer who didn't have a book out yet, they said. Policy, they said. Protocol, they said. Same old CBC, I thought. The closest they'd ever get to breaking a story was on *Hockey Night in Canada* for Christ's sake. Now sure they'd been good enough to break the Bull's once, but then he'd been broken long before that.

Yet that is jumping ahead somehow. That is jumping ahead to nearly the *Vanity Fair* release, coinciding naturally with the book's release, and at this point we were still laying the all-important Canadian foundation, as it were. Canadian foundation—I like that— Dominic used to say that. Sorry to hear what happened to him by the way, but then that is jumping ahead as well.

Canadian foundation: grassroots level stuff. Small stuff. Relatively low key, targeted impact, and therefore *Maclean's* magazine type stuff. Prior to *Vanity Fair*, the *Maclean's* feature was probably the most influential, if in all truth the least interesting to actually do—'One Hundred Canadians to Watch' the article was called, and in effect was just that: profiles of one hundred young Canadians supposedly something new. A few names I thought I recognized, but most I knew I did not, and that was probably as much my fault as it was anyone else's. After spending all those years in America I'd accumulated all the Canadian culture of a glowing red puck. Not that I'd been so up on it before. Actually, the closest I ever came to culture in my youth was drinking High-test from stubbies under the Bobby Orr sign on the outskirts of Parry Sound, Ontario. And if that truly be considered bona fide Canadian culture these days, I'm really not at liberty to say. One has no such liberty in here. But I did stand proudly for the anthem each game, and I did sing it quietly under my breath. I did watch the series in Seventy-two, and I did laugh when Esposito tripped and fell on his skates. I did cheer when Bobby Clarke took his stick to that Russian's ankle and *that*, I have learned, is the stuff of the quintessential Canadian hero. A radical foreign policy to be sure, but nevertheless Canadian through and through. Playing with pride; playing with passion; reaching down deep and finding something *mean* inside. You see my point then: I was raised outside of culture. I was raised inside a box. Sometimes I wish things could have turned out differently, but then they rarely turn out at all.

CHAPTER TWENTY

ONE AFTERNOON IN the middle of June I got bored of just sitting around. I was sitting in the café under the high vaulted ceiling of the hotel lobby, putting off the effort of heading out to the racetrack, when the idea suddenly struck me head-on. I had recently been contacted about my community hours at the hospice again, and had promised to show up again that night. Chris was there at the café too, and we were both reading our books when he informed me that he was heading out to see his wife. That was when I decided to follow him, if only because I had no desire to spend time with artificially stimulated horses or terminally ill children just yet.

Following him proved easy enough. I simply waited down the street while he caught the bus to White Rock, and then hailed a taxi to follow. Thankfully the bus went straight on through, with no stops en route, and all told the taxi fare was seventy-eight dollars including tip. It was not such a bad trip. I'd never been out that way before. Now naturally I'd brought along my father's book, but preferred reading the Canadian landscape as it swept past the car window. It was nice to see the horses in the fields, and the mountains beyond the fields, from a different perspective than an airplane window. And so it was that I was more talkative with the driver than I typically would have been somehow.

He was East Indian, or Indo-Canadian or whatever, and he sported, on his head, along with a bright red intricately woven turban, a long black beard of considerable merit. His accent was heavy, really very heavy, just as his ceremonial dagger appeared to be. He was very helpful and informative, this particular East Indian, and somehow we got to talking about booze. I asked if he'd ever tried something called absinthe. Absinthe is this greenish liqueur that I'd read turned milky white when combined with water. Actually, Pernod is a kind of imitation absinthe, complete with the colour and change of colour, but without the magic and little of the ritual and none of the discipline of the original. Pernod I'd discovered while rereading my father's book and had since sampled on several occasions. I was very disappointed with the results. I needed absinthe. I needed the genuine article. Apparently the genuine absinthe was something extraordinary all right, especially with regard to its particulars and its hangover.

Oil of wormwood. That is one of the key ingredients of absinthe, and precisely the one that furnishes all the notorious hallucinations. Over the years many famous artists have championed absinthe for its vision-inducing qualities, right up until the First World War or so when it was banned outright in most countries, all on account of the insane asylums. Evidently the majority of inhabitants of insane asylums in those days were in fact absinthe addicts, and at the time, I suppose, that was excuse enough to ban its production outright. That was too bad. There was a real ritual to absinthe apparently, a real ceremony and discipline, although what this discipline was I had no idea, and that was why I was in search of it in particular. I was really very much in need of the particulars, understand, and hence had taken to asking almost everyone I came across if they had tried it, or if not, if they knew where I could get hold of it. No one did. Few, if any, had ever even heard of absinthe. Though Dominic said he had. Sadly, however, he couldn't remember much in the way of feelings or impressions, and nothing at all in the way of particulars, and it was the particulars I was after here, specifically firsthand knowledge. No one could help me. No one could shed any light on the practice of absinthe until, as I said, I took the chance and queried this friendly and curiously knowledgeable East Indian cab driver here.

Now I will not recite the dialogue verbatim as I could never get the accent right. You have to get the accent right if you are going to do it justice, and not simply the disservice of lampooning the speaker into some kind of caricature. However, the gist of the conversation went like this: I asked the driver if he had ever tried something called absinthe, and he said he had, in England in fact. *The* England? I asked. Yes, yes, that very England, he laughed. As it turns out, he explained, they never got around to legally banning the use of absinthe in England; they simply banned its production. And so all one had to do, apparently, was order some up from the Czech Republic. I asked the driver if he spoke Czech as well as Indian and English and he said Punjabi. Punjabi and English, he said, not Indian and English. Then he said something else I didn't understand and I waved him off and said right. Of course. I'm the Indian and I'm the native and I'm the goddamned noble savage. He said what? Bull, I said. He shook his head and said he did not speak bull. No speak bullshit, he said. I waved him off and asked how one goes about ordering absinthe from Czechoslovakia if he doesn't speak Czech and he said the internet. *The* internet? Yes, yes, that very internet, he laughed again. And Czech Republic. Not Czechoslovakia, but Czech Republic. All right, all right, I said. Fuck the Indians and fuck the internet and fuck the goddamned Czech Republic. Then I asked if he had any absinthe with him here in Canada and he said he did not. No absinthe here, he said. Would be illegal, he said. That's a good point, I said. But we make our own, he said.

"What, like moonshine?"

"Yes, like moonshine. Very good and one cup all you need."

"But how?"

"How? Water distilling kit."

"*Water* distilling kit. But is it the same?"

"Same? No. Close though. Same percentage and therefore equal in most respects."

"Does it have oil of wormwood in it?"

"No, sugar cane. Sugar cane from Costa Rica," he said, writing down the recipe as he drove. Regrettably I lost that recipe later that night or else the very next day—either way the point is I lost it—not that it mattered anyway as I would never have made it as I was in search of the genuine article. I wanted the ritual of the spoon and the ceremony of the sugar and the visions and the madness of the wormwood. I wanted the absinthe. I wanted the real absinthe and I wanted only to have to pay for it. And so I decided right then and there that De Boer and I should probably get to the Czech Republic as soon as humanly possible.

I could hardly contain my enthusiasm. In fact, watching him get off the bus in White Rock I almost broke down and announced my plan right there. But then I thought better of it, and following along at a distance, maybe two hundred feet or so, ducked in behind successive telephone poles and the occasional shrub so that he wouldn't see me. He never did see me. Though he never did look, I suppose. We walked down the street, down past an elementary school, following the road as it curved off to the left, eventually turning right at a catholic church onto another downward sloping street—Fir Street, if I remember correctly—this street much steeper than the previous street with a tremendous view of the ocean stretching out and away to the southwest. I recall it was a catholic church we turned at as it was called the Star of the Sea, and the windows were shaped like t's. And walking down past the Star of the Sea Catholic Church I saw that the sea was indeed lit up like a field of stars, literally millions of stars, while directly below me a series of small scintillating waves rolled in past the occasional boat blinking lazily about the end of the pier. And away to the southeast stood the square flat top of Mount Baker, rising high and pinkish-white against the sun's slowly tiring glare.

I positioned myself below the house amidst a stand of pines, and at first glance could not see anything for the closed Venetian blinds. But later on, once the sun began to set, I could just make them out in there together, and finally, around nine, moving out onto the balcony alone, Jennifer. I had just finished crying when she finally appeared. Please allow me to explain. My knees had been getting sore from so much squatting, and so I had taken to bouncing gingerly from one foot to the other in hopes of alleviating some of the pressure. Bouncing around like that I had pretended to box with the tree, which in turn got my bladder working, and so I took to relieving myself against the tree, which struck me as funny somehow. In fact it struck me as so outrageously funny that I could not help but laugh out loud. I placed my hand over my mouth in an effort to keep from laughing, and when that didn't work, tried my fist instead. Still I could not stop laughing. I realized then that if I could not stop laughing, she would hear me up on the balcony. Naturally that only made it worse. Soon my stomach hurt I was laughing so hard, and I could feel my face turning red behind its clenched fist curtain. And in the end I was forced to dig my teeth into my fist in order to regain control, and that was when I noticed the tears trickling down the back of my hand— not that any of this relates to the story, I suppose.

She remained on the balcony all of a minute or so, just long enough to watch the last of the sun slip beneath the horizon. From my position down here amidst the stand of pines I could not see where the sun set, nor what it looked like when it did set, although I could see the sky above all yellow and orange and pink and dwindling into what I imagined was essentially every other sunset in the world. I felt dirty just then. I felt dirty and small down here amidst my stand of pines when I could have been up there watching the sunset like most any other citizen in the world. And I felt bad. I felt bad that she would resort to looking at sunsets when something like that was such an obvious cliché and therefore something to avoid. Still, I thought, as far as clichés go, this particular sunset might not be all that bad nor exhausted, indeed not all that painful, banal, nor commonplace, especially considering how truly pretty that sky is with the way all those colours fade to blue-grey and away from the bright red rim of the world. And therefore this sunset is probably worth looking at, I decided, at least for a time, if not by me then maybe by someone else with a far different view of things like that. And so, squatting down amidst the stand of pines with my fist in my mouth and my feet in urine, I decided to forgive her for that.

She looked different than I remembered. The wig was gone, and the hair beneath had grown back a dirty sort of blonde—still short of course, although longer than I'd expected, with some curl to it too, especially around the nape of the neck and at the front along the forehead. Her face seemed wider than I remembered, more round or robust maybe but just as pretty, and the eyes were enormous in that expiring light—for the token inspiration, I would wager. For that in fact she could have been ideal. And so, if I had to pick a real hero in all this, I suppose it would have to be her.

Chapter Twenty-One

THE DAY BEFORE we left for Prague I spent most of my time reading at the hotel café. I would have spent most of my evening reading at the café too, except for the fact I'd finished my book again and felt no obligation to return to it again so hastily. And so, avoiding the racetrack again, I headed over to Stone's instead. Mitch was there when I arrived, leaning heavily into the scratched steel bar, and we both got down to business immediately. That Latino actor joined us later, but true to form kept entirely to himself. I drank double Pernods with water, while Mitch drank his customary double Appleton and Coke. I couldn't tell what that Latino actor had. Melanie was very excited about our upcoming Czech adventure, and the fact that I was financing it made us both feel special.

I glanced over at a nearby table where an elderly woman was sitting with her middle-aged son. She was helping him prepare his coffee, but he was severely retarded and so refused to cooperate—he only wanted to play with his sock monkey. He spoke to the thing as if it were alive. His mother, however, and to her everlasting credit, remained calm and helpful and extremely patient throughout the entire ordeal, refusing to let his condition get the best of her. And anyway, he really only wanted to play with his sock monkey—on the list of recognized crimes it was certainly of the minor variety.

"I heard *Gavin* got himself a ticket," Mitch said, right hand underlining 'Gavin' all the way.

"He did? Are you sure?"

"Yup, same flight as you."

"Great," I said, feeling my ears burn red. "That's just great."

"Hey, you have to be happy for him though."

"I do?"

"Sure. Got himself another gig in town here starting the end of the month. Movie called *My Nine Wives*, with Rodney Dangerfield. Was called *My Five Wives*, but then they changed it to *My Nine Wives*—it's a play on words. Crew got their shirts and thought it was a misprint."

"Yes, I suppose they would."

I could think of nothing else to say to Mitch. In truth, I could never think of much of anything to say to Mitch—for Christ's sake, it was Mitch—and yet I was glad for this lack of common ground as I thought it somehow reflected positively on me. How this was exactly I had no idea, but I was glad for its possibility anyway.

Meanwhile, over at the table, the retard continued to play with his sock monkey, pitching it back and forth across the table, spilling the cream and upsetting the sugar, testing to the limit his mother's composure. His head was too big, and his ears were too small, while his eyes appeared puffy and slanted. I shifted my attention to that Latino actor. He was still drinking from a coffee cup in those days, but he wasn't fooling anyone anymore. He nodded my way when he caught me looking, and I nodded back before turning away as stoically as possible.

Mitch lumbered off to the washroom just as Melanie came sauntering up. The table with the retarded fellow and his elderly mother was hers of course, but of course she wanted nothing to do with it now. She pleaded for Fisk to take the table instead. He said he would as soon as he could, but that he had to tend to his own paying customers first. That Latino actor chuckled quietly to himself, nodding down into his cup, while Melanie rolled her eyes and walked away to pour a draft. The beer poured smoothly for the first half glass or so, and then, as though the patron saint of sock monkeys himself had been watching, sputtered up quite grumpily after that. Melanie shook the beer foam from her hands, swore repeatedly under her breath, and stomped away furiously into the back.

Finally, with a good long sigh, and decaffeinated coffee decanter in hand, Fisk meandered out from behind the bar in the direction of the retard's table. Upon his arrival he must have said something funny, however, as both mother and son began to laugh hysterically. He had a wild maniac laugh, that retard, and his grin was somehow wrong and unnatural, and I sure felt sorry for his mother.

Just then what I feared might happen did in fact happen—I had this strange feeling it was about to happen all along. Suddenly the mother was standing right next to me, fidgeting conspicuously, smiling awkwardly, and by the length and shape of her conspicuously awkward smile I knew exactly what was coming before she did apparently.

"I'm his brother," I blurted out before she could properly formulate the words.

She looked confused. "Really?"

"Don't worry about it." I waved her off. "Happens all the time."

She laughed out loud. She had a pretty sort of laugh. "Oh my gosh, you look so much alike!"

"Yes. Yes we do," I smiled. "In fact we look just like our father."

She laughed again, and pointed to her table. "You know, my Jacob there thought for sure you were Billy Purdy, and I must say, so did I. He's such a big fan of your brother's, my Jacob, and oh"—here she shook her head sadly—"oh he'll be so disappointed, too."

She introduced herself as Maureen. "And that there's my Jacob," she added, shaking my hand.

"Hello, Jacob. Hello, Maureen."

"Oh he's such a big fan, my Jacob," she frowned. "He'll be so disappointed."

"Like I said, I'm sorry, Maureen."

Tongue out and slobbering, Jacob plowed his sock monkey back and forth across the coffee-wet table. Meanwhile, down the long scratched steel bar, that Latino actor paid his bill and moved off towards the door. Maureen leaned in close, placing her hand gently atop my shoulder.

"Maybe you could do me a favour. You know, if it wouldn't be too much trouble. Maybe you could pretend to be your brother for a moment—just for a moment—and come over to the table and say hello to my boy."

"Can't do it," I said, and when I saw the protest rising in her face, added quickly, "Look, lady, it'd be unfair. To your son as well as my brother."

"Surely you could just scribble something on a piece of *paper*."

"No. No, I can't. Listen, it would be unfair. Not to mention unethical. My brother's autographs are worth a lot of money, and for me to fake something like that, well . . . it's just that you're asking too much of me here."

Maureen frowned, and my heart sank, but I refused to give in after having gone so far down this path.

"Maybe you could just go over there and say hello then," she said. "My Jacob, see, he won't know."

I glanced over at Jacob, then shrugged regrettably, "Look Maureen, I'm sorry. I really am. But like I said, it would be unethical."

At last Maureen walked stiffly away, and I returned once more to my drink. I glanced down the bar to where that Latino actor had been sitting, and then further down the bar and out towards the street he had fled to. Melanie stared down at the floor, beside me Mitch shuffled about uneasily, while across the bar Fisk whistled a requiem somehow befitting such pathetic theatre. We didn't speak. No one spoke. I took to shaking the ice around the bottom of my glass. And when I finally regained the courage to glance up again, that middle-aged retard and his elderly mother were already well out the door.

"You know you fucked up when even Chips leaves in disgust," I said, gesturing down the bar to where that Latino actor had been sitting.

"Yes," said Mitch, "he would be the litmus test for that sort of thing. But then he knew it could've been worse of course."

"How so?"

"Well he knew it could've been him."

After dinner, Mitch and I made our way over to the Ad. There was no queue when we arrived, but inside it was filling up quickly, and I was still stewing about Jacob and Maureen when I secured two barstools side by side. The Pimp, for his part, was upset himself. I had managed to Mitch him back at Stone's, managing to pay the bill when he was off in the can. And now, naturally, as we settled in at the bar and he nodded for his Appleton, he was hell-bent on getting me back. After pushing down two stiff Greyhounds in rapid succession I pushed down two more, and soon enough felt quite sure I had forgotten all about Maureen, Jacob, and that ridiculous toy.

A handful of patrons of the Devil's Advocaat that night had arrived solely on account of De Boer. Chris was the talk of his little circle at this point, if he hadn't always been before—a player of minor status with all the trappings of what was still a minor role. Exclusively young geek-chic art-nerds, they each smoked plenty of cigarettes while wincing with ironic seriousness, only occasionally taking a break from this tightly choreographed routine to smile in what I assumed was the starving artist's way. They each spoke condescendingly and with much cynicism through obscure cultural reference. Later on they would still be smiling and speaking of course, but through much nastier sneers and with far more obvious insinuations. But as for now they were still content to smoke and wince and smile in that token artist's way.

That night there was one hipster in particular, this tall thin geek dressed in too-short polyester pants, a puke-green cardigan and, of course, Elvis Costello glasses. His cigarette routine was painful to watch. I rarely saw him so much as take a drag. Still, he was consistent in his approach, if ineffective, choosing to hold the cigarette up close to his face with one hand clasped about the other in what amounted to a curiously affected embrace. Much like Mitch in a way, but with even more preparation and pretence.

"Fuck I hate these people," I said.

The galleys for the novel had been completed just days before. The words were all in place, the quotes were in position at the beginning of each chapter, and the jacket had been redesigned twice and then upgraded once more. The title itself was printed in this bright yellow handwritten-type typeface—Finehand thirty-three Bold

Condensed, I was told—behind which the cover remained mostly black, featuring the softly blurred image of a black-haired Indian girl crying down into her hands. Over the title appeared this little ditty in light blue ink, supplied by a certain Aimee Reid of *Vanity Fair*—

> 'Just as *The Sun Also Rises* did for the Lost Generation, and *On the Road* did for the Beat Generation, this astonishing novel seems destined to inspire, as much as document, this next generation, whatever De Boer himself decides to name it.'

—which I thought rather precious somehow. As for the back cover, it featured, along with a brief description of the plot, some more quotes from *Time, LA Weekly, Salon* and the *Washington Post*, along with this whopper from the *New York Times Book Review* under the heading Advance Praise—

> 'This is a wonderful book. Employing clear concise prose and vivid mind pictures, [De Boer's] manic economy and explosive force put most other writers of his generation to shame.... Echoing a vanished 1950's America, this wholly original novel is both a work of art and an incisive piece of cultural criticism, featuring enormous sociologic grasp, a revolutionary attitude towards sex, gender and political correctness, filtered through that old, stoic, cold-humored eye on class. AISOP's characters will continue to haunt the reader long after the final page has passed . . .'

—which I thought a rather precious sell as well. So none of these people had been around to read it the first time either. I supposed it was just as well. The first flap contained even more quotes, too numerous and too varied to list here, but still rather clever if one put much stock in such things, and the back flap featured a nice photograph of the author taken out on the deck of *Jade*, along with a brief caption describing vaguely who he'd been before the muse had taken him on such a wild and lucrative adventure. For such a brief caption, I thought it described him rather well, much like the one on the back cover did for the novel itself, although with much less fuss and bother. The first page of the book featured the title again as well as the author's name in **bold**. The page after that was blank. The next page featured the two epigraphs (from Henry Miller's *Henry Miller on Writing* and Fyodor Dostoevsky's *Crime and Punishment* to be exact) and the page after that the text began in full, printed in Bembo typeface on acid-free cream-wove paper of course. I don't know what any of that means, but I do know that it was very nice paper. The first letter of the first word of each chapter was larger than the rest, and dropped down into the body of the text. At the top of each page stood the acronym A.I.S.O.P. and of course the page number, and at the beginning of each chapter appeared the appropriate number. And that was it. That was my father's *Lovestiff Annie* as it now stood resurrected: *An Inverted Sort of Prayer* by Chris De Boer.

Mitch and I watched the cynical young hipsters crowding in around the end of the bar. Someone said hello and I turned to find Gracie. "Well if it isn't the hooker with the heart of gold," I said to her hair.

Gracie smiled, wrinkled up her nose, and shoehorned her way into her usual position between Mitch and me. Chris came over and took her order, and together we watched him make her a virgin Chi Chi. Eventually I placed my hand on her thigh—it was lean and hard to my touch—and Mitch looked over and smiled in his usual fatherly way, a smile that always managed to fill me with some measure of disgust and self-recrimination.

"How is everything?" Gracie whispered into my shoulder, adjusting my collar with long lingering fingers.

"What do you mean?" I asked, and she dropped her gaze to my lap. "Oh that," I said. "The same."

"Too bad," she sighed. "I sure wish you were feeling all right."

De Boer wandered over to wipe down the bar, and I told him Gavin was coming along on our trip.

"I heard," he said. "You must be pleased."

"Oh, ecstatic. All day I go around ecstatic having that bastard in my life."

I glanced over at Gracie, and then down at her dress riding up. If nothing else, I told her, I was certainly appreciative of the opportunity.

She sighed again. "I sure do wish you were feeling all right."

I watched De Boer work a while. When not chatting with us or pouring drinks for the waitresses, he was speaking, under the guise of professional necessity, with those cynical young hipsters crowded in around the end of the bar. At one point I heard him tell the guy with the Elvis Costello glasses how his wife in fact had cancer. Right across the bar he told this guy that. As if speaking of such things with strangers weren't entirely inappropriate in such an environment.

"Good move."

"Pardon?" Chris said in a surprised, unlikely way.

"Telling this guy something like that," I said. "Good move."

The young man with the glasses shuffled about on his stool, taking the first nervous drag from this his latest wasted cigarette.

"What's your problem?" Chris said, and I was about to respond, but having made the mistake of speaking my mind, and alarmed with what I had said, I tried my best to calm myself and undo the damage. Instead I only made things worse.

"Oh no problem here. Just impressed with your move, that's all. I mean a move like that must get you a lot of attention."

"Excuse me?"

"Yes, a real tool you got there," I went on. "Your wife's cancer, I mean. Musters up a great deal of sympathy, I'm sure."

He dismissed me with an acrimonious wave. In truth, it was not too late to put a stop to the lecture, but having started, and having felt it starting, I was in no mood to see it end so soon.

"I mean look at you. Look at both of you. Show some respect why don't you. I mean who the hell is this guy, Chris?"

Adjusting his glasses, the young man cleared his throat. "My name is—"

"Forget it," I interrupted. "Just forget it. Let's just keep it the way it is."

"Well no, I think—"

"Hey Chris, tell your little friend here to show some respect before I fill in his face with it."

The young man fell silent as De Boer turned his attention to the stacking of glasses along the back bar. In the crowd around me I felt a slight shift then a giving away on one side—the Indo-Canadian doorman, I suspected, no doubt intent on getting within range. And glancing about at the sea change of faces I had forgotten since the world had become no bigger than a bartender, I tried with every effort to calm myself.

"Go ahead, Chris. Go ahead and tell him that."

De Boer remained silent until he was certain I wouldn't interrupt him, and then, with a quietly affected sigh and a sanctimonious tone in his voice, said something like, "I don't know what the hell you're talking about, dude."

And in truth it was the 'dude' that did it. Enlarging my world by degrees until it included the geek in his Elvis Costello glasses and then, by extension, his acquaintances. I could feel all the guilt and anger I had inside me about Jacob and Maureen about to come out as violence at them. I could also feel that I was repeating myself without quite saying the same thing. Still, it felt good to get after him. I really did want to get after him. "What do you mean you don't know," I said. "Look at you. Look at *both* of you. I mean you are a writer, aren't you? That is what he does, isn't it, dude? He writes? Well of course he does. Isn't that right though—Elvis, is it?"

"Enough, Billy. You're embarrassing."

"Just a sec, dude. So tell me, Elvis. Tell me exactly what it is you're doing here. Come in for some advice, have you? Some sage advice on how to get published from the son of our former prime minister? Is that it? Or perhaps you're here to chastise him for selling out, is *that* it? Yes, that must be it. So tell me, Elvis. Tell me what it is you're doing here. Tell me *exactly* what it is a rebel like you intends to do with the big sell-out here."

"Jesus Christ, Billy, shut up," I heard Chris say, and feeling a hand on my shoulder I promptly pushed it away. De Boer shook his head at the doorman who wisely stepped back and away.

"And *you*," I said to Chris. "Quit carrying your wife's cancer around like some sort of trophy. Like some sort of prize. Like some sort of *badge* of honour for Christ's sake. I mean how convenient. How convenient to have it work out so well for you. It sure must be nice to feel so completely indispensable to the general scheme of things; to feel that everyone else must suffer so that you can achieve a sense of irony and self-satisfaction in the end. I mean look at you: you're such a con. You really are. You don't have friends, you have *followers* for crying out loud. Look at you. Look at the both of you. Show some dignity, why don't you. Some respect. Not only for your wife, Chris, but for yourselves too."

"Well you're certainly talking an awful lot of morality tonight," Chris said.

"Aren't I? Aren't I though? Forget it. Just forget it. Go on chatting up your charming little friend. Go on playing your charming little game, playing the great big charming author, and building up your charming little wife until you destroy her in every conceivable way. Go ahead and destroy her completely, see if I care. Christ, but you do have some nerve though, *dude.*"

And with that I stood up and, trying with everything I had to be insulting, tossed a fistful of twenties down onto the bar. Pushing a few people out of my way, I cleared a wide path to the door—the doorman was there and he let me pass—another wise decision on his part, I assured him with my most contemptuous smile so far. It wasn't until I was outside on the street that I realized I had company though.

"What the hell do you want, Gracie?"

"Dad thought I should come along."

"He did, did he. Quite the pimp isn't he. I mean how considerate of the old man."

"Well you're in a mood."

"Yes, I am. I am in a mood. Christ, I hate this town."

"Look, I'm just trying to help."

"Why, because we're such good friends?"

"You've got no friends like me," she said with a contemptuous little smile of her own.

"Knock off the charm, Gracie. Really. I'm not in the mood. Go on and charm your way under someone else's table tonight."

"You think you're the only one with your problem?" she said a few strides later. "Good God, you *are* vain."

"Yes, well, it's my problem, Gracie. So in that matter, yes, I suppose I am rather vain."

"Like I said, I'm just trying to help."

"Well I'm fine. Really. Now thanks and good riddance. Christ but I hate this town."

"How come?"

"I don't know . . . it's so boring. So—tedious. Tiresome. There's really not a lot going on."

She nodded knowingly. "Too many slants, that's the problem."

I looked at her. "Pardon?"

"Well there are," she shrugged. "Too many slants. Too many nine irons. There are way too many Asians in this town."

She kept abreast of me, high heels clicking repeatedly, little legs working overtime. Slowing some, I watched as she tugged something down from up under her dress. "Indian underwear," she explained with a frown.

"Excuse me?"

"Indian underwear. These three-quarter Calvin's, they keep sneaking up on me."

I just looked at her again, and then shook my head in wonder.

"Sorry," she winced. "Still, I really don't know how you guys stand them."

Finally everything seemed to be back in place.

"So I hear you're going to Prague tomorrow."

"Well you heard right," I said.

"What's wrong."

"Nothing's wrong."

"You seem, I don't know, upset."

"Oh you think so, Gracie? Massage drying up is it? You some kind of *psycho*therapist now?"

She stopped cold. "Look, if you really want me to leave, I will."

I shrugged and told her to come along. We walked in silence down Burrard Street to Robson and then over to Hornby and the Bacchus Lounge. Once inside, we secured a table near the window, and I ordered myself a Greyhound. The manager smiled that knowing Mona Lisa smile of his, hovering down closely over my shoulder.

"And for the lady?" he asked.

"Get the lady whatever she wants," I told him, smiling facetiously but in much the same way.

Gracie ordered her new favourite, a virgin Chi Chi, and together we settled in, waiting for the black pianist to start his set, which he inevitably did whenever I came in. For his part, the little immigrant manager managed to leave us alone for all of five minutes before he was right back to hovering over my shoulder again. Gracie watched it all play out with much delight. She especially enjoyed the way the little immigrant manager pulled over each of the nearby citizens to shake my hand, as if to say these men too were capable of joining our secret little band if and when I were so inclined. They would each come over, each citizen in turn, always polite until they had met me, and then rarely polite after that. It amused them to know that I had played such a game as hockey, and played it professionally, when they too had played it as youngsters themselves. Not one of them professionally of course, but always at some point and at some minor level to some degree suddenly more significant than most. Somehow it was always assumed that I was not half Indian, and as a result of this assumption the racial slurs against the little immigrant manager arose almost immediately on the heels of his every departure. I always took this as a kind of bonding process between the citizens and myself, and hence never really bothered to call them on it. There was no password, no set of questions that brought it out, only a vague sort of process of feeling out, rarely defensive and not always apparent, but forever accompanied by that same warm hand on my shoulder as if to say, "You, m'boy, you understand." Somewhat surprisingly, they refused to suspend their slurs with Gracie around. Perhaps because Gracie and I didn't speak much the entire time. Or perhaps because, being citizens, they didn't realize they were saying it out loud. Either way, I did eventually introduce my girlfriend Gracie, explaining how it was we were travelling to the Czech Republic the next day.

CHAPTER TWENTY-TWO

"WHAT'S THIS STOPOVER?"

"Oh, uh, we make one to refuel."

"Where?"

"Holland or something. Yeah, the Netherlands or something. Why?" I asked.

"I didn't know we had a stopover," he said.

"It's only for an hour or so."

"Still, you never told me, Billy."

"Well, Chris, I had no idea it was so crucial."

I didn't feel much like talking. Not to him anyway. Gracie and I had been up late at the hotel, and consequently hadn't gotten much sleep in. We'd taken our coffee at the café under the high vaulted ceiling of the hotel lobby, and later a little walk along the seawall to look out at the lights along Indian Arm. And then I had turned in early. Gracie, naturally, had turned in with someone else. The waiter from the café, I do believe, but in that I might very well be mistaken of course. It didn't matter anyway as I was asleep when they came in. And now, the morning after, my sinuses were stuffed full from all the smoke and my eyes were burning red. My head hurt. My clothes stunk. I felt as though I were getting a cold. Add in the fact that it was five in the morning and I was at the airport and I was hardly willing to utter a word. No one seemed too put-out having Gracie along. Even Gavin seemed indifferent to my last minute addition to the line-up. We were all quite tired and no one felt like talking. We were all planning to sleep on the plane of course.

As ugly as I was feeling, I took the time to be impressed with Gracie. To be honest, I'd half-expected her to be of higher maintenance than she was. One bag was all she brought, one carry-on just like the rest of us, and her black hair was pulled back in a thick tight braid revealing a little round face entirely devoid of makeup. She wore denim shorts. And a fleecy red sweatshirt. She and Melanie were immediately inseparable of course. It was going to be one way or the other. Women were always going to extremes like that, so much so that you soon got to wondering how much of it was simply for show. Whether it be clinging together or pushing away, it was not so much the direction taken as the passion with which they took to it on any given day. To be honest, before I saw them together, I had no idea how they were going to get along. I thought that maybe they were both a little more mature than most girls I knew, both a little mellower maybe and more developed, and being that way might just help to sort things out. Being a little more mature, they would have grown somewhat accustomed to such potentially awkward situations, and with experience tend to suppress that instinctive territorial rush. The younger ones were not so good at that. With the younger ones it was all cat and mouse. For a long time I thought that who was cat and who was mouse was determined by whom it was had been played with last. But then the older I got, the wiser I got to the fact that the player himself was not all that important. Not beyond playing a part. And rather than playing a part in the game, he was more often than not being played himself. Whether it was the cat or the mouse he was being played by, it was often simply to gain control of the house. Thus did they squirrel away the very essence of their being while managing to bring the same degree of intimacy out—a kittenish ploy for which there was little defence and rarely a chance of retort. And so it was less a game of who it was would be played with last than one to get away from all such gamesmanship itself. This is a very crude analogy of course, and hardly effective in its demonstration of my point, but I assure you it illustrates rather effectively my somewhat beastly mood that morning at the airport.

A long time later, we taxied into the Schipol Airport outside the city of Amsterdam. And once the plane finally came to a stop, some of us got off while others stayed on. Some passengers were staying on here in the Netherlands while the rest of us were going on to Prague, and those of us going on were given the choice of deplaning while waiting for the aircraft to refuel and whatnot. De Boer stepped out into the aisle. I asked where he was going, and he said he wanted to brush his teeth. I said that was a good idea, and so packs in hand we found the airport washroom and proceeded to clean ourselves up. Chris finished first and told me he would see me back on the plane. I told him we didn't have to board again for another hour or so, but he didn't seem to hear me. I told him to go ahead and see if there was anything good to eat in the airport, but he must have already taken off by then. And it was at that exact moment, I suppose, that he checked himself through customs, bolted clear of the airport, and escaped.

I had no idea he was gone until almost an hour later. Back on the plane I asked the others if they happened to know where he was, and they said they had no clue—why should they? I wondered where it was he'd gotten to. And I wondered that I should care. I wondered if maybe he was playing some sort of game here, but then I knew that he would never.

"He's gone."

"Gone?" Melanie said from her seat across the aisle. "What do you mean *gone*?"

"I mean he left," I said. "He's gone."

"Where?"

"How the hell should I know?"

"He *ditched* us?"

"Something like that, yeah."

"Well where the hell's he going then?"

"I have absolutely no idea, Mel. Now please, let me think a second."

I found myself feeling calm just then. I was proud of myself for feeling calm, and realizing I was feeling calm actually made me sort of nervous, and so I tried hard to feel calm again.

"All I know is he's gone," I said.

"Beautiful. Just fucking beautiful," Gavin said. As there were children present, someone asked if he might like to tone it down some, and in response Gavin asked this certain someone if he might like to kiss his ass. Always the ass with this guy.

I stood up. Melanie asked where the hell I was off to now.

"Well, to find him, I guess."

"But where?"

"I told you, I don't know," I said. And indicating the window through which the sun was presently rising up red over the great white wing of the plane, "Out there somewhere, I guess."

"Great. This is just great," Fisk said in what was, for him, a rare display of genuine distress. "What is this, some kind of joke?"

"Nope."

"But what about Prague?" Melanie said.

"What about Prague? I'm sure as hell not going without him."

"What, so we're all just supposed to *get off the plane?*" Gavin said. "Screw that, I'm not going anywhere."

"Suit yourself. Fisk?" I said, but David didn't answer, and so I shrugged and grabbed my bag from the overhead compartment.

"He's probably in the food court," Melanie suggested, her intended certainty sounding rather wishful at the moment. "Or maybe he's just chatting up some airport whore somewhere. Hell, he's probably back inside buying—something. Anything. Christ, I don't know."

"So what's your point?"

"My *point*, Billy, is not to panic. Why don't we all just relax. I mean my God, he could be anywhere."

She was being very maternal about it.

"But I am relaxed," I said, backing slowly up the aisle. "It's Chris who's panicking."

"Billy, wait!" she said, catching me by the arm. "So this is it then? You're just going to get off here in—in wherever the hell this is?"

"Amsterdam."

"In Amsterdam? You're just going to get off in *Amsterdam* of all places?"

"I suppose so. Yes, I am."

"Oh beautiful," Gavin said. "Just fucking beautiful!"

"But what if you can't find him?" Fisk asked.

"Oh I'll find him."

"But what if you can't?"

"Well then I guess I'll be seeing you around," I told them.

I walked the rest of the way to the exit, and then up the corridor and away from the plane. Someone ran up from behind—it was Gracie—swearing repeatedly and in Korean at me. It was of course impossible to know exactly what she was saying, although it was clear that she was rather unhappy with me.

We checked ourselves through customs after only a cursory inspection of the terminal. I knew that he wouldn't be there. I knew that he was gone. At the first real opportunity he'd bolted, and now it was up to me to find him.

This whole book thing must really be getting to him, I was thinking the whole time I was at the airport. That and the fact I wouldn't be getting my absinthe anytime soon. I supposed I could wait for that. And besides, I thought, there is always Pernod. I wondered, idly, if they had Pernod here in the Netherlands, as we walked out front to where we were told buses would be waiting. We must have taken a wrong turn, however, as we failed to find anything so much as resembling a bus out there.

Once Gracie adjusted herself to the situation, I thought she managed fairly well. I was still feeling fairly calm at this point, and after playing it so calmly for so long I realized I had no choice but to go on with it. Still, I was beginning to second-guess myself. After all, Europe was an awfully large place, with an awfully large and diverse population, and where Chris was headed we had no idea—we had no idea where we were headed ourselves. I exchanged some dollars for guilders, and then we caught the first yellow train into town. We didn't know where else to start. We didn't even know how far we were from town—from any town—and we had absolutely no idea where he'd hide himself. In the end, then, it was Gracie who stepped up and made the decision. She was managing fairly well. I might even have given her the title of seasoned traveller if I hadn't already branded her the fledgling escort.

Outside the train window the sun was coming up, and it didn't take long for us to reach the Centraal Station in town. By the time we arrived it was almost daylight, and I was thankful for that as I would have hated to have been arriving after sundown. First thing to do, then, was find a store. We found one inside the station. The lady behind the counter seemed pleasant enough and spoke fairly good English, and she happily sold us six bottles of beer. I placed four of the bottles in my bag and kept the other two to drink. They were those big green Grolsch bottles with those old-fashioned lever tops that you can open and close at your leisure. We immediately opened two, drained them off halfway, and Gracie suddenly felt a good deal better. We clinked our bottles and drank more Grolsch and soon enough I was not feeling quite so nervous either. I opened my wallet and passed her a wad. "In case we get separated," I told her.

Her eyes narrowed suspiciously. "Don't you ditch me. Don't you so much as *think* of ditching me."

"No chance, Gracie. Honest. But just in case," I said, pushing the money into her unwilling hand.

She frowned. "What if we do get separated though?"

"Then we'll meet right back here. Right here in front of this store."

She smiled, clinked my bottle with her own, and stuffed the wad of bills down into her shorts. Then she said, "Let's go find that son of a bitch, De Boer."

By the time we made it outside the station, morning had arrived in full. It was a warm morning, warm even for that time of year, and I removed my sweatshirt accordingly. I went to pack it into my bag, but with all the bottles there was no longer enough room, so right away I finished my bottle and opened another—one for each of us just to be fair.

"It feels like it ought to be night time," Gracie said.

"That's the beer."

"No, that's the jet-lag."

"Whatever," I said. "Have another beer and we'll see where it takes you."

I was really very nervous now. Finding someone in a strange city, in a foreign country, on a continent one was almost completely unfamiliar with, stacked up as a nearly impossible task at the best of times, let alone when that someone had no desire to be found. But then maybe he knows I'll come, I thought. Maybe he's expecting me now. But then maybe he intended that I come alone. Whatever the case, it was just as well. I drank my beer. It was good beer. And those stylish green bottles I thought I might just like to keep as souvenirs. I placed two empties in my pack only to have Gracie explain how this was in fact a stupid idea, as I would have no room left for anything else. She was right of course, and so I deposited the empties in the trash. There seemed to be no recycling program in place, so I felt no real guilt about that.

Once clear of the station we walked together through the open square out front. There were already a great many people milling about in the square, some coming and others going and many more just hanging around. Directly outside the station stood a loop of buses, and beyond these buses a row of quaint old buildings of smooth grey stone. I thought about De Boer and where he might be. I supposed he could have been anywhere. I'd been enjoying the beer so much along with the company that I'd only begun to appreciate where it was I'd gotten to here: the central square outside the Centraal Station in Amsterdam drinking beer with a Korean call girl.

A young woman came sauntering up. "You guys looking for a place to stay?" she inquired in an accent I initially misinterpreted as Australian. She was short, she was not very pretty, and with those ripped baggy pants and that long brown hair coiled chaotically at the nape of her neck I thought that she was probably a lesbian.

I told her no, but then Gracie squawked excitedly. "Well I suppose we might just as well," I said.

"Now I don't know what kind of budget you're on," said the girl, "but the hotels around here are all fairly expensive. And anyway you won't meet many people in those places."

"What else is there?" Gracie asked.

"Well there are a couple of places over on the Singel Canal."

I shrugged at Gracie, and Gracie shrugged back, and together we followed the girl across the square hand in hand.

"Sip of your beer?" asked the girl, and I handed her my bottle. She tipped it back heartily, then tipped it back again. "Thanks!" she said at last, handing it back. Unlocking a rather sorry looking bicycle from a nearby rack, she introduced herself as Krista something-or-other—I forget what. I told Krista we were looking for a fellow named Chris De Boer.

"SA is he?"

"Pardon?"

"De Boer," she said. "He's South African then?"

"Canadian. He's actually the son of the former Canadian prime minister."

Krista nodded knowingly. "Bald guy, gay, likes to talk about his balls a lot?"

"Not typically, no. Never in fact."

"He probably just got here," Gracie explained, and Krista shrugged.

"You two are Americans then?" she asked.

"Canadians, yes," we answered together as she tugged the bike free of the rack.

"Right," Krista nodded. "Sorry about that. I know how much that sort of thing pisses you off. You too, really?" she asked Gracie.

"Uh, yeah. Why do you ask?"

Krista, though, only shrugged in answer. In the meantime, she tried her best to mount the crappy old bike, but it seemed to be getting the best of her. Finally she shoved it at me. "Here, you take it—I'll walk. I've been trying to teach myself lately, but it's really not going so well."

"Yeah, well, it's just like riding a bike," I told her, but she seemed not to have heard me as she went about explaining how a little girl from Johannesburg stays in Amsterdam for over three months after having planned on staying only a week. I listened to her talk as

I rode alongside slowly and carefully, expecting at any moment the crappy old bike to disintegrate beneath me. On the far right side of the open square, next to a dirty body of water, stood what appeared to be an old telephone booth. Inside the booth stood a naked man. He appeared to be taking a shower of sorts. We moved along down the street with the body of water off to our left, Krista explaining how this was in fact the Singel Canal and a good place to get one's bearings. On our right, mirroring those across the canal to our left, stood more quaint buildings of smooth grey stone. Some had entrances atop ascending staircases while others you entered by descending some. It was morning now, and fairly bright out, and the street-sweepers were sweeping the old streets of the town. Actually, Amsterdam is a very nice town. It resembles exactly the very old European town of imagination, albeit one built up around a series of canals. Already, so early in the morning, it was getting hot on the street alongside the canal. We went further down the street alongside the canal and gazed out into the quaint old streets of the town.

"Now you have two choices," Krista announced once we had travelled a fair distance down. "There's a house right there"—she indicated the building to our right—"but that's a little bit more. And then there's the boat right here"—she indicated the first of a line of barges tied up alongside the canal to our left—"which is a little bit less, but naturally a lot more fun as well."

Gracie asked how much it was for a bed in the house.

"Forty guilders a night."

"And that barge?"

"Twenty-five."

"We'll take the barge then," Gracie said without consulting me.

"Good choice. It's for sure a lot more fun in there."

Slung low in the dirty brown water of the Singel Canal, the barge measured approximately sixty feet long and maybe fifteen feet wide. Krista removed a small chain hanging across the entranceway to the stern, and led us down a short ladder onto the open-roofed landing currently home to an old embattled refrigerator and an older orange couch. Across the landing stood a door, slightly ajar, and inside a row of bunk beds ran each side the length of the low-ceilinged barge. In back of the barge stood a small filthy kitchenette, and beside it a dubious looking toilet and sink. On the opposite side was a semi-private room, locked, supposedly used only for storage at present. There were no windows on the barge, and it stunk steadily and increasingly of old sweaty canvas with undertones of mildew and pot. Superimposed on these odours were the odours of all the memories here that did not include myself. There was also somewhere this distinct and uninviting smell of rotting flesh, and when I inquired into its origin, Krista explained dutifully, if a little too graphically, how it was that a big stinky rat had gotten caught up in the ceiling the week before. Completing the barge's altogether austere amenities were a guitar case standing sentry in the far rear corner of the room and a low wooden table squatting in the middle of the floor. Not that I'd expected much more. I noted something sleeping in the first bunk to our left, but otherwise the barge stood empty just now.

"Yeah, it's pretty desolate right now," Krista admitted with a thoughtful nod. "A bunch of us just moved out like a day ago."

"How come?" Gracie asked.

"We had to get away awhile," Krista said, and smiled suggestively. "Things can get pretty crazy on the barge."

"So we just take any bed then?" I asked.

"Yeah, any one you want. Though I wouldn't recommend those ones in the middle there"—she indicated the second set of bunk beds down the left-hand wall—"they're definitely the least comfortable of the lot."

I sat down on the second bottom bunk on the right, feeling the frame sag threateningly beneath me. On closer inspection the bunks proved to be little more than strips of stained battered canvas slung between pipes of severely corroded metal.

"So what do you think?" Krista asked.

"It's perfect," Gracie said. "It's absolutely perfect."

But all I could manage was, "Swell." And for the first time in what seemed like a very long time I wondered what the hell I was going to do now that hockey was over.

"If you're going to flush the toilet," Krista said, "flip this switch here. And there's a small refrigerator in back there, along with some dishes, but other than that you're sort of on your own. . . . Now Alex will be by at some point to give you some keys, but until then feel free to come and go at your leisure."

"What about this guy?" I asked, indicating the figure cocooned in the first bunk on the left.

"Oh him? He's harmless. Never even seen him wake up."

"Maybe he's *dead*," Gracie speculated.

"Na, he just gets really stoned. I reckon he's one of you Canadians too."

"You reckon, do you," I said.

"Sorry, bad habit that. Too many Aussies around. Yeah, Aussies and Canadians, they seem to be everywhere. The Dutch love you guys by the way."

"They do?"

"Absolutely. Apparently you liberated them during the war or something like that."

CHAPTER TWENTY-THREE

THERE ARE A lot of bicycles in Amsterdam. Now I realize this comes as hardly a revelation but Christ, it seemed as though they were everywhere in that town. There I'd be, just walking along and *Ring!* there would go another one, its merry little bell signalling its arrival, and with it very nearly my departure as well. Always walk in straight lines when walking in Amsterdam, I reckon. That seems to be the very best way to remain safe and sound, although absolutely the worst way to blend in with the local citizenry of course.

Back up the canal the way we'd arrived, I found what amounted to a small convenience store. Here I bought a dozen more green-bottled beers and a carton of orange juice, and at the last second a bunch of bananas as well. Across the side street stood a bakery. There I ordered two sandwiches with everything on them, along with two pastries stuffed with broccoli and cheese. I was impressed with how well the young man behind the counter could switch between his Dutch and his English depending on the particular customer he was presented with. He even managed to include all the appropriate slang. And after the bakery I returned to the barge and found Gracie sitting on the floor with a man. Gracie was talking and the man was listening and he inspected me closely as I made my way by. Closer still when I spoke with Gracie. His name, he said, was Mike, and he was Canadian like me apparently.

Mike was maybe De Boer's age, maybe a little older, with a short roof of scruffy brown hair over piercing blue eyes, a thin brown moustache and unbearably bright white teeth, the remaining few of which he displayed for me at almost every opportunity.

I offered Mike a beer to help ease the tension—the beer he accepted but the tension continued. Popping open the bottle, he promptly drained it off, at which point he picked up his guitar from the corner and proceeded to tune it vigilantly, managing to tune us out in just this manner. Gracie asked if he would play her something and he said he would, but not with the likes of me around, a remark for which my only preparation was the fact that he was a man, and I was a man, and here in the room between us was some semblance of a woman to be fought over.

"Is there a problem here?" I sighed, recognizing all the obvious signs of one.

"Only if you're looking to get one, big boy." Mike turned to Gracie. "You see me do that? I always challenge the big ones first off. First off," he said, "just to let them know I'm not frightened."

"Well just so you know," I said, "I'm not exactly a walk in the park when it comes to these sorts of things."

He did not respond immediately, nor did he even so much as look at me, choosing, for the moment at least, to focus on his instrument exclusively. He played one chord then another experimentally, and finally placed the guitar aside and said to Gracie, "I've no problem with going a round or two with your boyfriend here. I'm one with an awful big secret, see."

"What secret is that?" I had to ask, and he scrambled up quickly to set the toes of his brand new white Nikes carefully up to the toes of mine. He was lean and naturally muscular but far shorter than I, and yet standing under my chin and grinning like he was I could feel his impending violence all over me.

"It don't hurt."

"What'd he say?" asked Gracie excitedly.

"'It don't hurt,'" I impersonated. "What don't hurt, Mike?"

"It don't hurt getting hit," he told me, rolling forward on his toes and then backwards on his heels, slowly and rhythmically.

"Well you've yet to be hit by me."

"Won't make no bit of difference," he shrugged, waving me off. "I can take more pain then anybody."

Here he punched himself in the mouth—twice—and began to bleed profusely.

What a beautiful world it must have been once. A world where you could meet a man, shake his hand, and not have to worry about him trying to impress you with his toughness. Sometimes, though, things happen so quickly and unexpectedly that you have little to no time to put them in context. This is what was happening now as Mike went about boxing himself silly before me. He smiled goofily when he tasted the blood leaking from his face, and I shook my own head sadly.

"Good trick."

"No, no trick," he said, shaking his head in unison with mine. "Look, no nerve endings, see? No feeling in my skin." He grabbed my hand and arranged the reluctant fingers roughly around his fore-arm. "Ice cold, see? Can't so much as feel that."

"I'll have to take your word for it then."

"Truth," he said. "Can't feel a thing. Nerve endings've all been shot to hell. It's all that depleted uranium the fucking Americans like to pump into their weaponry over here. Fuckers love the stuff. Can't get enough of the stuff. It's far more dense than lead, I hear.

"Always hit myself in the gob too," he continued, almost as if in answer to something I'd asked, "because it ain't no big thing being hit in the guts." This next thing, however, he said quite on his own. "Tell me, y'ever been in a fight, big boy?"

"Oh I reckon I've been in a dust-up or two."

"Well be sure to be staying out of my guitar case there as I know how to take a big man like yourself out, and in a heck of a hurry too. How, you ask? Easy. Just go for the shins. Now you'll take your shots, see," he explained to Gracie, unexpectedly instructive, "but just keep going after those shins as best you can—it's all bone—and he'll fall sure as shit. See that scar there?" he asked me, indicating with the mouth of his bottle a long white line running from temple to neck behind his right ear. "Got hit with a mortar shell in a place called

Medak Pocket. Y'ever hear of it? Course you haven't. Fuckers sent me to Somalia too. Course I was just a little guy when I first joined up, so they tested me left and right—heavier packs and scraps and all that—but ol' Mikey, he persevered."

He shook his head ruefully. "Oh I've seen some places, big boy. Sure I have. Seen some fucked-up shit too. See that?" he asked, having pulled up his sleeve to reveal a faded blue tattoo. "Airborne, man. Fucking *Air*borne. You probably heard all about us in the news. Well 'conduct to the prejudice of good order and discipline' my ass—think what you like, but out there in the desert some guy's fucked off with your fuel, he might just as well have fucked off with your food. Should've just shot the fucker in retrospect of course, but at the time, well, at the time that seemed more like we'd be doing the kid a favour.

"Still," he shrugged, "we shouldn't have been there in the first place. We're Airborne, man. Fucking *Air*borne. We make war, we don't *keep peace*. Fuck that," he spat, "I'm a soldier. A trained killer. *I'm trained to kill.* Yes, we're rather alike you and me."

"Oh I doubt that," I said, and he regarded me sceptically.

"Well you're that hockey player, ain't you?"

"He's a writer," Gracie put in. "His brother's the hockey player actually."

"A *writer*!" Mike cried, looking to Gracie for confirmation before doubling back to corroborate this brand new impression he had of me. "Well I'll be damned! I used to write a little myself back in the army. Sure I did. Songs mostly. Occasional poem. Course the best poetry I ever heard was by this big Indian fucker we had with us. This big Hindu fucker—Hindu Hal, we called him—toughest bastard I ever saw. Talk about tough? This guy was tough. I mean *tough*—kill a man just with his hands. Course we all could, but then this Hindu Hal fucker, well he could accomplish the task just that much easier. Good poet though," Mike reflected, "and a real shame he ended up eating the business end of his rifle."

In the kitchen, in the back of the barge, I found a place to store my beer. So this is how it's going to be, I thought. All stoked up on angst the entire time I'm here. Well so be it: I'll find De Boer and get the hell out before Mike and I go at it right here. You could feel these things coming. Sure you could. You could always tell when you were in danger with an addict because with an addict you always were.

"Would you like to accompany me on my morning walk, Gracie dear?" Mike managed to ask just as I arrived back in the room. "You see me do that, big boy? I always ask the girls that sort of thing first off. First off," he said, "before they get to feeling too scared. I'm a drugger and a boozer but I ain't no faggot, understand? I know what's good for ol' Mikey here."

"Actually," Gracie said, trying hard not to smile, "we do need to go look for our friend soon."

"Won't find him," Mike said, shaking his head. "People come here because they don't want to be found. True. Ain't no finding no one round here."

"You sure are awful smart," I said. "How's the mouth by the way? Still bleeding?"

He looked at me, smiling savagely. "That's another secret I should've told you, big boy. Ol' Mikey's got a penchant for blood in his beer."

That said, he punched himself square in the mouth again. And again I shook my head as again Gracie laughed as Mike went about bleeding down into his beer.

"Come on, Gracie. We should go."

"But I want to stay," she protested. "I want to stay with little Mikey here."

"Ah," Mike smiled knowingly. "Well might I interest you in some chemicals, dear?"

"Chemicals?" she said. "What chemicals?"

Mike smiled his blood-soaked smile and opened his guitar case, revealing a fist-sized plastic bag of small white pills. "Had it checked myself at the lab downtown and it's the bona fide product to be sure." He looked at me. "A man like Mikey's got plenty of secrets, big boy. And he's got the chemicals to keep 'em too."

"What chemicals?" Gracie repeated.

"Why it's *E*, girl! Ecstasy! And for a hundred guilders I'll give you a full three."

"Five. I want *five* for a hundred," she countered obstinately, deferring final approval to me.

"I reckon five might be enough," I shrugged, having forced down a great mouthful of beer.

"All right, all right," Mike grudgingly capitulated, all the while looking hard at me. I must say, as much as he was devoted to his art of self-destruction, he seemed doubly intent on getting the best of me here. He faked punching himself in the face again, laughed triumphantly when I winced, then went ahead and punched himself anyway.

Eventually Mike set about the ecstasy's meticulous extraction from the bag, and once the exact five desired had been chosen, reached again into his guitar case for a roll of plastic wrap into which he carefully rolled the seemingly indistinguishable pills. His lip was fattening where his punches had landed, and bloody saliva was pooling down onto his lap from two lengthening cords dangling from his chin. Finally he passed the roll of plastic-wrapped pills to Gracie, who in exchange offered him one hundred guilders of my recently converted money. Mike packed away the money without counting it, and then proceeded to pack up his guitar. And before long he'd packed away all his various belongings and bidden us both a bloody farewell.

"But where are you going?" Gracie wanted to know.

"I have to go, dear," he told her apologetically. "Far, far away from here. And don't try and follow me and don't try and find me because Mikey's got an awful big secret about that sort of thing too."

And with that he was out the door and gone. Gracie and I looked at each other, her eyes as wide as I'd ever seen them as she continued to stare up at me from her spot on the floor. Quietly we both sipped at our beer. To my amazement, the fellow in the first bunk had somehow managed to sleep uninterrupted throughout the entire ordeal. I thought I might have heard him snore once, but then that might well have been the refrigerator kicking into gear.

CHAPTER TWENTY-FOUR

THE DOORS. THAT was what the coffee shop was called. And on our ensuing search for De Boer we made it just that far. The Doors was a small place, with a small functional bar along with a few sad but functional tables, and the walls were stained yellow from years of countless cigarettes and joints. One wall, actually the wall behind the bar, featured a wallpaper of foreign currency—a peeling multi-coloured plaster of various nationalities and denominations, affixed to which were all the token pictures and sketches of Jim Morrison one would expect to find in such a place. Some of these portraits had been scribbled out painstakingly on napkins, while others had quite obviously been purchased from a store. All conveyed the man in nothing less than a religious light, though not one was worth the paper or velvet on which it was printed of course. The fantasy was heightened by the small television implanted in the wall up near the ceiling behind the bar. Most everyone, with the notable exception of the bartender, ignored the television, preferring the aid of far different mediums. That is, until a Doors' tape was inserted into the VCR, and then of course everyone, especially the bartender, took to it with unwavering adulation for the duration of the video. The bartender seemed altogether too young and entirely too bored, and he was still caught up in the delusion of the ponytail as an effective mechanism of fashion. And yet he was pleasant enough with the customers and efficient enough with his work so that, as a result, I decided to let that go. After all, he was pouring and I was buying and there were the dynamics of that relationship to consider. All in all, then, the Doors was exactly the kind of cliché I'd have expected to find myself in had I expected to find myself in Amsterdam at all. And with this realization set firmly in mind I felt I was somehow above it all.

We chose a high-top table over near the window, and when no one came over to take our order I eventually made my way up to the bar. They had no pink grapefruit juice, I was told. Well no problem, I thought, and not yet wanting to drink Pernod, ordered a pair of drafts instead. The draft was Heineken, drawn into small stubby glasses with great heads of foam decapitated with a small plastic wand. Two aspects of ecstasy struck me immediately, and I should probably relate these to you now. One was obviously how good or 'ecstatic' it made you feel, and how you wanted to share that feeling with most everyone around you by way of what could perhaps be best described as unbridled affection. And the second aspect of note was how much the ecstasy allowed you to swill. My Lord, but it was a great deal. I must have hooked back thirty glasses of Heineken that day alone before I realized what in fact the deal was here. Gracie and I talked about everything. Not only amongst ourselves, but with others too. We had a good table, with a close proximity to the door, and with Gracie sitting near the entrance we soon had many different folks wandering over. She was like a magnet, that girl, she really was, not only for the men but for the women as well. Gracie, too, was greatly enhanced by the effects of ecstasy. She fit right in at the Doors. What with walls stained yellow and covered in currency she was everything that place was built for.

I don't know what this is, this insatiable need I feel to reinvent myself when out on the road. Perhaps it reflects a certain creativity, or else the need for an immediate change of course. Or perhaps it simply represents the opportunity to mask the reality of my own dreary self in the dream of someone more. Whatever the reason, whatever the pretext to this need for reinvention, it comes in much larger doses when out on the road. And tell a lie enough times and, well, so the story goes.

This one girl we met that day was an English model. Well of course she was. Another was a junior editor for a fashion magazine.

And these two young fellows from America here, why, they worked for some multinational conglomerate of dubious achievement not to mention questionable existence. I met this one fellow from Australia who, minus the ecstasy and his outspoken crusade for clothing made of hemp, would have undoubtedly proved one hell of a bore. He had that long stringy hair and those long traveller's sideburns that lent his face a perpetual expression of poverty, and his bottom lip, when not wrapped snugly around a self-rolled cigarette, bloated out whenever he spoke. He really did speak a lot that day. As for me, between fits of grinding my teeth and immersing myself in Doors' videos of dubious quality, I told this poor fellow such a slew of lies about my being a writer that he never really had a chance to refute me. The Australian himself was a blossoming young cartoonist travelling abroad on sabbatical. Well of course he was. The sabbatical, we both agreed, was an essential component of the creative process, not to mention a built-in bonus of sorts. We were all telling such wonderful lies and telling them out loud that I wondered how we'd ever managed without them. We were all living such wonderful lives that nobody even bothered to question them.

As it was, all these people had just arrived in Amsterdam that day themselves, and as such had yet to find a place to stay. Gracie offered up the beleaguered barge, and to a man they thought this a hell of a plan by the way. And so, late in the afternoon with that first bout of ecstasy wearing off, the two Americans, Gracie and I wandered the exactly two hundred twelve steps back to the barge.

I showed the two Americans where they could stow their gear. Naturally I was already playing the part. I was being awfully good in the room at the moment, something we veterans were always known for on the road of course. Actually, situations commenced and blossomed so quickly in Amsterdam that someone had to step up and take the helm. As for the two young men, they were very good at being polite behind their embarrassed American-in-Europe grins. Seemingly well aware of their countrymen's reputation abroad, they were intent on coming across as thoroughly nervous young citizens. And yet despite all that, and all that they would endure from me as insults to their country, they were actually rather good in the room, and there was certainly a future in that, I told them. The one was tall, black and altogether handsome, while the other was shorter, uglier and vaguely Hispanic. I never did bother to get their names. I could hardly get past their grins. They were just so intent on doing the right thing at every turn that, as I said, I soon got around to abusing their citizenship.

"Can we take these two here?" the black one said, indicating a pair of bunks along the left-hand wall. He was still grinning that citizen grin of his, but I decided to let it go for now.

"Absolutely," I said. "Any one you want. Though I don't recommend those ones in the middle there. They're definitely the least comfortable of the lot."

"Who do we pay?"

"Alex."

"Alex?"

"The owner."

"Any idea where might we find him?"

"Don't worry," I told them rather cryptically. "Alex, you better believe, will find you."

I turned to Gracie and smiled knowingly, and Gracie, she smiled too. In the meantime, the Hispanic cleared his throat nervously.

"Anyone know where we can score some pot?" he asked, gingerly placing his backpack near the head of the sleeper in the first bunk.

"You could have bought some up there at the coffee shop."

"What, like right over the counter? Is that shit true?"

"Oh that shit's true all right," I smiled patronizingly. "Just ask for the menu and they'll show you a whole list of supplies. I don't recommend the house bong though. Too many lips have been on that."

They asked me how much it cost.

"For the cheapest? Oh I reckon about the same as back home."

"How much is in a bag then?"

"No idea. Don't smoke. Hurts my throat, understand."

They settled in, and I eventually offered them a beer. "So you guys are American then."

"San Diego, yes," the black one said, accepting a bottle as politely as possible. "And you?"

"Lethbridge, Alberta. Either of you been there?"

"Don't think so, no," they answered together.

"No matter, not all that much to do there anyway."

"It's prairies, hey," the Hispanic ventured.

"Yes, but not all that far from the mountains," I told him, and together we drank some more.

"Canada," said the Hispanic, tipping his chin at Gracie, "I've been there."

"Oh yeah? Where?"

"Montreal, Toronto, Winnipeg, Vancouver," he said, naming them each carefully.

"So how long were you up then?"

"Just a few days," he shrugged. "On business."

We all nodded deeply at the word for a spell.

"So what do you do for work at home?" the black one asked me.

"Now? Nothing. Though I used to beat men up for a living."

"A fighter not a lover, huh?" chuckled the Hispanic nervously, obviously ignorant of the appropriate terminology.

"Something like that, yeah," I told him.

"Someone mentioned you were a writer," the black one said.

"You betcha," Gracie beamed. "He's my drinkin' fightin' writin' lovin' man."

"Man, that must be hard though," the black one said. "You know, to be so continuously creative like that."

I smiled. "Oh she's a bitch all right, but when you get her right, she's the greatest old broad in the world."

They both laughed at that, and the Hispanic turned to Gracie. "So what brings you over then? Just travelling?"

"Actually, we're looking for someone," she said. "He's gone—missing."

"Really? Here? Wow, that's going to be . . ." He looked like he was going to say something more, but then the effort of speaking so much American had apparently tired him.

CHAPTER TWENTY-FIVE

THERE ISN'T ALL that much to this game, I'd say. But then that is the secret right there. The key is the consistency of the effort, I'd say, and not so much the consistency of the final score. Each morning you score just a little bit, and if it's good, then each night you score just a little bit more. And with each day that passes, you pass along that much more of yourself, and in turn pass out just a little bit more. The point, I suppose, is to remain consistent with the effort, and in doing so, maintain a maximum purity of form. The purity of the line is the key to the discipline, and in the end discipline is what this game calls for.

Within two days of my arrival in Amsterdam I went from the person I'd been to the person I'd become—one who dealt designer drugs from the very last booth at the very back of McDonalds to acquaintances in whose company he wasn't always welcome. Now contrary to popular belief, at the time of this writing at least, drugs in Amsterdam are still quite illegal. It's just that the laws have been relaxed so far that simply doing them is considered legal. But selling them is illegal. And dealing them is illegal. And that is exactly what I'd been commissioned to do. The captaincy has been bestowed upon me in particular as I was obviously a little bit older, not to mention rather good in the room of course.

It's interesting to see how these things come together. You simply put the word out that you require something, and the market, it goes to work for you. Everyone involved is so very businesslike in their approach and handling of your needs, so very thorough and efficient, and yet never at the cost of your brotherhood, it seems. In fact, this sense of brotherhood which has seemingly sprung from nowhere is by far the most important element of the equation. There is simply this knowing between you, this common drive, this understanding that something is needed. There is no laughing, no kidding—it's all very sober and surprisingly serious—we have a buyer so where is the dealer? But then it never gets so serious that you willingly refrain from breaking out in sudden fits of laughter, wondering when you all became so theatrical. The entire scene, with its assorted series of one-way relationships and suspect characters, is just so strange in its efficiency, in its utter simplicity, that it all becomes highly intriguing. It gives you a part in something bigger, something in which you feel such an absolute kinship with all these others that you feel as though you can believe in it completely, literally, and with all of your being. It has in it that sense of something you have known somewhere before, but that you have not experienced now for some time. That something you give such a separate importance to, and rationalization for, that in comparison your own individual welfare takes on a degree of relative insignificance—indeed a topic to be avoided whenever possible in case it interferes with the deal. But by far the most important aspect of this sense of kinship is that there is always something more you can do to heighten it: you can do more ecstasy. And in doing more ecstasy, experience that same sense of expanded perspective and half-expected uncertainty that all those who abandon one life for another must deal with eventually.

Now this is not to say that I abandoned completely my search for De Boer. On the contrary, I did search the crowds as they moved past the barge, and I did search the disembodied faces as they drifted past the windows of the café. I did ride the Ferris wheel on several occasions, and I did check the carousel each and every day. In fact I did the very best I could considering my state of mind at the time—for the first time in what felt like a very long time I felt as though I really didn't care. For the first time in as long as I could remember there was absolutely no box to bear. And anyway, who was I to question the ethics of the transgression. Books were for sharing, and sharing was good karma, and any karma worth anything ought to be readily accessible through literature. So I let him go. Just like that I let him free. Free of every expectation, need and surrogate greed I had placed on him to this point—a somewhat elusive state he would enjoy for a little over three weeks at the beginning of summer while I managed little more than to chase after a whore.

There were these others on the barge now. By others I mean this freakish young couple from these islands just north of Scotland that apparently don't belong to Scotland at all. Then there was the pair of shockingly unattractive young women from Calgary who drank their vodka straight from the bottle. These two typically kept to themselves. And finally the token pair of Australians—two lean young men from Adelaide with clean-shaven faces and long matted hair. It was this last pair I took to most affectionately during my stay in Amsterdam, although I rarely referred to either by name of course.

Each day I arose from my bed around ten. The tightly stretched canvas remained uncomfortable at the best of times, and even at that time of year it was cold in the night with only a single blanket to protect me from the chill. The chill came up from the canal, up through the floor of the barge, easily penetrating the thin stretched canvas of my bunk, and each morning I promised myself that I would somehow remedy the situation for the following night, and then naturally break that promise sometime later on. Each night when I returned to my bed alone, and the lights were out, I lay there in the dark and listened. To the sounds of the canal and of the town beyond it, and to the rats scurrying about in the walls of the barge in between. I remember wondering if all rats scurried about like that, and if they did, whether they ever found anything to warrant the effort. And lying in my sagging canvas bed on a barge on the Singel Canal in Amsterdam I thought how different things might have been. If I could only have behaved a little differently, or else kept my head in a few key situations. I suppose it was instinct more than anything. No, more than anything it was a lack of control. Or if I had control, then perhaps I had relinquished some vital part of it a long, long time ago. Either way, there were times when you had to fight, no matter what the stakes. Men fight—there is a part of man that needs to fight—and to ignore that fact is to turn your back on what might very well prove your undoing.

And then, in the morning, when I'd finally awake, I always returned once more to my discipline. Staggering the two hundred twelve steps up to the store to purchase some orange juice, the occasional banana, and something for the inevitable headache waiting in the wings. The bakery waited across the street. Typically I went with the pastries, however occasionally a bagel would do. Finally I wandered the two hundred twelve steps back to the barge where I promptly swallowed my pill. And that was it. That was the extent of my daily Amsterdam discipline. The nights were far different though.

One night we were all sitting around the barge getting high. We had been getting high all morning and afternoon, and now of course the bar had been raised substantially. Gracie and the Americans had just taken more ecstasy, and were now following that up with some pot. As for me, I was still faring quite well with my own fix from earlier that day. Still, it was beginning to subside. The tide was starting to turn. And suddenly I was painfully aware of my hunger for actual food. That couple from those islands just north of Scotland had set up camp in the middle of the floor. The young male of the pair consumed so much pot in one sitting that he would often pass out right there on the floor. Over here, the two Americans were trying their American best with that hideous young pair from Calgary. Hideous being really no exaggeration here—they were both convinced they were witches. I suppose that's simply the way they talk these days, but in my day we called them bitches.

Outside, on the landing, it was getting dark, and the two young Australians were sitting on the couch. I could just make out their Quiksilver silhouettes behind the bright red glow of their stained yellow cigarette mouths. I stepped up off the barge and up alongside the Singel to where a string of lights described an arc up ahead. I approached the lights and the bridge across the canal they illuminated, and looked around half-heartedly for some sign of my friend.

I never really realized how young Gracie was. That's what I was thinking as I went up alongside the canal, feeling the very margins of myself. But then fully half the things any girl says when stoned are intended for her very next book of verse of course. I came to the lights of the bridge and leaned out over the stone rail, gazing up the length of the canal. In the distance I could see strings of lights at regular intervals—more bridges making the compulsory leap across the canal—while below me the water ran smooth and black beneath the bridge, making no sound as it passed. Meanwhile, a man and woman passed behind me holding hands, laughing quietly to themselves. I watched them drift away in the dark, drifting from themselves to dusky silhouettes of themselves to a single apparition floating of its own free will, and finally to nothing but the echo of some well chosen words drifting off into the night somewhere.

I crossed the bridge. By and by I came to the next canal, stopping just long enough to urinate against a set of ascending stairs. The sky was clear and the air was warm and I could smell my urine soaking the stones. Afterwards I followed the canal all the way up to an open square where the streetlights shone down through the leaves of the trees. Beneath the trees, a pair of matching white tour buses disgorged clots of senior citizens, and I walked over and joined in with the first of these there. We walked together across the square. Except for the lights filtering down through the trees it was mostly dark in there. Then I noticed these other lights, red lights, in the windows of the arcade surrounding the square. Through these windows I could see girls dancing. They all looked like Gracie in there. They were young, and Asian, and they were all dancing naked under the red lights of the square. Outside, on the streets, people were drinking and watching. I followed the group of senior citizens there. They were tourists from America having a good time, and they were touring about in the square.

I followed the group of senior citizens up the road and finally free of the square, and eventually we came to a walkway that crossed the canals one after another, heading off in the direction of the Ferris wheel. Arriving at the Ferris wheel, I didn't feel much like taking a ride. I meandered over to the carousel instead. It was an old carousel, in poor condition and in need of some paint, but the music came out a little better. There were a couple of children riding the carousel, along with an assortment of grungy looking drug addicts and waifs. I felt sorry for those children just then, forced to ride those big, red, rather beat-up looking horses in the company of such obvious degenerates. I watched them go around. There were only about five or six of them going around. But they were ruining it for the rest of us just the same.

"What kind are you?" asked a voice near at hand, and I turned to find one of the senior citizen tourists, a short, bow-legged fellow with dark wrinkled skin beneath a baseball cap that said Fighting Irish.

"The kind that drinks too much," I said.

"I meant what tribe?"

"I'd rather not say."

"Why not?"

"Because you'd find a way to hold me against them," I said.

I didn't see those tourists again until one afternoon a few days later. I was sitting outside the Doors reading my book, sitting there waiting for Gracie. She hadn't arrived when she'd said she would, but naturally I thought nothing of that. I returned to my book while I waited and when the bartender came up, ordered two more glasses of Heineken.

Gracie didn't turn up, and after finishing my beer I eventually returned to the barge. Along the way, I saw that same group of senior citizens shuffling quietly into the Bulldog café. I watched them a while through the window, watching them shake their heads in unison and wonder. I wanted to go in and find that Indian, that one with the Fighting Irish baseball cap I'd spoken with a few days earlier. But then I didn't know what I would say to him. Besides, I only wanted to meet him so that I might write about him one day. One day in the future when my imagination had absorbed him enough and worked him over enough to write about him truly and with an appropriate clarity. The only good writing is that achieved through experience—or so at least I had read—this so that your imagination can evolve the proper framework of authenticity in which to properly ground the fictional characters. It's important there be at least some truth to the story, I'd read, that way ensuring the highest level of entertainment and impact from the remainder. I didn't know how that Indian would fit into my story, only that he would, and that he would smile knowingly and stare stoically as all good Indians should.

Unfortunately, I couldn't find him anywhere. I checked my wrist where my watch would have been, and guesstimated it to be about six-thirty. Back on the barge, though most of the others were in, there was still no sign of Gracie. Someone said he thought she'd gone off to the Grasshopper with the Yanks. Someone else agreed whole-heartedly.

The young man from those islands just north of Scotland asked if I wanted to partake of some smoke. No thanks. Why not? Hurts my throat. One of the girls, whose name was Sue, offered me some cake. What is it? Try it, she said, it tastes like chocolate. I was hungry and felt like eating so I did. How much should I have? Have you ever had it before? Never. You're a big guy so have a whole piece.

I did and Sue was right: it did taste like chocolate. Chocolate and seed. I say seed here only because of the obvious connotations of grass, and one should always be subtle in such situations as these. The cake didn't taste very good, but I went about eating it anyway. I was really very hungry and this was the first real thing I'd eaten all day.

I sat down on my bunk and slid to the back to watch some of the others come in. Where's Gracie? I asked. I told you she's at the Grasshopper, someone said. The one from those islands offered me something else just then. What's this? Don't worry, he said, just put it on your tongue. I did and proceeded to forget about it entirely. Where'd this beer come from? I gave it to you, one of the Australians said. The young man on the floor giggled something I couldn't quite comprehend. I watched his face change in the light as others came wandering in. A circle was forming on the floor and over the bunks but Gracie wasn't part of the configuration.

When I asked where Gracie was, one of the Australians said something about grasshoppers. Thinking he was offering me some new drug, I said no thanks, and together they all had a good long chuckle over that. I chuckled along with them, although I had no idea what at, and wouldn't you know it but everything was by candlelight after that.

Two pipes and a bong were making the rounds, as well as a pair of joints the size and approximate shape of my middle finger. A plateful of cake arrived and made its way into the mix, and when the cake was gone, someone crushed some ecstasy into a fine white powder and formed the powder into thin white lines on the back of the plate. This, too, made its way into the circle. As for me, I passed on the plate. I could feel it coming. It was a long time coming. Here it comes. There it goes. Someone offered me a bottle of vodka and I accepted without reservation. It was clear and lukewarm and I gagged more than once, but it tasted just like the Sault going down.

Who'd I go down on? Sue asked with a laugh. No, I said Sault. Sioux. Whatever, I said, and when someone else came in I asked where Gracie might be. What's the matter, Billy? Nothing. Nothing's the matter. Just looking for her, that's all.

I tried not to look at the fellow from those islands just north of Scotland that apparently don't belong to Scotland at all. He was sitting on the floor looking up at me, but he was beginning to look very peculiar now. The table was full of candles and bottles, and rats were scurrying about in the walls. And those girls from Calgary, Sue and her friend, while sitting quietly on their shared bunk, were occasionally reaching over to massage each other's shoulders when a sort of subdued sexuality eased itself onto the barge. In that sort of halfway high that permits you to participate in any given scene, yet remain somehow partially detached, I watched as this energy of repressed sexuality began slowly to rise, radiating out to explore the room along suddenly very rigid, somehow almost crystalline lines. And this very same sensation, or its reciprocal, following inwardly the same irrefutable laws along the same irrefutable lines, sprung up inside me as my entire body began to actualize the dictates of a medium it had never before experienced firsthand. That which I could call myself contracted inward and away from my body's previously existent boundaries towards a bright centre of absolute understanding and conviction. And this tighter leaner core, ever smaller and increasingly concentrated, offset and indeed negotiated the web of sticky sensuality now on display on the barge. The smaller and harder and more concentrated I became, the more overtly soft and sexual appeared the scene from which I was currently being exorcised, and I felt for all the world like I was suddenly being born again.

What's a moor? No, I said *tour.* Have you been on the Heineken *tour.* What the hell's he on about? I asked with a laugh. What's the matter, Billy? Nothing, absolutely nothing—why? I asked. And as I looked down at that fellow alone on the floor, alone on his island, I thought to myself: Remember, Indians don't fight at night.

Don't fight who? Holy shit, I said, and tried to ignore the obviously telepathic Hispanic by concentrating more carefully on the fellow from those islands just sitting there on the floor. Speaking of which, I said, want to know something? I haven't taken a shit for three days. Sound like a problem? Well it isn't. I haven't eaten for four, except for cake.

I smiled with embarrassment as most everyone began to laugh at me then.

What's the matter with you, Billy? He's gone, someone said. I felt in my pocket and handed someone a hundred guilders. Bet on number five, will you? That's number five in the fifth. And if he wins, I said, take half for yourself. Here, Billy, have some more cake. I looked hard at her, this Sue from Calgary, currently sprawled out over her friend on the bed. She immediately pulled the cake away. Indian giver, I said.

What's that? Sue asked, tentatively handing it back. Don't look a gift-horse in the mouth, that's what I always say. He's thoroughly wasted, someone said. No, she's not. Not what? A thoroughbred, I said. I mean look at her—legs like sticks and lungs to match—she's a bleeder, and lucky to run seventh in a field of six, I bet.

Better eat, someone said, and so I ate some more cake. But all the time I was eating I was watching the others watching me, everyone except for that one from those islands just north of Scotland just sitting there on the floor at my feet. Every time I tried to catch him looking, he managed to catch me first, and it was all I could do to smile knowingly—just like the Mona Lisa would have, I said.

Lisa would have what? he asked, placing his hand on my leg only to pull it instantly away. Forget it, I said. Take the horns by the bull, that's what I always say.

Someone offered me a pipe. What do you think, Billy? What do *I* think? What is it, a peace pipe? Well no use shutting the barn door once he's out of the stable—here goes, I said, and inhaled deeply.

What do you think, Billy? Pot. P-O-T. Pots and pans, I said. What the hell is it anyway? African Haze. African *what*? Wheelchair weed, someone said. It hurts my throat, I said. Then as I removed my false front teeth and grinned and people laughed, from out of these hopeless depths Gracie appeared.

Hello, you bums, she said.

What do you mean? I asked, watching her approach. She had appeared so suddenly, and now approached so slowly, that I had this faint and funny feeling that she was somehow being made along the way. After a while in fact she got to be several inches tall, and I was proud with my part in her creation. She moved closer and closer, but beyond a certain point never became any taller, so I supposed that was how tall she was after all.

What do you mean, what do I mean? she said. I just said hello, that's all. She looked around at the others and shrugged. I'd never seen such eyes on an Asian before.

Look, Gracie, we either hang together or get strung up separately—it's your call, I said, and from what still seemed like a very long distance off she leaned forward and kissed me on the cheek, on the lips, and then somehow deep inside my mouth. Her tongue felt thick and rough and altogether unnatural as it rapidly explored my teeth and their assorted fillings. I wanted very much to bite down. It took everything I had not to bite down. Right up until my teeth clicked together with a resounding clash.

I continued to hit and miss the many different disciplines as they made their way around the circle. This hit-and-miss approach proved very good discipline in itself as I was rewarded with not becoming physically ill. Still, I began to grow paranoid. Suddenly I was all but saddled with the stuff. I tried to convince myself that it was all just the drugs, and that it would all soon pass, but I simply couldn't convince myself of that fact enough. I was watching them all from the safety of my bunk, and in the course of sampling the various drugs they all seemed to be watching me themselves. There was something innately strange about this group, I now saw, something not quite right, as though they were part of some secret inner circle I had never been asked to be a part of, or indeed, even remotely suspected to this point. The members of this tight-knit group seemed to alter their appearances from one moment to the next, becoming for brief flashes people completely unfamiliar to me, speaking in meanings much deeper and far more intensely real than any I had known previously, conveying a message that was altogether pressing and, for the time being anyway, entirely incomprehensible. What I mean to say is, that due to my lack of temporal relations, they were saying things I could no longer understand and saying them in no particular sequence. So then I began to think that maybe they were onto me. Just that—that maybe they were onto me—whatever that meant and whatever the ramifications might be. Whole volumes of thought swept past me in this quiet undulating manner, hinting at meanings upon meanings and levels of reality I had never really thought possible, all of which whispered of a conspiracy of truly epic proportions to which my simple trusting eyes and simple trusting mind had been entirely blind before. As though my entire life to this point had been nothing but a dream, or rather, that this barge and all these people on it were real and alive and what really mattered and that I alone was the dream—an insignificant minority suffering inside his self-induced prison who had never really touched anyone or anything meaningfully.

Turning in my bunk, I stretched out lengthwise on my stomach, placing my feet down through the bars at the end. Through the bunk, down through the floor of the barge and the canal, I felt somewhere an engine start, feeling it engage and accelerate, moving steadily up the Singel, at which point I happened to glance around just in time to find the black American hovering suspiciously over my legs. He was talking and the others were listening and I simply wasn't getting the gist of the conversation. My thinking at this point was incredibly crystallized and altogether mathematical, and yet the equations I was forming all featured myself as their common denominator, and so I recognized all these people for what they were: an underground sex-slave trade ring. So they're in on it too, I decided. Here I am alone in this town and this is how they got you: they brought you in, and they brought it out, and then they took you out to pasture just as they pleased. I wondered what all they would do to me. Sell me further into their underground sex-slave trade ring, no doubt. And what a perfect cover, I thought, having a black man around to deflect any and all suspicion of wrongdoing on their part.

Scrutinizing my enemies, I wondered when they would strike. I shifted in my canvas, feeling my boots get caught up in the harness at the end—well they certainly have me where they want me now, I thought. They're waiting for me to pass out—I knew this, I *knew* it— and when I do pass out they'll tie me up and remove all my clothes. I tried to kick myself free but my feet were stuck: I could feel the black one's hand gripping my ankles as with the other hand he lifted the branding iron up. With great effort I pulled myself free of his grip and struggled up to my feet. Someone asked me where I was off to now.

Out for some air, I said.

Just then the first-bunk sleeper awakened, standing up unsteadily alongside his bunk. It was the first time I'd seen him vertical. To be honest, it was the first time I'd seen him do anything at all. He was Greek, and groggy-looking, and spilt forth fat and flaccid from the stretched-tight confines of his boxer shorts. And standing there between the door and me, he was just enough to evoke my most violent of retorts.

I bull-rushed him. To his credit, however, he easily sidestepped the stampede, and I went flying out the door headfirst. Scrambling to my feet, I perceived immediately, in the diffuse elastic light of the canal, two figures seated on the floor of the landing smoking in silence, their backs against the couch for support. Full of friendliness, they were sure I had something interesting to say—why would I appear on the landing in such a way if I had nothing interesting to say?—but I had nothing to say, and ignoring their bleated enquiries, scrambled up the ladder and across the street to a set of stairs going up. There were only about a dozen or so stairs going up. And yet, sitting there at the top, I was afforded a fairly decent view of the altogether dubious reality of my environment. I awaited the inevitable attack. Naturally there was no way I was going to go down without a fight, but then what sort of opponent would I make? I could hardly stand, let alone swing. Still, I thought, they have no idea what they're in for with me.

I waited. And waited. I must have waited for hours like that, feeling the victim of a set of circumstances far too vast to even contemplate. Sometimes I would hear footsteps scuffling up behind me, and turning suddenly, find nothing of interest. At other times I would realize that the scuffling was not behind me but in front of me, and that I was no longer eluding but following the pricks. And always I would hear their voices plotting down between parked cars, only to scatter at faraway sirens.

I should probably go check on Gracie, I heard myself say later on, having consolidated enough of my reason, or what was passing as reason, into one more or less concrete thought. There's no way she could be in on all this, I thought, although the rest of them obviously are. Maybe she's in trouble on the barge. I tried to think rationally on the subject—it proved tough sledding—but one thing was certain: I had to get back on that barge. And with that in mind I cautiously descended the dozen or so steps to the street and negotiated the remainder of the gulf to the edge of the canal. Suddenly, though, the door of the barge swung open, and a knife blade of candlelight slashed out over the landing, sending me scampering back to the sanctuary of the stairs. No one was coming. No one came. A false alarm then. And so, searching painstakingly under each and every car within potential ambush range, I made my way cautiously back to the barge. Peering over the edge, I found the landing empty. I would just have to muster up the courage and look inside. That's all that can be expected of someone in my situation, I told myself. Although of course the girl was my responsibility in the end.

Still skittish, I made my way slowly down the ladder onto the landing and over to the open door. At first it was difficult to make out what was happening in there. Sometimes you happen upon a scene so strange, so utterly extraordinary, that you don't have the ability to comprehend it in full—either by acquiring a dim sense of the whole and then fitting in the pieces, or else by adding up the pieces until the essence of the scene makes itself more readily accessible. Standing there on the threshold of that barge, I paused a moment to drink it all in. I was only able to fit a few of the pieces together—they were dancing, though, that much was obvious right away. Or not actually dancing, but standing in a circle around a single glass of water, a secretly interconnected mass of humanity shifting its weight in unison from one foot to the other—hoping to see the water level shift, I'm guessing. Now perhaps such a scene would not have seemed so utterly fantastic, or ludicrous, or both, had I not suddenly observed the first-bunk sleeper blowing his nose into a pair of red plaid boxer shorts. He looked just so peaceful, just so completely natural and content blowing his nose into a pair of red plaid boxer shorts, as if he'd been doing so now for years, generations really, that suddenly it occurred to me that I'd been standing here on this barge, in exactly this position and context, for an incalculable length of time—my whole life nearly. At least that's the way it seemed to me at the time. But now, as I filter it through the sentimentality of memory, I realize that the entire scene and its various participants belonged to a fleeting and pastoral world where you could remain all day in bed on a barge in your underwear surrounded by strangers and not be considered a lesser man for it.

I called out to Gracie to see if she were all right. She said she was feeling just fine. She said I should join them. I said no thanks. And satisfied with my investigation, albeit not at all with my findings, I immediately aborted the rescue attempt and clambered back off the barge and over to the sanctuary of the stairs one more time.

After a while, however, with no more whispered voices or rapidly approaching footsteps, I began to entertain the thought that maybe, just maybe, I'd made it all up. But still I remained somewhat unconvinced. I mean something was obviously up. Still, I was glad to know that Gracie was safe, and within the hour mustered enough courage to walk the two hundred twelve steps up to the Doors. Once there, I order myself a single glass of Heineken, and in lieu of a second, a handful of Twix chocolate bars. I thought about heading over to the carousel. It might do me some good to see the children and the horses, I thought, or better yet, the lights of the town from way up high on the Ferris wheel. Finally, but by no means suddenly, sitting there alone at one of the sad looking tables, I shamefully crawled down from my high. The Twix helped. And eventually, feeling altogether foolish, I made my way back to the barge.

"Where'd you go?" asked Gracie upon my arrival.

"Out for a walk."

"You all right?"

"Just a bit of paranoia, that's all."

"You want some McDonalds? The guys are taking orders."

"I wouldn't mind some fries. And Gracie?"

"Yeah?"

"What's this all about?"

"What's what all about?"

"This," I said. "This whole thing here with you and me."

She looked up at me with those languid elongated eyes of hers. "I don't understand what you're saying, Billy."

"Look, just tell me the first thing that comes into your head when you think about me. No matter how silly it is, just say it. Please."

She reached up and kissed me, once, on the cheek. "Don't do this to yourself, Billy. It's not worth it. *I'm* not worth it. And besides, it wouldn't make any difference if—"

"But I'm not even a hockey player anymore," I said.

Grinding her teeth, she smiled up at me with some sort of acid understanding, seeming much older and somehow wiser than she was. "No, Billy, you're not. You're one of us now. And that's something you're just going to have to learn to live with, I guess."

CHAPTER TWENTY-SIX

THE DAY I left Amsterdam a very strange thing happened to me. As I had yet to experience anything more disturbing or adverse than that afforded by my own sordid activities, and as I had yet to locate that which I had come for—namely, De Boer—I still had no intention of leaving at this point—that is, until this very strange thing happened to me up near the train station where I had first entered Amsterdam proper some three weeks before. Until this thing happened to me, I had no idea it was coming, or indeed how very strange it would be. Or if I did, I certainly had no idea how immediate thereafter my departure would be. Until this thing happened to me, I was determined to wait as long as it would take to procure the desired result, and in the meantime make a go of it with Gracie. Indeed, until this very strange thing happened up near the train station I had always prided myself on my ability to avoid confrontation whenever it suited me.

When it happened, I was walking along near the Centraal Station where the others had sent me to acquire more ecstasy. It was the middle of the afternoon, and although there were some witnesses around to verify my experience, no one seemed to notice, or if they did notice, then no one seemed to care particularly. I was walking along in front of this seemingly respectable hotel adjacent to the train station when a green wine bottle suddenly flicked past my nose to smash against the wall on my left. That this bottle missed my head by no more than a fraction of an inch is the only reason I'm able to confess this story to you presently. I turned to find a short Middle Eastern man in a green military jacket moving aggressively towards me, sporting yet another green wine bottle (half-full) and only one eye (the left), the muscles of the raw and uncovered right twitching and bulging along as by common consent. The stare of his one good eye held me momentarily, until I realized what it was he was yelling: "Fuck you, American" at the top of his lungs, and in an accent with which I was completely unfamiliar at the time.

"Take it easy," I told him, backing away to the wall. "Just take it easy, my friend."

He came closer, and as he did the rest of his face came unfortunately into focus. Sweat-soaked lips pulled back in a nasty snarl, revealing enormous yellow teeth protruding from enormous yellow gums that had quite obviously been infected for months, perhaps even years. I wondered what had happened to his eye. I wondered why he wouldn't wear a patch. Still, there was this other eye at least, and I tried my best to focus on that.

"Fuck you, American."

I didn't say anything, but continued to hold my hands out before me just so. He was waving his half-full wine bottle at me now, slowly and rhythmically, and at this range, if he should choose to unload it, I didn't like my chances of avoiding the blow. Then I noticed another man, this one loping along perhaps twenty paces behind. That these two were a pair was obvious at once, although this second one, like the second socket, seemed somewhat empty of malice if not entirely of ugliness, and therefore content, for the time being at least, to simply follow the performance of the first.

"Fuck you, American," the first one said, the muscles of his open socket continuing to twitch and bulge as the fingers of his free hand continued to close and open, now into a fist and now into an open hand. "America the reason I have no eye."

Again I said nothing, choosing instead to focus exclusively on this half-full wine bottle wavering about before me. I was trying hard not to look into that one empty socket, and the wine bottle aided greatly in that. And all the while I was thinking, thinking hard of some way to get past him, and all the while I was thinking I was retreating slowly and uncertain.

"America takes my eye," he said. "Your America the reason I have no *eye.*"

"All right, all right," I said, still focused on this one wine bottle wavering about before me, still refusing to look into that one empty socket. I thought that if I could hit him as hard as possible I could probably get away with it and, conceivably, far away from here.

"America takes my eye!" he screamed, crying now, and around the empty socket tears pooled unpleasantly. He swiped his empty hand through the air, adding threateningly, "America takes my eye and so I fight them here."

"Well maybe that's not the best way of handling it," I said, not too wisely it turns out.

It was a delicate moment. He grinned at me, gap-toothed, and I thought for a second that I might just be making some sort of progress here.

"Well maybe I fight you and you join them," he suggested, dispelling that fantasy immediately.

"I'd rather you not."

He looked at me, tilting his chin as if to gain a fresh perspective on things. "Maybe I fight you now and make me feel better about things."

"Like I said, I'd rather you not."

I entertained a series of final thoughts. Eventually I came to the conclusion that this was the time to hit him, wine bottle or not, and I was moving into position to accomplish the task when out of nowhere he shrugged, "All right, I let you go then."

"Thank you," I said. "Thanks a lot."

"But first you give me five guilders."

"What? No way."

"Give me five guilders," he repeated, and I told him that, wine bottle or no wine bottle, I wasn't about to give him anything.

Once more I began to retreat, and when I did, he retrieved something from the pocket of his coat. "You know what this is?" he said, elevating the syringe for my inspection. "This is high-five. Positive *high-five.*"

Behind him his friend laughed drunkenly. Meanwhile, One Eye held the thick blood-filled syringe up before me, and with its appearance all thoughts of hitting him disappeared entirely. "You give me five guilders and maybe I forget I see America today."

"No way."

"Come on, give me five guilders," he said, moving forward, matching my rate of retreat to whatever was behind me. "It's just five guilders."

He stopped a moment. Then, approaching the problem almost elliptically, inquired, "Is it worth you life?"

"Pardon?"

"Five guilders," he said. "Is it worth your life."

"No, it's not. It's most definitely not. But I'm still not giving it to you," I maintained, and quite rightly.

He moved slowly towards me as I backed away. Trying not to look into that socket, I instead watched the syringe dance up and away. I remember it dancing back down around my face when I first felt something slide open behind me, and stumbling back quickly into the hotel lobby watched the glass doors slide automatically closed between me and my adversary. He didn't follow me in, and neither did his friend, and so I retreated into the lobby, all the way to the reception desk apparently. As mentioned, it was a nice hotel—very clean and very well appointed—and I explained to the nice young lady working behind the desk what had in fact happened, and she listened with what seemed like the concierge's respectful concern and genuine empathy.

I asked her to call the police.

"I am sorry, sir."

"But he just threatened to stab me with a needle. He just threatened to *kill* me."

"I am sorry, sir, but this is Amsterdam. It takes a lot in Amsterdam," she told me.

I chanced a quick glance outside. There he was, alone, just beyond the glass doors, shouting obscenities and threats to my life while dancing about with his bottle and his syringe. I checked into the hotel and got myself a room on the very top floor, far away from him. Safely installed in my room, I sat on the edge of the bed cracking my knuckles and watching European MTV a while. I thought about calling someone. Anyone. But then really, who could I call? In the end I called Dominic Reid at home. No one answered. I left a message. And waiting for the Englishman to return my call, I lay down on the bed and tried to sleep, but it wasn't a very comfortable bed, and so I ended up pacing around the room instead. It was a square room, nearly a perfect cube, and none of the windows would open. They were double-paned windows and well-insulated, and through them I could hear absolutely nothing of the outside world. Additionally, and as luck would have it, the air-conditioning seemed to be out of order. I called down to the front desk to complain about the broken air-conditioning and the ineffective windows of the tight little box they'd installed me in, and the lady said she'd send someone up shortly to deal with my unfortunate but, for whatever reason, not entirely unexpected situation.

After an hour or so of waiting without seeing anyone, I checked myself out of the hotel. Peering out from the sliding glass doors of the hotel lobby, I could see my adversary sitting at his bench and laughing with his friend, tilting back his seemingly bottomless wine bottle. I stepped out from the lobby and into the street, heading immediately in the opposite direction. Offering him and his companion a respectful berth, I took the long way back to the barge by way of the carousel, past the station. By the time I arrived at the barge, most everyone had left. All the really fun ones were gone. The sleeper in the first bunk, he was still there of course. Gracie, however, she was nowhere to be found. Probably out with the black one, I thought as I went about collecting my things. And it was then that Krista the South African showed up.

"Where are you off to then?"

"Home, Krista. I'm going home."

"So soon?" she said, leaning out the door to indicate where a pair of young men might park her bicycle before coming onboard.

"I've been here three weeks."

"Yeah, but usually it's longer though."

"What are you talking about," I said. "I've never even *been* here before."

"Yeah, I know. It's just that guys like you usually stay longer, that's all."

I shrugged and moved past her to the ladder. Then I stopped. "Listen, Krista, could you do me a favour?" I opened my wallet and extracted a wad. "There's five hundred some-odd guilders here," I said, "and I want you to give it to Gracie as soon as you see her. Can I trust you to do that?"

"What, she's not going with you?"

"No, I think she's probably staying on here."

"She likes it here then, I reckon," Krista smiled knowingly, folding the money once and tucking it away.

"I reckon she does," I said, looking up the length of the canal. It was a grey day, and the water too looked grey, and in my mind vaguely unnatural.

"Yeah, well, I'm sorry it didn't work out for the two of you."

"It's nothing."

"Yeah, well, it's sad anyway."

"In a way, I suppose," I said. And pack in hand I walked off the barge, over the nearest bridge and across the canal, taking the long way around to the station, by way of the carousel.

BOOK FOUR

CHAPTER TWENTY-SEVEN

THAT PLACE. IT was both strange and comforting to be returning to that place. And as I'd never yet written about that place as eventually I would, never yet writing about it in a way that showed how I understood it enough to write it well, and as I'd yet to discipline myself into seeing things as they happened—not simply as a spectator but as an observer who would later dictate it as it was, more real than it was, and not merely as it had been—I did not bother to watch it all come into view through the window of the plane. I did not watch the glaciers of the blue-green mountains relinquish control to the green foothills and greener valleys from which the yellow fields came strolling out unattended, nor did I watch the long grey roads laid out like an iron latticework in between. I did not watch the mottled grey suburbs overwhelm those same green hills and valleys before making a final desperate ill-fated run at the snow-capped coastal mountain range, nor did I watch the city itself sprouting up somewhere in between—its highways and its bridges swelling up so rapidly beneath the belly of the plane straining on its slow downward trajectory before touching down ever so gracefully on the tarmac again. I paid no attention to the stewardess with her tall awkward arrangement of immigrant hair telling us to remain seated with our seatbelts fastened until we were safely docked at the terminal, nor did I pay much attention to the prettier younger stewardess requesting my empty liquor bottles who, after being refused said liquor bottles, turned an embarrassed and angry red towards the immigrant one as if to complain—the immigrant one smiling coolly and plainly as, souvenirs in hand, I

calmly exited the plane. I paid no attention whatsoever to the young
child being carried over his father's shoulder before me, his nose
running crusty beneath a Kansas City Chiefs baseball cap, nor did I
pay much attention to the ground crew at work outside—the one
member berating the other over an obvious lack of workmanlike discipline and pride. I paid no attention to the young man watching me
from the corner of his eye to see if I was really that one, that one who
had fought so hard and so often for so long, nor to his mentioning
this fact to his girlfriend before chuckling something under his breath
and falling casually into line behind me. I paid little if any attention
to any of these things that meant real observation albeit painful eval-
uation as I'd as yet no idea how I would later wish to write about that
place, and how very much one needed to think clearly about something as it happened and not just see it happen in order to write it
well. And realizing this as I struggled drunkenly down the long hallway towards the terminal, I began to observe all those things around
me as much as possible, with as much conviction and discipline as
possible, framing them in so as to get them right if indeed I should
choose to write about them later at the café. And there were many
such photographs on the airport walls that day.

As soon as I returned to Vancouver, I learned that De Boer was
neither dead nor lost but in fact splitting time between New York and
Los Angeles. After disappearing in the Netherlands, he'd shown up
in Prague seven days later for his scheduled flight home, apparently
no worse for wear for the escapade barring perhaps a vague technical
awareness that he couldn't run from our collective fate anymore. He
never did bother to explain his whereabouts, nor his reasons for suddenly running off, except to say that some cousin in Rotterdam was
apparently a Born Again Christian *again* and therefore no fun whatsoever anymore. And waiting for De Boer to return to Vancouver, I
spent most of my days reading under the high vaulted ceiling of the
hotel café, or else drinking alongside Mitch at the long scratched steel
bar at Stone's opposite Fisk and Melanie. Melanie and I didn't speak
much anymore, as for some time now she'd wanted nothing to do
with me. Mitch asked about Gracie. I said I didn't know. The last

time I'd seen her she was sleeping in a black man's bunk on a barge on the Singel Canal. Sometimes even now I wonder what happened to her, but then wondering about something like that can get a guy in an awful lot of trouble in here.

Gavin returned from Los Angeles a week or so later, some five days after the first draft of the *Vanity Fair* article, together with a long excerpt from the novel, arrived at the hotel for De Boer's preliminary perusal. Chris, however, for whatever reason, had not accompanied Gavin home. On top of that, our telephone at the hotel was ringing off the hook, and so I soon stopped answering it altogether. It was getting all built-up like that. Speaking of the December issue, well it was to be a real piece of work all right; Aimee Reid's article a real piece of crap. Outlining a promising future, colouring in an irreverent past, it would offer a good sell if nothing else—and sell him they did for that was the task. As for the prospective cover, it featured, surprisingly or not, the newly appointed author and artistic crossover sensation Ethan Hawke standing sullenly on the roof of some highrise in suit and tie—a rather unattractive tie at that—with what appeared to be a fog-filled New York skyline in behind. Naturally it would go on to sell well. How could it not with the sensational Mr Hawke hawking himself like that.

Sitting near the rear of the long scratched steel bar, his eyes rimmed a telling red, Gavin yawned a "How 'bout a beer there, comrade?" at Fisk, and upon receiving said beer proceeded to ram the accompanying lime down its long narrow neck. I can only hope the same fate might befall him soon, I imagined myself saying aloud to a roomful of surprised but appreciative laughter.

"So when's Chris coming back?" I heard myself ask instead.

"What's that? Oh, not sure he is, to tell you the truth. How about another lime there, comrade? Cheers. I mean it's utterly fantastic when you think about it. It really is. Not to mention utterly well deserved." Gavin shook his head and laughed, hoisting his beer for a toast. "Look at that," he gasped, indicating his trembling hand. "Oh dear, that's not good. Must get more sleep. Still, I've never seen anything quite like it before. Not for a book at least." Did any of us realize that by the way? That this was a *book* we were talking about here? Or was Gavin the only one who thought this was all just a little bit—oh how should he put it—bizarre. "Comrade Fisk, another round down here at your leisure."

"You're just jealous," Melanie observed.

"What's that?" Gavin asked the mirror, fascinated by the handsome albeit exhausted fellow doing all of the talking and none of the listening there. "Oh yes, I know. I know I am. In fact I'm rather jealous of Bill here too." He graduated his focus to include Fisk gathering the next round together. "You know what's weird though? How neither of you seems to be talking to the other. Interesting. I think I'll delve into that a little deeper."

"Where is he then?" I asked, and his eyes slid towards me in the mirror.

"What's it to you?" he said, offering me his Gavin-in-profile once more.

"Well I was thinking of maybe meeting up with him somewhere."

"Don't bother." He shook his head and tried to belch. "Doesn't want you there. Believe me, he wants nothing to do with Buffalo Bill Purdy right now."

"What do you mean?" I asked in a voice I hardly recognized.

"Fix your eyes on my mouth, Bill: *he doesn't want you there.* He wants to be alone. And that's the joke of course. I mean he's anything *but* alone right now."

I flexed my fingers and cracked my knuckles and watched Gavin belch some more.

"Oh but don't ask me why," he eventually went on. "To be honest, I really couldn't say. All I *can* say is that he's already too far gone for me to honestly give a damn either way." But then that was hardly unexpected, was it. After all, he was the great big shining Star now. And it was awesome, in Gavin's opinion. "Don't you think so though? Don't you think it's absolutely *awe*some?"

"Oh look here," Melanie said, "the voice of reason."

"Indeed," Gavin said, smiling at himself in the mirror. "It's awesome for him though, don't you think? Don't you though? Well it is. It's awesome and it's appropriate and it *is* a book after all—honest to God, it's got pages and everything—oh dear, sounding awfully jealous again now. Sorry about that. Frightfully sorry, ladies and gentlemen. Comrades. Now where were we, comrades? In arms? In good hands? Or was I just being an ass? Speaking of which, don't bother trying to call him, Bill. After all, he's so very far above us now, frightfully removed in fact—at least five degrees in separation and climbing steadily—and hey, he just wants to be alone, that's all. I repeat, ladies and gentlemen and comrades in arms, he just wants to be left alone right now."

Gavin hooked back his beer. And eventually, when no one seemed willing to step into the breach, he said, "Now is there anything I've somehow neglected to make you aware of, comrades? Any message I've somehow failed to pass on? If there is, well then you really ought to speak up. Go on, Bill, make your query. Query up." He paused. "No? Nothing? Then I'll close on this note," he said, relaxing back into the vicinity of authenticity. "No, I really just think he's stressed, that's all."

"Well how is he? I mean does he seem all right?"

Gavin stared deeply into the mirror, trying to discern which of the ignorant creatures there had so erroneously addressed him now. Finally, having successfully identified the perpetrator, he offered her reflection one final disparaging inspection before saying, "Well he *seems* fine, Mel. Heavens, why wouldn't he though. The literary world is all *abuzz* after all." He hooked back his beer, then sighed at length, "Na, he's just stressed, that's all."

"Even from me?" I asked, regretting having said it as soon as it was out there. Still, you have never really sat at a bar until you have sat at a bar with someone like Gavin and let him insult you out loud and for others to hear. With the aid of the alcohol the individual words and phrases containing the insults gradually lose their meaning, leaving only a steady stream of syllables spewing forth from a faceless orifice. Liquor, then, although it doesn't completely eliminate the insults, does seem to diffuse some of their nastier effects somewhat.

"Especially from you," Gavin smiled with grim satisfaction prior to opening up wide, wide enough for me to see all the way down that big black hole, all the way down to his overworked asshole perhaps. "Es*pec*ially from you, Billy Boy."

"He actually said that."

"No, but I could sure as hell tell he wanted to though."

Fisk returned with another round of drinks while Melanie cleared away the contents of the glass washer. Together Mitch and I took good long pulls while Gavin took a good long look in the mirror.

"Christ, I'm tired though, comrades. Really, I am. And I really ought to get more sleep. Getting so old I need more sleep. Or is it less. . . . Doesn't matter," he shrugged, "I never sleep anymore as it is. It's my curse. And we all have our curse—even Chris."

"So when's he coming back then?"

"Oh I don't know, Bill . . . soon, I guess. Maybe later though. Sooner or later anyway, that much I do know." He giggled, opening up painfully wide before simmering down once more. "Christ, I've got to get more sleep. Really, I do. I mean all this shit over one god-damned book. AISOP *my ass*. Christ Almighty, what a load it is too."

"All of us in general, or me explicitly."

"Pardon?"

"All of us in general or me explicitly," I repeated.

"Oh no question, you're all the goddamned load," he told me, managing to maintain this serious front for all of a second before launching off once more. He continued to laugh even harder, opening up an even greater bore. "Still," he sighed at last, "I've got to write a book. I really do. I mean his is still, what, two months away, and I bet it's not even that good." He took another drink and flexed his neck in the mirror, eventually turning his attention on me. "Say, what-ever happened with you and Gracie?"

"How do you mean?"

"You know, in Amsterdam. What happened with you two in Amsterdam."

"He left her there," Melanie put in.

"Thanks, Mel. Really," I said. "I think I can handle it from here."

"What do you mean he *left her there*."

"Just that," she smiled, anticipating. "He left Gracie over there."

"You *ditched* her?" Gavin said to me.

"Sure did," answered Fisk and Melanie together.

Gavin looked from me to Mitch, and then back to me in the mirror. "Are you serious? Well what the hell's she doing then?"

"One, two, three, four," I shrugged. "Take your pick."

"And you just *ditched* her? And you're *okay* with this?" he said, whipping a hard look at Mitch. Mitch didn't blink, so I blinked for him. It was the least I could do, I guess.

"Why shouldn't he be?" I said. "I mean come on, man, he's her Daddy."

"Yeah . . ." Gavin said slowly.

"So Gracie's a whore. She's a hooker. And Mitch, being her pimp . . ."

"Mitch is her *foster father*," he told me.

"What do you mean?" I asked, and Gavin rolled back his head to laugh but nothing came out. He was long past laughing now. I looked at Mitch, then at Melanie, then at Fisk and Gavin, then finally back to my drink on the bar. "Oh well, what does it matter," I said, convinced this was simply the preamble to yet another joke at my expense.

"It matters, Billy, because she's seventeen years old," Mitch said.

CHAPTER TWENTY-EIGHT

AMONG THE MANY messages awaiting my return home that evening were a pair from the fellow in charge of my long overdue community hours, my third, forth and apparently final notices before my case was to be returned to the courts. I returned his call the very next morning, and we set up my very first appointment. I was to show up at Canuck Place the following Monday, and when I did show up, I was greeted by a very friendly staff member telling me which form to sign in order to prove that I'd actually been there performing my hours for the community. As I think I've mentioned, Canuck Place was this old Victorian house revamped into an extended care facility for sick children. Some of the children were bald, others were in wheelchairs, and all of them were dying apparently, and the one I got stuck with was unable to move her head from where it appeared to be anchored to her left shoulder. She had to speak to me from way down there. Her name, she said, was Sam, and she had just turned eight years old. I was told Sam had some sort of progressive degenerative nerve disease, and even though I'd never heard of this particular nerve disease, I knew for a fact this wasn't some sort of con she was working on as no one in their right mind would willingly place herself in such an uncomfortable position for such an extended period of time. Still, I was glad none of my ex-teammates were there as they so often were in the television commercials. I didn't know what they would think of my being there, although I did wonder that I should care.

This kid, Sam, she was a mess all right. She was wearing a Canucks' jersey, one of the old white ones with black, red and orange trim, and she asked me to sign it and I did—she was still under the impression I was playing then. I answered some of her questions, even most of her questions but certainly not all of her questions—she had a lot of questions—as some I simply had no idea what the answers were anymore. I told Sam I'd get her a new jersey if she was still around a week from now. She took that pretty well, I think. Children like that could surprise you sometimes. Still, sometimes I thought she was going to croak right there in front of me and what would *that* have done for my community hours, I wondered. Nothing, I was told by one of the nurses. He assured me it happened all the time. Besides, he said, I was just supposed to spend time with them. It wasn't like I was expected to cure them or anything like that.

One time Sam told me, from way down there on the left, that she thought I'd be different. It hurt her to speak, you could tell it did, and so she spoke awkwardly, but all things considered quite admirably and coherently, I think.

"How so?"

"Well I thought maybe you'd be more serious," she said.

"Oh I reckon I'm fairly serious, Sam. In fact I've been told I'm one of the most seriously screwed-up guys you'll find."

"And I thought you'd have blonde hair," she went on.

"Well I reckon you must be thinking of someone else then."

"Well you're the Indian one, aren't you?"

"Half Kainaiwa, yes."

"Half what?"

"Blood Blackfoot."

"Blood what?"

"Half Indian, correct," I said.

"I knew it," she smiled triumphantly.

"You did, did you. Well I reckon you're a regular little racial profiler then."

"How come you keep saying that?"

"What?"

"Reckon."

"Well probably because I do," I said.

"Do all Indians do that then?"

"All the ones in this room, sure."

"That's neat," she said. "I want to be an Indian and wreck everything too."

We watched television, Sam and I. We had a good time together in her room.

"But what about the Indian with the blonde hair?" she asked after a time.

"I don't know a lot of blonde-haired Indians, Sam."

"There's one in *Pocahontas.* Look at the box," she said, indicating a videocassette on the desk beside me, the cover of which featured a handsome young blonde man courting what appeared to be a younger black-haired Indian maiden.

"He's not Indian."

"He's not?"

"No, look at his features compared to hers. No, he's definitely white," I said.

"I thought he was Indian."

"Well he's not, he's Caucasian. He travels around and gets in adventures."

"And wrecks everything?"

"Well I don't know. I've never seen the video in question."

Sam seemed content with that. For a time at least she did. But then eventually she said, "Na, I still say he's Indian."

"Look, you want me to put the tape in? You'll be able to tell by what he says."

"What do you mean?"

"You'll be able to tell by the dialogue," I said.

"I can't hear it."

"What do you mean you can't hear it."

"My hearing's gone," she explained. "It's been gone a long time, so now I have to read lips. But it's hard to read lips from the television."

"I'm sorry."

"Huh?"

"I'M SORRY," I articulated loudly, and she started to laugh, only to have it congeal all too quickly into a loose rumbling cough.

"I can always make you guys do that," she eventually hacked.

"Funny. Funny little Sam," I said, and she frowned.

"Now you're too serious."

"Well I reckon I'm just like you thought I'd be then."

"Actually, I thought you'd wear a tuxedo."

"Tuxedo?" I said, sitting up stiffly. "Why, do the other players wear tuxedos?"

"No, just you. I figured you're so serious because you're going to an important meeting afterwards."

"Oh yeah? What else'd you figure?" I said, relaxing back into my soft, fuzzy Scooby Doo chair.

"That you'd have paperwork."

"Paperwork? What kind of paperwork?"

"I don't know," she shrugged. "Just paperwork. For all the stuff you do when you're not playing hockey and helping kids like me."

"And what stuff should I do, Sam?"

She considered that a moment. "You should make buses," she concluded.

"Buses? Why buses?"

"Then you wouldn't be so late all the time. Or wreck everything like you do," she said and I laughed, and fairly soon I was crying I was laughing so hard. And Sam, she was laughing too. In fact she laughed so hard and so long that eventually it hurt her too much to continue. We talked some more about this and that until finally she fell asleep. I watched her sleep with her head anchored down to her shoulder. She had sandy yellow hair and plenty of freckles, and I found myself wondering, briefly, if she had freckles all over.

Ten straight days I went back to see Sam at Canuck Place until they told me not to come anymore. I asked why not and they told me my community hours were over. I asked if I could come back anyway and they told me not to bother. Besides, they said, I would need to reapply through proper channels. And so I did not return for two days. But then the third day I did return, proper channels be damned, and with a brand new Purdy jersey to boot, I might add. And that was when they told me that Sam was no longer with us. No longer with us? What the hell did that mean, no longer with us? She's passed away, they said. She was eight years old, they said. And all the way home in the taxi all I kept wondering was whether or not I had set Sam straight on that whole blonde Indian thing. I thought that I probably had set her straight, but naturally couldn't be positive. So then I called up Canuck Place to see if perhaps they taped their conversations there. To see if perhaps they had video cameras installed in the rooms to which I could somehow gain access in order to put to rest my fear. Oh dear. Of all the rotten ways to die. No, of all the rotten ways to die this had to be the worst. This was back on the Blood Reserve. I remember there were horses in the barn, and that beside the barn was the rink. And I remember that behind the rink stood the lake, across which stretched the wharf in the direction of the western mountains purple and dark to the snowline and then white and marbled in the sun beyond. Beyond these mountains I saw a second range of mountains, these ones slightly lighter in colour with their peaks covered in even more snow, beyond which stood a third range of mountains I couldn't tell if I really saw at all. That was where she first came to find me. I remember how she looked that day. That was funny. That was about the last funny thing, I'd say. But I didn't laugh of course as they had already informed me of her condition by then. Then she made that wonderful speech: "You an Indian *and* an English"—to her any white man was an English—"you have a chance for more in this life." And then she looked away. I thought that maybe she was looking for another cigarette, but then I realized that she was crying, desperately. I could feel her crying as she pressed up against me. She refused to raise her face to mine. She simply sat pressed up against me with her hands pressed up against her mouth, looking out the length of the old grey wooden wharf towards the lamppost at its end. We sat together like that a while, just looking out at the lamppost and the mountains beyond it and listening to the wind on the lake, each of us trying hard to console the other, feeling sorry for the other, but for different reasons apparently. I put my arm around her and she pressed closer still, sobbing quietly down into her hands. I couldn't make out what all she was saying, but I do recall the feeling of her horsetail wig scratching my cheek, the hair long and straight and probably the blackest I'd ever seen. Fastened to her skull by means of a single piece of tape, that wig remained with me for the longest time, far longer than she did then.

Over in the corral they were branding the horses. I could see my father with the iron in there. One horse managed to break away and through the fence, bolting its way down the length of the wharf and into the lake, breaking its leg in the process—oh dear. Of all the rotten ways to die. Still, it was a decent enough speech in the end. She never said anything. My mother never did need to say anything. Good stoic Indian girl, she was putting herself in our place, I guess.

CHAPTER TWENTY-NINE

TO BE HONEST, I have no idea why I would go there. Now I have proposed various theories for why I would *choose* to go there— including the one that it was no choice at all—but nothing has proved too telling, at least not thus far. Perhaps I took going there as a kind of challenge, the impetus of which a certain curiosity for which there was simply no solution but experience firsthand. Perhaps it was a calling of sorts, something I had to risk the reality of or else risk a further ambiguity of self in the end. Or perhaps I was simply drawn there by this somewhat absurd desire I had to be a writer at the time. Whatever the reason, it proved reason enough, and in retrospect it was only a matter of time.

We were drinking at the Bacchus Lounge the night I went down. I had been back from Europe a month or so, and De Boer had yet to make his return to town. He was, or so we had heard, spending a lot of time in Manhattan with actors Jon Favreau and Vince Vaughn. The waitress came by and we ordered another round. The black pianist was just about to start his second set, and we liked to be well stocked whenever he began.

"Gavin here's got something to tell you," Fisk told me through the collar of his T-shirt, intruding upon my comprehensive inspection of this one particular painting presiding over our table.

"Shut up, David," Gavin said.

"Oh really?" I said, trying hard not to care, failing horribly in that regard however. The painting was of a centaur—or was it a minotaur—and I studied it more purposefully than ever.

"Gavin here's gone and gotten himself engaged."

"I said shut up, David," Gavin said, settling lower into his chair. He had his toque pulled down snugly over his skull as I remember it. As cold as he was, he liked to keep his ass warm, I take it.

"Hey, he's going to find out eventually," Fisk shrugged as the waitress returned with our round. She explained how the manager had bought it, and that he hoped everything was fine. I looked over and nodded at the little immigrant manager, and he smiled back knowingly, confident and proud.

"To whom?"

"Pardon?"

"To whom is Gavin getting engaged this time?" I inquired, trying hard to sound condescending but serene.

"Why, to Melanie," answered Fisk without the slightest hesitation, relieving me of the latter immediately.

"You're joking."

"Believe me, I wish I was. Turns out they've been going to church together."

"Is this true?" I asked Gavin.

"It is," he rather sheepishly admitted. "Though what for I have no idea."

I must have taken it fairly hard as the little immigrant manager immediately approached the table. "Swell. Everything's just swell," I told him when he asked if everything was all right over here.

"I wanted to make certain," he said, smiling knowingly, his hand clasped firmly over my shoulder. "Especially with training camp tomorrow."

Gavin sat up in his chair. "Uh, training camp?" he said. "What training camp?"

"It's nothing," I said, waving him off.

"*Ah*," Gavin beamed from beneath his toque. "*I* understand. You think Bill here's still playing, don't you."

The manager shrugged in confusion.

"You think Buffalo here's still a player," Gavin continued. "You think he's going to start training camp tomorrow."

"I do not understand," shrugged the little immigrant manager.

"HE'S NOT PLAYING ANYMORE."

"Shut up, Gavin," Fisk whispered harshly.

"Well it's true, isn't it? He's not going to camp tomorrow, is he? No, he's not. He's just another drunk like the rest of them now."

"Shove it up your ass, Gavin."

"Well it's true, isn't it?"

"Shove it up your ass," I said.

The little immigrant manager glanced about, embarrassed by all the gathering attention. "I do not understand."

"Tell him, Bill."

"Shut up, Gavin."

"Just a sec, David. Tell him, Bill. Tell the man so that he understands."

"For Christ's sake, shut up."

"Hold on, David. Tell him, Bill. Tell him the only thing you'll be playing with now is yourself. But hey," he said, "from what I've heard, that might not be so, um—hard after all."

Gavin smiled, not saying anything. Then he opened up wide. And I felt the glass break off inside his mouth as I shoved it up deep inside. I waited for it to come. It seemed to be a long time coming. Then it came. Here it comes—I watched the blood come pouring out onto the table in gobs. The music stopped. The manager shouted. Hands clasped down firmly over my shoulders from behind. I did not resist. How could I resist. I was being escorted towards the door by the silver-haired citizens of pride.

Outside, on the sidewalk, I offered to pay the bill, but the little immigrant manager declined. I was standing on the pavement and he was standing in the doorway, appearing altogether agitated now. Inside the bar, Gavin was still seated at the table, bleeding down into his hands. It's difficult to say what exactly I was feeling at that point. After all of the build-up you might have thought that it would somehow feel better than it did.

"Where's Fisk."

"Pardon?"

"Fisk," I said. "David Fisk."

"The other one at table?" the manager said.

"Yes, for Christ's sake, the *other one at table.*"

"He is inside. I do not know what for."

"Well is he coming out?"

"I do not know. Now please, sir. Please. You must go."

I looked down at the little immigrant manager sweating along his upper lip and forehead. Collections of spittle were beginning to gather in the corners of his mouth. I requested he wipe his lips and head.

"Pardon?"

"Wipe your goddamned lips," I said.

"Look, you go," he shot back, having smacked my helping hand away. "You go or I call the police."

"You're kicking me out."

"You must go." He pointed away and down the street.

"He had it coming. You know he had it coming. Trust me when I tell you that asshole had it coming," I said.

"You cannot just do that. You cannot just go and hit. Now go, please. Go. *Go.*"

I laughed as he pushed me on the chest. Fisk appeared in the doorway, but didn't say anything. He had the collar of his T-shirt pulled up over his mouth instead.

"Oh come on, David, you knew he had it coming." I turned to the little immigrant manager. "He's an asshole, and he definitely had it coming," I said.

"What's going on?" Fisk asked through the collar of his T-shirt.

"I believe I'm being kicked out," I said.

"He must go," explained the manager, lips hinged with spittle. "He is not allowed in anymore."

"You're barring me?" I said, attempting to wipe his lips, only to have my hand smacked away again. Other than that the little immigrant manager didn't respond, pointing away and down the street instead. Fisk said something, but I couldn't make it out through the collar of his T-shirt. His voice seemed a long way away. I walked towards Stone's with the collar of my own shirt pulled up over my mouth. It was a nice night out, and Robson Street was crowded for the Labour Day weekend, and when I arrived at Stone's that Latino actor was sitting halfway down the long scratched steel bar, hunched down over his coffee mug in glassy-eyed contemplation. I didn't feel much like drinking with him, though, and so I continued on to the Roxy instead. When I arrived there was quite a queue. I considered bypassing the queue, I'm sure, but then in the end must have decided against it.

I walked down Granville Street in the direction of the hotel. As I said, it was a nice night out for walking—the stars were out and there was quite a warm breeze coming up and I walked along enjoying the evening. By and by I came in sight of the hotel. Instead of heading in under the high vaulted ceiling of the hotel lobby, however, I turned right and kept going, heading down Hastings Street to Main, eventually arriving outside the flat fortress-like police station. Easy enough to spot, it was the only reasonably half-decent building around. All the others were decrepit. Some were abandoned. Many more were burnt-out and crumbling in places. Somewhere within a single city block the entire town had changed. Gone were the towers of concrete and glass, in their place tenements of timber and brick instead. Kitty-corner to the police station they were filming a movie. A long line of gleaming white trailers stretched out of sight down the street. Enormous klieg lights engulfed the nearest abandoned hotel and, adhering awkwardly to its moorings, the dangling makeshift remains of a fictional fire escape. Beneath the fire escape, clouds of dry ice-mist drifted past legions of beggars, drug-peddlers and dope-fiends roaming languidly about the set. Whatever the movie, they wanted the scene to be authentic, I take it.

Most of the crew were loitering perfunctorily about the buffet, and I wandered over to ask one—the best boy, it turns out—where the best place might be around here to get a beer. He asked me what kind of bar I was looking for.

"One with a whole bunch of Indians," I said.

"In that case," he said, and pointed to a bar on the corner. Inside it was a typical beer hall, its only distinction being that, at present, it was jam-packed with adolescent American soldiers. Dressed in their civvies, they were anything but civil. On the contrary, they were young military men and women on leave taking advantage of the lower drinking age this side of the border. But I could still tell. I could always tell. I had always had an eye for such citizens and details. They took up half the bar—the front half—leaving the back half to the regulars and locals. Although there were some whites, most of the regulars were Indian, and most of the Indians were men, and of the men most were beyond middle age, so there is little to be said about them.

The soldiers' tables were crowded closely together. There was a close, crowded feeling coming off them there. The soldiers were loud and boisterous, even for Americans, and they were buying round after round of the one-dollar beers. Their tables were littered with glasses, many of them full, most of the contents flat. I found a seat way back in the rear of this squalid context, and when the waiter eventually came around and found me, I asked if they happened to have the pink stuff here. He indicated the front door and told me with a world-weary sigh that I should probably do my drugs outside.

"You a soldier too?" someone asked, and I turned to find a thin ugly Indian in a tight red shirt and tighter red cords kicking out her corrugated chest and hips. She had a little belly. Apparently she was showing. She would have been older than I was, I bet.

I told her I wasn't a soldier at all.

"You're not with them?" she asked, indicating the Americans with one swift acrimonious wave of her hand.

"No, I'm here alone," I said.

"Do you want to buy me a beer then?" she asked, and looping an arm around her shoulder I told her there was nothing else I'd rather do. Then I kissed her. On the head. She tasted readily of cigarettes and, in there somewhere underneath, the slight tang of stale urine, I guessed. I kissed her again anyway just as the waiter returned, at which point I requested a couple of beers for me and my lady friend.

Another Indian came sauntering over, this one sporting a thick gold cross around her neck. I found myself troubled by her accent too, and by the fight with a broken beer bottle still visible as a crescent moon on her cheek. "Me too?" she said.

Pointing at the waiter, I told her to catch him before he left, and to her credit she did, managing to snag him by the pant leg. I bought her two glasses of beer and, in time, myself a table full of Indians this way. It was really very easy when I think about it, and really I think about it every single day.

The first one moved closer. "Do you have a cigarette?"

"No, but have another beer," I said.

"You must be rich!" she smiled through small determined teeth.

"Why do you say that?"

"Because welfare doesn't hit till next week," she said.

We watched the Americans a while.

"I hate when they come in," one of them said.

"Me too," said another.

"So why the fuck don't you go to another bar?" asked a third, a male, with bristling irritation.

"Henry," growled the first, "why don't you just fuck off."

Henry was old, and wrinkled, and apparently in the mood for a fight. He wore a baby blue visor with an appliqué of fake bird shit on its bill. This for a joke no doubt.

"Fuck you, Henry," the second one said.

"No, fuck you. Fuck the *both* of you," Henry shot back.

"Easy now," I said. "We four ought to be getting along quite fabulously here."

"So?"

"So shut up and watch the show," I said.

The show, of course, was the Americans. One after another they stood atop one of their close crowded tables to tell a joke or to sing a song before downing their token glassful of beer. Some of the jokes were discriminatory while others just crude, but most of the songs, in a way, were good. One of the Indians had her shirt pulled up. Some of the male soldiers were spitting beer onto her chest. I watched the beer shoot forth from their mouths in great arcing jets to burst against her exposed flesh with a splash. She just stood there laughing, the

Indian did, with the beer running down into her jeans. The soldiers repeated the feat over and over, all to a chorus of appreciative applause and knee-slapping laughter from the rest of the troops. The waiter tried to stop them but could not get at them—the tables were crowded too closely together. One of the Indian men went over—he was young and large and altogether angry—but the woman, she just pushed him away. And when two of the female soldiers offered her a beer for such a gutsy display of feminine independence, she accepted it without reservation. Then, with a truly savage laugh, she dumped the entire glass over her own head. Still there was plenty more where that came from. The tables were full of dollar beers paid for, for the most part, in American.

I asked the first Indian at my table where I might find the toilet. She pointed down the hallway in back. I excused myself and went back to find it. Well it certainly was a disgusting sight. The first Indian from my table followed me in, checking inside each stall to confirm that we were in fact alone in here. I told her no thanks when she offered her services.

"What, you don't like women?"

"Well, to be honest, I can't."

"Hey, it's only twenty dollars."

"Oh it's not that. It's something—else," I said.

"*Ah*," she nodded with sudden understanding. "So then maybe you want to piss on me then."

"Excuse me?" I said, and she held up both hands with fingers spread wide.

"You can piss on my tits for ten."

"You want ten dollars to let me urinate on you."

"Fine. Make it five then," she said.

"Good Christ."

"What?"

"I can't believe you're saying this," I said.

She smiled proudly, almost as if providing oneself as a willing receptacle for urine were a positive reflection of one's character. "Come on, five dollars. They do it all the time," she said. Then, tilting her head back, and regarding me from this fresh perspective, she added, "But if you want to do it in my hair, it's ten."

"Who does it?"

"I don't know," she shrugged. "Guys who like that sort of thing, I guess."

"What kind of guys."

"White guys—like you," she said.

And that was when I had the bright idea of telling her I was Indian.

She shrugged, thoroughly unimpressed. "Well you sure don't look it."

"Doesn't mean it's not true," I said. "I'm Blood. Half Blood. My mother was full-blooded Kainaiwa Blackfoot Nation."

"*Ah,* buffalo hunters," she said. "Well good for her—and you—aren't you the spiritual thing. You and Shania Twain."

She checked each of the stalls again. Whatever else, she was certainly a thorough little thing.

Finally she said, "So you come down here to be with your tribe, is that it?"

"I didn't mean it like that."

"No, of course you didn't. People like you never do."

"So you don't know who I am then?"

"Sure I do. You're the guy who can't get it up."

"Besides that," I said.

She studied me closely just as one of the Americans came sauntering in. "Sorry about that!" he said, making a quick about-face at the door.

I told him it was quite all right.

"You sure?" he said. "I can always use the ladies' room."

"Absolutely. We were just finishing up."

The soldier stepped awkwardly between the Indian and me and up to the trough. Not surprisingly, he seemed a little uncomfortable with the company I was keeping.

"Hey soldier, let me ask you something," said the woman. "You recognize this guy here?"

He glanced back over his shoulder. "Can't say I do," he said, turning back to the trough. "However, I'm sure he's whoever he says he is, ma'am."

She turned triumphantly to me. "There you go. He doesn't know you either."

"Why would he, he's American. No offence," I said to the soldier.

"None taken, sir!"

"But you should," I said to the woman just as another soldier came sauntering in.

"Why? Because you think you're Indian like me?"

"Actually, I was thinking . . ." But my voice trailed off as she began to laugh. In time she was laughing hysterically. Eventually, though, she did stop laughing, and the last thing I heard as I walked out the door was the second soldier petitioning five dollars American from his friend.

CHAPTER THIRTY

ONE AFTERNOON IN September I was sitting at the café getting some work done. It had been raining all day, and so I was glad for the high vaulted ceiling of the hotel lobby painted to resemble the sky itself on far better days than this one. Robert Redford came up.

"Hello," he smiled. "You must be Billy Purdy."

We shook hands and he smiled again. He spoke slowly and confidently, and in retrospect I must have taken exception to that. Otherwise I have no explanation for my exceedingly puerile behaviour that afternoon at the café.

I tried to relax with some humour. "Nice hat," I said.

"Uh yes, the hat. The extent of my disguise, I'm afraid." Sighing, he played with the worn rim of his Indian Motorcycles cap until the waitress crept up, blushingly eager to take his order. He ordered another Pernod for me, and for himself a small bottle of purified water. "What's that you're reading?" he inquired eventually.

I held up my book for his respectful assessment. "Ever read it?"

"I don't think so, no. New is it?"

"I suppose," I said. "In a way."

He smiled as the waitress blushingly brought the drinks. We sat and drank quietly together, Robert Redford and I, and eventually he said, "So I suppose you'd like to know why it is I'm interrupting your studies."

"Oh I have a fairly good idea," I said, having, it's fair to say, no idea whatsoever.

"It really is a fantastic book, Billy."

"Isn't it though, Robert."

"Bobby."

"Isn't it though, Bobby. But tell me, don't you find it a little, you know, malicious?"

"Only on the surface of it," he said. "Actually, I haven't read a book this good in a very long time. Years in fact."

"Oh there are a few around—Bobby," I said. We smiled plainly at each other as he paused to gather his thoughts for his next assault on my petulant façade.

Finally he just came right out with it. "I'm interested in a film treatment of AISOP, Billy. And Chris assured me I'd need final approval from you."

"He did, did he. And why do you suppose he'd do that, Bobby?"

His blonde eyebrows furrowed slightly. "Well I suppose because he values your opinion."

"Oh I don't know about that."

"He did say that any such project would require his agent's full endorsement."

"His agent, huh." I held up my book. "Well you should read this, Bobby. Now *this* is a damned good book."

We drifted into a prolonged silence at this point.

"Exactly what kind of film is it you're looking to make?" I eventually inquired.

"How do you mean?"

"Well for one, there wouldn't be any horses in it."

He laughed long and hard at that. "No. No, I suppose there wouldn't."

"Will you be in it then?"

"Probably not, no. No, the story really calls for someone a little—younger, I'm afraid." He leaned closer. "I assure you the production will be of the highest quality."

"Who's going to be in it then?" I asked, and he shrugged noncommittally.

"As yet that's undecided."

"That's too bad. I'd really like to know who you'd put in it."

He shuffled forward in his chair. "Can I tell you something off the record, Billy?"

"Were we on the record, Bobby?"

His eyes narrowed slightly, but he offered no comment.

"The director then? Can you at least tell me about the director?"

"There has been some discussion, but as yet that's undecided too. You understand why I can't commit to anything right now."

"Well naturally, Bobby. Naturally I do."

He shuffled sideways in his chair. "AISOP is a fine book, Billy. A damned fine book. And it'll make a damned fine picture when we're through. And you may or may not be interested to know that most of the Spanish scenes will most likely be shot right here in Vancouver."

"Yes, well, that's all fine and dandy, but to be honest I do have some concerns."

"Well perhaps I could help alleviate some of those."

"Perhaps." Sadly, however, I couldn't think of any genuine concerns, and so I asked him how long he'd be in town for. I was thinking that maybe we could hang out together.

He glanced at his watch. "I was actually hoping to be back on a plane tonight."

"That's not a lot of time."

"Meaning?"

"Meaning, Bobby, it's not a great deal of time you've given me to make any sort of informed decision here."

"You're absolutely—"

"And taken to its logical conclusion," I continued, "which, incidentally, is the only conclusion I choose to take to here, this tells me you already consider it something of a done deal. And I have to say, that bothers me immensely."

"You're absolutely right," he said. "It's rather presumptuous of me and I do apologize for that. But under the circumstances I assure you it cannot be helped."

"You do realize it's not a matter of money."

"Chris assured me it would not be, yes."

"Because it's not. I reckon if there's anything I still have in this life it's a great deal of that."

"I understand completely," he said.

"So Chris wants you to make the movie?" I asked a little later.

"He seemed a little, what, hesitant maybe, but then that's not entirely unusual. A book's author so often . . ." He shook his head, unhappy with the direction his thoughts had taken, and then tried again: "Well anyway, it's a damned fine book. It's very unusual in its quality. In its—authenticity." Picking at the corner of his eye, he checked over the findings carefully. "You see, I too was raised an Irish Catholic and, well, when my mother died . . . Anyway," he said, tacking again, "I suppose there's a certain nobility in any writing that refuses to draw attention to itself."

"Oh sure," I said. "Sure there is. I mean hey, the book's not even out yet, and yet here you are trying to secure the goddamned film rights from me."

We sat silently a moment, staring up at the high vaulted ceiling's fictional summer sky.

"So he just left it up to me then?" I asked.

"Well like I said, he did say I'd require his agent's approval."

"And what do you suppose that means, Bobby?"

"Well, again, I suppose that means he values your counsel."

"Tell me now, honestly, do *you* believe he wants me to sign?" I asked, at which point he leaned back in his chair and took a good long look at the deep blue sky.

"This I can't say. Not for certain anyway. He seemed a little, what, doubtful before he left."

I stiffened. "Left? Left for where?"

"Well I'm not exactly sure. Though I got the impression from his father that he was headed down to Central America some-where."

I finished my Pernod and called for another. "So let me get this straight," I said, holding up *Lovestiff Annie*. "You've never heard of this writer before?"

"*Edward Purdy*," he read, shaking his head. "If I have, then the name escapes me."

"He was a writer back in the late fifties and early sixties. I really do wish you'd have read him."

"I very well may have. But again, the name escapes me." He frowned. "There really are a lot of writers, Billy. And one can't be expected to read them all."

"Yes, but this one—well now how shall I put it—he and Chris, their styles are very, um—similar," I said.

"Imitation is the sincerest form of flattery, they say."

"Yes. Yes, I suppose it is," I said, studying the book's worn cover some more. "But then you say you don't remember him."

He looked up at the summer sky again for what seemed like a very long time. Then he looked at me. "I'm sorry, Billy. It appears as though you need a little more time."

"No, no, I've made up my mind—I'll sign. I'll sign whatever it is you want me to. That is, if you'll do me this one small favour."

"Name it."

"Punch yourself in the mouth."

"Excuse me?"

"Punch yourself in the mouth," I said. "Right here, right now, punch yourself square in the mouth—for me."

He didn't react like I thought he would. In fact, and to his credit, he didn't react at all. He simply continued to study me with that same sense of controlled curiosity he had since the beginning of the encounter.

"You see, I saw this one guy do it once, and I tell you what, it impressed the hell out of me."

Still he said nothing.

"Come on, Sundance, say something. Don't just sit there like a statue for Christ's sake."

We sat there staring at each other for what seemed like forever. Finally I caved.

"All right then, fine. You win. I sign. Now don't get me wrong," I said, "the man who'd punch himself in the mouth still deserves the shot, I reckon. But then a true horseman like yourself deserves a fighting chance too, no question."

He leaned back in his chair, smiling the only way it was possible to smile in his profession. Despite myself, I felt happy for him. And we talked a little more about this and that as he reached down to pull a stiff square of stationery up onto the table for my inspection.

CHAPTER THIRTY-ONE

THE FLIGHT DOWN was a milk-run: Los Angeles to Mexico City to Guatemala City before finally settling for good in San José at around ten in the morning local time. In Los Angeles I made it as far as the airport Burger King. Of Mexico City I saw nothing more than the tarmac. Guatemala City was interesting—insofar as gun turrets placed alongside the runway are interesting—not to mention the scrapped husks of old military aircraft strewn here and there throughout the surrounding area.

It was cloudy and muggy the day I arrived, and it rained in several hard punishing bursts during the ride into town. The taxi set me back ten dollars American, although naturally it wasn't really a taxi at all. It was simply a man with time on his hands with access to a small red car. The real taxis, those few licensed ones around, were always red, and hence having access to a small red car could prove a somewhat lucrative opportunity for the local entrepreneur, if and when he were so inclined. But then it was important he operate his business in the appropriate fashion. Evidently this consisted of accosting travellers the moment they cleared the customs area. As for me, I was met by a whole swarm of miniature people milling about just outside the terminal. They pressed in, yelling things in a language I claimed to be familiar with but had yet to fully understand, and finally I allowed this one small moustachioed fellow in an *Ally McBeal* T-shirt the pleasure of driving me the twenty or so minutes into town. Actually, he did seem pleasant enough. He didn't speak a word of English, though, and as I was still nervous to try my Spanish, barring the radio and the lightning it was a fairly quiet journey into town. The radio pumped out the *Lion King* soundtrack all the way along. There was a sticker on the passenger's window that said 'DENVER BRON-COS #1 SUPER CHAMPS!' and when I pressed the little driver on it he smiled with smug satisfaction. The lightning came in two strikes, the first strike hitting a telephone pole no more than twenty yards away, and the second hitting a tenement just up over the ridge across the highway. I jumped each time it struck, and the little moustachioed driver seemed to enjoy that immensely. Actually, he seemed to enjoy everything immensely. He was a Latino with access to a small red car and he was driving me into town for my American money.

He took me to the Gran Hotel Imperial, downtown San José, an old three-storey construction sporting iron grates on the windows and a chained iron gate across the entranceway. Regrettably, the Gran Hotel Imperial was located in a rather questionable part of town. I asked the driver if there were any other accommodations nearby that were a little more reasonable—a little less budget-conscious maybe—and he replied in his monosyllabic way that this was the cheapest one by far. That said, he was once again on his way, off to the airport to earn another ten dollars American in his own small red way.

People were beginning to stare at me now, and so I ducked inside and out of the natural light of day. I hadn't yet learned that this was simply their custom. That the women were simply very advanced in their promiscuity and paid attention, and that they made no attempt to hide their curiosity in this way. Within hours I was to learn that prostitution was in fact legal in Costa Rica, and this too helped explain my unexpected charm and magnetism in this country.

The Gran Hotel Imperial was without question a real dive, my room itself a real hole. Consisting of four particleboard walls reaching for, but not quite achieving, the ceiling, and no windows to speak of, the room contained only a single cigarette-scarred particleboard bed without benefit of mattress or pillow. Clean sheets were to be found at the front desk, I soon discovered, and after making my bed I tried to make amends for some of the sleep I'd missed out on the night before. It didn't come off too well. With the Third World racket going on outside, combined with the heat and humidity inside, not to mention the hardness of my particleboard bed, I didn't fare too well. Every few minutes that part of me pressed against the particleboard would go numb, and I would be forced to roll over into the heat and humidity once again. It was very hot that first day in Costa Rica and, suffice to say, my first attempt at sleep was more or less a restless one.

Postponing the effort of sleep, I spent most of the afternoon wandering around town getting myself acquainted with its particulars. Just a few blocks away, in the central square, an outdoor market was humming along. There were many interesting items for sale in the market—knickknacks, ceramics, hammocks and the like—and I purchased myself a hammock and some kind of decorative mask, both of which I'd later forget at the café. It was called the Café Parisienne, and they served me cup after cup of good Costa Rican coffee in a booth way back out of the way. The coffee was very dark and rich, and since I could drink it comfortably without benefit of sugar or cream, I decided the Café Parisienne might just be the perfect place to work one day. I decided to return there later on. Unfortunately I never did. There was a Taco Bell nearby, and unfortunately I ended up eating lunch there instead. All of the shops and most of the fast-food restaurants in San José employ their own security at the door. These guards all carry on their person some sort of firearm, some of which, surprisingly or not, are of the automatic rifle variety. They open doors for you and nod pleasantly at you when you bother to thank them, smiling joyously whenever you manage to do so in their native tongue. I was confident enough to thank them in Spanish, but really nothing more just now.

It was so very hot that day. It was so very hot every day. My shirts were forever clinging to my back, and several times each day, in the beginning anyway, I was forced to change into a fresh one. Until I was acclimatized, that is, and then of course I could go a day or two or more before any change were necessary. But that first day I wasn't yet acclimatized, and I wandered around the city sweating and avoiding eye contact with the female contingent of the local citizenry. I have mentioned how forward they can be down here, and I really can't emphasize that fact enough. They often stare at you for so long and with such intensity that you are forced to look away entirely. It's easy on your ego until you realize they see only your money, and then it's every bit as easy on your wallet after that.

Wandering down one of an assortment of seemingly identical streets, I happened upon my first bona fide Costa Rican tourist bar. La Esmeralda, the bar was called, and inside a mariachi band was playing energetically and for American money of course. Sadly, though, after just two quick songs they were done. They wore tight black sequined suits and large white sombreros and I missed them as soon as they were gone. I sat down at the bar and ordered a beer. The beer was called Imperial, and it tasted very good going down. They had a Heineken too, and one called Pilsen, and I ordered one bottle of each of these just to be sure. I liked the Imperial the most, however, and so I decided to make that beer my signature one. The bottle had a red and yellow label featuring the silhouette of a bold black eagle, and it came in the small dark hands of a nice young Spanish girl. She was thin and dark and took away the bottles as I finished them. I really did finish a lot. And because she was so very nice, and the beers so very cheap, I tipped the girl enormously until we were all trying on our sociable citizen smiles.

I drank at La Esmeralda for an hour or two, and met up with no one of particular interest and learned nothing of real value, except of course that a taco in Costa Rica in any place other than Taco Bell isn't really a taco at all. At La Esmeralda, for instance, I discovered I'd somehow ordered myself a limp red wiener on a bed of limp wet fries. Needless to say, I didn't enjoy it. I did enjoy my bocas however. Bocas are these little side dishes that accompany your cervezas. Some resemble burritos and others enchiladas and so, except when I was in Taco Bell, I didn't order Costa Rican tacos anymore.

After my shift at La Esmeralda, I wandered around feeling light-headed from the beer and lack of sleep until I happened upon that familiar rapid-fire exchange of random ill-formed ideas characterizing the token locals' bar. It resided off a quiet side street, its decor as plain as its clientele, and to my delight a fight broke out soon after I arrived—I settled in quite comfortably and ordered a beer. I hooked back several more Imperials in and around the usual suspects absorbed in a soccer game on the television up behind the bar, and afterwards walked alone back to the Gran Hotel Imperial. It was dark when I arrived. Along the way, someone asked me in broken English if I would perhaps like to sample one of his girls. I looked at the fellow, then at the girl—young and plain and altogether unappealing—then shrugged and said, No gracias. Con mucho gusto, he said. I continued along towards the hotel, and at the very next corner two girls approached me from behind, calling me their *amor*. One flirted with me in almost every conceivable way while the other one went for my wallet. I pushed them both away and carried on, and as a result the one after my wallet fell hard to the ground. She swore at me in Spanish as I continued along, until finally someone yelled out from a balcony, again in English, to *please keep it the fuck down*. Back at the hotel I fell asleep immediately, and barring the particleboard bed and all the noise, heat and humidity, remained that way almost until dawn.

The following morning I took my breakfast in the restaurant on the second floor of the hotel, and then my coffee on the balcony overlooking the town. In those days the Gran Hotel Imperial was a traveller's hotel, and thus most of the clientele were on the younger side of thirty. I met a young couple from Germany who spoke good English, and we proceeded to talk about hockey. I mentioned my old team in Mannheim and they said they thought they remembered me. I could tell they were lying though. He was tall and thin and altogether ordinary, while she was tall and thin and extraordinary. While he was away in the washroom I asked her several questions about the local customs, such as whether there were any bullfights in Costa Rica that she might have seen. She said there were bullfights, although none that she had seen, and then I asked her about Jaco and she said it was out west somewhere. West of San José, she said. It was a bright morning in San José, but the air pollution was awful, and so I was looking forward to getting out on the road again. With the German girl's help I discovered a Budget Rental Car, but after much heated debate with the manager ended up taking my business across the road to Thrifty instead. Budget wouldn't allow me to rent a car without a valid driver's license, nor would they allow me use of my platinum credit card to cover the required insurance. Even if I could, then, I wasn't about to rent from them. When one is travelling in such places as Central America, one should try his best to never be wasteful. It's the spirit of the thing that matters of course, and to have spirit one must always appear frugal.

Thrifty didn't ask to see my driver's license, allowed me full use of my credit card and, on top of that, rented me a nearly brand new car—a Ford Taurus in a colour, described in the provided literature, as Matador Red, wouldn't you know. I asked about Jaco, and they directed me west and out of town. I passed some gardens on the way out, wild and colourful, and then I was out in the country beyond. Costa Rica is a very green country, green and rolling, with the long rising-falling road rolling out ahead of you all the time. At first I was nervous behind the wheel, as I hadn't driven now in some time. But then as I grew more comfortable I began to take more chances, passing plenty of automobiles and, further out in the country, some oxen. One farmer had his cattle strewn out ahead of him on the road, while another hauled his behind in a provisional queue. I bypassed them both, and later on some houses all white-plastered in the sun. In the country all the land appeared rich and green while the villages and houses looked clean. San José had been dirty—the streets full of garbage and the people only occasionally pretty, many even filthy, and even with their big easy smiles and flirtatious demeanours I'd often found cause to doubt their respectability. But then the road started to climb into the western hills and everything started to change. All at once the landscape began to resemble some green and over-foliaged country of my memory. Suddenly the vegetation was all very different in the hills, and in the valleys the rivers picked their way through nests of sun-bleached stones. All along the crests of the hills I saw what appeared to be coffee plantations, while in the valleys those favouring bananas seemed that much more abundant now.

Sometimes I'd stop alongside the road to pick bananas, gazing out in the direction of the mountains. I couldn't actually see the mountains. I only knew that they were there. I could see hills, however, and beyond those hills even more hills, beyond which I knew the general direction in which the mountains lay. Other times I'd look for monkeys. If I were patient enough, I'd catch some hanging about in the trees by their tails. Sometimes I'd see them by the dozen and other times in only twos and threes. But I always saw trees. Really so many trees. Many types I didn't recognize and others I knew only as palms. Other times I'd stop at one of the roadside cantinas and have myself an Imperial cerveza. There were many such cantinas along the roadside, and I made many such stops that day. These particular cantinas were rundown by anyone's standards, but then again so was the entire country. I didn't yet know that these cantinas were in actual fact called *sodas*—not that access to such information changed my perception of them at all. That each soda matched so perfectly that Third World neglect in my head made them all seem cantina enough.

I continued west and over a bridge crossing a river running deep and blue in the gorge. After the bridge the road began to climb, and in time my right front wheel reached out and caught itself a pothole. It wasn't so much that I had been drinking—although naturally I had been drinking—it was simply that the roads in this country existed and continue to exist in such utter disrepair. There are potholes literally everywhere. The locals use inner-tubes in all their tires, and these two factors, together with all the roadside repair shops and road-improvement crews I saw, led me to believe that my situation here was neither all that hopeless nor unusual. Since then I've learned that the brutal road conditions can be blamed solely on the inclement weather. It rains so hard in areas so often dry that the sand beneath the pavement simply drains away. I suppose they could lay the asphalt on gravel of some sort, but then this is Costa Rica and the money simply isn't there. Despite the fact Costa Rica is relatively wealthy in comparison to its neighbours, it's still very much a Central American country down here.

Luckily there was a spare tire in the trunk, and so I exchanged it for the flat one alongside the road, then drove cautiously the next few kilometres until happening upon the next available roadside repair shop. The dark old fellow working there spoke not a word of English, but he certainly understood my predicament well enough. He patched my tire quickly and inexpensively and afterwards, with a sledgehammer, hammered the rim back into some semblance of a circle. I thanked him repeatedly in Spanish for his quick efficient service, and the old fellow smiled from ear to ear. His smile wasn't so nice in comparison to others I'd seen—they actually have access to some terrific dentistry down here—but still quite fetching coming as it did from such an inky veneer.

Soon thereafter it began to rain, and I knew I'd arrived in that season. When it rained hard like that, I immediately pulled off the road and into the very first soda I could find. The roads were simply too narrow to negotiate in any sort of bad weather, especially with all those nasty potholes waiting to trip you up. I remained in the soda until the short rain burst ended, and then I was right back on the road after that. Eventually I encountered a delay of some sort along a narrow portion of the winding road. A bus had collided with a truck, it seemed, and now the ensuing glut of traffic was grinding slowly past the scene of the accident. The passengers had gotten off the bus and out of the truck to huddle together along the roadside in the rain. Some were crying. Others were talking. All were huddled quite close together, however, although some quite obviously in vain. One young entrepreneur had taken the opportunity to implement some rudimentary commerce, peddling bags of round prickly fruit to the traffic as it passed. Several drivers partook of this strange prickly fruit, but I didn't, thinking it would somehow be in bad taste. Afterwards, as I emerged from the hills, there were still trees along both sides of the road. But there were fewer monkeys. No mountains. And only the occasional soda. And even with the flat tire and all the prickly fruit stops it took me only five hours to reach the beach at Jaco.

CHAPTER THIRTY-TWO

JACO HAD EVERYTHING I had come to expect from a small town in this country, having pictured it for so long in advance. The one main street, two blocks removed from and running parallel to the beach, was paved, yes, but only in parts, and the discos and hotels stashed away from the main road and closer to shore offset the scores of sodas and stores on display out front. When I arrived beachside, however, I was surprised to find it littered with clutter (from the earlier rainstorm, I gathered), the sand and waves both dark and grey and thus, unlike the town itself, nothing like I'd pictured it would be. I parked the red Taurus at the end of the road and walked out onto the grey, clutter-covered sand. Abruptly a mangy old dog appeared, stepping out from behind a nearby palm. He woofed at me inquisitively, his eyes wide, his blonde belly muddy, while staggering about in a haphazard way. Again he woofed good-naturedly, then settled into a spinning satisfaction on the sand. I found an old white table leg and, waving it about in his face, threw it out over the incoming waves. For his part the dog almost fetched the table leg, but not quite, much to my frustration and dismay. Woof, he commented perfunctorily. Woof, I retorted in kind. I mumbled a few choice words regarding his laziness until I noticed the table leg washing up against my sandals, and then laughed quite good-naturedly after that.

Except for the surfers, there were very few people out on the beach. As for the surfers, they were a long way out—it was too hot to spend much time on the beach. Feeling the heat, I scampered back to the shade of the Taurus—the air conditioning felt good and I was suddenly glad to have it. I hadn't even thought of it before.

I drove back up the side street onto the sunlit main drag where some ticos (slang for local Spanish folk) and some foreigners, their white soles winking at me, walked along together in a daze. I passed them, and then a small surf shop followed by a pizzeria and some more surf shops down the road a ways. I pulled over to the side of the road to ask directions to the Copacabana Hotel where I remembered De Boer saying he'd stayed before. The foreigners told me in an accent I failed to place that they didn't understand me all that well. I asked where I might find the nearest beer store and they pointed me further down the road in the sun. I was about to drive off when a dark young tico came up and offered to take me there himself—for one American dollar of course.

"How about colónes," I said. "Say, fifty."

Levering his Oakley's up to his forehead, he repeated the figure carefully, translating it into his native tongue. Then he shook his head. "American dollars, por favor."

"Seventy then. Final offer."

"Hasta luego, amigo." He stepped back and away from the Taurus as I pressed the accelerator hard to the floor. My Spanish was improving with time and confidence, and whatever I was going to be had by in Jaco certainly didn't include my very first tico. I parked the Taurus next to the beer store, and inside purchased a dozen Imperials. As well I bought a bottle of vodka and some ice—I was hoping that perhaps they had absinthe here but apparently they didn't, and to be honest I was a little surprised. Nor did they have any of the pink grapefruit juice either, and so in the end I was forced to settle for regular. And when I asked the squat little woman behind the counter where the Copacabana was, she pointed back up the road with a large blue feather.

"Restaurant with a bar on top. Turn there."

I asked if there was a name to this restaurant or if that was all she could give me, and she scratched her head with the stem of the feather and checked her watch thoughtfully. "Happy hour in an hour," she told me.

"In the restaurant or the hotel?"

"Qué?"

"Happy hour," I said, "is it in the restaurant or the hotel."

"Sí, in the bar. Bar above the restaurant. Me entiende, América?"

"Canada."

"All the same to me," she shrugged, and returned to doing nothing in particular.

Back in the car I opened a beer and drank it down. I was already hungry, and becoming increasingly cranky from the heat, and so it was that a restaurant sounded like a hell of a plan just then. Off to my right, a pale grey iguana eyed a long line of ants marching along the side of the road. I got back out and followed the procession, triggering the iguana to skitter off into the bush. The ants were red, and each one carried a uniform piece of leaf in its pincers, carrying it up over its head. There must have been a thousand such flags marching alongside the road that day, and that struck me as amusing in a way. Eventually curiosity got the best of me, and I followed the pageant of red and green down the road and into the jungle. There was no path leading into the jungle, and so I was forced to make my own, breaking branches and muscling through undergrowth in hot pursuit of the lost empire of the ants. Eventually I entered a secret clearing where sunlight slanted down through a high canopy of palms. On the far side of the clearing stood a flat brown swamp with a large brown crocodile stretched out alongside. He appeared to be sizing up a long-legged bird. I let out a warning yell when I thought he was about to strike, managing to frighten away, and in turn save, the bird.

Back at the car I finished another beer before driving up the road to the restaurant. The restaurant I thought the beer store lady must have been referring to was this open-air, café-style restaurant, and the tables were covered in those red and white checkerboard tablecloths so ubiquitous in these equatorial climates. The menus were written in both English and Spanish. I opted for the English side that day. I ordered the pasta with butter sauce and a large fruit smoothie, but the tico waiter, looking very Spanish behind his thin black moustache and black bow tie, yet speaking very good English, informed me that the smoothies were only for breakfast regrettably. I asked him to suggest something else then in lieu of the smoothie. He suggested the Imperial cerveza. Lazy spic, I thought, and thanked him very much for all his help, then spitefully ordered the Pilsen instead.

I was the only one eating at the restaurant that late in the afternoon and the meal was very tasty. While I was eating, the tico waiter stood over at the bar speaking quietly with the bartender, and when he wasn't speaking quietly with the bartender, he was over at the table silently serving me. For such a quiet man, he actually proved an excellent waiter, offering a truly excellent level of service, and the gratuity I left him acknowledged as much. He didn't seem to care or even notice. He simply gathered up his change and went back to his long quiet discussion with the bartender, the latter occasionally lifting his large fat head to shoo an emaciated cat away from the grill.

Near the end of my meal I inquired about happy hour. The bartender told me it took place upstairs. I asked about the specials, and trying to answer he coughed, and so I asked him for la cuenta instead. That is the word for bill. And while I was waiting for the bill, I watched a group of young white girls come shimmering up the street from the beach. They disappeared around the corner of the restaurant in a fit of giggles, and I followed them there and up a set of stairs to a crowded bar where they all ordered Imperial cervezas. They ordered by shouting, "Una Águila!" very loudly and rudely, and I decided to order my own cervezas that way. Afterwards I watched the girls a while from the corner of my eye, but they didn't seem all that sociable, really.

After several more Imperials I made my way back to the car. It was beginning to cloud over. The sun was starting to go down. Just like under the high vaulted ceiling of the hotel lobby I'd lost track of time once more. And now of course the sand fleas were out, and as I'd not yet purchased any repellent I was forced to seek the safety of the car. After an hour or so in the Taurus, and the last of my Imperials, I ventured off down the road on foot. As I didn't yet know what the laws were in this country regarding drinking and driving, I decided to leave the car where it stood. Pack in hand I walked down the dirt and gravel road in the direction of the beach at its end. There were palm trees along both sides of the road, and at the end of the road a building stood off to the left. It was two storeys high and painted beige for the most part, with a broad strip of black down near the base. A sign on the wall said Hotel Copacabana, but I was far too tired to be all that excited, feeling a sort of smooth drunken satisfaction instead.

Around the corner I happened upon what I assumed to be the hotel lobby. A dark young woman sat behind a darker wooden desk.

"Hola."

"Hola," she said. "Cómo estás?"

"Are there any rooms available?" I said.

"Sí. Yes. Several without the gorgeous view and one with the gorgeous view."

"I'll take the one with the gorgeous view then, I guess."

"More money."

"Cuánto?" I asked, and she studied me closely, or not actually me but a spot on the wall just behind me, eventually coming up with the rather inflated figure of ninety dollars American.

"Muy caro."

"Ninety," she repeated. "Take it or leave it."

"All right then. Fine. I'm sure the view is worth it," I said.

She told me I didn't have to pay yet if I didn't want to, but that she would require my passport either way. Being low on cash, I passed on the payment and gave her my passport. She noted I was from Canada. The owners were from Canada.

"Oh yes? Where from?" I said.

"Toronto maybe?" she shrugged, unsure. "Now come on and I'll show you the way."

She led me upstairs to my room with a view. Inside it was dark, and smelled gamely of suntan oil and pot. Something small skittered over my feet. My hostess pulled a cord that switched on a light and in turn launched the blackened blades of a ceiling fan into a shaky rattling revolution of the thick humid air. The room contained two stiff single beds and an en suite bathroom along with a few sparse pieces of furniture of indefinite make. I nodded my approval, triggering the young woman to smile, even though I could tell that she was bored. They were always bored. But even in her boredom she found ways to be flirtatious. Conning was simply in their nature, I supposed.

I stepped out onto the tree-enshrouded balcony. "Tell me, is there a room available with a view a little more gorgeous than this?" I asked, indicating this veritable wall of palms arranged so effectively between me and even a glimpse of the beach.

"They do need to be cut back," she admitted with a nod.

"Yes, well, is there a more gorgeous view available now?"

"No, this is most gorgeous. There are other rooms down on the concourse though."

"Thanks for everything," I told her, and she turned to leave. "Con permiso," I said.

"Yes?"

"Is there a Chris De Boer here—aquí?"

She shrugged noncommittally. "Why, should there be?"

"I think so. Maybe. You'd probably know him. He's Canadian—like me."

"There are a great many Canadians in Jaco," she sighed, rubbing her forehead. "All of your country comes here."

"Is that so? Why? Por qué?" I asked, and she shrugged again.

"I guess because they like the view," she said.

After she left the room I walked out onto the balcony to enjoy my gorgeous and uninterrupted view of the nearby trees. From the balcony to my right I could hear music playing (Ricky Martin—remember him?) and I leaned out and introduced myself to two young girls from Moncton, New Brunswick. I could see they were drinking and thus offered my vodka. They offered me something harsher instead. One of them passed over a capful of something called guaro. "It's brewed from sugar cane," they said.

"Distilled."

"Huh?"

"Spirits are distilled," I said. "Beer is brewed."

"Whatever," they shrugged, and asked me my name. I told them. "La Cuenta Grande!" they said. Big Bill. They were Canadians on vacation in Central America and they were eager to practice their Spanish on me.

"Do you speak much Spanish, la Cuenta Grande?"

"No entiendo," I said.

They laughed at that, and more so as we continued to pass the guaro back and forth from balcony to balcony. They were fairly easy drunks of course. And by and by they invited me over to their room where I promptly drank them under the table. Eventually they offered me some of their pot, but naturally I declined, citing how much it irritated my throat since smoking so much of it in Amsterdam. They liked that I'd lived on a barge in Amsterdam. They thought that was neat. And all this time I was scratching hard the tops of my feet, scratching to bleeding where the sand fleas had bitten me.

I asked what their plans were, and they said they were heading to the festival.

"Festival? What festival?"

"The Columbus Day festival in Puerto Limón."

"Where is Puerto Limón?"

"Other side. Caribbean side—la Cuenta Grande," they said.

I asked them when and they said they didn't know. Then the one passed out. Soon enough her friend got sick. I moved out onto the deck after that. And it was here that I discovered the full and entirely unobstructed ocean view I had requested, and for which the girls from New Brunswick had apparently paid in advance.

CHAPTER THIRTY-THREE

THE TWO WEEKS leading up to the festival in Puerto Limón were very busy for me. I met many people in and around the swim-up bar at the Copacabana, including the two young owners, Brian and Steve. Twin brothers originally from Edmonton, they both went big and blonde. They both kept ticas as wives and, as far as I could tell from the ridiculous number of children running around, kept them both in a nearly perpetual state of pregnancy as well. I didn't see Brian all that much. He was out running the fishing charters most of the time. Steve, though, for his part, took care of most of the day-to-day duties in and around the hotel. I liked Steve. He treated me very well. He always allowed me to stock my own Imperials at the swim-up bar, and when for whatever reason I ran out, always allowed me to run up a tab as well. They both knew who I was from my years of profession-al hockey, and I was able to take further advantage of that now.

Two days into my stay in Jaco I got hit with my first bout of diar-rhoea, and so abstained from water after that—even bottled water—sticking instead to my diet of Imperials and guaro. In the few days I had the diarrhoea, Steve learned that I hadn't brought any malaria pills with me, and so he promptly got me started on a regimen of these as well. It was a trying time for Steve, let alone myself. I man-aged to piss all my strength out my rectum, and with it whatever I had left of pride as well. Steve honestly thought I might die at one point, and I must say, so did I. That is why, despite my feelings of guilt at being such a burden, I couldn't muster the necessary enthusiasm or even the energy to be embarrassed, let alone moved, when he proposed taking me to see the local doctor one day. I was stubborn. I wanted to die right there, comfortably, in the hotel. I didn't want to get up out of bed just to find a better place to die in for crying out loud. For me, the Copacabana was the perfect resting place, and a justifiably absurd end to what had become of late an entirely absurd existence. But then soon enough I was back on my feet, despite my willingness to go out on my back right there in Jaco Beach.

On a typical day, after lunch, say, I would go for a dip in the pool, followed by some cervezas in the shade of the swim-up bar. Television became a regular routine for me again, especially baseball and the ongoing endeavours of the visibly juiced-up Sammy Sosa and Mark McGwire. Then, some time late in the afternoon, I would slip back to my room for a siesta, typically emerging again around seven or so. Then it was off to the bar above the restaurant with my New Brunswick neighbours to catch last call for happy hour—the two-for-one special. In the evenings they televised the new season of hockey games at the swim-up bar—the brothers were both big fans—but then I rarely went in for that. To be honest, it seemed ridiculous to be watching hockey in such a tropical environment anyhow.

The remainder of the evening typically revolved around one of two discos located along the beach a few blocks south of the hotel. The one disco played good music with not too much Bob Marley or Ricky Martin, and there was always plenty of interaction to be had with the local ticas as well. Still, some of the younger ones would offer me opportunities of which I couldn't bring myself to take advantage. Some of these younger ones couldn't yet have been in their teens. Sometimes they'd corner me up at the bar, and other times they'd try to drag me outside to the beach. In the end, however, and although it often proved difficult, I always declined their various invitations and recommendations.

I didn't always stay in Jaco. Sometimes the New Brunswick neighbours and I would take the Taurus down the coast to places like Quepos, and other times even further south. Other days we travelled up the coast to Puntarenas and over to the Nicoya Peninsula, occasionally heading east and inland to such tourist meccas as the Arenal volcano. And sipping Pina Coladas in the evening in the natural hot springs at the base of the volcano, I soon got to wondering how I would ever get to leaving this place. Gazing up at the volcano from one pool or another, I could see the crooked lines of red lava running down, and afterwards we took the Taurus around the backside of the volcano, heading up just as high as the road would allow. For a while the country was much as it had been, until crossing the crest of a ridge onto a nearby plateau where the road, no more than two parallel ruts in the moonlight by this point, wound back and forth on itself several times in succession and we were really somewhere we'd never been before: far below, the valleys and the plains shimmering in the moonlight, with the world itself turning on some suddenly more significant axis than before.

The road knew enough to go up by itself, but required some real convincing to come back down. After crossing a stream-cut gorge it continued to climb before turning out along another ridge quite a bit narrower than the ridge before. Here the moon disappeared from view, and with it very nearly the road as well. Eventually we came upon a locked gate barring any further ascent, and so we piled out into an impenetrable darkness the likes of which I had never experienced before. I don't think I have ever been in such a darkness as that night on the backside of that particular volcano. Believe me, a darkness like that is quite inconceivable until you have experienced it firsthand somehow.

After Arenal we returned to the coast and the rapidly disintegrating port town of Puntarenas. From Puntarenas we took the car ferry across to the Nicoya Peninsula and along the peninsula to the hippie village of Montezuma. The dirt road leading into Montezuma proved tough on the Taurus, and we went through two more tires that day. We drove fast whenever possible, and soon came upon the rising dust of other cars making their way along the road that way. Where the road curved we saw three vehicles ahead of us, all identical black Toyota trucks well-equipped for the terrain, and the dust boiling up from their wheels through the surrounding trees gave us pause—but then we caught them and passed them anyway. Driving in convoy is not all that unpleasant an experience when you are the lead vehicle, and so I was able to settle in and watch the country much of the way. We were in some foothills now, surrounded by jungle, and as the road went up the tops of distant hills came up, beyond which blinked the far-flung ocean through gently swaying palms. In my rear-view mirror I saw the three black trucks climbing along the road behind us spaced by intervals of rising dust. Later, they seemed to vanish altogether, and there was only the dust and the sound of stones tossed up by the tires against the undercarriage of the Taurus. Occasionally we bottomed out on a shoulder of stone muscling up through the middle of the road, twice managing to scrape the oil pan and jar loose the muffler, but otherwise nothing especially detrimental arose. Suddenly, however, I had to stop for a crush of cattle coming towards us along the road. The herd parted naturally, one slow moving line on either side of the Taurus, and we reached out and stroked their soft fuzzy flanks as the cows brushed past our open windows.

After the cattle the road ahead was clear, climbing further into the hills before dropping down and over the shoulder of a long descending hill. We were headed in the direction of the ocean again. It was getting very near. There were trees spaced unevenly along both sides of the road, and through the left line of trees I could see the water with the waves breaking slow, white and methodical along the shore. The sand was whiter here than further south, and from some-where in the jungle above a river ran down to meet us. I parked the car at the far western perimeter of the village where the road ended and the river gorge began. At the river's source, we were told by some locals, we'd find a waterfall, and so we climbed on foot alongside the river running wide and shallow in the gorge. Further up, in the gorge's narrower and livelier passages, we were forced to climb around one tree or another or else, arching over the river from either side, makeshift timber bridges connected far-reaching jungle trails. The river led us a long way up before culminating at a large deep pool. Over the pool hung a slight mist so that, as I approached, I felt myself increasingly isolated from the civilized world. Eventually I noticed two young ticos climbing their way up the wet stone cliff flanking the waterfall. Friendly boys, they showed us where to scale the cliff in order to reach the jump up near the top. I followed them up a steep slippery ridge cutting alongside a wide flat expanse of rock, then doubled back towards a steep incline leading to a ledge some twenty meters up. From the ledge I looked down through the trees below and saw, where the sunlight reflected off its surface, the line of the river running down through the gorge. It looked nothing like the river we had followed to get here. In fact it hardly seemed aquatic at all. A series of smoothly constructed curves, it appeared, from this vantage point at least, to be little more than a water slide switching back on itself several times in succession, as though making certain it had thoroughly betrayed itself. It was a farce then. A joke. The wildness of its nature assimilated to the confines of a culture it ought to have cast aside long ago. Still, I could see the girls swimming, and I could see the boys gawking, and I tried my best to take a visual imprint of the moment. That was when I realized that I couldn't recall either girl's name. If I'd ever even known them in the first place, that is. I considered asking them their names now, but then really, what would it matter. They'd be out of my life soon enough either way.

From the ledge, then, we jumped into the pool at the bottom of the falls. You had to be careful when climbing the slippery stone staircase so as not to slip and fall onto the jagged rocks below. But once at the ledge the feeling was immeasurable. Much as it was on the quick flight down. One time up, in complete disregard of my young guides' more adamant warnings, I climbed further up the ledge and over the crest at the top. Here, by virtue of all the water rushing past, I could no longer hear the girls whining nor the ticos warning—I had this idea that no one had ever been this high before. I felt as though I were breaking new ground. Following another ridge, this one larger and more clearly defined, I allowed my eyes to wander up towards the central plateau of the peninsula where, shimmering in the heat just beyond, a range of mountains stood purple and dark to the snowline and then white and marbled in the sun beyond. Beyond these mountains I saw a second range of mountains, these ones slightly lighter in colour with their peaks covered in even more snow, beyond which stood a third range of mountains I couldn't tell if I really saw at all.

Girls made such swell friends. With the older ones, the women, there was so much more to it that you ended up with so much less in the end. Not so with the younger ones. With the younger ones it was so much easier an equation to maintain. You never had to bother seeing things from their perspective, or if you did, you could always claim an utter lack of maturity on their end. It was very much a taking relationship—something for nothing—or at worst, something for something you didn't care to lose. It really was such an awful way to go about being with people when you thought about it, and worse still when you remembered it afterwards. Still, I thought I'd paid for everything by now, but then realized that we never really stop paying for girls. The relationship with the younger ones, it was always the simplest equation to figure: they never went making things too complicated by expecting to spend time with you for any obscure reason. If you wanted a younger one to like you, all you had to do was sacrifice a little money—not time, just money—a minor sacrifice really, and one for which they seemed to like you steadily and increasingly and with a great deal of energy. They appreciated your economic qualities. They were glad to take you in. And so you took them out and spent a little money, and they took care of you as you went along with them. And it was sincere because they were young and as yet knew no other way. I had sacrificed for Gracie this way. Sure I had. And Mitch, he had sacrificed too. Naturally I had always been the one to blink first, but then I suppose I had wrecked all that too. It all got wrecked sooner or later, and sooner was better from my point of view. The complication coming was never a mirage, though it was an illusion for which no amount of money could ever prepare you. But with the younger ones it was never so complicated as that. With the younger ones you could always count on a certain relaxation of the rules. With the younger ones you could pay your way in or you could pay your way out and they would be no wiser for the view. Either you paid to have them, or you paid to leave them, or else you paid to have them leave you be. Either way you got your money's worth and walked away no worse for wear. They had that eagerness to impress, that was all—they were all emotion, oozing love and devotion—they had yet to learn the value of controlling the cloth, and always got gored by the bull. But then somehow the younger ones got older, and the older ones got bolder, and you were left to play without knowing all the rules. It was not as though she knew the game so well herself, but simply that she knew it better than you. And now all you wanted to do was learn. If you could somehow only learn to play, you thought, you could somehow learn to look the other way. No longer was it simply enough to play with emotions—no, they had to play with your balls instead. And that was where the real damage was done—not to your heart but to your balls—and then later on to your head. And even when you learned to protect yourself, you were still the one to blame. Love is all about sacrifice, understand, and sacrifice for love has always been somewhat in vain.

After a few days, we came back down the coast from the peninsula and there were trees along both sides of the road. There was a stream too, and ripe plantations of bananas, which the rising, falling road went straight on through. The road continued straight for a time before lifting off to a rise up ahead. Off to the left and east, amid shimmering waves of heat, stood a hill crowned with what appeared to be a half-finished castle. Groves of banana-laden branches shifted in the wind. Eventually we crossed a wide-open plain, and along the shoulders of the road ahead I saw crews and vehicles working where a narrow muddy river had risen with the recent rains. Fortunately an alternative route over the river had already been established: beside the washed-out bridge a makeshift one had been hastily erected. We crossed the new bridge slowly and cautiously, and all the time we were crossing I was looking out to the east where I could see the plateau shimmering in the rising heat. In back of the plateau were the mountains, and every way I looked there were more mountains, and ahead the road stretched out white towards some other country there.

CHAPTER THIRTY-FOUR

THE LIMÓN FESTIVAL began the twelfth of October. I decided to partake of it alone. The neighbours from New Brunswick had made it clear they wanted to partake of it too—I'd initially told them they could—but then in the end I decided against it as a matter of principle. They were very angry with me as I remember it, and I think the one might even have cried. I was about to tell them they could take the bus, but then naturally thought better of that. They were standing at the swim-up bar when last I saw them, drinking Imperials and trying their best to pretend they wanted nothing to do with me. I remember I was readying the Taurus for the trip. I remember that because a young tico came over to show me a scorpion he'd found in his shoe earlier that day. He kept the thing in a clear plastic Coke bottle: brownish white and black in parts, it measured about the length of my thumb, I'd say. I remember that moment clearly as I've checked my shoes for scorpions ever since—although in truth I've never yet inspected the cans of cola in this place.

Despite the heavy traffic and the poor road conditions, the drive east to Limón via San José took only eight hours all told. Still, by the time I reached the Caribbean coast the sun was already waning over the country, and soon enough had disappeared entirely. In the night, then, it was difficult to find my way through the maze of ramshackle streets and houses in which I suddenly found myself ensnared. As the festival had only just begun, and as it wasn't due to hit its stride until later on in the week, there weren't all that many tourists around as yet. Not many ticos either, for that matter. One aspect of Limón that struck me immediately—and really this goes for the entire east coast of Costa Rica—was the general colour of its populace: almost entirely black. At first I found this more humorous than anything, especially considering how no one had ever bothered to mention that.

The first thing I did in Limón, then, was seek out the bullring. Sadly I couldn't find it anywhere. I did find the area where the majority of the festival would be held, however, a large plaza in the middle of town cordoned off with banners into some semblance of a square. Some banners said PILSEN and others BAVARIA, but it was really the red and yellow IMPERIAL banners that dominated the town that week. The air was humid. Flags hung stiffly from their poles. It was hot out without much benefit of a breeze. Located in and around the central square were the various amusement rides and beer gardens, along with the token food courts and makeshift dance halls, the latter rumbling heavily already to deep jungle rhythms of rudimentary design. There were people walking around laughing and drinking under the strings of lights strung up around the perimeter. It was all fairly tame. Still they were all fairly black, and for the most part that concerned me all the same.

I drove around in search of a decent hotel, but nothing was available. All the rooms had been booked well in advance by the ticos set to descend upon the town for the festival. However, I did find what appeared to be a church, and parking the Taurus, went reluctantly inside. As I hadn't been inside a church in decades, and as I didn't want to appear too odd or out of place, I chose a pew somewhat removed from the pulpit and knelt down and began to pray. I prayed the only way I could think of—that is, as I'd read it was done in my father's book—feeling beneath me the wooden pew worn smooth by countless hands over countless years of torment. And while kneeling and not getting sad at remembering, I prayed I'd somehow find De Boer. I repented anything I'd said and how I'd said it, and regretted not having seen him in so long now. And all the time I was praying, I was thinking of myself as praying, and feeling a little silly because of it, even a little guilty and ashamed, especially with my scarred and

beaten hands held up alongside my head where, despite the fact it
made for perhaps the best discipline going, prayer had so often failed
me in my childhood. And thinking of my hands as beaten and
swollen made them feel as if not really my own, almost as if separate
entities in themselves, and thinking of them as such made me feel as
if these hands were someone else's entirely, someone far more com-
passionate and worthy of feeling sorry for in fact. And thinking of
these hands held out before me in fists, and of them falling hard and
punishing against another—so many others really—I thought of the
first time they'd been petitioned to do so and by whom, and thinking
of him in his collar and what all he'd done to me I became steadily
and increasingly ashamed and even regretful that I was such a rotten
man. Still, realizing there was nothing I could do about it, at least not
for a time, and maybe even never considering my heritage, I thought
about my mother who had always been a damned fine person, even
if a little naive, but always a damned fine person before she had taken
her leave, and thinking of my mother I naturally thought of my
father, and of my brothers, and of my wife and children, and thinking of my children I began to feel my heart race, feeling it race out
and out and out, approaching the line prancing, wet and nervous,
anticipating the rush as the gate snaps open and the bell goes off.
Then sweeping past the people all bunched up in their pews before
spreading out around the turn, growing smaller and smaller and gliding fluidly from afar, up close though bunching and muscling and
flogging in a rhythm separating out until there are two of them, or
rather my heart in two parts, one rhythm superimposed on the other,
the original running rhythm being still the base rhythm, but overrid-
ing this rhythm a newer lighter rhythm that together with the runner
form an immensity of motion mending itself into one boneless grace
and seamless precision. And with the prayers of the people still far
away and removed and silent, I feel yet another part of my heart separate out, moving out and out and out, only to impose itself in a
returning rage upon these other meeker members of myself, questioning myself, wondering if I will hold this lead until what remains
are the rhythm of the runner, the rhythm of the rider, and this third

rhythm raging apart. Eventually, however, all three rhythms move in one upon the others until finally rage rejoins rider atop runner and there is but one rhythm remaining—a trinity I do believe to be the runner, but then I could be mistaken of course. And coming now into the final long turn, stretching out the lead on the pack, stretching it out and out and out, I feel the anticipation growing again as something separates not out of myself but out of the pack itself and moves around the outside and it gains. And it is chasing me, this thing, it is chasing me and it is gaining on me as I approach the last of the people in their pews not praying but raging against runner and rider that it is gaining on me, this thing it is gaining on me and it is passing me, coming faster and faster and suddenly neck and neck with the screaming and the flogging and the muscling with all my legs pounding heart racing veins pumping breath rifling lungs flooding beneath a lathered sweating hide, so that I dare not look for fear of seeing it pass me and then of course the photo finish at the wire. Always the photo finish. And the waiting. The clutching the ticket and the trembling and the waiting. Jammed in with the others all eyes waiting to see if I hold it off and sometimes I do and sometimes I do not because this is a race and that is the way it goes in a race. That is the way it goes and no one ever made me do it because I always loved to do it having always known the rules. Because I never liked to lose. Because I always loved the feeling, the feeling of the fight, that indescribable feeling running right on through the victory and right up through the gate.

And as I knelt there calming the last sobs in my throat, feeling the burning tingling pain of my hands rubbing hard against the wood, from some great distance someone spoke to me in Spanish, asking what it was I prayed for here. The question and the voice posing it suggested that if I were to stand up and turn around I would somehow find a priest.

"What is it you pray for?" repeated the voice, but in English.

"Myself," I said, feeling a fluid of some sort seep its way into my lungs. "I pray for myself. I have something of an irregular heart rhythm, it seems."

"An arrhythmia," he said, and I stood up and turned around. The priest approached slowly, his hands clasped formally behind his back. "You are Catholic then?"

"I've had some in me."

"Here for confession?"

"Not yet anyway."

He smiled benignly, adjusted his collar, and eventually inquired as to my confirmation name.

"Bull," I said, pulling the collar of my T-shirt up over my mouth.

"Bull," he repeated, smiling again. "Well where are you from then, Bull?"

"Oh, uh—Lethbridge," I told him through the collar of my T-shirt, startled by the simplicity or else the complexity of the question. "It's in Alberta. Though my old man, he was from Paris originally."

"Romantic city, Paris," nodded the priest appreciatively.

"You've been there?"

"A long time ago, yes. And you?"

"When I was a kid, sure," I said, coughing whatever it was pooling in my lungs up into my throat, only to swallow it at once. "I took a bus there once from Sault Ste Marie."

He nodded, slowly, and I looked around and out the windows for a time.

"What is it?" asked the priest eventually.

"I'm looking for someone."

"A friend?"

"Yes, a friend."

"Well then you've certainly come to the right place," he smiled benevolently, a man of the cloth in every conceivable sense apparently. "Now this friend you're looking for, he is in Limón?"

"I'm not sure. I had a feeling he might come in for the festival. I assume he'll probably come in by train."

He frowned a little as I secretly coughed and swallowed behind the cloth of my provisional T-shirt curtain.

"What?"

"Nothing."

"What is it? Speak, priest," I said, having released my T-shirt so as to speak freely again.

"Well it's just that the trains here, they haven't been running for some time."

"What, there are no trains in this country?"

"Well," he said doubtfully, "there are still a few tours that run out of San José—on the old lines."

"That must be it then," I said, and he frowned again. "What? What is it now?"

"It is nothing."

"Speak, Father."

But he didn't, and so I turned to leave.

I turned again and found him smiling. "What is it, Father? You don't believe me? You don't believe that he's coming?"

The priest ended the ensuing silence by saying something to the effect of, "He will come if you call him," or else some other such crap, and I turned to leave again.

"Where will you go?" he wanted to know.

"Well, to the train station, I guess."

"But it is closed."

"Then I'll wait for it to open."

"I assure you it has not been open for some time. Years in fact."

"Then I'll buy some tickets for the bullfights. Or do those not exist now either."

"Oh there are fights. Though perhaps not of the—calibre you are accustomed to."

I asked the priest to explain himself and he was about to, but then he shook his grey speckled head instead. "Go. Go and see the bullfights. You will see."

I walked towards the door and stopped. Somewhere outside a woman was laughing. It was both strange and difficult to hear a woman laughing inside a church.

"It's just that sometimes I like to make-believe," I told him.

Again I heard the woman laughing. Soon it was joined by another such laugh, a strange sort of laughter in its pitch and its duration.

"Seagulls."

"Pardon?"

"Those are the seagulls you hear," he said. "Feeding. Down at the dump."

"They sound like women. Laughing women."

"In a way, yes, I suppose they do." He paused. "But then the question is, are they laughing at you?" he chuckled.

I returned outside and felt the full heat of the evening descend upon me. It had been cool inside the church, and I hadn't really noticed the change going in, but now, in coming out, I felt it immediately and in waves. I began to sweat, and suddenly felt like returning inside the church, but then thinking of the priest and his condescending way of speaking, I rubbed the sweat from my fore-head and continued on instead.

Somewhere out there I could hear the laughter of the seagulls. It seemed to be coming from over near the square. I crossed the street and headed in the direction of the laughter. And it was some time after that that I again found myself in the company of Chris De Boer.

CHAPTER THIRTY-FIVE

WHEN I WAS a child I had a definite aversion to praying and not having my prayers answered, and so I wandered around a good long time before actually finding the bastard. When I finally did find him, I actually thought he might be someone else, but when I looked a second time and then a third I suddenly realized that it was him all right. He had taken up with a pretty young Nicaraguan named Heriberto—'Harry' for short—a very pretty and informative Nicaraguan interpreter who, despite the fact he provided such a service, I initially had no idea why he was kept around. I suppose he was good enough company, though, and whenever I inquired of something of interest, Harry always seemed to have an informative answer. He had decent enough teeth for a Nicaraguan, which was decidedly poor for a Costa Rican, and yet when he smiled he was somehow very polite and attractive and even unassuming, and his dark complexion made him seem very much like a local. Of course I'm now convinced that he was a working boy, but back then it was difficult to tell. I never did see them together, not really and never in that way, although I do think that perhaps they would have been had I not suddenly gotten in the way. De Boer was Harry's meal ticket, nothing more, and in turn Harry kept him company along the way. They had a good working relationship, one in which time spent together still held a definite value for them both, and who was I to comment on the situation, being as I was now an outsider of sorts.

Chris seemed his usual self and, at first glance anyway, barring perhaps a little lost weight, appeared relatively no worse for wear.

Initially eye contact proved impossible, though, and I got the impression early on that he was overly conscious of my presence in some way. Still, he seemed genuinely pleased to see me, even if a little distant, and we both agreed that it had been far too long since we'd spent time in each other's company. I inquired immediately as to whether he had been avoiding me, and he said he had, but now that he was with me again he was really very glad to have me back. We didn't discuss *An Inverted Sort of Prayer*. We didn't need to. The inevitable ending had already been written, and discussion of that ending wasn't something either of us would willingly fall into.

We stayed that night at Harry's sister's house, a battered, broken-down, clapboard affair located in the poorer district of Limón—if indeed a poorer district somehow separate from the rest existed in that battered, broken-down, clapboard town. Harry's sister, though, she was nice, as was her husband, and they set me up with a comfortable hammock in which to sleep—I'd always liked the idea of sleeping in a hammock, and here I was presented with my first authentic opportunity to accomplish the feat. I slept fitfully, and the following morning we took our coffee at a soda on the way into town, reclining in comfortable wicker chairs and gazing out over the too-blue water below. At some point a bald little tico separated himself from the scenery and tried his best to sell us a figurine. As an ensemble he was remarkably unattractive. In all honesty, he was the filthiest human being I've ever seen. As for the figurine, it looked gold, and had about it a vaguely Mayan look—squat and square—but unfortunately it was broken, missing one arm and pitted in several places. A brief yet amazing sequence ensued. Chris asked the filthy little tico where he'd acquired the figurine, and the tico explained how he'd dug it up. Dug it up from a grave. We told him we weren't interested in such rare antiquities, no matter how cleverly acquired, but he wouldn't go away without a fight, or so at least it seemed. He kept insisting we buy the figurine. Suddenly, and seemingly for no good reason, he reached under the table and grabbed De Boer's leg. Chris slapped him repeatedly on the top of his bald head until he let go, and eventually, with a measured gait, obedient but un-intimidated, the little fellow retreated from the table. But not before I'd taken my own turn with him. Suddenly I, too, had developed this passion to slap a filthy little grave-robbing tico on the head. I'd never before been aware of such a passion, but now it quite literally overwhelmed me. I leaned around from my side of the table and tried my best to slap him, but he'd been slapped before and by experts, and so in the end I missed him completely. Still I felt better for the effort, and for several seconds he looked back at me in somewhat surprised indignation, as if he couldn't believe that he'd been set upon by *me*. It was to become a moment frozen in memory. And of course he took with him his broken figurine.

When I inquired into the subject of bullfights, Harry informed me there were some in fact scheduled for the weekend. There were no tickets required for admission, however, as apparently one just showed up and went in. And when I asked about the running of the bulls, he said he'd never heard of such a thing. He looked to De Boer for an explanation. But Chris, of course, was not listening. Lost behind a pair of recently stolen sunglasses, he had a red elastic band wrapped around his left wrist that he flicked at repeatedly while mumbling incoherently under his breath. I seemed to bring out that sort of thing in him. There was a tanker far out on the ocean. We watched it slide along the horizon for a spell. Chris continued to flick at his elastic band, the accompanying murmur of words occasionally rising up to a point where I could almost recognize them—only to slip down and out of reach once more. I decided we ought to go for a drink. Harry thought we should head out of town. He said he knew this nice place up the coast a few kilometres that always had plenty of working girls around. I told him I wasn't really interested in that sort of thing, and winking he said there were plenty of boys working there as well. We asked De Boer what he thought of that idea, but he chose to ignore that as well.

On the way north, we stopped to fix a tire I'd blown on my way into town. Harry, for his part, struck up quite a conversation with the operator, managing to strike us quite a deal in return. Not that it was expensive, this type of repair, but to broker us a deal like that seemed to make Harry feel rather good about himself, so I let him have his little victory for now.

After the tire was fixed, we began our trip north in earnest. Soon we were out of town and on our way to the beach. Suddenly, though, I felt like fishing. I asked Harry if he knew where we could rent some equipment. He said he did, but that it would cost us. I told him I was filthy rich. And so, on that note, we returned to town to collect some fishing gear, ending up right back at the plaza in the center of town. Not much was happening. The square was empty. An old man was watering down the sun-baked brick with a hose. He reminded me of my father on our old backyard rink in Alberta—it was the same back and forth motion of the hose, I suppose. A few of the amusement rides were open, as were some of the sodas, but it was simply too hot to remain out in the square too long. A few blacks were milling about in the shade killing time, waiting for the night to come.

Harry was hungry for lunch now, and so we decided to eat inside and out of the sun. We chose a restaurant in the corner of the plaza down under cover of the arcade, and Harry and I went with the chicken casados while Chris stuck with his diet of Imperial cervezas for now. That was when it first occurred to me how much weight he'd lost, especially through the neck and face. When I made a point of this, he immediately turned sour, pointing out how much weight I'd gained. Harry laughed at that until I quietly asked him not to, at which point he moped off in search of the gear. Eventually he returned with three rods and some bait and I immediately went about settling the bill. It was stupidly hot in the plaza, and before we left town I stopped for another dozen bottles of Imperial. When I returned to the car, I was glad to see that De Boer was still with us. It wasn't so much that I thought he might run again, but simply that he had a habit of not staying put when and where you wanted him to.

We travelled north along the road with the ocean wide, flat and blue on our right, and once we were out of town the scenery bloomed—the sand as white as my palms and the palms a vibrant green in the sunlight. The road was paved most of the way along, and eventually we passed the beach where Harry had first wanted us to go

for a drink. A little further along we came to a turn-off in the road
leading to a dirt parking lot near the shore. Adjacent to the lot stood
what must have been, at one time, one heck of a fine hotel. Little
remained now beyond that of the sun-bleached, vine-covered
frame—perhaps a cracked and splintered floor or two, but really
nothing more. At over ten storeys high—this according to Harry anyway—the *Vista Del Mar* had stood, at one time, as the single most
expensive private undertaking this part of the country had ever seen.
When I asked what happened, he mentioned something about an
earthquake a decade or so before. Then he told us to follow him
inside. Dozens of iguanas scurried clear of our path, slipping off into
piles of crumbling concrete and trash. One iguana, the bull, larger
and more muscular than the rest, raised his chin repeatedly at our
intrusion on his turf, but when I called his bluff he immediately
scrambled away to safety. Later on I saw him attempt to mount more
than one member of his harem, unfortunately without much success.

Beer and fishing gear in hand, we made our way out to the ocean
side of the hotel where we happened upon a peculiar sight: as far as
I could see in either direction the entire reef had risen some two
meters clear of its natural environment. The *Vista Del Mar* had been
built upon the reef, Harry explained, and when the earthquake hit
and the reef shot up, the resultant shockwave had all but obliterated
the hotel. I asked if it was safe to be walking around out here now,
and he laughed and told me not to be such a girl.

We set ourselves up on a shady part of the dead grey reef surrounding what amounted to a deep blue aperture in the coral. The
bottom of the aperture revealed the bottom of the ocean—sandy,
immaculate and beautiful. Between the sand down there and ourselves up here a variety of fish darted about nibbling at the coral. And
although the waves were rolling in large beyond the reef, the water
here in the aperture remained, for the most part, quite peaceful.
When I asked De Boer if he'd like me to bait his hook, he did not
answer, not straight away, choosing to strum his red elastic band
instead. He mused a moment, his clear blue eyes fixed almost hyp-
notically on mine, so that I couldn't tell what he was thinking or even

if he was actually with us at the time. Then he blinked and said no. When I asked if he was nervous about the book coming out, he laughed and said God no. Then he mumbled something else to himself, all the while strumming his red elastic banjo.

"It's a prayer," he said when I asked what all this mumbling and strumming was about.

"Prayer? What prayer?"

"One my wife used to use. When she was sick," he added for Harry's benefit.

"How pious of you," I said. "I didn't think you put much stock in that commodity."

"Up till now I haven't," he said.

We watched Harry fish a while, his eyebrows pinched together in concentration. He thought he had a good solid bite at one point, and suddenly leapt up excited, but from my vantage point I could see clearly that he only had a good solid hold of the coral. Still, he was excited at the prospect, and so I let him wrestle at it a while, the tip of his wet red tongue exposed at the corner of his mouth with the effort of being such an imbecile. And a little later, having finally figured out what it was that held his hook so staunchly, and determined not to give it up without a fight, he peeled off his shirt and dove down into the aperture all skin and ribs and muscle. In due time he surfaced, hard-fought-for hook in hand, but now there was no way to scale the remaining yard or so of reef in which he suddenly found himself surrounded. As a means of escape, Chris suggested swimming out and under the coral. Harry took a deep breath and did. I watched his image fracture and disband as he dove deep for the sand, and promised myself that one day soon I too would learn to dive like that.

He didn't appear again for almost a minute, finally popping up triumphant beyond the distant edge of the reef. And finding a suitable place to scale the coral, he was soon back to fishing the aperture in vain once again. Meanwhile, out over the water, a pelican glided by. Then another. Then another. I tried to talk to De Boer again. However, unable to compete with his red elastic banjo, I had to be content with just being there beside him instead.

CHAPTER THIRTY-SIX

PRIOR TO THE Friday evening the festival finally commenced in its entirety, there had been some action in and around the plaza—a few sparse gatherings of ticos mixed in with the local blacks—but until that evening rolled around the festival had demonstrated a remarkable lack of activity, especially in comparison to all the expectations I'd established prior to my arrival this far out in the country. Ticos had been funnelling in all week long from throughout the provinces, filling the hotels to overcapacity. At night the plaza came alive as one solid moving body, but during the day remained mostly empty. These people weren't fools. They'd grown up under the merciless rule of the sun. The heat to them was not so much a blessing as it was a stipulation of an inescapable end. And so, counterpoised against its punishing proximity, they stuffed themselves into the sodas and bars and makeshift cafés leaving what little was available for beaches to the blacks. As a city, Limón lays claim to few nice beaches, if any, but just north and south of town there are some. Chris, Harry and I typically remained in the shaded cafés under the arcade surrounding the plaza, but occasionally we went out to the beaches, myself in a T-shirt most of the time. I didn't want to put on display the gut I'd grown in recent months, what with the likes of the recently trimmed-down De Boer and his skinny little Nicaraguan around. I poked around at my abdomen, finding it soft and weak, and made a vague promise to myself to start losing some weight at the end of the week.

With the bullfights scheduled for the next two days, we stuck mostly to the plaza that night. There was to be a parade and some kind of fireworks. Well the parade turned out all right. Fireworks, naturally, were never very good. They were always so built-up like that. In an unguarded moment I pondered aloud whether we as a species would ever tire of celebrating mediocrity, and Chris just looked at me and smiled. I suppose it was a rather profound insight.

Sitting in one of the makeshift cafés at the edge of the plaza we drank mostly guaro that night. The chairs and tables were of that cheap folding variety—not so comfortable or stable but certainly functional—and the tables were covered in cheap plastic red and yellow tablecloths featuring what else but the Imperial águila. I had the waiter bring me some water along with a spoon and some sugar. I was attempting to prepare my guaro in the manner of absinthe. Initially, I admit, it didn't go so well. Later on, however, I saw a woman preparing her tea with some sort of strainer that fit over the top of her cup, and so I petitioned from the waiter one such device for myself. He brought me one and I placed it over my glass, then placed the sugar on the strainer and poured water over the sugar—it mixed well with the guaro, but certainly made it taste no better. And all the while I was preparing my absinthe approximation, Harry was frowning—that is, until he got into the spirit of the thing. Then, of course, he went along without complaint, and later on even became quite fond of it. Chris refused to take part in out little ritual, but then I'd never expected he would. Guaro was certainly no absinthe, and preparing it in such a way was certainly a stretch, but then with the situation one inherited one had to make do, I guess.

The people of this country appreciate good drinking, but frown on a really bad drunk. That said, they naturally do a great deal of drinking themselves. But then who can blame them. It's always so very hot down here, even too hot, and on many occasions it's all you can do just to crack open an Imperial and say to hell with it. Still it's not good to drink in the sun, especially in a country such as this one. Drinking guaro at any time is itself no small feat, but drinking it in the sun this close to the equator can finish you in a matter of minutes. But it was not too hot now. It was evening in the plaza before the day of the bullfights, and we were in one of the makeshift cafés drinking guaro as though it were something else entirely.

The fireworks had just ended when I wondered aloud when all these people had arrived. There were suddenly so many bodies milling about in the plaza that I could no longer see the far side. All I could see were the ticos and the blacks—mostly blacks—Chris and I being the only white ones around. And sitting at that table in that makeshift café I studied the diversity in the local citizenry. The ticos and the blacks were at odds in far more than just skin colour. For one, the blacks were far larger than the ticos; far more athletic and muscular. As well, their collective conduct was far more a caricature of something sadly American, and the ticos were very much intimidated by that behaviour somehow. Both sets of youth were decked out in the colours of American athletic teams in and of which they had no vested interest or working knowledge, but in truth the ticos had nothing on the blacks. The blacks wore it all with so much more style. Savvy. Affectation and attitude. One could say the blacks were far more American than the ticos were Spanish and that, I suppose, was the crux of it.

I immediately ordered another round. I didn't want to lose hold of what feeling I'd gained as, like any endeavour for me, drinking was very often an uphill battle. This time Harry took his guaro with something called *Lift*, a clear carbonated beverage so popular in these countries crammed down around the equator. That was how De Boer took it anyway, and now of course they both took it the same way. Myself, I was very excited about the bullfights the following day. True, I hadn't yet seen the bulls, or the bullring, but then really, what did I care. Just so long as I witnessed the main event I would be happier here than anywhere. And sitting in the makeshift café at the edge of the plaza, I explained the bullfights to Harry, and what all to expect from the bulls, as he'd never actually seen a fight before.

"They've been bred for the sacrifice," I heard the guaro say. "Generation after generation, the bulls have been cultivated towards this single point in time when they enter the ring for the contest."

"So it is dangerous then."

"Oh very dangerous indeed," I joined in. "Especially when the bull is alone. You see, in order to keep the bulls calm, they keep them together in herds. But detach one from the herd and look out, he charges right at you. The bull only kills when he's alone."

Harry considered that thoroughly. "Watch closely tomorrow," I said. "Their horns, they use them like fists—like an enforcer, jabbing and striking in close."

"En-forcer?"

"Boxer," I said, putting together a few quick combinations to further demonstrate my point. "It's all a very sweet science."

"Sweet science," he said. "I have not heard it put that way before."

"Oh yes, the matador's science must be extremely sweet if he is to avoid being mounted on one of those."

Another round of guaros arrived, but this time I prepared mine in a slightly different manner. First, with a borrowed lighter, I caramelized the sugar, then poured the water over the sugar and watched the mixture trickle down into the liquid below.

I explained to Harry how fighting a bull required strength, balance and grip, all three of which required equal mastery if one was going to be at all effective in such a dangerous forum as this. The first component, strength, was of course self-explanatory: it took a strong man both mentally and physically, not only to maintain that level of energy, but to dole it out effectively as well. But the second component, balance, may have been the most significant, structurally speaking at least. "Balance is lost, and found, in the hips."

"Por qué?"

"As goes the means so go the extremes," I said. For starters, a narrow stance was good—"difficult to get knocked off your feet like that"—toes together, legs straight, hips held in under the body, allowing the momentum of the charge to send the fighter spinning around a central point. "Tight and effective, good balance can be the one crucial difference leaving you standing at the end of the tilt."

"What is the third then?"

"Grip," I said. Just as important as balance but far more complicated, it was with grip that so many young matadors made their crucial mistake.

"Grip on the espada—I mean the sword?" he said.

"You might think so but no, grip on the cape." Overly concerned with landing the money shot, typically the overhand right, too many young fighters forgot to make better use of the cloth instead. And while it was true that the bullfighter required a variety of attributes and skills in order to excel in this line of work, above all he needed a good left hand. Any fighter worth his title would tell you a fight was won more with the hand controlling the cloth and guiding the bull than with the one shoving in the blade. "Remember, Harry, the bull uses his horns like fists. Like a boxer. The trick to remember here is *corto y derecho.*"

"Short and straight," he translated.

"That's right. Short and straight," I said. Short and straight was always the most efficient way to maintain a maximum purity of line, and in doing so, minimize the gap between bull and cape.

"You see, Harry, instead of establishing an effective grip on the cloth, thereby limiting the bull's mobility and effectiveness, a less accomplished fighter typically holds on for show, for balance, or simply for life in general." Typically, say, with a right-handed bull, a fighter established his grip somewhere in the middle—"out too far and he risks being pulled off balance, while in too close and he risks the very bone structure of his face"—thus nullifying any undue generation of power, speed and punishment on the bull's behalf, all the while manoeuvring his sword into the proper position for the corto y derecho. Typically. Because it was when a left-hander was involved, or a bull of greater experience, breeding and ability, when the complexity, speed and beauty of the dance tended to grow together almost exponentially.

"Left-handed bull?"

"Left-handed bull," I said. "He's the one that makes it a thing of beauty out there."

"I see," he said, although naturally he did not. "Were you a good matador then?" he asked a little later.

"You bet I was. In fact, I was exceptional. I was known for standing quiet and motionless before a fight—like this," I said, standing up to demonstrate.

"Are you still?"

"No. No, now I am too old unfortunately."

"Still you must have been good at one time to know all that you do now," he said. "Tell me, though, were all the bulls you fought left-handed?"

"In the end they were. Things are different now though. Vastly different. The game has changed—or *evolved* as they so annoyingly like to say."

We were drinking guaro at the makeshift café readying ourselves for the festival. Harry asked whether I'd ever been gored by the bull and I told him I'd taken far less than I'd given anyway.

"Oh but he has his scars," Chris said after a prolonged silence.

"Really? From the cuernos?" Harry asked as I looked hatefully at De Boer.

"Oh yes. Show him, Billy. Show Harry here some of your wonderful scars."

"They're nothing, really."

"Por favor—please," Harry implored. "I must see the scars from the horns."

"I would, believe me, but a truly accomplished matador never reveals his sources."

I flexed my fingers and cracked my knuckles, but couldn't get the last one to go. Harry turned to Chris. "Were you a matador too then?" he asked.

"No, I only kill when I'm alone."

Harry laughed. "You make a broma then."

"No," I said, "he's far too corto y derecho for that."

"Is that another broma?"

"Yes, another joke," I said, cracking that final knuckle at last. "You'll find his writing very witty like that. What, you didn't know, Harry? Your boyfriend here is a writer of stories."

"Truly?" Harry said, truly impressed. "What kind of stories you write?"

But Chris merely shook his head in answer.

"As I told you, he's a wit," I said. "Everything he writes is witty. You'd probably recognize it, though, as his style is achingly familiar."

I don't know why I was going after him like this. Of course I do know. As it was, though, we didn't speak again for some time as the parade was fast approaching the plaza. From down the street you could hear them coming: the pipes and the drums of the various bands marching along to the square. Very soon it was all you could hear. The crowds of people preceding the parade were pouring into the plaza, packing themselves in with those already there. Everyone was smiling. Some were singing. Others were dancing alone or in groups. Through the crowds, amid the dancing and the singing, I could see the parade approaching: the floats seeming to hover under the lights strung up around the plaza's perimeter. Some of the floats resembled giant cartoon characters, while others were simply flower-covered automobiles. One float, larger and more extravagant than the rest, featured as its centerpiece an enormous poster of a man's face, the poster itself framed in bright multicoloured garlands and painted red around the perimeter. Coming into the square, the poster trembled and swayed within its framework of flowers, swaying to the rhythm of the music. I asked Harry which saint it was pictured on the poster and he said Cristóbal Colón, or something to that effect.

"Cristó-what?"

"Bal. Cristóbal. Christopher Columbus," he said. "It's in his honour this festival is held." And all the while the pipes kept piping and the drums kept drumming, the pipes so high and the drums so low that soon they were almost out of range of hearing altogether.

The square was almost full. Along with the floats came painted clowns and parades of children darting in and around the dancers already there. They all pressed in tightly together as the music grew louder and the crowds came closer—some dressed in shirts of red and yellow with little more than crudely knotted black bandannas for underwear. At the edge of the café, maybe ten feet from our table, a young couple came together amid these Imperial colours. Adjusting my head to the proper angle, I was just able to make them out through the press of bodies in between. He was a black and she was a tica and they were both soaking wet from dancing in the square. Suddenly he wheeled her around, and I watched as the bottle in his hand slid up under her skirt. I watched it slide up. It went a long way up. Then I noted the bold black eagle on the label.

"Bull's eye!" Harry smiled, smacking me on the shoulder to ensure I was watching. I was watching, and so was De Boer. His shirt said Georgetown—the black man's, I mean—and he was pressing the bottle up into her from behind. Fascinated, I continued to crane my neck, only to lose sight of them through the dancing crowd. Off to the left some policemen were wrestling another black to the ground, taking from his person what appeared to be a pistol. As the skirmish continued, I experienced something of a mild and pleasant shock. And allowing the burnt sugar-water to mix with the liquor, I hoisted it back into my throat in one greedy gulp.

"Déjà vu," I said, watching the poster, now detached from its float, come bobbing along atop a circling of dancers. A bit of the drink had dripped onto my chin, and I found myself wondering briefly if Harry had noticed.

"What?" Chris laughed, unable to hear me over the music and the crowd.

"Déjà vu," I repeated. "I feel like I've been here before."

He laughed again, but I knew he hadn't heard me. It didn't matter either way. We were sitting together in a café at the edge of the plaza drinking absinthe as the fiesta began.

CHAPTER THIRTY-SEVEN

LATER THAT NIGHT, good and tight, we found ourselves wandering aimlessly around the plaza. Harry was probably in the best condition of the three of us, and try as he might Chris just couldn't stop smiling. It was good to see him smiling again, though, and I was glad the guilt had receded far enough to permit such a reversal of character. The crowds had dissipated somewhat over the previous few hours, and once again we were able to move freely about the plaza. The dancing and the singing had died their inevitable deaths, dispersing to remote corners of the square. It must have been late as all of the children were gone. All that remained were the ticos and the blacks—mostly blacks—Chris and I being still the only white ones around.

The heavy bass beat brought us in. One of the makeshift discos, its walls constructed mostly of palm fronds held together with Imperial banners, resonated a deep bass rhythm to all four corners of the square. Inside, the blacks were dancing. There must have been three hundred or more in there. We three moved to the center of the throng where we took up with a pair of young girls. One couldn't yet have been in her teens. She wore an Imperial bandanna tied snugly around her small close-cropped head, and her flat hips and smooth chest suggested but a handful of years. Her friend, however, might have been a little older, what with her enormous breasts and massive afro. Both wore cut-off denim shorts and neither one spoke a word of English, and so naturally we spoke English a great deal.

Both girls hopped to it immediately, but then not in a manner I might have expected. Their expressions never changed throughout the entire ordeal—they rarely took notice of us, and when they did, it was with an air of grim duty but otherwise general indifference. It occurred to me then that this might well be a con. After all, what they did was anything but civilized, and I still can't explain it in any other manner.

On cue they wheeled about, bent forward from their waists and arched their backs, then shuttled their buttocks up and down against our crotches, all to the rhythm of the bass of course. The smallest one shuttled me, and I doubt she was too impressed with my response. She was too short to position herself properly against me, and so took to standing atop my sandals in an effort to somehow account for the discrepancy. Together we made quite a tandem. The fact that she was standing on my toes made for a large part of my discomfort, but then I wasn't about to rock the boat and ask her to get off or anything like that. As it was, I simply grinned my stupid grin and bore it all as best I could. To my right, Chris seemed to be receiving the same sort of treatment from his, while to my left Harry was left dancing by himself. I could see De Boer's was performing the dance properly, however, shuttling up and down both vigorously and rhythmically to the deep bass beat, receiving the expected physical response. They were dancing like this all over the disco. The pressure to perform was immense. It was all very exciting what they did, even erotic, and I was tempted to compare it with the copulation of animals. Like Harry, those few young men unlucky enough not to get paired off still danced, albeit quietly and by themselves.

Next thing I knew the place was half empty. The blacks were leaving in droves. Within minutes the place was all but deserted, all except for ourselves and our girls. Eventually even the girls left. I asked Harry why everyone had disappeared so quickly, and he said it was because of us gringos.

"What, we soured the place?"

"It only takes a few," he shrugged.

"A few what? Us?"

"No, a few of them," he said. "A few of them decide you no belong, and the rest just follow along. Don't take it personally," he shrugged again. "They just not used to you here in Limón."

"Why not just ask us to leave then?" Chris asked.

"Not the way," Harry smiled. "Not the way here in Costa Rica, my friend."

We exited the suddenly empty disco and wandered aimlessly about the plaza. It was very late and some of the makeshift sodas were closed. We did find a place still serving noodles, however, and giving Harry some money I sent him off with our orders. Chris chose a table off in the corner. One of the legs was broken, and I tried but failed to fix it with a roll of napkins. A basket on the table contained a variety of hot sauces, and I was excited about putting some on my noodles. Whatever else this country has to offer, it certainly has some terrific hot sauces, let alone those rather spicy mating rituals.

While Harry was away at the counter, a black man approached our table introducing himself as Noël. Just like Christmas, he told us twice, scraping back a chair. Noël did seem friendly enough. He was powerfully built and wore his tan button-down shirt wide open, revealing a narrow muscular torso. Though heavily accented, his English remained relatively comprehensible, and I was glad for that at this point of the night. I didn't feel much like conversing in Spanish or worse, that awful Spanglish anymore.

"Man, you two being *watched*," he said, his pronunciation of 'man' as 'mon' more than enough to make me laugh. To conceal this reaction, I asked what he meant by *watched* and he said, "Look," in a low and sober tone, implying serious advice was imminent. "Look, Noël been to New York, and Noël knows what people be considering. Knows what people be considering hostile, understand? And here they be considering *you.*"

"Now what do you mean by 'considering,' Noël."

"Watching. I told you."

"And who's watching?"

"People, man. People maybe want to confront you."

"What for though?"

"Money, man. What do you think what for? Limón port town, no?" He frowned, watching Chris flick at his elastic band. "Why do you do that?"

"What, this?" said Chris, staring at the elastic. "My wife once tied her hair back with this."

Noël nodded once, feigning comprehension.

"So then Noël, he will help us," I continued on in an ironic tone of incantation clearly wasted on our guest.

"That's right, man. Noël, he been to New York, and in New York they help him plenty." He leaned back in his chair and added with pride, "Noël just spreading the karma, understand."

"Mighty white of him," I said.

"You know why they not come for you yet? Because of this," he said, and reached across the table to trace a finger along De Boer's upper arm, snapping the latter out of his latest prayer session. I should probably mention that Chris had this tattoo of intertwined vines wrapped around his upper right arm. It was a nice enough tattoo, but then considering the proliferation of those sorts of things these days, hardly worth mentioning till now.

"That's right, man. People down here, they don't know what it means. But Noël, he understands. Noël been to New York and knows all about devil's paint and point of view. But down here, down here in little Limón, they still think it be some kind of *voodoo*."

"You're joking," I said.

"Occasionally, yes," he admitted. "But understand, Noël no joke here."

I glanced over at Chris as he continued to strum his red elastic band, content, it would seem, to regard the matter as a mystery not worth solving just now.

"Well I suppose we'll just have to take your word for it then."

"Yes," Noël said, suddenly very serious, "but not for granted, man. The fear only keeps them away so long, understand."

And with that, Noël politely excused himself from our table, cueing Harry to return with the noodles. I doused mine in hot sauce and washed them down with Imperial. For whatever reason, De Boer refused to touch his food.

After the noodles and the beer we made our way free of the plaza. I thought it was smart we had Harry along as, indeed, most everyone seemed to be watching us now. And walking east of the plaza in the direction of the ocean we came upon those two young black girls from the disco leaning against a fence alongside the street. They offered me some of their joint but naturally I declined, citing how much it hurt my throat. Harry took some though. As did De Boer. It came around once more. It really was a very ugly joint—dark brown and wrinkled—and listening to the rhythm of the distant bass I watched the four of them smoke it down to a roach. I suppose at some point I must have moved with the rhythm as the little one once again set to. And setting my jaw I awaited the inevitable pain and discomfort as she clambered awkwardly aboard my sandals and into position.

Following her friend's lead, sporting a look equally devoid of expression, De Boer's girl assumed the position evidently required of one of her station, superimposing her young black indigenous rhythm on his own very tired white Imperial one. It was all so very strange in its ritual and implication—all so very primitive and crude—and yet they made it seem as though it were nothing at all, as though it were all simply understood. I wondered if Chris was aware of that. I wondered if he saw that too. I wondered how it was a prejudice was formed, and when it was if it was always untrue.

Once the joint was finished, we sent Harry back to the plaza for beer. A few cars had crept by slowly and suspiciously of late, and so we decided we required some place a little more secluded. Once Harry returned with the beer, we went off and found the Taurus. No one bothered to speak too much. I suppose it was just as well. I suppose we could have employed Harry as interpreter, but then really, what more could he have possibly gotten us.

Under the occasional glare of infrequent streetlights, we drove north and out of town in the direction of the demolished *Vista Del*

Mar, and upon our arrival at the hotel, Harry and the little one went out for a swim beyond the jutting shelf of coral. The other one remained with De Boer and me in the Taurus, and soon they were together in the back seat. I was thinking that maybe he wanted to put on some sort of show. Truth is, he didn't seem entirely taken with the girl, and yet seemed to know exactly what it was I was looking for here. I settled in as she again assumed the position—not so easy an assignment, believe me, not when you considered the overly cramped conditions afforded by the car. I could hear it happening. It made such an awful drawing sound happening. It was a disgusting sound to be sure. And I swear I was just about to take my leave when Chris asked if maybe I wouldn't mind taking off for a few.

I wandered out to the reef alone, three cans of beer in hand. It certainly was a beautiful night—the stars were out and the ocean was calm, though I didn't recognize any of the constellations. The ones I would have recognized were all too low on the horizon where there was too much of an artificial glow out over the water. I thought the glow might well have been Havana, but then with my geography having suffered along with the rest of my childhood education, I really had no clue. Now of course I know I was wrong—it was not Havana at all—but back then, well, it just goes to show you.

Far above the glow on the horizon the moon sliced a bright minstrel smile against the black backdrop of sky, mocking my predicament down here. In the moonlight I could just discern their silhouettes out there on the edge of the reef, Harry very much in behind her. I wondered if they knew any other way of doing it. Fucking savages, I thought. Now how funny is that. How funny is that for the pot calling the kettle black. Still, it wasn't such a difficult leap when you thought about it. What was difficult was not to box them in like that. Besides, I doubt I was too far off in my diagnosis. And although I'd like to think that I'm not at all like that, the truth is that trip cemented the fact. I suppose it was funny. I mean in a way it was funny. It was just so easy to be branded like that.

After a long time watching I made my way back to the Taurus. I didn't think I should be away too long, and back in the front seat I sat quietly drinking my Imperials and watching them via the rear-view mirror. Christ, what a stench, I thought. He was at her breasts and she was at his arm, gnawing aggressively at his tattoo. I decided I might try to join in. I didn't know what I was going to do when I got there, but then I didn't want to be branded as some kind of queer. Chris had her pinned into the far rear corner of the Taurus where she was still all tooth and nail at his tattoo. Christ, what a stench, I thought—I couldn't get over it—a smell like hot tar and fresh tanned leather. Cramming myself awkwardly between the two front seats, I directed her head over and down. Truth is, I envied her the specificity of her task, so unlike the elusive nature of my own. Regrettably she began to scream, and so I backed off immediately, apologizing profusely, but still she continued to scream bloody murder. I apologized again and scrambled free of the car, De Boer hustling along behind with shorts in hand. And side by side we sat on the edge of a shattered, pitted concrete slab just inside the frame of the hotel. I thought it might well have been the bar we were seated at, but of course in this light it was difficult to tell. I knew I would be lucky to find one out this far.

"She seems pretty upset in there," Chris said, gazing back over his shoulder in the direction of the Taurus. I looked around, shrugged, and popped open another Imperial. Then I remembered that I'd left the keys in the car. No matter, I thought, and shuffled up closer to the bar. Outside the window, the heat continued to pour down. I reached over to close the curtain for now.

"Don't block out the light like that."

"What's that?"

"When you moved up on her like that, you blocked out the moonlight," Chris said. "She got scared."

Fucking savage, I thought. "You're right," I said, looking out the window at the car. "She does seem pretty upset out there."

We watched her shuffling about inside the Taurus, presumably getting back into her gear. I wiped the moisture from each of my beer cans onto my shorts and sighed tremendously. The *Vista Del Mar* was so very quiet this time of year.

We sat drinking our beer in the old hotel bar waiting for the girl to come around. Or at least to unlock the doors. I ordered two more, waiting until the bartender returned with the drinks before inquiring as to whether he'd said something about my condition to Harry or the girls. He said he hadn't, but that they could probably just tell.

I stood up and thrust myself clear of the bar. The girl, I could see, was still locked in the car.

"What are you thinking about, Billy?"

"Nothing."

"What?"

"Nothing, really. Just about the horses back on my mother's family's farm." I coughed once, and cleared my throat. "I just thought of something else."

"I don't believe it."

"Trust me, it's true."

"Trust? Who said anything about trust? I could've sworn we were talking blind faith here."

I poured out two quick shots. "Gentlemen, to getting blind," I said, and we hooked back our shots together.

Still wincing from that shot, I poured out two more. "To the piss," I said, and we hooked back our shots.

"It sure was off in there," I said a little later.

Chris said nothing.

"Christ it was off," I said. "It stunk like shit in there."

He looked at me, but still said nothing. Finally I went one further.

"I suppose you used some protection though."

"Well then I guess you'd be wrong. And besides," he said, rising slowly from the bar, "she's probably got more to fear from me than anything the other way around."

Just then, Harry and the little one came sauntering back from the reef arm in arm. Somewhat surprisingly, she didn't seem all that upset at the prospect of her friend having locked herself in the car. In fact, she took to it with that same air of indifference and disconnection she'd taken to everything else that evening thus far. I asked

Harry if he had found her all that indifferent out there on the reef. He said he had, but then no more than he had, and we both laughed at that and finished our beers. We waited for the other one to come out of the car. She was a long time coming. Here she comes. There she goes. I asked Harry if he could tell I was injured. He said he couldn't tell, not by looking anyway, but that the girl had mentioned something about it out there on the coral.

The girls must have walked back to town soon after that, as suddenly I couldn't find them anywhere.

"What was all that screaming, Cristóbal?" Harry asked.

"Oh, uh, Billy here blocked out the light."

"Blocked out the light—is that another joke then?"

"No," I sighed. "Unfortunately it's very much a fact of life."

Chapter Thirty-Eight

SUFFICE TO SAY, the day of the bullfights neither De Boer nor I were in a very good mood. Suffering through a hangover like that would have proved difficult at the best of times, but in the heat and the aftermath of the previous night swelled to a nearly impossible endeavour. It was so very hot the day of the bullfights. There was hardly anyone out on the streets. Still, there was no way I was going to miss out on the spectacle, and so I dragged Chris along just to spite the jerk.

Even the plaza was dead. What few flags had been replaced after the previous night's debauchery clung passively to their poles in the heat, while in the shade of one corner a few people were dancing languidly, but then these were ticos and I no longer cared. We took our coffee in one of the makeshift cafés, and sent Harry out to gather information. He returned a few minutes later. The fights were set for five o'clock that afternoon, he said, and were scheduled to continue into the early evening. I rubbed my hands together expectantly. Despite the hangover and the heat of the day I was eagerly anticipating the contest. Harry was interested too, he said, but naturally De Boer could not have cared less.

"Don't look at the horse after the bull hits him," I told Chris at one point. "I doubt your poor Liberal heart could handle it. Just hide your eyes when the bull makes his run and I'll let you know when it's safe to come out again."

We bitched and groaned this way—or rather, I did—all the way up out of town. The bullring was situated atop the plateau to the northwest of Limón where even now a steady procession was making its way up. There were people on foot going up, as well as those in open-bed trucks, and the cars and trucks going up the hill swirled the dust up over the heads of the people on foot forced to cover their faces with their Imperial bandannas. We took the Taurus to avoid the heat, but still ended up making the trip at a crawl. The dirt road was narrow, only one double-rutted lane wide, and the traffic crawled along in a general stupor much of the time. I checked and rechecked the Taurus's temperature gauge throughout the journey, but found no real cause for concern. Certainly it was hot, and the air-conditioning certainly worked doggedly, but as was always the case in this country it was the tires that bore the brunt of one's worry.

"Por qué, Cristóbal?" Harry whined when Chris informed him he would have to be returning home soon. *An Inverted Sort of Prayer* would be out in less than two weeks, and naturally he would be expected back for the launch party. "But why, Cristóbal? Why is it so soon you must go?"

"Because he's a martyr," I snapped. "He's a martyr and eventually all martyrs must go."

"Look, Harry," Chris said tenderly, refusing me the decency of a proper retaliation, "I have things I need to take care of back home."

"But what kinds of things, Cristóbal?" Harry asked again in that whine, and again with that ridiculous nickname.

"Things you really need no knowledge of," I put in. "Political things. Saintly things. What, didn't you know he was a saint, Harry? Well of course he is. He's the patron saint of thievery and plagiarism."

Chris sighed and shook his head. Harry narrowed his already narrow eyes further.

"Oh sure he is. Just ask him. Go ahead and ask him," I said. "In fact he's the one for which we hold this entire celebration."

"All right, Billy, enough," Chris said, slowly removing his sunglasses.

"Sí, enough," echoed Harry.

"Oh come now," I continued. "Surely you're familiar with the story of the great Saint Christopher? I mean you did say you were

Catholic didn't you, Harry? Well didn't you? Well of course you did. All you little Latinos are. Latinos and Indians," I said. And Cristóbal here, why, he *preached* to Indians. Sure he did. In fact he was called, as Harry was no doubt aware, the great *apostle* of the Indians. He had that kind of faith in him that moved mountains, I said. That kind of faith that got him into *Vanity Fair* for all the customary reasons. "Just imagine though, Harry! Vanity Fair! How's that for the conquering hero? How's that for personal sacrifice? How's that for power to intercede on all our Indians' behalf? Yes, a great saviour we have here," I said. "A real philanthropist. A veritable soldier of the Lord. At one time he wanted to change the world, but now he only hopes to save himself."

I explained how Chris had given his wife cervical cancer, via some kind of venereal virus he'd picked up while cheating on her, and how guilty he was understandably feeling as a result. But then who could blame him? Certainly not us Indians, I said. No, not us Indians whatsoever. After all, we had our own faithlessness to deal with, our own lack of discipline, let alone this fabulous new religion he'd given us.

The heat of the day overwhelmed my hostility as we parked in a field next to the bullring. The ring looked a little shoddier than I'd hoped it would, less majestic and more, what, functional, but then I saw the horses shimmering in the hot currents of air rising up beyond the ring and everything began to click once more. They were running the horses through their paces on the hard sun-baked earth. One horse, a white charger larger and more muscular than the rest, moved about under saddle, picking up his legs first the one then the other, playfully engaging his rider. He certainly was a beautiful horse, one it would be a shame to have to sacrifice to the bull, but then that was the nature of the bullfight of course, and there could be no sacrifice without something getting butchered.

The big red gate was open, and inside I could see the sand of the arena dragged clean and smooth. Red and yellow Imperial banners draped from the wooden barrera at regular intervals, while the walls behind had been freshly postered with the logo of the Imperial eagle.

Matadors, banderilleros, and the occasional picador shuffled about in the shadows of the amphitheatre. I pointed to a dignified young matador strutting by all tanned, healthy and athletic looking, his silver-brocaded coat tossed casually over his shoulder. He was playing with the length of scarlet sash at his waist and his black hair was glistening in the sun.

"But where is his sword?" Harry asked. "I thought they had swords."

"His handlers must have it," I said, having coughed to clear my throat. That was when I first started bringing up blood. Or rather, when I first started taking notice of it.

"So where are the bulls?" Harry asked.

"Oh you'll see them," Chris said. "They're the ones with the horns being tortured."

Although we still had plenty of time prior to the first scheduled bullfight, I hustled them both along and inside. I wanted to make sure we got the very best seats, the berreras along the first row out of the sun. As expected, there was no one around to charge admission at the door, and we went in through the red gate uncontested. Once inside, we secured three berreras directly across from another red gate, behind which stood the crate from which the first bull would eventually emerge infuriated. Sitting and sweating and glancing about, I noticed how few people there actually were in the stands. True, there had been quite a procession making its way up the hill, but then this was a large albeit largely makeshift bullring, one which would prove difficult to fill.

Watching the amphitheatre slowly fill with people, I explained to Harry what exactly he was in for here. I explained about the bull again; about the carriage of the great horned head by the great hump of muscle rising up from its shoulders, and how the entire fight would be fought to bring about that muscle's weakening until the great head came down. And I explained about the picador, and how with precision and strength he would drive his long-poled pic perfectly into that hump of muscle, using the momentum of the bull's charge against itself to weaken its strength and to bring the great head down. I explained about the banderillero placing his slender barbed sticks into that hump of muscle to further weaken its strength and to further bring the great head down, and I explained about the matador who would finally dance with the bull, driving his sword over and past the great head now down, past the horns now heavy, deep into that muscle once swollen and tight but now injured and bleeding, ragged and weakened, to that precise point high up between the shoulder blades, past the vertebrae and atop the ribs to sever the aorta that would finally see the great head come all the way down and instantly dead to the ground. I explained about the horses again, and how they would be gored in the belly until their entrails dangled out, often catching up in the feet of the animal, tripping the animal, and how the matador would use his cape to take the bull away from the fallen horse with a series of two-handed veronicas, smoothly and suavely, never wasting the bull. I remember clearly Harry's confusion with that. His confusion with not wasting the bull. If the point was to kill it, he said, then why not kill it as quickly and painlessly as possible? I explained that almost any bullfighter could kill a bull, but that only a truly gifted matador could turn that killing into an art. That is, saving the bull for the very last when he wanted him, and never the other way around. The point was not simply to kill the bull, I said, but to kill him with discipline and honour. The entire phenomenon was a sacrifice, a religious sacrifice whose ecstasy, while momentary, remained as profound as any religious one.

"What is a veronica then?"

"A two-handed pass with the cape," I explained, offering a quick demonstration.

"Why is it so called?"

"I'm not altogether sure, Harry. But to emulate Saint Veronica wiping the face of the Christ with a cloth, I'm guessing."

"The matador wipes the face of the *bull*?" he said in wide-eyed disbelief.

"It's only an expression."

Next I explained about the terrain of the bullfighter and the terrain of the bull, and how, in my best days, I worked always in the terrain of the bull. This gave the feeling of imminent tragedy, I explained, and people came from miles around to see it and to feel it, hoping to see me gored by the bull. Harry thought it both odd and horrible that people would want to see a great person fail. I explained how that was the way of people, and the way of sport, and that, if possible, he would be wise to maintain a safe distance from both. The bullfight's ability to move you depends on the faith you have in its performers, I said, and in faith there is nothing more moving than the sacrifice of one's good judgment.

Finally the first fight was set to begin. The amphitheatre was hardly half full. Those few people in attendance seemed completely misplaced—mostly teens, a few elderly women, and certainly no aficionados to help solidify a rapidly unravelling event. Setting my jaw, I awaited De Boer's inevitable barb, but for now he only prayed, aloud but to himself, strumming his red elastic banjo to the red elastic rhythm in his head.

Eventually the procession made its way into the ring, dragging their lengthening shadows behind. Heads up and swaggering, right arms free and swinging awkwardly to the tinny canned music, the matadors stepped out and across the sun-baked sand. Behind the matadors, a rough looking crew of banderilleros and horse-riding picadors shuffled out side by side before breaking up into their various components around the ring. The matadors stood around the edge of the ring laughing and sweating in the sun. Most were squat little ticos with bellies jutting out over cheap red sashes, drinking from jugs of cheaper red wine. I awaited the arrival of the servants to come out and sweep the sand. No one appeared quite up to the task. Too hot, I thought. Too bloody hot. I waited impatiently for the bull to arrive.

Harry brought my attention back to the young matador strutting about before us, the one we'd seen outside earlier with his silver-brocaded jacket glittering in the sun. To his credit, he looked young and strong and confident. However, on closer inspection, the silver brocade of his jacket proved to be nothing more than tin foil shaped and crushed to appear as such.

Finally the red gate opened and out bounced the very first bull. Charging headlong from the crate, he skidded to a wavering stop somewhere near the middle of the ring, and I breathed a sigh of relief. The bull, too, stood there breathing heavily, his coat a shimmering sweat in the heat. Primarily white, he sported here and there some pale red markings of no particular shape or design, as well as a pair of smoothly curved horns that, at first glance anyway, appeared more than capable of accomplishing the task of some overly plump tico's disembowelling. The bull lowered his horns slowly and menacingly, and then, possibly for effect but probably just for exercise, raised them mechanically again. Some half-chewed something-or-other swung limply from an ever-lengthening cord of saliva before falling for good and forever from his lip. Reluctantly he turned and started to prance, soft and slow at first, then aggressive and stiff-legged as he went along, the idea of putting on a show apparently coming rather gradually to him, if it were actually coming to him at all. The sparse crowd cheered in the heat. The bull responded by crashing headlong into the wooden barrera and promptly losing his feet.

Chris nudged Harry on the arm. "And that, my friend, would be the bull."

The bull continued to charge the barrera perhaps forty feet down to our left. He seemed to be caught up in one of the banners—the red and yellow seemed to be catching his attention. Thus engaged, the bull refused to acknowledge any of his true combatants out there with him in the ring. One of the picadors on horseback moved in unsteadily to challenge—nothing doing, the bull only wanted the advertising. The bull continued to run and tear at the red and yellow banners placed all along the barrera until, finally, they were pulled up and over by some drunken spectators seated nearby.

Eventually the bull offered one of the horses a legitimate run, and I breathed another legitimate sigh of relief. Harry, however, offered up another good point when he noted that the pics themselves were actually blunted on the ends. When the bull rushed the horse, then, the picador simply held him off with the pole's blunt end. The bull was afraid of the blunt-ended pic, and couldn't get near the soft fuzzy underbelly of the stallion.

"I have no idea why the pics are blunt," I said. "Perhaps it makes for added danger."

"Go bull," Chris chuckled, almost but not quite to himself. Meanwhile, rapidly losing interest in the picador and his mount, the bull took a wide strutting turn around the ring, silent except for the several ragged breaths issuing from his mouth.

"That must be a right-handed bull," Harry observed.

True, it was not very big. Again Chris chuckled quietly to himself, yet loud enough for me to hear. As for the astute and literal-minded Harry, well he raised yet another good point when he noticed that the bull's horns were somewhat blunted themselves. Sawed-off more bloody likely, I thought, and panicking, explained how a dull horn could often inflict far more damage than one that was sharp. "It's been proven," I heard myself say more than once.

"Go bull," Chris laughed a little louder. I scowled at him, trying my best to ignore him, and failing horribly in that regard, thought about the horses instead. I focused all of my attention on them.

Eventually one of the matadors—the young one—stepped out boldly into the centre of the ring. He managed to take the first run relatively closely, his body held almost perfectly in line. I winced at the next pass. Harry shifted in his seat.

"He's not taking the charges too closely, is he."

Chris chuckled. "He does look a little scared. Not you, Billy, but your matador there."

"What are you talking about," I said. "I've yet to see him do a damned thing."

We watched the young matador leap about like a fairy on the sand. "Where is his sword?" Harry asked.

True, there was as yet no sword on the scene. And with the third pass, the matador took the bull with a rather crude veronica at full arm's length, his body twisted into an awkward chaos of limbs.

"He's not taking the charges too closely," Harry whispered to Chris.

"No, he does seem a little timid doesn't he."

I told them both to go to hell.

"Go bull!" Chris shouted as the crowd cheered, the great majority of which seemed fairly enthralled with the entertainment provided by the skittish young matador and his blunt-horned bull. Lending strength to my frustration, someone tossed one of the Imperial banners into the ring. Well the bull made a quick mess of that. Soon the horns were so caught up in the banner that their owner couldn't see where to go to get laughed at next. Much to the joy of the peasants in the bleachers, he crashed headlong into the barrera several times over, each time further injuring and exhausting himself. The picador rushed over and poked him daintily with his pole, but in legitimate combat the bull seemed completely uninterested—he only wanted his Imperial banner. Eventually his head ripped clean through the logo, and everyone laughed at the resultant cartoon-like effect. I told Harry to go find out what the hell was happening here, and eventually he returned, visibly deflated.

"No killing."

"What do you mean?" I said, spitting a wad of bloody saliva out onto the sand.

"It is only simulacro. There is no killing of bulls in simulacro."

"What do you mean no killing of bulls. It's a bullfight, isn't it? Yes, it's a bullfight and *bullfights kill bulls.*"

"Not in simulacro. No killing of bulls in simulacro."

"Well when the hell's the real fight then?"

He shrugged. "Only simulacro in Costa Rica," he said.

"Go bull!" Chris shouted, standing and laughing along with the rest. I could no longer look. I could no longer see. My eyes were filling up with red. I imagined myself outside the ring but could no longer see it. The Taurus's air-conditioning would have felt good at that moment, I bet.

BOOK FIVE

CHAPTER THIRTY-NINE

I LIKED THE ocean here. And I liked the beaches too. These were postcard beaches certainly, and the ocean was postcard ocean too. I thought that if there were some postcards around I might just send some to people back home. But then really, who would I send them to. Melanie maybe. Dominic probably. Anyway, what did it matter. This was paradise and I had everything I wanted right here.

That particular morning was like any other morning since my arrival this far down. I awoke around ten to my token headache and hacking cough, but considering what all I had poured into my system the night before, the gamble had more than paid off in my favour. Almost two weeks had passed since the festival in Limón. I was no longer sore about the fight. Now sure it had hurt, at least for a time, but since De Boer had seen fit to take it relatively easy on me in the aftermath, I had no real festering wounds to lug about. That is not to say I didn't have a sick feeling inside. I could feel it coming now, and I didn't want it to come at all. And yet, after all of the build-up, I thought the expected conclusion might make it all seem worthwhile somehow.

I made my way out to the sink in the common area to wash up, cough up, and shave. Neither De Boer nor the others were around that morning, so I put together a bundle for the laundry then headed into the washroom for a shower. The toilet was plugged and the stench was awful—someone had placed toilet paper in the bowl again and not in the appropriate basket alongside. It must have been that couple from Chicago. He seemed experienced enough, but then she was certainly no traveller. What with the way she dressed and the way she flirted she was more of an ornament, I gathered.

After successfully unclogging the toilet, I went ahead and showered, washing whatever blood I coughed up out of my lungs down the drain. Then I went out for breakfast alone. Even on a hot day Puerto Viejo has a certain quality of morning about it. A few hours' drive down the coast from Limón, this quiet little beach village abutting the Panamanian border never really gets going at all. This general feeling of lassitude has more to do with the heat than anything else, as even at the best of times it's absurdly hot down here. And at the worst, well, one is better off spending whatever he can spare of his waking hours submerged to the neck in water. At least that is how we found it, and in turn that is exactly what we did. Each day we had our little routine, starting out at the inland cabanas before heading a couple of hundred yards down the dirt road to the beach. Along the way there was an excellent little restaurant. Most often we ate our breakfast right there. And afterwards it was on to the beach to spend the rest of the afternoon up to our necks in water.

That morning De Boer was not at the restaurant either, so I assumed that he'd already made it as far as the beach. After coffee and an omelette I returned to my room, and tried my best to get some more sleep in. Unfortunately, though, due to my nagging cough I couldn't sleep, and so returned to my book instead. When I finally awoke again it was nearly four o'clock and my pillow was stained with red. I removed the case and washed it by hand in the sink with cold water and salt, then hung it to dry from a peg. And finally, pulling on my swimsuit and sandals and donning a T-shirt, I made my way down to the beach. The tide was in and the dogs were out, playing about in the surf. On any given day in Puerto Viejo there are any number of stray dogs roaming the beaches and streets. One gets used to them eventually, or tries to anyway, but the truth of it is they really need to put some sort of sterilization program in place.

I walked to the north end of the beach under the shade of palms spitting blood-laced saliva into the oncoming waves. Naturally both Chris and Harry were there already, climbing the cliff in the direction of the tree at its crest. Stated simply and affectionately and actually quite accurately, this was the Bug Tree, and in reality was just that— a tree covered in bugs—ants, spiders, centipedes and all other manner of tropical insects of which I had, and continue to have, no real working knowledge. The challenge, then, was to climb the cliff to the base of the tree, and once at the tree, climb out as far as possible along the length of the trunk. This rough black arm extended almost horizontally over the waves some thirty or more feet, and it was no easy task to complete. It required good discipline and a great deal of faith in oneself. At least it had in the beginning. In recent days of course we'd grown somewhat immune to its charms, and thus no longer really feared the journey. Still, during the course of the inverted climb out along its trunk the Bug Tree tested your faith. And by the end you were so covered in all manner of insects that it was all you could do not to let go of it. That was the test then. Not to let go. Naturally, once you had furthered the mark placed by the climber before you, you were free to let go without fear of ridicule. It was maybe a twenty-foot drop into all of five feet of water, so you had to be very disciplined upon entry. It was a fun game, especially when played with that girl from Chicago, and we were apt to play it on and off all day. Other times, she and her boyfriend would accompany us out for dinner, and afterwards out for drinks somewhere. He drank beer and she drank rum and she always wore this faded yellow bikini regardless of the temperature. She usually wore cut-off denim shorts to cover her bottom half, but then she never wore anything else to conceal the remainder. She looked nice in the yellow bikini and she knew it, and she wanted everyone else to know it too. Still she was a nice enough girl, and her boyfriend was a nice enough fellow, and I do wish I could remember their names too.

As it was, only Harry and Chris were there at the cliff that day, and I joined them for one climb of the tree. I didn't make it very far out before I let go, but then that had little to do with any insects bothering me.

"Book comes out day after tomorrow," Chris said. He reached down to pick a shell from the sand and hurled it out over the water.

"I thought it came out on a Tuesday," I said, hanging upside down from the trunk.

"It does," he said. "And it's Monday tomorrow."

I looked over at Harry. I could tell he was disappointed. And for the briefest of moments I considered asking if he might like to accompany us back home. Naturally I didn't, knowing full well how ridiculous that would appear, let alone the stink Immigration would raise at some point.

Still suspended upside down from the tree, I looked out the gnarled length of the trunk. In truth, there were hardly any insects remaining. It occurred to me then that we must have taken most of them with us over the previous two weeks of climbing and falling. And a few seconds later I plummeted into the ocean, emerging at once to examine my skin.

"Nope," I reported, "not much left now."

That night, we took our dinner at this open-air restaurant located right down near the beach. As usual, the sand crabs were out in full force that evening, all bone white and tan in their armoured skin. They emerged from their holes just after sundown, slipping across the roads in slow stubborn parades. At dinner, as one saw fit to poke its hammer claw up through a hole in the floorboards, the girl from Chicago carefully placed her joint in its grip. That was funny. As I recall, that was about the last funny thing. Because despite the fact we all drank excessively that night, it refused to come off all that easily. I fed them each a steady diet of guaro and tequila, allowing them the occasional luxury of a beer as chaser. In hindsight, however, I could have done better. Much better. The last supper always deserved something slightly more special than the Imperial eagle.

The owner of the restaurant, an obese, middle-aged, perpetually perspiring tico with too many jokes and not enough teeth, had taken a shining to us almost immediately upon our arrival that far down. A generous man was old Manuel. A real philanthropist in the making. After we purchased at least twelve rounds of shots, he saw fit to make it a baker's dozen. In addition to owning the restaurant, Manuel was very much a fisherman by trade. Or at least he had been

until making it big in the far more profitable venture of shark mutila-
tion. A traditional fisherman, by which I mean one with his very own
skiff, Manuel eventually made his small but respectable fortune peddling shark jaws and cartilage to foreign markets through middlemen
of questionable character and dubious means. That a market still
existed for such a gimmick as shark jaws was depressing enough, let
alone that it could prove so lucrative a venture.

And yet the cartilage racket was where the real money was.
Apparently shark cartilage was really taking off in America as an alternative therapy of sorts. Therapy for what, I had no idea, but apparently people put it in their smoothies and such. Or so at least Manuel
maintained. Furthermore, he said, Europeans and of course the occasional Chink still enjoyed purchasing the occasional jaw for their kids,
some of the Chinks even making soup from the fins. In the beginning,
or so the story goes, Manuel only shot those sharks caught up in his
nets. In the beginning he carried it for that purpose alone, and then
only at night, but eventually he brought it along for comfort and then
respect. Too many of his friends, not to mention two of his brothers,
had been robbed of their nets at night. Panamanians, he said, stealing
up from over the border, took great pride in stealing your nets. It was
one thing to be robbed of your shark cartilage decanters apparently,
but quite another to be taken for the nets you caught them in.

Eventually Manuel hooked up with this gentleman from
Germany who offered a very sweet deal for fish. That is, if the fish
were sharks and the sharks were harvested in something resembling
marketable condition. And naturally harvesting was where Manuel
excelled. No longer would he waste time fussing over the nets when
all he need do was cut them with a knife. The sharks themselves fed
out along the edge of the reef a few hundred meters offshore. Along
the edge of the reef they were easy enough to spot, caught up in the
nets lost there years and even decades before. The water was clear
around the reef, and when the tide was low he likened it to shooting
fish in a barrel. Then he sliced off their fins, ripped out their jaws,
and cast whatever remained of their still living carcasses overboard,
hoping the blood and flesh would attract even more would-be guests

to his nets. None of this is really part of the story of course, but it does offer some insight into the rifle in question.

He kept it on a rack behind the bar when he was not out work-ing the nets, an Italian-made bolt action hunting rifle with a cracked scope and a well-rusted barrel. It was an old rifle to be sure, really very old, and altogether poorly designed. And yet I liked it despite all its shortcomings, and even went so far as to ask Manuel where he'd acquired it, and if he'd be willing to part with it at all. He said he wouldn't part with it, but that he knew a fellow who could get me a similar one, especially if I were willing to enter the cartilage market as something like his business partner. That discussion had come just days after our arrival in Puerto Viejo. We never did broach the sub-ject it again. As it was, we were drinking heavily in his restaurant that night as it seemed as good a place as any to get drunk in.

I was quite intoxicated when I realized De Boer was no longer around. Assuming he was off with Manuel somewhere, I stumbled off to search the disco a few hundred yards south of town. When I arrived, the disco was only one-third full. That would have been some time after ten. Far too early for them to have gone out to the reef, I thought as, like the disco, it was still very much out of season out there.

Right about then I heard the first report. Strangely, it came from back up the beach. Typically they came from much farther out, but then really, what was typical these days. By the time I arrived, sever-al more shots had been fired, and the echo was really carrying. Floating about in the skiff a few yards from shore, Chris and Manuel appeared to be hunting something there in the shallow lagoon. Despite their activity, the surface of the lagoon remained relatively calm, and the moonlight clearly illuminated their faces. I asked what it was they were shooting at this far in, but neither one chose to answer me.

"Look!" Chris said, his one eye closed, the other eye squinting down the barrel of the rifle. "Look, there goes another one!" he said, indicating something there in the shallows I couldn't make out from my place here on the sand.

"Sí, friend. Take it presently," Manuel said, wiping sweat from his forehead with that same soiled handkerchief he always seemed to have in his hand. De Boer leaned forward, carefully aimed the rifle, and squeezed another round into the shallow lagoon. He certainly is getting comfortable with the rifle, I thought, as whatever he was hunting—if his reaction were any indication—he'd evidently hit again. Glancing about nervously, I asked what it was they were shooting at, knowing full well a shark could never make it this far in. Again, though, neither one chose to answer me, and then the tico moved the skiff slightly closer to shore. Behind me, on the beach, people were starting to make their way down, coming down from the restaurants and the bars. They, too, were uneasy with the proximity of the reports, when typically they came from farther out. I could hear them mumbling something to this effect up under the cover of trees. I asked again what it was they'd shot if not a shark, but then neither Chris nor Manuel were paying all that much attention to me.

And then I saw it, floating upside-down near the edge of the lagoon, its wide flat underbelly glowing white in the moonlight. It certainly was a small one, far too young to have survived the gunshot, and its tail twitched spastically as it died.

"Why do they keep coming back though?" Chris wanted to know, sighting his rifle for yet another shot. "It makes no sense to keep coming back."

Another shot rang out, another one died, and another group of curious onlookers made their way down to the lagoon. Alongside that couple from Chicago, I saw that Harry too had arrived, a look of concern complicating his features. And as the echo of the next shot evaporated down the long smooth curve of the beach, I watched another one float dead to the surface. Then once more the lagoon resumed its glassy façade. Focusing on the shoreline, I could just see, hovering there just under the surface, the schools of young stingrays feeding silently on the beach—I could just barely discern their smooth flat silhouettes spread in two-foot diameter veils. With each shot they scattered back to the depths, only to slowly return to the surface once more. Then another shot rang out, and another ray slid upturned and convulsing to the shore. I turned to De Boer standing there in the boat. He went to load in another cartridge but apparently he was out—he held out his hand for more. Manuel, to his credit, said they'd probably already taken their quota, but Chris would hear none of that at this point.

"Why do they keep coming back though?" he said in disbelief, the red elastic band doubled around his right wrist. "I really don't understand why they keep coming back."

Eventually Manuel caved to the pressure, and reaching into his breast pocket handed over a fistful of shells. A flat white underbelly floated upturned near my feet, and I poked at the flesh with my sandal. It hardly moved and felt heavy to the touch. Something like that must be all muscle, I thought.

"Why though? I mean can't they *see*?" Chris said. He slapped open the breech to expend the empty casing, then deposited a new cartridge and slapped the breech closed once more. "It makes absolutely no sense that they'd keep coming back."

I heard the faint wail of a siren from far away to the north, and in time flashing lights appeared along the long smooth curve of the shore. The threat was still a fair distance off when Manuel mumbled something in Spanish and scrambled his way clear of the skiff. He pleaded for De Boer to come with him, but he wouldn't, at least not without first engaging in some kind of fight. I made my way to the bow of the boat where Chris stood regarding me with something like amusement. His lips were moving and his one eye was closed. I quickly snatched the rifle away by the barrel.

Finally, with sirens closing in, we made our way up to the car. The couple from Chicago appeared alongside us quite suddenly, and together with Harry we piled into the Taurus. No one spoke as we made our way up the long dirt road, driving slowly in the direction of the cabanas. Long drooping palm fronds clawed over the roof as we passed further into a darkness made more desolate with the howling of distant dogs. We drove around cautiously on the back roads a while, our headlights extinguished, the hot rifle angling down alongside my seat. I could feel the barrel burning the skin of my thigh as I coughed up blood again and again. Meanwhile, in the passenger seat, De Boer settled into his usual role as navigator, sighting the targets as we crept slowly along, crushing them under our right front wheel. The moon provided all the light required, and we hunted many a sand crab that night in this manner. It was an entertaining game, but one played before and for hours at a time, and so it was somewhat inevitable that we'd eventually grow bored with it. However, in an effort to prolong the game beyond its natural limit, the fellow from Chicago offered me some of his joint. Naturally I declined the invitation, citing yet again how since I no longer smoked, pot tended to irritate my throat. And driving along slowly under the light of the moon and abstaining as I did, I soon came to feeling quite sober. Closing my eyes and clenching my fists hard around the wheel, I could feel the crackling crunch of the crabs shuddering up through the frame of the Taurus. Occasionally, if it were a big enough shell, and the tire hit it at just the right angle, I swear the car would actually shimmy and slide to one side or the other prior to finally bursting through. Opening my eyes, I could see behind me in the rear-view mirror dozens of smashed white bodies stretching out in a line in the night. Sometimes a dog would come padding along to sniff at the scattered remains, occasionally even chancing a bite. One poor survivor, its legs crushed on one side and its hammer claw missing, pulled itself with its remaining limbs up out of the wheel rut and over towards the roadside and safety. Shifting into reverse, I managed to finish him on the very next pass. We continued this way long into the night—it was a clear and wonderful night, but still the sun eventually made its way clear. And looking back over that last strange dawn, I realize now why even the sand crabs regarded it with fear.

CHAPTER FORTY

SHE WAS CAREFUL not to wake him. Gently, and by the wrist, she raised his arm from about her waist and placed it down softly next to me. I watched her get dressed through the mosquito tent a moment before moving back to my own bed across the room. It's difficult to say what exactly I was feeling at that point. After all of the build-up you might have thought that it would somehow feel better than it did.

After she left the room, I allowed a suitable grace period to pass before rising to start the day. It was well after one before I finished shaving and showering, and thinking De Boer might sleep too late, I finally went in to wake him. He was already up packing his things. I felt that he should talk first, in order that I might reciprocate, and so we went about passing all the cursory greetings I suppose two people do in such awkward situations. The conversation grew sparse, remaining for the most part, however, extremely polite, with volleys of ill-fated goodwill rebounding back and forth over the red and white checkerboard floor.

"You're repellent."

"Excuse me?"

"Your bug repellent," he said, his back to me, elevating the bottle over his shoulder. "You want me to leave it here?"

"Oh, sure. That is, if you don't mind."

"No, I don't mind."

"Great. That'd be great," I told him, trying to sound both composed and unconcerned at the same time. I wondered, briefly, why we never wore the bug repellent while climbing the Bug Tree. Not as much fun, no doubt.

Eventually I returned to the common area where the others were waiting. Having made coffee with his portable coffeemaker, the fellow from Chicago promptly offered me a cup, and I accepted without reservation. Still it was good coffee, and so I really had no problem drinking from his cup. The girl from Chicago looked at me and smiled. I knew that smile. Harry emerged yawning from his room. When he asked if we were going to get some breakfast soon, I said I wasn't sure—why, was he buying? He scowled, and the man from Chicago looked at me and smiled. "Quite a night."

"Quite a night indeed," I smiled back.

"You sleep all right?" asked the girl.

"Fine, thanks. And you?"

"Not bad," she smiled, and I smiled too. The conversation went like this as we continued to smile our knowing smiles. She liked it that her boyfriend had no clue.

"You want to get some breakfast before you leave, Chris?" I asked, having returned once more to our room.

"Sure," he said. "If you want."

"I could go ahead and order," I offered.

"Fine. Great. I'll have my omelette. Actually no, you know what? I might try something different today."

"Speaking of different," said the girl, poking her head in through the door. "Good morning, boys."

"Good morning," said Chris.

"Sleep well?"

"Not bad," he sighed. "Maybe a little cramped near the end."

She shuffled about in the doorway, biting her lip and trying not to smile. "So what time's your flight back to Vancouver?" she eventually inquired, slipping a foot free of its sandal to rub the toes against the back of her calf.

"Actually I'm going to Toronto," he said, turning to me. "I fly out at midnight remember."

"Midnight tonight?" said the girl. "Well you'd better get going."

"Not really," I said. "San José's only, what, eight hours away."

"When's your flight, Billy?" she asked, still biting her lip and smiling that smile.

"I haven't bothered to book one yet."

"And you're coming back here after you drop Chris off?"

"No, I think I'm heading out too—to Paris," I said.

Her shoulders sagged. "What, you're going to drive him all the way to the airport and then book your flight from *there*? Good luck."

"You don't have to."

I turned to Chris. "What do you mean I don't *have* to?"

He studied me a moment. "Just that you could stay down here if you want to."

"Don't be ridiculous. Of course I'll drive you. Besides, how the hell else would you get there."

He shrugged. "I could always get the bus from Limón."

"And you could hitchhike to Limón, no?" suggested the girl, ever the eager travel agent and personal advisor.

"Look, I said I'd drive," I told her prior to coughing up blood into the palm of my hand. Together they frowned as I scraped the blood from my hand onto the edge of the windowsill, and eventually Chris returned to his packing.

"Well then you'd better get your stuff together," he said, and so I shuffled reluctantly across the room to my own pathetic collection of gear.

"On second thought," I said, "you're right. I think maybe I'll just come back. I mean it's not like I have anything else to do," I elaborated for no one in particular.

"Retirement must be a wonderful thing," smiled the girl.

"Oh it is that," I told her.

At that moment her boyfriend called out to her, and she responded quite curtly as she advanced further into the room, "Hold your horses, dear." And jerking her thumb in her boyfriend's direction, she whispered that they were unfortunately heading down to Panama that very afternoon. Then she went up to Chris and gave him a hug. I watched her press up against him. They were kissing. They kissed. I stood there watching them kiss.

She told him to have a nice trip then.

Next she came up to me and, briefly embracing me, said they'd be back up this way in no more than a week. It was both strange and exciting to feel a woman pressing up against me, especially after having gone so long without. I turned my face down to hers to find her smiling. Smiling in that knowing way. As though what happened the night before was now a very deep secret between only the two of us, a rather shocking but very real secret that only she and I could fully comprehend. She was smiling as though there were something outsiders would never really understand about our little secret, as if it were somehow lewd to those not in the know but to us was simply an age-old passion better shared—like the shooting of stingrays or the pissing on Indians or the fostering of the fight in the child of a friend. We didn't speak much. We didn't need to. It was simply the pleasure of discovering again and again that little secret for which we both held so much passion. Smiling in her knowing way, Mona Lisa let me know that she alone would always understand our little secret, and would never dare expose it to anyone outside our little band.

She left the room just as her boyfriend appeared in the doorway, eager to shake each of our hands. He wished us well. We wished him well. It was the least we could do after all.

"So you're staying on then?" he asked, still shaking my hand.

"Actually no, I think I'm heading out too."

He smiled knowingly. "Undecided, huh?"

"I suppose you could say that, sure."

He gave each of us his address and telephone number, and then he left the room. I thanked him for the coffee and for everything else he'd shared, but he mustn't have heard me—I listened to his girl-friend laughing as they strolled up the road together.

"I thought you said you were coming back?" Chris said, his back to me, his attention once again on his packing. Suddenly it seemed very lonely in the room.

"Well now I've changed my mind," I told him.

Sitting on the edge of my bed, feeling the mosquito tent tugging gently at the back of my head, I reached back with both hands and pulled a portion of the cloth down over my eyes.

"Check it out," I said, pointing down at the red and white checkerboard floor to where a locust stood transfixed in the midst of one red square. "That fucker must be as long as my finger."

Chris nodded, "They do grow them big down here."

Studying the locust through the mosquito cloth now draped down over my face, I poked at it several times with my sandal. Still the locust refused to move from the square. Harry came in and asked when we were going for food.

"Soon," I said, speaking through the cloth. "And hey, free ride ends today too."

Wounded by this remark, Harry asked if we wanted him to go on ahead and order.

"Sure," Chris said, smiling him out of the room. "What the fuck was that all about, Billy?" he asked once Harry was out of earshot.

I shrugged. "Just tired of carrying him, that's all."

"What, like I've been carrying you?"

"What's that supposed to mean?" I said, exploring with a finger the long beetle-like scab that had formed where the barrel of the rifle had burned my thigh the night before. With a wave of his hand Chris dismissed the subject entirely.

"So what are you doing then? Are you staying or going? Look," he said, "if you want to stay, I can always find a ride. It's not like we're trapped down here."

"To tell you the truth, I'm not sure what I'm going to do," I said through the cloth, still staring down at the locust on the floor.

"Look, before you say anything, I have to go. I *have* to."

"But why?"

"*Why?* Because that's the punch-line, pal. That's closure. Closure to this whole ridiculous affair and . . ." He paused. "I just don't want to pretend I'm something I'm not anymore, that's all."

Somewhere outside a woman laughed, and I went back to watching the floor. The locust was gone though, and so, releasing the mosquito tent, I turned instead to the study of my hands rusted and reconstructed against the blurring backdrop of the floor. Purple and dark to the knuckles, and then white and marbled beyond, I flexed them several times while trying to form a decent fist—the arthritis was coming along. I wondered how Gretzky was coping with his arthritis. I wondered how he could. I wondered if maybe he'd already discovered a cure for arthritis, as, no doubt, he would.

Leaving Chris to his packing, I went outside to retrieve the rifle from where I'd stored it in the Taurus the night before. I opened the breech to ensure that it was loaded. I closed the breech and returned inside. There he stood before the open window with the dried blood on the sill, while outside the window stood the car. And somewhere out there a woman laughed as I watched him fall hard to the floor.

Laying the rifle across his punctured chest, I grabbed my swimming gear from the back of the chair next to the open door. Then I walked out to the open road, past the Matador Red Ford Taurus looking almost blood red in the sun, and down towards the shore. It was hot on the road in the glare of the sun, and whenever possible I retreated to the shade. Still, I found it difficult to breath. I watched the people coming out of their homes, coming out onto the road in waves. Standing there alone in the shade, alone and outside myself, I saw their bodies shimmering in the heat. Flexing my stomach muscles, I poked around at my abdomen, managing to make it feel hard and lean. I felt hard and lean and athletically serene in the heat rising off the road, but still it was difficult to breath. I recall seeing Harry run past. I don't recall his face, but I do recall him saying something to me in Spanish.

I walked on down the road. Despite my shortness of breath, it felt good to be back in the sun. The beach was smooth and white and gave way softly under my sandals while each wave appeared sharply described against the others, one undulating rhythm amongst all these undulating others. I removed my sandals and walked barefoot for a time. Soon, though, the sand was too hot to continue, and so I returned to my sandals, noting how few people there were out on the beach. A few hundred yards offshore stood an island. An island covered in trees. And the clear, sharply defined waves were breaking slowly around the tree-covered island one after another, and then once again on the nearly empty beach. I went down to where the waves broke smooth and shallow against the sand and, removing my sandals and T-shirt, waded out into the oncoming waves. And once it was deep enough to dive safely, I dove forward into an oncoming wave, feeling it break over me as I swam under and out and free. That was good discipline, I decided, and so I swam out towards the island, sliding beneath the waves this way. We'd gone out to the island a few days before to snorkel around the coral and the caves. It had been good snorkelling, and I had promised myself to return if I were ever alone. This was my first real opportunity to do so then.

Once at the island, I pulled myself up onto the reef. I thought about travelling inland—the island measured no more than a couple of hundred yards in diameter—but then seeing how dark it was in the shaded parts I must have thought better of it in the end. I stretched out on the reef until I was dry, and afterwards, dove off the reef into the clear blue water, repeating the feat several times. Once I dove down as deep as possible, all the way down past the coral to the sand. I dove with my eyes open, equalizing the pressure in my ears with a controlled series of air-bursts as I descended, just as Harry had done. And down there at the foundation of the coral-based island the water was clear and clean. I could see where the coral met the sand. The island made a shadow all about me, and I was diving in the shadow of some distant and exotic land. There were fish down near the bottom, of several different species and of a variety of different colours, and I tried my best to touch them, but naturally they wouldn't allow me that pleasure. And finally, when I could no longer stand it, I returned to the shimmering surface for air. I was very pleased with the depth of my dive, knowing I'd never been deeper. I stood on the reef and dove deep several more times, though none so deep as the first. And after I finished diving I went ashore once more to see what all was happening there.

I walked down towards the cliffs and the Bug Tree. The tide was in and a breeze was rising, but after a while it got too hot on the sand and I made my way back into the sea. Wading out to chest depth, I felt something tickling my chest, and looking down, discovered a school of minnows nibbling at the hairs. It tickled as they nibbled and I laughed aloud, otherwise allowing them to continue unabated. There must have been twenty or more fish feeding on me. Suddenly I started to cough, and coughing up blood, spit it down into their midst. And while the minnows attacked the gradually extending rope of bloody saliva with increasing ferocity, I flexed my burnt red chest, burnt a rusty red from the sun, and poked around at the various muscles. They felt lean and hard under the pressure of my fingers. I felt like maybe I was losing some weight after all.

Following the meal with the minnows, I returned once more to the beach, and gathering my things, made my way down to the Bug Tree. I managed one good climb, managing to further the previous mark considerably, but then it didn't mean all that much as, except for a few minor ones, there weren't all that many insects remaining.

At the base of the cliff I sat in the shade of the Bug Tree and watched a family of bathers come strolling down the shore. They looked so very small and black from this distance. Almost tragic. And the children were playing in the waves away from their parents now. Gathering my things into a neat little pile, I waded out into the water, and then down along the beach. By the time I arrived, duck-diving all the way, the children were back on shore with their parents though.

I walked up the beach. "Can any of you speak English?" I said to the father. He had slightly bulging eyes, and his large bald head was sweating profusely in the sun. He looked at me bulgingly before turning to his wife.

"Hello there," I said to the wife over the weary sigh of waves behind me. "Are there any English here? I'm afraid I've some rather unfortunate news."

They both regarded me in that typical citizen's way. Of the children, one of them came up and hugged my leg, but then the father bulged his eyes in a way that quickly told him not to.

"That's okay," I said, patting the child's head affectionately. "Are there any English here? I'm afraid there's been a terrible accident. You see, one of the horses . . ."

But they didn't answer. Why would they answer? I was talking complete and utter nonsense here. One of the children—not the one who'd hugged me but the other one, the girl—pointed to the several khaki-clad officers making their way down the beach towards me. Behind the officers stood the town in profile.

"Christ it's hot," I said to no one in particular.

"Sí," said the mother with sudden recognition. "Sí, hace calor."

"Isn't it?" I smiled. "But then it's always hot in Spain at this time of year."

And in this little border town on the southeast coast of this country the roads are fringed with large swaying palms. And in the nearly vertical sun of early afternoon there are very few shadows, but what shadows there are, in quiet deference to the trees, take up this little town in their arms. Forming a fist, I too took up an arm, and squinting hard, sighted with my one open eye along its outline reaching up through the shadows of the trees and the houses towards the central plateau where, shimmering in the heat just beyond, a range of mountains stood purple and dark to the snowline and then white and marbled in the sun beyond. Still squinting, I aligned the peaks and valleys of my knuckles with those of a second range of mountains—one undulating rhythm superimposed on these undulating others—these mountains slightly lighter in colour with their peaks covered in even more snow, beyond which stood a third range of mountains, the whitest of them all.

Still squinting, I stepped over to the little girl and offered my hand. She took it, and I hugged her narrow brown shoulders with my burnt red arms. She hugged me back, smiling, but I could tell she was thinking of someone else—she was trembling and felt small in my arms. Still I appreciated the effort and told her as much.

"Darling," I sighed, rubbing the red from my eyes, "I've had such a hell of a time."